"Yes . . ."

His nostrils flared ever so slightly. "Why?" he asked, brows lowered in confusion. "Why now?"

She understood perfectly. A few days ago she'd insisted on professional distance. Yet how could she explain it? They were high above the city, just the two of them, in a cocoon of warm July air. "Does it matter?"

"It does to me. I'd like to know why you've changed your mind."

Because she wanted him, wanted him to do the same wicked things he'd done on the ship. The insides of her thighs grew slick just thinking on it. She went with a coy answer instead. "Isn't that what women do?"

One side of his mouth kicked up. "Most women, perhaps. However, you're not most women. There's no one else who can begin to compare."

By Joanna Shupe

The Four Hundred series
A SCANDALOUS DEAL
A DARING ARRANGEMENT

The Knickerbocker Club series
MAGNATE
BARON
MOGUL
TYCOON

JOANNA SHUPE

A SCANDALOUS DEAL

THE FOUR HUNDRED SERIES

WITHDRAWN

AVONBOOKS

An Imprint of HarperCollinsPublishers

A SCANDALOUS DEAL. Copyright © 2018 by Joanna Shupe. All rights reserved. Printed in the United States of America. No part of this book may be used or reproduced in any manner whatsoever without written permission except in the case of brief quotations embodied in critical articles and reviews. For information, address HarperCollins Publishers, 195 Broadway, New York, NY 10007.

First Avon Books mass market printing: May 2018

Print Edition ISBN: 978-0-06-267891-1
Digital Edition ISBN: 978-0-06-267893-5

Cover illustration by Kirk DouPonce, DogEared Design
Design and art direction by Guido Caroti

Avon, Avon & logo, and Avon Books & logo are registered trademarks of HarperCollins Publishers in the United States of America and other countries.

HarperCollins is a registered trademark of HarperCollins Publishers in the United States of America and other countries.

FIRST EDITION

18 19 20 21 22   QGM   10 9 8 7 6 5 4 3 2 1

For Michele, Diana, and JB,
who keep me sane and always make me laugh.

Chapter One

"My buildings will be my legacy . . . they will speak for me long after I'm gone."
—JULIA MORGAN,
ARCHITECT OF HEARST CASTLE

July 1890
Somewhere on the
Atlantic Ocean

Lady Eva Hyde hated boats. Yachts, schooners, steamships, barges . . . all tiny enclosed prisons made of steel and brass and boredom. She preferred a structure on solid ground, tall and wide, one she designed herself. Granted, this floating torture device was a luxury steamship, with all the modern conveniences that entailed, but she'd much rather be on terra firma.

Stack of drawings in hand, she left her cabin and locked the door behind her. The warm July sun greeted her once she arrived topside. She tilted her face up to the sky, pausing, and the heat sank into her bones, relaxing her a fraction. One day into the voyage and all that she'd left behind in London still pressed down on her shoulders. Her father's illness, the whispers and stares directed at her . . .

Look, there is Lady Unlucky.

Three dead fiancés tended to turn one into a spectacle—not that she'd ever truly fit in before. Her longtime governess had called her a hoyden, saying Eva was more comfortable in mud and dirt than swathed in petticoats. An entirely true statement. Eva had forever been chasing her talented, famous father about, desperate to learn everything she could about buildings and basic construction. Dashed good thing, too, considering how rapidly his mind had deteriorated in the past two years.

Her father was E. M. Hyde, Lord Cassell, one of England's premier architects who had designed buildings all over Europe for nearly four decades. Last autumn E. M. Hyde had been approached to design a luxury hotel in New York City, what would end up as the biggest and most modern in America, a crown jewel to be remembered for centuries. Unfortunately, her father's illness had worsened and he hadn't been able to design for two years. Oftentimes he didn't even recognize his only child. Those days broke Eva's heart.

However, Eva hadn't been ready to give up the prestigious and lucrative project. She knew her father's work inside and out, and she was ready to complete the Mansfield Hotel in his stead, as she'd been doing with his other recent projects. God knew quitting was not an option considering their dwindling finances.

The only thing to do was to carry on the Hyde legacy so no one would learn of his condition. Of course this meant pretending her work was his, as no one would believe a woman capable of designing a one-room hut, let alone a massive thirteen-story hotel. Yet if it kept a roof over their heads and paid for his care, then pride be damned. Her own career would begin eventually, after her father . . .

No. She did not want to contemplate that just now.

She headed toward a deck chair facing the ship's promenade. Beyond that was the wide expanse of blue ocean, sparkling and shimmering like glass. She was still focused on the water when a small figure darted in front of her. A child. Eva tried to slow down but there was no hope for it—she collided straight into the tiny boy.

He started to fall so she reached for him, hoping to keep them both from tumbling to the deck. Her grip on her designs slipped, however, and she watched in horror as three of her pages fluttered away in the ocean breeze. "No, no, no!"

"Sorry, miss," the boy mumbled and scampered away.

Eva paid him no mind, panic gripping her insides. Those pages . . . she absolutely had to get them back. They were ideas for the hotel project, ideas on which she had worked terribly hard. A brilliant spark of inspiration that could never be replicated. She darted after the twisting papers, determined not to let them get away.

She trapped one page under her boot, while the other two blew and flipped along the promenade. After collecting the first paper she hurried to the others. Her lungs froze as they drifted toward the railing—and then they slapped against the leg of a well-dressed man standing there. She blew out a sigh of relief and raced toward him.

Bizarrely, the man did not move. Never glanced to see what had pressed against his leg. Never reached for the precious papers, the irreplaceable ideas she'd labored over. No, he stood as still as a statue, staring out at the water.

Heart in her throat, she dove for the man's leg. She nearly tackled him, bumping into his tall frame and grabbing at his trouser-covered calf like a deranged lunatic, relieved when her fingers closed around the drawings. *Oh, thank God.*

She shut her eyes and exhaled. The wooden deck bit into her knees through her skirts and no doubt she'd made a spectacle of herself. As always.

The man completely ignored her, which both comforted and irritated her. She would appreciate his help in rising. "A hand, sir?"

He remained perfectly still, other than his throat working as he swallowed. Was he hard of hearing?

"Good, you are alive. I had worried there for a moment." She grasped the railing and pulled herself to her feet, after which she smoothed her skirts.

Not ready to walk away from this puzzle, she took a moment to study him. Little to see from his profile, unfortunately. Around thirty years of age, she guessed. Tall and fit, with dark brown hair tucked under a straw hat that somehow hadn't blown away. Clean-shaven. Dressed smartly, expensively.

He still hadn't acknowledged her, his hands clutching at the wooden rail, and it became a sort of game for Eva. She normally kept her distance from the other passengers when she traveled, taking all her meals in her room to avoid the pity and suspicion when they learned her identity. Often she made up names, assumed a completely different persona to avoid the awkwardness. It was easier. But at this moment, she needed some sort of recognition, some sort of answer for his rudeness.

Then again, he seemed rather pale.

Leaning against the railing, she said, "I've heard taking gingerroot helps."

Nothing. Not a twitch.

"You know, there's likely an officer or surgeon on board who carries a supply for sick passengers. I'll go and find someone—"

"Not. Sick," he gritted out through clenched teeth.

She resisted the urge to roll her eyes. "I see. You are attempting to will the nausea away. Does it work?"

His nostrils flared as he dragged in a series of deep breaths. Then a shake of his head.

"You may feel better if you go ahead and empty the contents of your stomach over the side."

Another shake of his head, more vigorous this time.

"Has anyone ever informed you of your stubbornness?"

"Yes," he wheezed. "Many times."

A full sentence. This was progress.

His coloring still indicated he might be ill at any moment and she started to feel bad for him. He obviously preferred to suffer staunchly, bravely. Alone. A soldier on the battlefield, ready to be cut down at any moment for king and country. Sometimes, however, these things really were mind over matter. "Thank goodness," she said cheerfully. "I did not relish being the bearer of such news. No one wishes to hear of one's foibles."

"Like garrulity?"

She laughed, not offended in the least. Her second fiancé had said getting information out of a plant was easier than talking to Eva. "I'm afraid you are the only person to lament my loquaciousness."

"Lucky me."

He had a sharp wit. She liked that. "Give me your hand."

His head swung toward her and she had her first full look at his face. The air left her lungs like she'd been punched in the solar plexus. *Good heavens.*

He was . . . unexpected. Faces were nothing more than basic construction, with tissue and muscle stretched over bone and cartilage, much like a building's steel, wood, and plaster. But this was no ordinary face. Strong, bold features, perfectly symmetrical, and patrician bone structure that spoke of great past civilizations. Greek columns and Roman aqueducts. Men who had built, conquered. Discovered and settled.

Even ill, he had confidence fairly oozing from his pores. "Why?" His gaze swept over her face and red hair, which must have appeared a total fright in the wind.

"Because I said so." Not awaiting a reply, she tucked her drawings under one arm, securing them, and peeled his left hand off the railing. She pushed up his sleeve and placed three fingers across his wrist, then centered her thumb below, just over the large tendons there. She began making circular motions, using a little pressure.

He said nothing for a long moment, just took deep breaths. "What are you doing?" he finally asked.

"It's a Chinese practice to rid nausea." Not that she would explain how she knew this. Most men believed a construction site no place for a lady.

After several minutes, she reached for his other wrist. Measured then rubbed. He had strong forearms and hands, with veins that popped under golden skin and shifted with her movements. These were working hands. Capable hands. Not the hands of a gentleman, though he was dressed as one.

Who was this man?

Though they were hardly touching she could feel him begin to relax. Perhaps this was working after all. "Were you on holiday in England?"

"Paris, actually. Coming to shop our Ladies' Mile?"

She tried not to make a face. They were strangers, so he had no idea she was the daughter of E. M. Hyde. Her ailing father's work and legacy was the reason for her journey, not that she would confess as much to this man.

Heaven knew men didn't appreciate any woman who desired a career. Eva had quickly learned this lesson from Robert, fiancé number one. He had been the wealthy one, who'd informed her no fewer than seven children would do.

"However did you guess?"

He lifted one broad shoulder, somehow the movement both arrogant and charming. "I have sisters."

"How many?"

"One older, one younger. Both meddling."

Still, that sounded nice. "I am an only child. I would have adored meddling sisters."

"We all want what we do not have, I suppose."

True. For example, Eva had long wished she'd been born a man, the son her father always wanted. If so, all this would have been much easier. Instead, she was forced to hide the true nature of her father's illness and secretly carry on his work herself. Subterfuge was exhausting.

"Do you see them often, your sisters?"

"I do, regrettably. Though they are married and busy with their own families they still find time to harangue me."

"How utterly terrible for you, all that love and concern over your well-being."

He made another noise above her, almost a laugh. "The lady has bite."

Warmth slid under her skin and she released him. She avoided his eyes by pushing her hair out of her face and staring out at the ocean. "You must be feeling a little better."

"Perhaps the sea air finally agrees with me."

"Or perhaps I have charmed you back to good health."

"Possibly. Where did you learn this?" He held up his wrists, turning them. The light cream-colored coat pulled across his arms and shoulders, revealing muscles not of a bon vivant but a workingman's physique, like the laborers on her father's construction sites, the ones who wielded heavy hammers and steel girders all day.

"Here or there. I cannot remember exactly."

"You must travel quite a bit, then."

Not lately. Not since her father's illness had grown considerably worse. "I tend to stay on dry land," she hedged.

"Smart of you."

"Are you always ill on a ship?"

He closed his eyes and rolled his shoulders. "Would you believe it if I said no?"

She shook her head. "Indeed, not. I think you view it as a weakness, yet many others suffer the same affliction. It's a common enough condition."

The color was returning to his face, yet he tensed at her observation, his expression pinched in discomfort. She wasn't certain he would actually admit to the nausea. This man seemingly had pride to rival her own. "It's only the first one or two days with me," he explained quietly. "I'll be fine tomorrow."

"There. Was that so difficult to confess?"

"Yes. I usually stay in my cabin but thought the fresh air might help."

"You hoped no one would notice you here, gripping the rail as if you might leap over at any moment."

"Obviously—and if not for your papers the scheme would've worked. Are they letters?" He tipped his chin toward the pages in her hands.

"Something like that. How do you feel now?"

"Tired, but better. Thank you."

"You are welcome." He stood staring at her and she was uncertain what to do. His eyes were dark, a deep brown with golden flecks dancing in the sunlight, the lids framed with long lashes. She could see a few cuts on his face, the kind from shaving, and she wondered if he had a valet with him on the trip. "Do you require assistance back to your cabin, then? I could find a porter . . ."

He pointed across the deck. "No need. I'm right there, on the end."

The biggest of the first-class cabins. Of course. He must be one of those wealthy American tycoons. Railroads or stocks, probably. Her cabin was at the opposite end, the smallest of the first-class cabins, paid for with money from the hotel project.

Even still, with another six days on the ship, the two of them might bump into one another, if she ventured out again.

He has no idea who you are. You can be anyone. The possibility exhilarated her, the chance to interact with someone ignorant of her past, free of her father's illustrious reputation. Indeed, that could prove a very good reason to leave her cabin.

She clutched her papers to her chest and gave him a small smile. "Well, I'll leave you to it, then. Good day."

"Indeed, I hope to see you around the ship." He tipped his hat. "Good day, miss whomever you are."

THE BOAT DIPPED and Eva's pencil slipped once more on the paper. "Blast." She reached for her eraser and cursed the ferocious storm raging outside.

For six hours now, the steamship had tossed and

turned in the rough seas. Beyond her tiny window the rain pelted down from leaden, angry skies. Fortunately she'd not yet experienced *mal de mer*. Her stomach remained steady the entire time, possibly because her concentration stayed on her work and not the surroundings.

They were due to arrive in New York Harbor tomorrow. For the past eight days she'd kept to her cabin to review and polish her new ideas, hoping to impress Mr. Mansfield, the owner of the new hotel project. Now that time was almost up. Nerves fluttered in her chest but she pushed them down. It would be fine. Mansfield would be agreeable and the building would be finished on time.

Honestly, all the financiers she'd dealt with merely wanted her father's name on a project. They didn't give a whit about whether her father actually showed up to meet with engineers and plumbers. As long as the benefactor could brag about owning an "E. M. Hyde" masterpiece, they were happy. Mansfield would be no different. He hadn't even come to London to meet with her father, as many preferred when hiring an architect. He'd cabled and written some letters in which they'd settled on terms. Three weeks ago, she'd sent the final revised drawings to his home in Manhattan and hadn't heard a word since.

What worried her was Mansfield's reputation. Upon digging, she'd learned he was widely regarded as an exacting, even ruthless, hotel owner. The entire restaurant of his Boston hotel had been ripped out and redone at his behest because the tile had been manufactured in Greece, not Italy as promised. His employees respected but feared him, and his letters to E. M. Hyde had been quite specific in outlining his expectations with regards to quality, timing, and budget.

For example, if the building went over schedule, E. M. Hyde would forfeit one thousand dollars every day until completion.

If the building went over budget, E. M. Hyde would forfeit 15 percent of the total architect fee back to Mansfield.

Furthermore, if any of the materials were substituted without Mansfield's prior written approval, the job would be redone at the expense of E. M. Hyde. Considering the budget for the hotel was around three million dollars, Eva couldn't fathom having to cover a portion of this cost herself. Redoing one part alone would bankrupt her and her father.

More than anything, the hotel must succeed. She needed to keep her reputation away from the project; otherwise everyone would associate her bad luck with the hotel. No one wanted to stay in a building designed by Lady Unlucky. As long as Mansfield was kept happy and the work completed under E. M. Hyde's name and not hers, all would be well.

A weak knock on the adjoining door caught her attention. Her maid, Mollie, appeared in the doorway, her hand clutching the jamb. "Milady, will you . . ." The girl swallowed hard. "Will you be wanting to dress for dinner?"

The gray hue of Mollie's skin alarmed Eva. She shot to her feet and quickly crossed the cabin. "Are you unwell?"

Her maid swayed and Eva reached to steady her. "Just a bit queasy," Mollie said. "I'll be all right in a moment."

"Nonsense." She turned Mollie around and led her to the narrow bed. "Lie down, please. I am able to fend for myself tonight."

Mollie sat on the bed and frowned. "I am not so ill that I cannot—"

"You need to relax and stay calm. Let your stomach settle. We have no idea when the storm will pass."

"Thank you, milady. I don't know if I am able to take much more of this rocking." Mollie laid flat on the mattress, and Eva went to the small sink to wet a cloth. She returned and placed the cool cloth on her maid's forehead.

"Shall I bring you anything to eat?"

If possible, her maid's complexion turned even whiter. "No," she wheezed.

The ship dropped into a swell, water lashing the sides and spraying up past the tiny window. Mollie groaned and closed her eyes. Eva patted her shoulder. "Rest. I'll check on you a little later."

She returned to her room where her stomach rumbled, not from seasickness but hunger. With Mollie ill, perhaps she should eat in the dining room. A quick squint at the clock told her that dinner service had just begun, so she wasted no time, changing her clothes and slipping into an empty corridor. Odd that no one was about, not even the ship's officers. Perhaps everyone was already in the dining room. Holding on to the brass rail attached to the wall as the ship swayed and rocked, she made her way toward the stairs.

When she reached the dining room, rows and rows of vacant chairs greeted her. That was strange. No one was here. The long wooden tables had not been set, the bare wood gleaming in the low light. "Dash it all," she muttered. Perhaps someone in the kitchen could give her some bread or cheese. Anything to hold her over until morning.

She walked toward the swinging door in the back. Presumably the kitchens were there.

As she drew closer, the door swung out and she exhaled in relief. Of course someone was here. They had probably been waiting for passengers to arrive.

A man stepped out from the kitchens, a man she didn't expect. The American from the railing.

She came to an abrupt halt. "Good evening."

"Good evening." The side of his mouth lifted as he hefted a tray in his hands. "The waiters are all ill, apparently. There's one chef but he appears a little green. I do not believe he'll—"

A huge clatter erupted, the crashing of dishes and ringing of silver. Eva and the man both winced. "I think it's safe to say we are on our own for dinner."

She glanced at the different meats, cheeses, bread, fruit, and nuts on his tray. She was starving. Any of what he held would be a welcome meal. "Is there more in the kitchen?"

"Of course. There are also bottles of champagne on ice as well as a fillet of beef entrée."

"That sounds delicious. I'll help myself."

His jerked his chin toward one of the long tables. "What kind of gentleman would I be if I allowed that? No, please have a seat and I'll fetch everything for us. Let's eat before the ship sinks in this storm."

The words jarred her. She hadn't been frightened until now. Ships sank all the time in bad weather. "I hope you are wrong about that."

"Don't worry. If you grow scared, I will happily comfort you."

He said it casually, but there was something in his voice. She walked to the end of the long table and sat, wondering if he was . . . flirting with her? The idea was preposterous. They hardly knew one another and she was hardly the type of woman to inspire flirtation. Her second fiancé, James, had repeatedly chastised her about her unladylike tendencies. *I don't fancy having a wife with ink-stained fingers, Eva. Why don't you give up your sketching and drawing and act like the other girls?*

To be fair to James, none of her three fiancés had encouraged her interest in architecture or pursuing a career of her own. Each man had been properly horrified at the very idea of it. They'd all wanted to marry her for various business reasons related to her father, like his notoriety or a specific project. None of them had actually cared about *her*.

She'd always been a bit different, a bit odd. Like her father. While society tolerated eccentricity in men, however, a woman could very well be outcast for wearing the wrong dress, let alone striving for a career.

This man doesn't know you. Be whomever you wish, even a woman who flirts back.

"You are too kind," she said with an easy smile when he returned. "Might as well enjoy our last meal together, then."

"That's the spirit." He placed the tray between them and took the seat opposite. "Let's eat and drink ourselves into a stupor. Then we'll hardly notice when the boat goes down."

THEY ATE QUIETLY at first, the only sounds that of the storm raging outside, each taking pieces here and there from the plates he'd procured in the kitchen. The champagne flowed freely. Usually she moderated her consumption in public so as not to embarrass herself, but she saw no reason not to imbibe tonight. Why not enjoy this one last night of freedom before she reached New York?

He speared a piece of pear and brought it to his mouth. "I don't even know your name."

"Evelyn." The name popped out of the part of her brain that longed for anonymity here on the ship. "And you?"

"Phillip." He chose another pear slice. "Odd that we are the only two passengers not suffering from *mal de mer.*"

"I thought for certain yours would return."

The boat rocked back and forth as the ship struck a wave. They both reached to keep the contents of the table steady, and he refilled her champagne glass with his free hand. "Mine only lasts the first day or so, then I'm steady as a rock no matter the weather. Have you sailed to America before?"

"No. I've not traveled much outside of England."

"Not even Paris?"

"I went there a few years ago. Spent most of my time wandering through the churches."

"Are you religious, then?"

"Not at all. I like the design of them. So forbiddingly beautiful. I am fascinated by the contradiction."

"Like the gargoyles atop Notre Dame."

"Exactly." She grinned, pleased he understood what she meant, and he smiled back at her. Goodness, he was handsome. She cleared her throat. "They were originally waterspouts, you know. Clever, wasn't it?"

"I didn't know that." He popped a grape in his mouth and chewed, his eyes never leaving her. "So tell me, how does an English girl with a Mayfair accent come to learn about gargoyles?"

She swallowed a mouthful of champagne, discovering it made lying easier. "Oh, I read quite a bit."

"I read as well, though mostly contracts and reports for business."

Yes, definitely some sort of rich American tycoon. Probably owned oil fields or a silver mine. "How long do you think the storm will last?"

"No idea. I hope we are not delayed in reaching New York tomorrow afternoon."

"Me, either. I am on a tight schedule this trip."

Eva reached for a dried date—and her hand collided with Phillip's, his rough skin sliding over her own. She jerked her hand back and put it in her lap, heat flooding her cheeks. Undoubtedly she'd turned the color of a tomato, the curse of fair skin.

Smooth, Eva. If he hadn't thought you skittish before, you've cleared that right up.

He lifted his glass and gestured to the plate. "Please, I insist. Ladies first."

Without hesitation, she snatched the date and slipped it into her mouth. "Thank you. What is your favorite color?"

His head snapped up from his plate. "Pardon?"

She loved to talk about colors and shapes, how other people saw the world. "Color. The one you prefer best." When he did not answer right away, she nudged the plate of dates toward him. "Come now, we must pass the time somehow."

He selected a piece of fruit. "My favorite color is blue, though I am coming to appreciate red." He flicked his gaze toward her hair. "And yours?"

"White."

"White? Is that even a color?"

"Yes. White is the sum of all colors so therefore is a color." White meant new and clean, like new buildings, new walls. A blank canvas on which to draw and construct.

He reclined in his seat and cocked his head, studying her. His dark brown hair hung a little over his ears and collar—a slight rakishness at odds with his polished appearance. He was otherwise impeccable, dressed in a fashionable, well-fitting suit of light gray wool. She had a strange urge to know more about him. "Are you staying in a hotel while in New York?"

"I live there. What about you?"

"I shall be staying with a friend, actually."

There was the slim possibility that he knew her friend, Lady Nora, so she dared not elaborate. *Do not get acquainted. There's no point.*

"You have the most interesting eyes," he said, leaning in. "They are the purest brown, but every now and again there is a glimmer of green . . ." He instantly shook his head. "I apologize. That was terribly forward of me. Blame the champagne."

The words heated her insides, like warm honey working its way through her veins. She'd heard the occasional compliment here and there, but none so earnestly offered as this one. "Thank you. Are your wife and family anxiously awaiting your return?"

If he thought the question bold he gave no sign of it. "No, I am not married. Much to my mother's dismay, I'm afraid."

She raised her glass in a toast. "To disappointing our parents."

Chuckling, he lifted his glass and touched it to hers. "May they come to forgive us someday."

They both drank and then set down their glasses. An easy silence settled between them, with none of the expected awkwardness of strangers. There was something freeing about pretending to be a woman with no cares or worries. No father whose memory had failed him. No dwindling finances, thanks to years of overspending and forgetfulness. No deception to keep from losing the most important job of her life. No whispers and stares behind her back.

All those things awaited her when they docked in Manhattan.

For now, however, she could set that aside and merely enjoy this man's company. Bask in his attentions. Revel in the anonymity.

"Are you traveling alone?" he asked abruptly. "I realize that is forward of me, but it is helpful to know if an angry spouse might appear at any moment."

She didn't blame him for asking. Unattached women never traveled alone. If she were a normal unmarried female, she'd have a chaperone with her at all times. Better he assumed her a widow or a wayward wife. "I am traveling alone. No one shall seek retribution for you having dinner with me on the ship."

"Good."

In an effort to change the topic, she nodded to the tray. "I notice you aren't eating the Stilton."

"Hate the stuff, actually. Cannot stomach the smell."

"That's because you have not been shown how to properly eat it." She took a toast point and layered it with a thin slice of pear, a small wedge of Stilton, and topped it with a date. "Here."

He took the precariously balanced bite from her hand, his lips curled in adorable distaste. "Must I?"

"Yes, you must. I insist."

Opening his mouth, he put the entire thing between his lips and chewed. She watched, pleased that he hadn't refused or spit it out. Finally, he chased the bite with some fresh champagne. "Would have been better without the cheese."

"Perhaps hold your nose next time, as a child might do with medicine."

One dark brow shot up. "I believe you've just equated Stilton to foul-tasting medicine, which proves my point."

She laughed, unable to help herself, the sound much louder and sharper than her usual tone. She was enjoying herself immensely tonight, despite the storm and the threat of danger. Phillip was witty and intelligent, two qualities she greatly appreciated in a person.

"I adore your laugh," he told her, his voice strangely husky as he regarded her. "It's quite genuine and captivating."

She snatched her champagne and took a gulp, suddenly self-conscious. How did one begin to respond to such a compliment?

He cocked his head. "Have I embarrassed you? I would think you'd be used to flattery, considering."

Considering, what? "I've never had anyone comment on my laugh before."

"You haven't?"

"No. I stay fairly busy in London. There's not much time for play."

"Now I'm truly intrigued. I thought ladies were all about teas and parties, and here you're learning Chinese remedies for nausea."

He had quite the low opinion of women. Were all American ladies so boring, then? "Have you ever been to teas and parties? If so, then you'd know they are exceedingly tedious."

The side of his mouth hitched. "I am well aware of their tedium. I've just never heard a woman admit it before. I thought you were required to love them."

"Well, I've never been one for doing as society requires."

"I am gathering that." He lifted his champagne once more. "To disappointing society."

She clanged their glasses together. "To disappointing society."

Chapter Two

The night wore on, the two of them chatting easily while consuming more food—and champagne. She couldn't remember a time when she'd enjoyed herself this much. Why hadn't she dined with him every night?

"That's the last of this bottle." He righted the empty champagne bottle and rose. "I'll fetch another from the kitchen."

She watched him walk away from the table, enjoying the sight of his fine shoulders shifting beneath the wide cloth. No, *wide* shoulders beneath the *fine* cloth. Yes, that was it.

Oh, dear. I have definitely had too much champagne.

To be fair, though, the man was sinfully attractive. She was having a hard time following the threads of their conversation, content to merely stare at him. She'd even caught herself giggling like a schoolgirl at some of his comments.

What was wrong with her? She never, ever flirted. If she batted her lashes it was because plaster dust had lodged in her eye, not to play the coquette.

For a woman who spent so much time around men she was hopeless on how to attract them. Her father had plain given up on trying to marry her off after William, her third fiancé, passed away. Her reputation as Lady Unlucky had taken root by then, so Papa had whisked them both away from London for a bit. Eva hadn't minded; she would much rather learn about buildings and design than worry about dances and afternoon calls.

It hadn't helped that each of her three fiancés had laughed when she'd mentioned an interest in architecture. None had understood her passion or her drive, instead saying she'd be too busy with children and the household to pursue a career of her own.

Despite their unenlightened views, she had mourned their deaths. She'd been truly sorry that each man lost his life, but she hadn't ever mourned the lack of a husband. Who needed a lord and master to curtail her activities?

No, this was perfect. She was here, sharing a meal with a charming and appealing man she hardly knew. What more did one need?

The door swung open and Phillip emerged from the kitchen, two china plates in his hands along with a bottle of champagne tucked under an arm. He somehow kept his balance and managed not to spill a thing.

The plates each contained a huge fillet of beef with fingerling potatoes. Her mouth practically watered. *No more making a fool of yourself over him. Stay quiet, eat, and then go to your cabin and fall asleep.* "This looks delicious."

He topped off their champagne. "There's more if we want it. Additionally, they have baked vanilla pudding and chocolate éclairs."

"I plan on eating all of it," she said, cutting into the perfectly rare beef. The piece nearly melted on her tongue, it was so heavenly. She must have made a noise because his head snapped up, his eyes locking on her mouth.

The air went still, growing heavy, as if she'd done something wrong. But the ferocity of his stare, the way his jaw tightened, hinted she'd done the opposite. It was a look that stole her breath, her wits. Why did his attention fluster her?

She forced a napkin to her mouth and slowly dabbed her lips. He looked away and she heard him exhale. Mouth now dry, she downed the rest of the champagne in her glass. What was happening? Did he feel this strange pull between them as well?

The ship bobbed and dipped, and both of them reached to secure the champagne bottle. His hand covered hers over the cold glass, and the feel of his warm palm sent a rush of sparkling heat along her spine. She couldn't move, her limbs frozen in place, muscles useless, while the beat of her heart seemed to pound in her ears.

Why were his hands so rough?

"You do not have the hands of a gentleman."

He released his hold on her and the bottle, relaxed in his chair. His lids swept down over his eyes, shielding his thoughts. "Who said I was a gentleman?"

Good point. She'd assumed because of his cabin and his clothing. She plucked her glass from the table and took a long swallow of champagne. "You're right, I made assumptions. I apologize."

"Maybe I'm a famous bare-knuckle boxer."

"I doubt it. Your nose would be crooked from being hit."

"Unless I'm the one doing the hitting. I might be just that good." He toasted her with his empty glass before refilling it. "What do you plan to do while visiting New York?"

Why the abrupt change in topic? "I'm hoping to see as many of the new buildings as I can. I hear there are some extraordinary ones."

He blinked a few times, clearly not expecting that answer. "That's true."

"Any suggestions?"

"Definitely Trinity Church."

That was on her list. "The spire is the tallest point in Manhattan, they say."

"Indeed, it is." He settled deeper in his seat as he cut his beef with a knife and fork. "Though Pulitzer's building on Park Row is rumored to be taller. Won't know until it's completed."

"How many stories are planned?" She leaned in, fascinated. Americans were obsessed with building higher, these skyscrapers that seemed to defy gravity.

"They say twenty."

She could not hide her shock. "That is astounding. The foundation must be quite deep."

"Quite." He forked up a bite of meat. "I hadn't expected a woman to know that sort of thing. Do you fancy architecture?"

Even through the haze of champagne she knew

not to admit her true passion to this man. "Oh, I merely guessed. With all that steel and . . . heaviness one could only assume the bottom would need to be strong."

"You would be right."

Worried she'd revealed too much, she soldiered on. "No, I merely like to look at buildings. I'm curious to see how your landscape differs from London and the other European cities." She lunged for her champagne to rinse the awful lie from her mouth.

"New York is unlike any city to which you've ever been, I guarantee it. Any idea how long you'll stay?"

All that depended on Mansfield. If she could satisfy him to where he'd leave the project alone, then she could return to England for a few months while construction continued. She hadn't planned on leaving her father alone for long. He was well cared for, but she felt a responsibility to be close to him as his health declined.

"I am not certain," she told Phillip. "I've not seen my friend in a long time. I'm taking as long a holiday as I like."

His brows lowered. "Did you just say 'holy day' or 'holiday'?"

She covered her mouth with her hand, stifling the urge to giggle. Had she slurred her speech? Her head was buzzing and there was no way to be sure. "Holiday," she enunciated. "I said holiday."

Eyeing her champagne glass, she pushed it away with two fingers. Perhaps she'd overdone it tonight.

At that moment, the ship wrenched sharply again and they both lunged to steady the champagne bottle. This time their hands collided and knocked the heavy glass piece onto the floor. Champagne spilled over the carpet in a dramatic spray. Their eyes met—and they both broke out into a fit of laughter.

She had no idea why the accident was hilarious, but they kept laughing while he righted the bottle. "That was a waste of perfectly good champagne," he said.

"We should say a few parting words. To show the appropriate amount of sorrow."

He nodded. "Give me your hand." When she did, he gripped it and bowed his head. "Dearest Wine Gods, forgive our clumsiness in wasting this bounty produced from the finest French grapes."

She snickered even as he gave her a mock frown. "And do not blame this woman for her jocularity. She knows not what she does. More importantly, we hope this spilled champagne finds eternal peace in the afterlife."

She snorted a laugh and he grinned at her, his handsomeness sending a thrill through her. How was a man this charming and eye-pleasing unmarried? He stared down at where their hands were still joined and she realized her thumb was rubbing the inside of his wrist, almost absently, intimately.

Horrified, she released him. "I apologize. I hadn't meant to . . ."

He reached across the table to find her hand once more. "I didn't mind."

A mighty wave crashed into the side of the ship, jostling everything in an explosion of movement and sound, and the lights flickered. Her breath caught and Phillip froze. The flickering finally stopped and she exhaled, relief cascading through her. "Thank heavens. For a minute I thought—"

Blackness engulfed the dining room as the lights cut out.

THE MOON OFFERED hardly any light and inky darkness surrounded them. "Phillip?"

She heard the fear in her voice and suddenly a warm, heavy hand landed reassuringly on her shoulder. "I'm here, Evelyn." He'd risen and crossed to her side of the table, thank goodness.

"What should we do?"

"We should go." He helped her out of her chair. "Perhaps the cabins still have light."

"Yes, good idea."

She stood and clutched his shoulder, unsteady from both the rocking of the boat as well as the champagne. He quickly wrapped an arm around her waist, anchoring her. They stood pressed together a moment, her breasts smashed into his chest, their legs tangled. Thank heavens for the darkness. Her skin felt as if it had gone up in flames, the sensation of his hard frame so foreign next to hers. Yet she didn't move away.

She wanted to move in farther, wrap her arms around him, and never let go. Was that fear . . . or something else? She wasn't certain.

"Are you all right?" His voice sounded strained, not his usual tone at all.

She patted his lapel. "Perfectly fine. Lead on."

He guided her into the corridor. None of the

lights were working, so they groped their way down the dark staircase and then stumbled along the first-class passageway. The pitch of the ship was considerably worse belowdecks, making walking extremely difficult.

Eva clung to him, uncaring of propriety. Her heart pounded behind her ribs, loud to her ears even in the fierce storm. *The boat is strong. Constructed of iron plates riveted over an iron and steel hull, with a screw propulsion system that will keep us moving through the storm. We won't sink. Probably.*

"Where is your cabin?"

She swallowed and shook her head, though he couldn't see it. She didn't want to be alone. "I believe yours is closer. Let's go there."

He didn't argue, merely stopped at a door and unlocked it after a few fumbles with the key. He held open the wooden panel and she stepped into the darkness. He tried the switch on the wall and nothing happened. "Dash it," he muttered and she heard the door close behind him.

Eyes now adjusted to the darkness, she could make out the sitting area and the wooden platform bed beyond. The scent of leather and cigar caught in her nose, unmistakably the intimate domain of a man. Nervous giddiness bubbled like champagne in her chest. She'd never been in a man's apartments before. All her fiancés had maintained a respectful distance, with only William, her last betrothed, sneaking a tepid kiss during a turn in the gardens late one night. It had been akin to drinking a bland cup of tea.

Would she die before ever experiencing any passion in her life?

"Shall we sit?"

The deep whisper slid over her skin like a caress, the question almost a dare. *He doesn't expect you to stay.* Did he think she'd faint at the sight of rumpled bedsheets? She hated to be dismissed. Underestimated. Some days it felt she'd spent her entire life trying to prove herself.

"Yes. We might as well get comfortable."

She heard him move, the soles of his shoes sliding over the carpet, clothing rustling, just before a large hand closed around her wrist. Before they took a step, the ship tilted and she lost her balance. His arms shot out to steady her, with one hand going to the wall for support and the other wrapping securely around her waist. Every part of her was flush with his frame and she leaned in, curling her fingers into his evening coat. "You are unusually strong. Are all New York gentlemen like you?"

He chuckled. "I believe this is the part where I say that no man in all of America is like me."

"I would almost believe that." He was certainly a contradiction. A man of good breeding, clearly wealthy, with hands like a laborer and a body like a longshoreman. He'd taken care with her tonight, made her feel safe despite the storm. Not only that, he'd made her feel pretty. Desirable.

There was something about him that both relaxed and excited her. A deep thrill erupted low in her belly each time she looked at him, a hum of attraction she'd never experienced with a man before.

"Stop moving," he told her.

"*I* am not moving. The *boat* is moving."

"I realize that, but you're . . . rubbing against me and I fear you'll discover more than you bargained for in a moment."

What did he . . . ? Was he *aroused*?

She couldn't imagine any other meaning and the idea that he wanted her as well sent a rush of heat through her veins. This beautiful, intelligent man desired *her*, and for once in her life she wanted to be reckless. To replace the gossip and sneers she'd endured during the past three years with the memory of one night where she'd allowed herself to be someone else, someone daring.

To prove there might be a little good luck for her after all.

Without realizing what she was doing, her palm landed on his jaw. "You are exceedingly handsome. Even when we first met I thought you were perfectly lickable."

One dark brow shot up. "Did you say 'likable' or 'lickable'?"

You'll never make your mark on the world by playing it safe, her father had often said, words now echoing through Eva's skull as she rose on her toes and dragged the tip of her nose over his chin. He smelled divine, all clean skin and woodsy cologne. Her tongue darted out and swiped under his jaw. He inhaled sharply but did not pull away. "Hmm," she murmured. "Definitely lickable."

In a blink, his hands cupped her face, holding

her still as he captured her mouth with his own, kissing her hard. She responded instantly, eagerly, returning the kiss and parting her lips to allow him inside. And *oh, goodness*, the slick, warm softness that met her tongue. It was heaven. He drove deeper, angling and shifting, stroking, stealing her breath.

Her fingers found their way under his coat and she dug her nails into his strong back, tugging him even closer. He pressed her against the door, nearly pinning her with his delicious weight, hands feeling and testing everywhere he could reach. Her hips aligned wonderfully with his and she immediately felt what he'd been referring to earlier. His erection dug into her, fascinating in its thickness.

She felt drunk on him, much more so than from the champagne. She bit his bottom lip, teeth sinking into the plump flesh. He growled in response, a primal, raw sound that matched exactly how she felt at this moment. Like she wanted to tear off his clothes and explore every inch of him.

He dove for her mouth once again, consuming her. She couldn't get enough of his taste, the demanding way he chased her tongue with his own . . . He rolled his hips to drag his erection over her pubic bone as he cupped her breast over her clothing. She gasped, surrounded by pleasure and sensation. Overwhelmed by the fierceness of her reaction, as if she'd explode at any moment.

He began trailing kisses along her jaw, down her throat, and she nearly collapsed into a puddle on the floor. No wonder girls risked their reputations over a passionate encounter. It was bliss and torture all at once. "We should not be doing this," he murmured as she arched to allow him better access. "But I've been dying to kiss you all night."

"You have?"

He nipped her collarbone through the silk of her dress and a shiver coursed through her. "Indeed. It's all I've been thinking about."

Just then, the ship rocked and dipped, forcing them apart, and they both teetered. He put a hand on her hip as they stood there, breath powering out of their lungs as if they'd run a race. No, no, no . . . she wasn't ready to stop yet. Would he send her away? Or would he lead her to the bed and ravish her?

He jerked a thumb in the direction of the sofa. "Perhaps we should sit, before we're knocked to the floor."

Relief nearly weakened her knees and she hid a grin. "Sitting sounds like a fine idea."

ONCE ON THE sofa, her skin burned with the feverish desire to touch and be touched. The kisses . . . Dear Lord, *the kisses*. Eva hadn't been able to get enough.

She wanted more.

That is the champagne talking. You'll regret this tomorrow.

Perhaps. Perhaps not. And she couldn't think on that right now, considering Phillip was staring at her as if he might pounce at any second. A thrill skated down her spine.

"Are you shocked?"

She blinked at his question. "Shocked?"

His face was cast in shadow but she could see the

dark smile twist his lips. "I was talking about the kiss by the door, but I guess the answer is no."

What she felt could hardly be considered shock. *Ravished. Excited. Enlightened.* All those words were more apt, though she kept this to herself. Instead, she asked, "Are *you* shocked?"

"I am, actually. I lost myself for a moment there." He reached to tuck a strand of her hair behind her ear. "You are quite unexpected."

The compliment buzzed through her like more champagne, making her even more light-headed. Did all Americans just say what they were thinking at any old time?

"Yes, we do. It's part of our charm."

Had she said that aloud? "I suppose I'll need to get used to it during my visit. We English are a bit more reserved."

He relaxed and stretched his arms along the back of the sofa. His waistcoat outlined his impressive chest, each expansion of his rib cage straining the fabric. "Are you certain you'd like to stay? I can escort you back to your room."

She didn't want to leave. At all.

"I'd like to stay, if you don't mind me here."

"I don't mind a bit." Sliding closer, he lifted her fingers to his mouth where he kissed each one lightly. "In fact, I'm quite glad of it."

Her muscles grew heavy, sinking into the soft fabric of the sofa. "Are you?"

His teeth gently scraped one knuckle before he murmured, "Yes, and I promise to restrain myself from doing anything improper tonight."

That implied there would be another night,

which Eva knew to be patently false. Even if the boat stayed afloat in this terrible storm, they would never see each other again once they arrived in New York. Eva hadn't the time or inclination toward romance while there. The hotel project would consume all her focus and energies.

She studied him through her lashes. "What if I said we only had tonight?"

He released her and put up his hands, palms out. "I would still say no. You're inebriated and I'd be taking advantage of you."

Inebriated? "I'm merely tipsy—and you drank far more champagne than I did."

"I'm also twice your size. And you passed tipsy three glasses ago."

Had she? Whether it was Phillip or the champagne she felt *alive*, more alive than ever before. She didn't want this to end. Tomorrow brought reality, with work and responsibility. Pressure and loneliness. Tonight was for abandon, with steamy kisses that curled her toes. "If you're inebriated as well, then aren't I also taking advantage of you?"

"A dangerous combination. It means neither of us is thinking clearly. I wouldn't care to be a source of regret for you."

His consideration both reassured and frustrated her. "What if we took advantage of one another?"

His gaze glittered in the darkness, his mouth hitching in amusement. "You wish to take advantage of me?"

She flicked a glance over his wide shoulders, the rough hands and strong jaw. The thick thighs spread slightly apart on the sofa cushions. She fought the urge to lick her lips. "Yes, I rather do."

"Well, then. I am at your service." He gave a wave of his hand, as if magnanimously granting a wish.

Giddiness and desire surged throughout her and she angled closer. "Endeavor not to complain, if you please."

"I shall certainly try." He tracked her approach, anticipation crackling in the air between them. She was nearly panting by the time she settled next to him, her thigh tucked snugly against his. Heat rolled off his frame and her nipples tightened behind her clothing. She had never been this bold, this *eager*, yet she could not seem to help herself. The storm raging outside, traveling alone on the ship . . . none of this seemed real.

Like in a dream, she placed her hand on his face, the evening whiskers rough against her palm. "Kiss me, Phillip the American."

He bent his head slowly, as if giving her time to reconsider, but she merely moistened her lips and waited, breathing him in. His lips brushed hers gently once, then twice. Then he turned toward her, hands threading through her hair. Their mouths opened as if by silent agreement and his tongue twined lazily with hers. He controlled the pace this time, the kiss slower but thorough, as if he were memorizing her. Savoring her. She put her hands on his chest, the hard planes of his body a solid anchor under her fingers.

The boat twisted and dipped in the fierce waves but she hardly noticed. Phillip was driving her mad

with the perfect rasp of lips over hers, the master-
ful suction of his mouth. Each flick of his tongue
sent sparks along her limbs, the place between her
legs now pulsing with desperate yearning. Everything inside her strained to get closer, begged for
more. She canted her head to deepen the kiss, her
fingers jabbing into his soft hair while her breasts
crushed against his front.

The kiss grew frenzied, their chests heaving and
hands grasping. She'd never felt like this before, so
light and brave, as if she could do anything. She
had the urge to touch him everywhere she could
reach. Arms, throat, chest . . . He jolted when her
palm skimmed over his thigh.

The world tilted as he quickly lifted her. He settled her on his lap, his arms banded around her,
holding her tight to his frame. *Hot. He's so very
warm.* More deep, drugging kisses. A noticeable
erection rested beneath her buttocks and she loved
this proof of how much he wanted her.

Yet the kisses weren't nearly enough to satisfy
the ache building inside her. She wriggled, need-
ing to get closer, nearly climbing him from the
urgency, every part of her body throbbing and
pulsing, scorching with desperation. As if he read
her mind, his fingers pushed up her skirts. A gentle nudge parted her thighs and he delved into her
drawers, right to the very heart of her.

She froze as one digit swept the slickness surrounding her entrance. He tore away from her
mouth. "You are soaked. I feel as if I've died and
gone to heaven."

Thank goodness, because she had no idea if that

was normal or not. She had a basic understanding of the act but the details were a mystery, other than what she had discovered during her own explorations. Without a mother or sisters, Eva had been left to piece together knowledge from books. In short, she had no idea what men expected when it came to intimacy.

He began kissing her jaw, nipping along the skin of her throat. "Relax and I'll make you feel extraordinary."

Words eluded her as his finger brushed the tight bundle of nerves where every bit of sensation had now settled. Her hips lifted, seeking, and he rewarded her with another caress, stronger this time. Then he began to circle the taut bud, sending shivers of white-hot pleasure through her, while he licked and sucked on her skin. Hard.

"How is that?" he whispered. "Tell me."

"Oh, God." She tried to pull air in her lungs. "Do not stop."

He hummed in his throat, teeth sinking into her earlobe. "Rest assured, I won't."

She clutched his shoulders, the torment continuing to steal her wits, as he made good on his promise. Her insides coiled and tightened as she climbed higher. He kissed her again, taking her mouth ruthlessly, almost brutally, while his hands worked magic between her legs.

One thick finger slid inside her entrance, filling her, and the heel of his hand ground down on her swollen nub. The fullness, the way he surrounded her, his blistering kisses . . . it was too much and yet not enough.

"Please," she rasped, rocking her hips.

"I have you." His voice was low and dark, a seductive whisper of silk. He picked up the pace, stroking her in earnest. "Let go, beautiful girl. Show me how good this makes you feel."

He continued with words of encouragement, humid gusts of tantalizing sin in her ear. Soon her muscles seized and time drew to a stop, pleasure gathering at the base of her spine until it burst. Eyes screwed tight, she trembled, a shout torn from her throat as the sensations dragged her under.

When she floated back down, she couldn't lift her lids, just laid sprawled in his lap like a limp rag doll. She clung to his warmth and enjoyed the languid, boneless feeling. *This is bliss.*

He pressed a kiss to her forehead and she felt him right her skirts, covering her legs. She yawned, nestling closer to his big frame. Somewhere in the tangled cobwebs of her mind she realized his erection hadn't deflated one bit. In fact, it had grown bigger.

She would just rest for a moment and then ask him about it.

Chapter Three

Phillip Mansfield arrived home in a foul mood.

The morning had not gone as expected. Unfortunately, the ship had docked in New York Harbor sooner than anticipated, and he hadn't been able to find Evelyn before he disembarked—not for a lack of trying, however. While on the ship he'd searched the promenades, the dining area, and passageways. He'd even ventured into the first-class walnut-paneled reading room, which was where all the women congregated and chatted during the day.

She hadn't been anywhere.

He hadn't seen her on the pier, either. Every face, every hint of red hair came up lacking. Even the ship's crew knew of no Evelyn in the first-class apartments. It was as if she had disappeared.

There had been no choice but to accompany his valet and trunks to the waiting carriage. They rumbled north through the city until they reached Eighty-First Street, the welcome sight of his home greeting him. Built to his specifications three years ago, the house was modeled on the Loggia del Capitanio in Venice. Long columns adorned a brick and limestone front with a balustrade running the width of the five-story home. A mansard roof capped off the structure, one of the tallest on the street.

When he walked in the front door, Roberts, his butler, greeted him. "Good morning, sir. I trust you had a pleasant stay in Paris."

Phillip grunted as he shrugged out of his top-coat. As pleasant as Paris had been, he could not picture the woman he'd entertained there. All he could see was red hair and greenish brown eyes. Why had she not stayed this morning? The rumpled bedcovers on her side of the bed served as the only reminder the previous night had even taken place.

He had enjoyed every minute. Bold and responsive, Evelyn had certainly been an unexpected surprise. He'd been painfully aroused when she fell asleep in his arms after her orgasm. The only remedy had been to put her to bed, secure himself in the washroom, and use his hand to find relief.

"It was pleasant enough," he told Roberts. "I am glad to be home, however."

"I imagine so, sir. Incidentally, Mr. Gabriel awaits in your office."

"Excellent." Gabriel was his secretary, and Phillip was more than ready to get to work. "Have some luncheon sent in, will you?"

He strode deeper into the house, past the Italian sculptures and priceless works of art. Over the marble imported from Carrara. Through the wide arches and intricate plasterwork. The sight of it normally calmed him, but he was entirely too distracted today. Distracted by one elusive young woman.

Upon waking this morning, he had instantly reached for her—and discovered cold sheets. That she'd left his room without even waking him to say good-bye bothered him. The woman snuck out like a thief in the night, as if she'd regretted what had happened between them.

He, on the other hand, had absolutely no regrets. He had been eager to touch her again, feel her soft and willing. Warm and wet. Revel in the urgency of her kisses, hear the need mewling in her throat. Then they could finally complete what they had started last night.

Yes, they had slept in the same bed but he hadn't bedded her. They'd both been drunk on champagne and he would much rather possess his full faculties when fucking a woman. He also preferred a partner who was complicit and fully engaged, one who could approach the situation with logic and reason.

In the clear light of day, he'd been planning to broach the subject, to woo and seduce her until he had her melting into the mattress. Only she'd crept out of his bed before the sun rose. Being denied what he'd craved made him . . . surly. He was not used to disappointment, especially when it came to women.

Mistress, he told himself. *I need to find a mistress.*

Perhaps he should find a nice widow, a woman he could talk with and who wouldn't expect marriage. A woman who wouldn't distract him.

His projects were more important than anything else in his life. The risk with a mistress was that she'd grow unhappy when he stayed at the construction site instead of her bed. He must secure a mistress with reasonable expectations, one with no interest in a serious relationship.

He opened the door to his office, where the familiar hum of the electric lights and stock ticker proclaimed business as usual. A reminder that the world kept turning, no matter his mood.

Gabriel rose and adjusted his glasses. "Sir, you've returned early."

"Yes, by a bit." Phillip crossed the room. "A storm pushed us closer to shore."

His secretary gestured toward the ornately carved walnut desk that took up a good portion of the room. "I have organized your things into several piles, each in order of importance. If you start on the left . . ."

"Fine, fine. I'll get to it in a moment. I have one immediate need first. Get a list of the first-class passengers on my steamship from London to New York. I want to see if I can locate someone I met on the journey."

Gabriel wrote all this down on a small pad of paper. "That should not be difficult. The shipping line will have a manifest of the passengers."

"Excellent. I am looking for a woman. Goes by the first name Evelyn. Find out everything you can about her." His secretary nodded. Satisfied it would be handled, Phillip asked, "Have we received the final arrangements from Hyde? Any idea when the man is coming?"

"Yes, the final plans are there on your desk. Hyde should arrive any day now, as expected. Milliken's crew is assembled and waiting to break ground."

Excellent. He was eager to have something to occupy his mind. Lazing about and obsessing over a woman was not his usual style.

"Incidentally, sir—"

The door swung open and Phillip's mother appeared. He sighed, the familiar pinch between his shoulder blades pulling at his muscles. How had she known he'd returned? She had an uncanny ability to predict his schedule, like a medium with a single-focus crystal ball.

As always, his mother was expensively outfitted. Her dress was a heavily embroidered navy silk, and a sterling silver pin dripping with diamonds rested above her heart. Her light brown hair, now fashioned into an elaborate hairstyle, had started to gray at the temples, a fact he happened to know vexed her greatly.

New York society both loved and feared Ellen Mansfield, and most in the Mansfield family were no different. She relished her roles as both matriarch and one of the reigning queens of Fifth Avenue, never hesitating from offering up an opinion—even when unsolicited. The woman brought meddling to an entirely different level.

He approached her, bending to kiss the cheek she presented him. "Hello, Mother. I thought you were in Newport."

"I brought the railcar in yesterday because I wanted to see my son. When did you return from your little holiday?"

"Just now. I had planned to cable you this afternoon. Shall we sit? I can ring for tea, if you like." He led her to the chairs opposite his desk and helped her into one. Then he took the other chair, sitting beside her rather than behind his large desk. Gabriel left, softly closing the door behind him.

"No need for tea. I won't be staying long." She smoothed her skirts and arranged herself. "The hotel project is ready to begin, I hear."

"Yes. We break ground in days."

"And E. M. Hyde is in New York?"

"Not yet, but I expect him imminently. Why?"

"I am having plans drawn up—"

"No."

She blinked, her shoulders shifting in irritation. Ellen Mansfield did not like to be told *no*. "You haven't even heard what I wish to do."

"Because it's irrelevant. You do not need to build, redecorate, adjust, or add on to any Mansfield property."

"I disagree, and I am perfectly within my right to do whatever I wish to Stoneacre."

Ah, so it was Stoneacre this time. Would she never leave well enough alone? First of all, Stoneacre, the Newport cottage, was more than adequate for the family's needs. With forty-four rooms, no additional space would be required, ever. Second, Hyde was not traveling to New York to bow to the whims of Ellen Mansfield. There was a hotel to build, for God's sake.

"The answer is still no."

"That is unreasonable, Phillip. Your father built

that house for me, in case you've forgotten. It was a gift after five years of marriage. Stoneacre is mine to do with as I please."

As expected, she was digging in her heels, using guilt and nostalgia to wear him down. He had to hand it to her; his mother was crafty. "I realize as much, but there's no space issues and you had the interior remodeled two winters ago. You are merely bored, Mother."

One eyebrow rose, the barest of movements but one that spoke volumes. "Perhaps I would not be so bored if I had more grandchildren."

He closed his eyes and drew in a deep breath. She was like a dog with a bone. "*Stop.*"

"Fine." She rose and pulled on her gloves. "By the way, I am having a dinner party on Friday evening and I expect you to attend. I need to even out the gentlemen."

He noted she hadn't given in on Stoneacre and he foresaw more future conversations on this topic. Oh, the joy. "I'll check and let you know. Who else will be in attendance?"

"The Wilsons, the Halls, the Bends. Hardly anyone is in town."

He saw right through her. "This would not have anything to do with Miss Hall, would it?"

She stopped and held up her hands, palms out. "We cannot have the Halls thinking you've changed your mind."

"I never agreed to anything and you know it. Merely because you wish me to marry the girl does not make it so."

His mother had been trying for two years to convince him to marry Rebecca Hall. The girl was lovely, well mannered. Good fun, really. She was one of the young unmarried ladies of society he actually liked. But there was no spark, no burning attraction between them, and he sensed Rebecca was as uninterested in him as he was in her. Hardly seemed fair to start a marriage off in such a lackluster fashion.

"It is a good match and all but decided, Phillip."

A familiar anger rose in his chest, the burning resentment of having his affairs out of his control. "You do not get to decide when and whom I marry. That may have worked with Meredith and Beatrix, but it will not work with me." His sisters hadn't had much choice in husbands, even though both claimed to be content in their matches. Despite this, Phillip did not want to be managed.

"You've always been like this." His mother glanced up at the portrait in Phillip's office, one painted of the entire family while his father was still alive. The lines of her face softened and he knew his mother missed his father. They had been the rare couple where love had blossomed from an arranged union. "The more I try to push you toward something the more you back away. I'm not your enemy or rival; I only want what is best for you."

Not entirely. Sometimes he believed she only wanted what was best for *her*. His opinions held very little weight when it came to his mother. "Do not assume I will marry Miss Hall—or anyone, for that matter."

Her eyes grew large with horror, yet he didn't

retract the comment. This was not the first time he'd said this but she needed to hear it again, apparently.

"It has been more than ten years, Phillip. Is it not time to let it go?"

He said nothing. The incident was brought up so infrequently these days that he hardly knew how to respond anymore. The humiliation still pricked, however, as fresh in his mind as it had been all those years ago when he'd nearly been tricked into marrying Caroline. "My feelings about Miss Hall have nothing to do with that."

"Nonsense. I let you choose that Boston girl, even though I had my doubts. Always supported you and did everything in my power during the worst of it. Let me choose this time. I promise, you'll be satisfied."

A marriage in which he was merely "satisfied" sounded positively awful. He wanted the perfect wife, someone beautiful and refined but who also dazzled him; an intelligent woman who never argued and would not mind a husband who traveled most of the year overseeing various endeavors. Settling for less would never satisfy him.

"No. When—and if—the time comes, I'll be choosing my own bride."

Disapproval carved deep lines on his mother's face, and still he would not give in. He did not need children to build a legacy. He would have his buildings, his hotels.

"Well, I've already told them you are coming Friday night. What am I supposed to say?"

As always, his mother had already moved her

pieces on the chessboard and he was struggling to catch up. He did not have it in him to be cruel, however. "Fine, I'll be there—but only if you promise not to make any more promises on my behalf."

She lifted her chin and stared at his father's image in the painting. "He was so young when he died. I always thought we would grow old together, but no one lives forever." She lowered her gaze to Phillip's face. "I expect you promptly at eight o'clock."

MORNING SUN SPARKLED outside the glass of the Cortland breakfast room the next morning as Eva entered. "Good morning," she called.

"Eva, good morning." Nora gestured to a chair. "Please, join us."

A footman assisted Eva into a seat next to her friend and across from Mrs. Cortland, Nora's aunt. A servant stepped forward and reached for the coffee urn. She held up a hand. "I'd prefer tea, actually."

"The coffee is here for my husband," Mrs. Cortland murmured as the footman poured. "He's the only one who won't switch over to tea."

"Julius is also one of those obnoxious coffee drinkers," Nora said with a small, fond smile. "Yet I love him anyway."

Her friend and Mr. Julius Hatcher had married a few weeks ago. The marriage was to be kept a secret, however, and a big society wedding would follow in September. At least Eva would be there for the second ceremony, where she would serve as Nora's maid of honor.

Eva had shared dinner with Nora, Mr. Hatcher, and the Cortlands last evening, and it had been instantly clear why the pair were perfect for one another. Hatcher was grounded in practicality and reason, which suited Nora's impulsiveness. Eva couldn't be happier for Nora, even if it was hard to believe her headstrong, fearless friend had married. Though, as Eva could now attest, American men were nothing like British men.

A shiver went down her spine as she recalled Phillip's drugging kisses. Even if the night they spent together remained hazy in her mind, she did remember those kisses, ones she'd needed more than air.

The morning after, she'd been gifted with plenty of opportunity to study his well-delineated muscles and golden skin as he'd slept. The man hadn't a bad side, apparently. She hadn't found fault with him at any angle. Dark lashes rested on his cheeks, full lips parted, with morning whiskers covering his jaw. Broad, strong shoulders. She hadn't ever witnessed a more glorious man.

And she prayed never to see him again.

The mortification over her behavior hadn't abated. Thank goodness Phillip did not know her real name. Whatever happened on the ship would stay there, never to be repeated or reported. They would not encounter one another in the future and this whole episode would be forgotten.

The end.

She shook herself and offered Nora's aunt a grateful smile. "Thank you again for opening your home while I am in New York, Mrs. Cortland."

"My pleasure, and you must call me Aunt Bea. We have more than enough room and Nora is thrilled to have you here. We all are, in fact."

They chatted easily over their breakfast until a footman arrived with a note for Nora's aunt. She excused herself from the table and left, leaving Nora and Eva alone. Her friend ordered the staff from the room. "Now we may speak privately," Nora said when the door closed.

"That sounds ominous." Eva took her plate to the sideboard, where a large collection of covered dishes awaited. She selected three pieces of buttered toast and some eggs. Now recovered from the champagne headache, she found herself ravenous.

"I never had a chance to speak with you alone last night." Nora sighed and lifted her china cup. "What did you think of Julius?"

"He's intelligent and kind. And absolutely perfect for you."

Pink swept over Nora's cheeks. "I swear, that man. I am utterly and completely mad for him."

"I noticed," Eva said dryly as she scooped up some ham. "I'm happy for you both. I do wish I could have attended your real wedding, however."

"Father rushed it all through. You know, protecting my sterling reputation."

"As well he should. That is what fathers are for."

"Oh, Eva. I am so very sorry your father's health has worsened." Nora's gaze swam with sympathy as she watched Eva retake her seat. "Perhaps a handsome American will sweep you off your feet and you'll end up in a hasty marriage yourself."

Eva must have turned the color of a tomato but

Nora just slyly smiled. "Why, Lady Eva Hyde, you are blushing. What are you not telling me?"

She shook her head, not meeting her friend's eyes as she chewed a bite of toast. "Absolutely nothing."

"Oh, and I suppose absolutely nothing is responsible for the love mark on your neck?"

Eva's hand flew to her throat where the bruise-colored mark was covered by her dress. "How did you . . . ?"

"I saw it last evening. I thought I should let you have a good night's sleep before I wrestled that information out of you. So, who was he? Someone on the ship, obviously."

Eva sighed and rubbed her forehead. Nora would never let this go, not without the truth. "Yes, a man on the ship. An American."

"Hmm, I see. And?"

"And that's all."

"That's all?"

Eva shrugged and began eating, ready to move on from this conversation. Nora made a noise in the back of her throat. "I don't believe you. You would never let some stranger leave love marks on your neck. The two of you obviously had a spark of some kind. Who was he?"

A spark? More like an inferno. "No one important. Merely a shipboard dalliance. Caught in the storm with no one else about. We had dinner together and then the lights cut out. He took me to his cabin and I'm afraid the champagne caught up with us."

"Champagne or no champagne, that's hardly like you. I've known you a long time and I do not believe you've ever been in an improper situation with a man. Me, on the other hand . . ."

Eva didn't answer and Nora started drumming her fingers on the table. "Spill, Eva. It's plain you are holding back. What are you worried about, that I'll judge you? Please, I am the last woman to ever cast judgment on a dalliance. Julius and I certainly did not wait until marriage and then there was Robert. You may trust me."

"It's not a matter of trust. You *know* I trust you. Goodness, you're about the only person I would ever confide in. But the whole thing was so strange. I went from eating with him one minute to kissing him in the next. And I don't even know his last name."

That caused Nora's eyes to widen. "You don't even know his last name?"

"No, and I told him my name was Evelyn."

"Good lord. What are you, some sort of wartime spy?"

"It's silly, of course. I just . . . I didn't want him to know who I was."

"Why?" When Eva did not respond, Nora said, "Oh, that ridiculous nickname."

"Not so ridiculous when you consider the circumstances."

Nora leaned in, stabbing a finger at the tabletop. "You are aware that you had nothing to do with the deaths of those three men, correct?"

Eva loved her friend even more for the fierce response. "Of course, but society hardly sees it that way. Nor do the newspapers—and neither will the owner of this hotel I am building. I'm considered cursed."

"They can all hang. You lost your betrothed three times. It's a bit odd, granted, but young men do foolish things. One of them died after being thrown from a horse, one from influenza, and another drowned when his boat sank. Good heavens, Eva. You're to be pitied, not vilified."

"I don't want pity, either. My father wanted those matches, not me. I liked them each well enough but there was never any emotion attached to it."

"Not a spark?"

"No, not a—" Eva saw what Nora was trying to do. "You may cease that line of thinking right there. I don't want to get married. Not to him, not to anyone."

"You say that now, but marriage isn't so bad. Not with the right man."

"Spoken like a true newlywed. The last thing I need is another dead fiancé—or worse, a closed-minded, controlling husband who will try to curtail my activities at every turn. I need to focus on my father's legacy then begin planning my own."

"Fine. I'll refrain from matchmaking." She picked at her roll. "Tell me, was he handsome?"

"Absurdly handsome. Big, like one of the workers on a construction site." Eva held her hands to her shoulders to indicate Phillip's muscles.

"Oh, my."

"Indeed. He was . . . Well, a nice distraction for a few hours." She checked the time. *Oh, no.* She would be late if she didn't leave soon. After a few quick bites of ham, she pushed her chair back from the table and stood. "I need to be going. They're expecting E. M. Hyde at the hotel construction site to go over a few things before we break ground tomorrow."

"How exciting. I am looking forward to seeing your work here in New York."

"My father's work."

Nora shook her head. "No, *your* work, Eva. Make no mistake—this is yours. It may carry your father's name but this is your building."

THE CARRIAGE STOPPED at a giant empty lot at Thirty-Fifth Street and Fifth Avenue. Eva turned the latch and threw open the door without waiting on the driver. A group of men were gathered at the corner, a circle of brown and black hats, while the morning traffic of New York continued around them.

Clutching her large case, she descended from the carriage, careful to watch her step. If she tripped or appeared weak in any way these men would sense it and lose all respect for her.

James, the Cortlands' coachman, appeared in front of her, blocking her view. "Are you all right, milady? Wasn't expecting you to jump down on your own."

"I know, James. I tend to be a bit more independent than other women. I don't believe I shall be long but if you want—"

"I'll stay. I'll just settle in and wait for your ladyship." He tipped his cap and started for his perch.

Breathing deep for courage, she started for the group of men. This was a meeting with Mr. Mansfield, his construction chief, and some of the foremen who would oversee the job. The tone of this meeting would dictate all future encounters, so it was imperative she make a good impression.

There was something familiar about the largest of the men. He had his back to her, broad shoulders pulling the fabric of his coat tight. Short dark hair. For a moment, she almost thought it was Phillip.

She nearly laughed. One night of his kisses and she was seeing him everywhere. How pathetic.

And then he turned.

Her breath caught, heart leaping into her throat to strangle her.

Dear God, it was *him*. Phillip the American. Tall, square-jawed, brawny-shouldered Phillip.

She took a step back as he pushed forward and headed toward her. What on earth was he doing here?

Something in her chest fluttered at the sight of him once more. She tried to analyze the reaction and decided it was half embarrassment, half a basic biological attraction to the opposite sex. A silly female reaction. She clutched the leather handles of her case and tried to school her expression.

His brows drew together, wariness on his handsome face as he reached her. "Evelyn, what are you doing here?"

"I . . . Wait, what are you doing here?"

He took her elbow in a strong grip and led her away from the other men. "Not that I'm unhappy to see you, but I am quite busy this morning. Perhaps we could have dinner this evening? Just tell me where you are staying and I'll make the arrangements."

"You think I . . . ?" What, that she'd been driving by and saw him? The idea was so ludicrous she couldn't finish it.

"I assumed you noticed me standing here." Confusion clouded his dark gaze. "Whatever the reason, I am glad to see you. After you disappeared on the ship I thought I'd never find you again. I looked everywhere before we docked."

She shook her head as if to clear it. "You did?"

"Of course. I wanted to . . . Well, I wanted to see you again. To take you to dinner."

"That's not a good idea."

That set him back on his heels a bit. "Then what are you doing here?"

"I'm here for a meeting. Why are you here?"

"For a meeting." He studied her face. "With whom are you meeting?"

Phillip . . . here for a meeting. Could it be? Puzzle pieces began to fall into place.

Oh, no.

No, no, no.

She forced the words out. "Oh, my God. You are Phillip Mansfield."

He put his hands on his hips, annoyance and impatience staring down at her. "Yes, I am. I realize we never exchanged surnames on the ship but I hardly see why learning who I am caused you to go white as a sheet. And I still have no idea who *you* are."

For heaven's sake, she would have to tell him. There was no way to avoid it. Yet the words were not easy, not when she knew what they meant. This was the man who'd hired her father, who had entrusted E. M. Hyde to design his spectacular hotel.

To deliver, as Mansfield had called it, the greatest building America had ever seen.

She was here to oversee the project. For this man she'd drunkenly kissed. Slept next to all night in various states of undress. God, he'd been shirtless in front of her . . . not to mention whatever happened the night before. She could die from mortification.

And he was her employer.

"Evelyn, what is wrong with you? You are scaring me. Are you ill?"

"No," she said instantly, aware of the many curious eyes a few feet away. She could not appear weak, not in front of these men. "I'm perfectly fine. But there is something you should know."

He shifted his weight from one foot to the other, impatient, as she tried to summon the courage to speak. "Well," he prompted when she remained mute. "We need to hurry this along. I'm expecting the architect for my hotel at any moment."

"No, you are not," she wheezed.

He peered at her. "I'm not?"

"Not waiting, I mean. The architect is here."

"For God's sake, I don't have time for this. Get to the point."

"Me. I am the architect." She cleared her throat and repeated it, stronger this time. "I am the architect."

After a beat he threw his head back and laughed, the strong cords in his throat standing out in sharp relief. "You had me there for a—"

"I am. The architect." Anger sparked at the base of her neck, quickly spreading to every part of her body to replace any lingering embarrassment over their past. Of course he did not believe her. He was no different than any of her fiancés, or any of the other men who believed women should not have their own careers.

Slowly, he quieted, his amusement dying off when he realized she wasn't joining in. He blinked, his lips pressing together into a flat, unhappy line. "Are you saying . . . ?"

She held out her hand. "I am Lady Eva Hyde, E. M. Hyde's daughter. And I shall be overseeing this project."

Chapter Four

Phillip could barely rein in his fury as the brougham bounded up Fifth Avenue. He kept his gaze on the familiar streets and limestone buildings, the city he knew and loved so well, while attempting to keep his emotions from bubbling over. Evelyn—no, *Lady Eva* sat silent next to him, her large leather satchel resting on the floor of the vehicle.

Lady Eva, also known as Lady Unlucky, the daughter of E. M. Hyde—or Lord Cassell, as he'd become a few years back—and Phillip's architect.

Christ.

Phillip ground his teeth together. No wonder she'd kept her identity a secret on the ship, considering her reputation. Not that he cared about her history with fiancés; he didn't want her working on his hotel. Not in any capacity.

As soon as she had introduced herself, he'd taken her arm and hustled her into his carriage, ordering Gabriel to finish the meeting. He needed to sort this out with Lady Eva and they did not require an audience.

"Were you planning to speak or merely grind your teeth the whole trip?"

He clenched and unclenched his fists. He wished to pummel something, to expel the dangerous energy coursing through him like a cancer. Perhaps he'd visit McGirk's this evening. The boxing club in the Bowery was the only place in New York where he could truly lose himself and his polished upbringing. Drown in rough physical activity for a few hours. Regain his equilibrium.

"Will you at least tell me where we are headed?"

"My office," he ground out, not looking at her. He watched the blur of people and carriages outside the window instead.

"Why?"

"Because I wish to speak with you in private."

"We are in private now, in case you hadn't noticed."

"We are on a public street in a very crowded city. *My* crowded city. This is hardly private."

"In other words, you wish to yell at me and you are afraid someone might overhear."

"I never said that."

She made a noise in her throat. "You didn't have to. I can see it plainly on your face."

You have your father's temper, his mother often said. *You must find a way to control it.*

He tried to relax, tried not to think about the three million dollars he'd put up to build the hotel. The hundreds of jobs this project would provide. The income the hotel would generate once it opened. This project was to be his goddamned *legacy*.

And the construction timeline was ambitious; he

didn't have time to find another architect and have the plans redrafted.

"Damn it," he swore under his breath. She stiffened but said nothing more.

They reached Eighty-First Street and the carriage slowed. Heart thumping, he pushed open the door and climbed out before the wheels even stopped moving. He held out his hand and helped her to the walk, then escorted her into his home.

"Is this . . . ? It's the Loggia del Capitanio." Her chin tilted as she assessed the exterior of his home. "Goodness, it's stunning."

Of course she recognized it. *No, I merely like to look at buildings. I'm curious to see how your landscape differs from London and the other European cities.* A lie. The woman was the daughter of the greatest living architect in the world. What else had she lied about?

Even when we first met I thought you were perfectly lickable.

That too? Had she been playing him the entire time?

The front door opened and Roberts appeared. His eyes widened at the sight of his master tugging a small, well-dressed lady at his side. "Good morning, sir."

"I'm not to be disturbed, Roberts."

"Very good, sir. May I take . . . ?"

The words were lost to the empty room. Phillip had already left the entryway and was leading Eva farther into the house. He noted the way her head kept turning, the soft gasps at the artwork and details throughout the interior. He slowed his pace to allow her to keep up, though his hand remained securely wrapped around her upper arm.

He'd touched her before, of course, and thoughts of those touches had haunted him since waking to a cold bed on the ship. Since searching for her in every nook and cranny on that floating hunk of steel. He hadn't wanted to lose her. So, he'd raced about, looking, certain what they'd shared had been real, that her touch had perhaps been more real than any he'd ever had.

How wrong he'd been.

Throwing open the heavy wooden door to his office, he motioned for her to enter. Shoulders set and spine straight, she strode past him and lowered herself into one of the chairs opposite his desk.

He stripped off his morning coat and tossed the garment over a chair while taking a deep breath, preparing for the sight of her. He steeled himself against the glossy red hair that was every bit as soft as it appeared, the smooth, creamy skin that had given under his lips and teeth. The lush mouth that kissed like an angel and tormented like the devil.

He recalled every detail of their evening together, from laughing and talking over dinner to the breathy sound of her orgasm in his ear. It had been one of the best nights he'd had with a woman in ages, perhaps ever. Those memories were now tainted, ruined.

On the ship he'd assumed her to be . . . experienced. Women didn't travel alone, especially wealthy English women, and there hadn't been a chaperone anywhere in the vicinity. He'd guessed her to be widowed. Hell, she could've been married for all he knew and cuckolding her absent husband. He hadn't asked.

You didn't ask because you wanted her to be experienced.

Also, she'd acted bold and responsive—not like a virgin at all. She'd been warm and wet, a pleasant surprise. He could still hear the little gasps she'd made in her throat as he pleasured her.

"Are you an innocent?"

Her pale skin turned a dull red. "I hardly see how that is your business."

"You would be wrong, considering what happened on the ship. Not to mention what could have happened. You should have told me."

"If things had progressed I would have informed you."

"I hope you mean that. I do not care for surprises."

"I'm gathering that fact," she said dryly, shifting toward him. "But this changes nothing. We must put the past behind us and not think about what happened on the ship."

"I am not upset over the ship," he lied. "Yes, I was disappointed when I could not find you, frustrated you left without saying good-bye, but there are worse problems at the moment." No need to mention he'd ordered his secretary, Gabriel, to track her down, that he would have found her eventually. "I'm upset you lied to me."

"That I *lied* to you?"

He pointed at the leather case on the rug. "When those plans were filed, when the contracts were signed, I was promised that E. M. Hyde would be in New York to oversee this project—not his daughter."

She swallowed hard but her voice did not waver. "He has fallen ill and asked me to come in his stead. I am entirely qualified. He's been mentoring me all my life—"

"I did not pay a bloody fortune to get second best, Eva. This is a three-million-dollar hotel with my name on it. I paid for E. M. Hyde and I damn well want him!"

"You are passing judgment on me without even giving me a chance. I'm more than capable to do this."

A woman . . . serving as the project's architect? The idea was ludicrous at best. At worst, it was dangerous.

He clenched his fists and watched the blazing fire in the hearth. What was he supposed to do? Construction was scheduled to start tomorrow. He hated feeling this way, as if he'd lost control of the project before it even began. "When will he recover?"

"The physicians are uncertain, but he is able to answer cables and letters. I know the plans inside and out. I can do this, Phillip. I would never claim otherwise, knowing what his reputation means. He's spent a lifetime building his legacy. I would not dare do anything to ruin that."

"It's more than knowing the plans. You'll be expected at the site, which is hardly a safe place for a lady. Not to mention the crew. These are rough, often crude, men who are not well versed in genteel manners. Have you thought of that?"

"This is not the first project I have overseen. I promise, I have dealt with all of this before."

"Yes, but not *my* project and certainly not one this high profile. *Goddamn it.*" He dragged a hand through his hair. "I should fire you on the spot."

"But you won't." She reached for her satchel. "I'll prove to you that I know the project. I have a few ideas for the ladies' drawing room on the main floor."

Despite his anger he was intrigued. "Your father and I settled on Italian marble and frescoes."

"I prefer French. I'd like to recreate Marie Antoinette's apartment."

"Fine, let's see these ideas. But Eva?" He threw her a hard glance. "They had better be good."

AT LEAST HE hadn't discharged her. Yet.

Eva tried not to fumble as she opened her satchel and removed the revised sketches for the ladies' drawing room. He hadn't raised the issue of her nickname, so perhaps he hadn't yet heard of it. God knew she certainly had no intention of telling him.

Especially since he appeared on the verge of losing his temper.

The man behind the desk was entirely different than the one she'd met on the ship. On the journey he had seemed . . . playful. Charming. Relaxed. This version was all hard edges and sharp focus. A ruthless scion of business who commanded a room with his mere presence.

Shocking to admit, but she'd much rather deal with the charismatic bon vivant. At least then she'd have known what to expect.

Standing, she unfurled a long piece of tracing paper on the desk. Phillip came around the large piece of furniture to stand beside her. "The room is already oval," she explained, "so we merely need to add some recesses and lower the ceiling height to inset it a bit." She pointed to a detailed sketch of the front view. "Glass mirrors here, here, and here, with chandeliers in front of each. All white enamel woodwork with French furniture. We'll have an artist paint a fresco on the ceiling."

"You're certain this is close to the original?"

"Yes, it's almost identical."

He stroked his jaw and studied the drawings. "I've written to Will Low to see if he'll do some original paintings. Perhaps I can add this fresco to his list."

Hope sparkled in her chest. "So you like it?"

"It's different. No one's attempted anything like this, not here, and I think the publicity will help when the time comes." He turned his head toward her. "Your sketches are quite good. No one helped you with them?"

She clenched her jaw, tamping down the urge to shout at him. "I did them all by myself."

"It is clear you've inherited some of your father's talent. However, this does not alleviate my concerns." He leaned a hip against the large rosewood desk and folded his arms, calling attention to his ridiculously broad chest. A flash of bare muscular shoulders on white cotton bedclothes ran through her mind, a sight she was unlikely to ever forget.

Suddenly itchy and uncomfortable, she pulled at

the collar of her shirtwaist. His gaze dipped to her throat—and his nostrils flared.

The mark. He must have seen the fading mark he'd left on her skin the other night.

She dropped her hand but not before the dark, primitive satisfaction reflected in his eyes caused gooseflesh to erupt on her arms. Awareness buzzed between them, the memories of passionate kisses and heated words. Part of her expected him to gloat, to throw her wanton behavior directly in her face.

Instead of commenting, however, he spun on his heel and returned behind his desk. Her skin went up in flames, a reaction she prayed he wouldn't notice.

"And what of your reputation, Lady Unlucky?"

So he had heard about her. She struggled not to let him see how much the nickname bothered her. "A silly exaggeration by gossips with nothing better to do with their time."

"While you and I may believe it silly, the public are a superstitious lot. If there's any hint the building is cursed not a soul will ever stay there. Your involvement alone jeopardizes the entire project."

"I am not cursed."

"Three dead fiancés in as many years says otherwise."

She flinched but did not evade his scrutiny. "I did not murder them, if you were wondering."

"I wasn't, but thank you for clearing that up. Were you in love with any of them?"

The question caught her by surprise and she gaped at him for a brief moment. Finally, she managed to ask, "How on earth is that any of your business?"

He lifted an arrogant shoulder. "Three seems a high number for such a young woman. Did you not mourn them properly? I think likely not, which makes me wonder: Why was your father so desperate to marry you off?"

Her ears buzzed with embarrassment. Each fiancé had been a calculated business move on the part of her father, either for a project or money. She'd been a pawn in the schemes of men, something she'd sworn never to become again.

Still, Phillip had no right to any of that information. "Not that it matters, but he was not desperate to marry me off. I was quite fond of each man."

He made a disbelieving sound in his throat but didn't argue the point. "This project must run smoothly. Even if the workers are fine with working under a woman—which is a big *if*, I might add— the nickname ensures they'll be looking over their shoulders for trouble at every turn. I cannot have them skittish and causing accidents. I am afraid—"

"I won't tell anyone who I am," she blurted. No idea where the thought came from, but now that she'd said it this appeared the perfect solution.

"What do you mean?"

"I'll pretend to be Hyde's secretary instead of his daughter. We'll make up a name."

"In which case you'll have no real power. As his daughter and a lady, you would command a certain level of respect. As a secretary, you'd be merely an ineffectual substitute for your employer until he arrives in New York. Is that truly what you want?"

After all the hours she'd spent laboring over these drafts, poring over every detail of the hotel's interior and exterior, she could not walk away. And seeing as how her father would never arrive in New York, she had to see this through for him—for *them*—even if she had to battle every foreman, mason, carpenter, and imperious owner to do it.

"Yes, that is what I want."

"Why?"

Because she needed to see her work finished, the final result towering over the city for generations to come. Not to mention the money that ensured her father would receive the best of care as his health declined. But Phillip need not know any of that. He believed this her father's work. "This project means a great deal to my father. He is quite passionate about what you hope to accomplish here and is invested in ensuring the hotel lives up to expectations."

"His name lends incredible weight to the publicity. People shall travel from all over the world to stay in this hotel."

A hotel completely designed by her.

Eva tried not to rub her hands together in glee. "Is it all settled, then? Have we completed our chat?"

"No." He leaned back in his chair. "I have agreed to nothing. None of this is ideal."

"I realize I've caught you by surprise. But it's merely temporary," she lied.

"How temporary?"

She lifted a shoulder. "A month. Six weeks at most." Hopefully she could convince him to let her stay at the end of that period.

He heaved a sigh. "As long as you stay in constant

contact with your father during that time. I want him updated regularly of all that's happening and offering guidance. That way, it'll be like he's really here."

Instead of you.

Like nearly every male Eva had ever encountered, Phillip believed women were incapable of anything other than gossip and menial tasks. They distrusted any female with half a brain and attempted to demean her at every turn.

You know you can do this. Tell him what he wants to hear and then prove yourself indispensable.

"Yes, I shall do exactly that."

His frown had yet to diminish. "There is one more item I'd like to discuss and it pertains to what happened on the ship."

She had hoped he wouldn't raise the topic. Ever. Was it not bad enough she'd always remember making a fool of herself with him? "There's no reason to discuss it. *That* shall not be repeated."

"Agreed. Any sort of continuation is out of the question. As your employer, I must maintain a professional distance to not affect the project on which we are collaborating."

"Rest assured we are in agreement on this."

He dipped his chin. "Go home and I'll see you at tomorrow's ceremony."

"Does this mean you are letting me stay?"

"Until I am able to figure out another solution, it seems I have little choice."

PHILLIP SURVEYED THE crowd gathered in the warm summer morning. Politicians, reporters, friends, and acquaintances had all turned out for the announcement regarding the hotel's construction. He adjusted his cuffs and tried not to stare as Eva hurried toward the platform erected for the event.

Thank goodness she'd worn a high-necked gown to cover that ridiculous mark he'd left on her skin. What man of his age did something so foolhardy? He hadn't given or received a love mark since he was in his teens, for hell's sake. All he could recall was drowning in her delicious smell, the softness of her skin, and the way she'd held him tighter as he nibbled and sucked her throat. A wave of sharp awareness rolled through him, one that he tamped down immediately.

He'd lost his mind, apparently. That he was allowing this, allowing *her* to stay on the project, smacked of recklessness. *She's worked her way under your skin, Mansfield.*

No, absolutely not. She had not affected him, nor would she. He would not allow it, no matter how well she kissed. Three dead fiancés meant scandals—and Phillip abhorred scandals. Hated negative attention of any kind.

Eva reached him, her boot heels thumping on the wooden dais. Her red hair was neatly tucked under a wide straw bonnet secured with a peach ribbon under her chin. She appeared young and fresh-faced . . . and damn delectable.

"Is something the matter?" Eva stood in front of him, staring at him as if he'd gone round the bend.

"I'm fine—and you are late."

Her eyes flashed then cleared. Had that been anger? "I apologize. I had difficulty securing a hack. Shall we get started?"

"Yes, but have you decided on a name for this ruse?"

"Oh." She bit her bottom lip and studied her shoes for a moment. "How about Miss Ashford? That was my mother's maiden name."

He nodded and motioned to the mayor that they should get started. Mayor Grant quieted the crowd and spoke first. After a brief welcome, he talked at length about the Mansfield family and their contributions to the city, as well as the progress happening all around them. He thanked Phillip on behalf of the city and then a round of applause went up.

Phillip stepped forward and shook the mayor's hand. Then it was his turn. He put forth his vision for the hotel, discussing the designs Hyde had produced, and how they hoped to change luxury travel in the United States forever. "Allow me to introduce the team behind the Mansfield Hotel. On the end is John Milliken, the head of our general contractor, Milliken Brothers. Beside him is Alfred Carew, the project's construction superintendent. Then Miss Ashford, here on behalf of our architect, E. M. Hyde, Lord Cassell. Anyone have any questions for me this morning?"

"Mr. Mansfield," called a heavily mustached reporter. "Is E. M. Hyde planning to travel to New York to oversee the project?"

"Yes, though it's uncertain exactly when. His lordship has fallen ill in London and cannot travel at the moment. Miss Ashford will serve as the liaison in the meantime."

"Does that concern you?" another reporter asked.

Yes, for several reasons. "No. Miss Ashford is entirely competent and modern advances in communication allow us to stay in close contact with his lordship. Without a doubt, the hotel shall not only meet my standards but also the standards of every New Yorker."

A pencil went in the air. "The timeline for your hotel is ambitious, Mr. Mansfield. Any worries you cannot fulfill it?"

"Not at all. We are extremely confident the project can be completed in two years. I plan to be directly involved on the day-to-day decisions and moving this forward as rapidly as I can." Eva made a small noise behind him but he remained focused on the crowd.

The reporters scattered a few minutes later and Phillip thanked the mayor and the other politicians on the dais. Just as he was turning to find Eva, a hand landed on his shoulder. Turning, he found James Keene, second in command at Tammany Hall, the powerful—and corrupt—political machine that ran New York.

"Mr. Mansfield," Keene said with a well-oiled smile, reaching to shake Phillip's hand. "Congratulations. You must be quite excited to get under way."

"Hello, Keene. Yes, indeed I am." He hadn't been surprised to see Keene and a few of his cronies in the crowd today. No one built a property as big as the Mansfield Hotel without Tammany trying to get a slice of the pie. They had pushed to control the construction and Phillip had resisted. When the permits had stalled at the city, however, he'd been forced to appease Tammany with a large "donation" in exchange for the demolition work. Very large, in fact.

So what the hell did Keene want now?

Keene surveyed the flat area that had been cleared. "I came to wish you luck. Should be a beautiful hotel when it's finished."

"That is certainly my intention."

"Boys did a thorough job on your demolition, wouldn't you say?"

Phillip crossed his arms over his chest. What was this parlor-room talk really about? "They did. I have no complaints."

"You know, it's not too late to let us help with the construction. We have some of the best masons—"

"That's not necessary." Tammany was like a Hydra; every head you cut off sprang two more. Phillip refused to give them another opening. "Our contracts are signed and we are set."

Keene slapped Phillip's shoulder. "You drive a hard bargain, Mansfield. I like that about you. Not much different from your father. He was a tough one when the mood struck him, too."

Phillip had heard this many times over the years, though his memories of his father were scant. Phillip had been just five when his father died.

"But he also knew how to keep the peace," Keene finished. "You don't want to make enemies on your first project here in New York, do you?"

"Is that what we are now, enemies?"

"No, no. We're not looking to start trouble here

but you must spread things around, especially with a British architect instead of a New Yorker like Mr. White or Mr. Mead. And Milliken and his crew are from Chicago. Carew's certainly not one of us, being a Negro and all. We cannot have the locals resentful at being locked out."

Phillip didn't give a damn what the "locals" were feeling. He'd hired the best people for the job, period. Not to mention that most of the laborers were immigrants living right here in the city. But he wasn't fooled: Keene's supposed concern was reserved exclusively for the wealthy politicians looking to skim off the project through graft.

He struggled to remain calm and keep his voice even. "What you fail to see here is that my money is backing this project. That means I get the final say. I won't be strong-armed, not even by Tammany."

Keene stroked his jaw thoughtfully, gaze sweeping over the empty plot. "If that's the way you want to play it, Mansfield, then I'll be certain to let Croker know."

"You do that," Phillip said and turned on his heel, ready to find Eva.

He found Milliken waiting instead. His general contractor wore his usual unhappy expression, looking a bit like a fireplug, with flat, hard features. "Mr. Mansfield, may I have a word?"

The two of them stepped to the edge of the platform for privacy. Phillip slipped his hands into his pockets. "What is it?"

"Sir, that woman, Miss Ashford. Is she overseeing the plans? I'm afraid I don't understand."

"She is managing them on behalf of Hyde, who cannot travel at the moment. I know it's not ideal but we have little choice in the matter."

"The other men, sir, the crew members? They won't care for a woman being underfoot. They're not thrilled about Carew as it is."

His construction superintendent was one of the best engineers in the country. Phillip didn't give a damn about the color of a man's skin. What mattered was finding the most qualified person for the job, and Carew had more than proven himself on previous projects. These petty complaints had to be thoroughly quashed for things to progress smoothly. "I understand Miss Ashford's presence is unusual for the men. Believe me, if I feel she's not up to the challenge, I'll have her on the first boat back to London."

Milliken nodded though he hardly appeared appeased. "Fine."

"I'd like you to meet her." Raising his head, he found Eva standing a few feet away, clearly waiting for him, and motioned her over. "Miss Ashford, this is Mr. Milliken, the head of Milliken and Brothers. Milliken, this is Miss Ashford."

Milliken tipped his derby. "Miss Ashford."

"Mr. Milliken. I look forward to working together."

She was self-possessed and polite but Milliken did not thaw. His jaw remained tight, lips flat and lifeless. He gave her a brief nod and strode away.

"Well," she said, facing Phillip. "He seems quite thrilled to have me around."

"You had to expect it. The workers won't be any easier to win over, you know."

"I can handle them. You needn't worry—this

project shall come off without a hitch. In no time at all you'll be welcoming your first guest."

He wished he shared her confidence. Surprises were unwelcome with millions of dollars on the line and he'd already had his fair share thus far. "Did you meet Carew?"

"Yes. He was a good deal more welcoming than Milliken."

"What did you think of today's ceremony?"

"I thought it was the perfect amount of pomp and circumstance. The reporters were eager and your answers were to the point. A success, I'd say." She shifted from one foot to the other. "What did you mean when you said you plan to be directly involved in the day-to-day process?"

"Precisely that. I plan to be here every day." Color crept up her throat and over her cheeks, a reaction he noted with rabid interest. Had she been hoping he would disappear? "If you thought I'd summer in Newport while construction began I am sorry to disappoint you."

She kept her gaze on the emptying crowd. "No, no. This is your hotel, of course you should do as you please . . ." Her voice trailed off and he had the impression there was more she wanted to say.

"However?"

"No, nothing." She peered up at him. "It's just that most of my father's clients trust the plans and the crew. They don't bother themselves with the small details and the tedium of the job."

"That may be the case but last time I checked you were not E. M. Hyde. So let's merely say I am entirely invested in watching over my investment."

"I'll quickly prove to be entirely capable, Mr. Mansfield."

Mindful of the crowd still milling about, he leaned in a hair's breadth closer. She didn't retreat, merely stared up at him with her stubborn chin high in the air, defiance simmering in her wide gaze. "I do hope so, for your sake. You'd best accustom yourself to my presence because I'll be looming over your shoulder until your father arrives."

Chapter Five

Eva sat on the stone garden wall, a pile of pebbles at her hip that she organized into shapes and mounds. Squares, rectangles, pyramids. Anything to keep her hands busy and her mind occupied.

Phillip Mansfield was nothing like the wealthy patrons she'd encountered over the past few years. This building meant something to him. He actually cared about the result, much more than merely putting his name on the cornerstone. The echo of his words from this morning sat ominously in her stomach, a sour apprehension of all that could go wrong.

I'll be looming over your shoulder until your father arrives.

And what would happen when her father never arrived? Would Phillip stand over her shoulder like a hawk for two years? Lord above, she'd be an utter wreck by then.

"What are you doing out here?"

Eva glanced up from her rock pyramid and found Nora sauntering along the garden path. Her friend had been out with Julius last evening for dinner so she and Eva hadn't had a chance to talk since Eva discovered the identity of her boss. Eva was dashed glad to see her friend. "Thinking."

"Brooding, you mean. I know that look you're wearing." Her friend perched on the stone, half turned toward Eva. "Now, why so glum?"

There was no use hiding the news from Nora; she would find out regardless. "The Phillip from the ship?"

Nora's eyes twinkled and her mouth curved into a knowing smile. "Mr. Love Mark?"

"Turns out he's Phillip Mansfield, who also happens to be—?"

"Your employer." Nora covered her mouth with her hand, mirth quickly morphing into horror. "Oh, no. I cannot imagine his reaction. What did he say? Did you tell him about your father? What of Lady Unlucky? Had he heard of the nickname?"

Eva rubbed her brow as she sorted through the mess in her mind. "At first, angry. Said he paid good money for my father and had been promised E. M. Hyde would personally oversee the project. When I explained my father is ill and I would be stepping in until he is able to travel—"

"Wait, I thought he couldn't travel."

"True, but Mansfield need not learn that fact now."

"Oh, goodness."

"Do not give me that face, Nora. You, of all people, understand why I am doing this."

The two women had been friends for years and Nora knew how hard Eva had worked. How many years she'd studied and practiced to learn her father's craft. How her father's health had deteriorated along with the money. If Eva hadn't accepted this job, she and her father would soon be destitute. "Almost two years now since Father has been able to work," she explained. "I don't have a choice."

Nora grasped Eva's hand. "You know Julius would be more than happy to help with your debts, if I asked. So would my aunt and uncle. It's appalling how terrible your father was with his finances."

The offer touched her deeply, but this was not Nora's problem. Eva had to handle this in her own way, not borrowing money and keeping them dependent on the kindness of others. "I cannot disagree, but getting angry won't solve the past. And thank you for the kind offer, but I need to handle this myself. I'll think of something to tell Mansfield when the time comes."

"Perhaps you can stall until it no longer matters. You are talented, Eva. Once he realizes you drafted those plans, he'll come around."

Eva wished she shared her friend's confidence. "He almost sacked me, saying my reputation will cause the crew to believe the site cursed."

"Oh, dear. Is that not what we feared?"

"Yes, most definitely. To keep from losing the project, I promised to keep my identity a secret from everyone."

Nora blinked a few times and then swatted at a nearby bee. "Wait, you are not telling anyone other than Mansfield that you're Lady Eva? What are we to call you in public?"

"I doubt the crew will attend the opera so you may continue using my real name," she said dryly.

"If you visit the construction site, however, I am Miss Ashford. Thankfully Mansfield has agreed to the scheme for now."

"He has? I find that surprising. Mansfield is not known to be flexible. He's . . . rigid. Very old money and proper manners."

After today, Eva believed it. "You make him sound like a stodgy old duke."

"The comparison is a fair one. His family is at the very top tier of New York society, richer than anyone save the queen." Nora squinted as she studied Eva's face. "You know what else I know about Mansfield?"

The carrot had been dangled and Eva couldn't resist, desperate for any sort of information. "What?"

"He's quite handsome."

Eva rolled her eyes heavenward. "Tell me something I do not already know."

"Fine. Do you know he has a mistress? At least, he did. One of the most well-known actresses in the city."

She tried not to react to that news, but the truth of it settled on her tongue like a spoiled sardine. *Did you believe him a monk? Of course he has a mistress, one who is probably beautiful and talented. Revered and successful. A worldly woman with social graces, one accustomed to showing men a good time.*

In other words, the exact opposite of *her.*

Nora's jaw dropped. "You like him."

"Do not be absurd. He's my employer. And he's much too . . . unyielding for my tastes."

"Come now, this is me. I know you better than anyone so there's no need to lie."

"Fine. There was something there, aboard the ship. He was much different." Nora's brow quirked in question so Eva continued. "He was charming. Humorous."

"Do tell." Nora nudged Eva's arm with her elbow. "And spare no detail."

Eva laughed and proceeded to tell Nora about his *mal de mer* and then the night of the storm. "There were all these open bottles of champagne and we couldn't let them to go to waste," she finished with.

"Oh, an act of public service. So what was kissing him, then? Generating your own electricity?"

Electricity, indeed. Eva could still feel it buzzing through her whenever Phillip was near. "A night of drunken hedonism, nothing more. We are entirely unsuited. He actually called me 'second best.'"

"Well, you can hardly blame him. As far as he knows, the architect who drafted the plans for the Mansfield Hotel is in London."

A fair point, but Eva was not finished. "He asked why Father was so desperate to marry me off." Nora gasped but Eva continued, "He also asked if I was in love with any of my fiancés. Can you imagine the cheek?"

Nora looked down and began smoothing the wrinkles in her perfectly pressed dress. "This is all very interesting."

Eva knew that tone, knew that expression. Knew it well enough to be frightened. "Do not start hatching a plan. Whatever scheme you're imagining is unwise and unwanted."

Her friend pushed off the wall and brushed her skirts as she stood. "Eva, you have been engaged

three times. Three different men who might have
been decent husbands, with their only crime boring you to tears in six months. You wouldn't have
been miserable but none of them put a spark in
your eye and brought a flush to your skin. Not one
of them affected you as Phillip Mansfield does."

"But—"

"And there is one thing Mansfield clearly has
going for him those other three did not."

Broad, delectable shoulders? The ability to kiss
her senseless? A shockingly low opinion of females
in general? Eva could list a hundred reasons how
Phillip was so unlike any of her fiancés, but none
appropriate for polite conversation. "What?" she
asked when Nora fell silent.

"Mansfield lives here, in New York. I also happen
to now live in New York, and it would please me
greatly to have my closest friend here as well."

Panic began to flutter inside Eva's chest, her
heartbeat stuttering. Nora was a locomotive when
she set her sights on something, barreling straight
ahead without considering the consequences for
anyone else. "Do not start plotting. I mean it. Whatever you are contemplating, forget it. Even if I were
amenable to an American husband—which I am
not—my father is in London and I cannot desert
him, not now." To desert him was the height of cru-
elty, even if he didn't always recognize her these
days. He may not ever recover, but he was still her
father. He was her responsibility.

"He would want you to be happy—as do I."

Eva rose as well, rocks scattering to the ground.

"Then leave it alone. A man like Phillip Mansfield would never understand my ambition or me. It would be a waste of everyone's time."

THE BOWERY WAS no place for a gentleman.

Thieves, whores, murderers, and toughs abounded, these streets a safe haven as the city's police force had long thrown up its hands and given up here. Street gangs were the Bowery's ruling class, the saloons their drawing rooms. The sounds of a brawl were as common as ragtime piano.

Anything could be had in these blocks of vice for the right amount of coin. Tattoos, liquor, opium, or a roll in the sheets with a woman—or a man, if that was your preference. Phillip came for a different reason, the one type of physical exertion the uptown men deemed too violent to try.

Sullivan, Phillip's driver, dodged an oyster cart and hurried to catch up. The Irish-born servant insisted on making these trips with Phillip. "You certain this is wise, sir?"

No, he wasn't. These outings always happened at night. The Bowery was more dangerous then but there was less chance of being recognized. Phillip took great pains to keep his pastime hidden. He could only imagine what society—including his mother—would think if they learned how he kept himself sane.

But there was no help for it today, not when a pair of sultry brown eyes haunted his every breath.

What if we took advantage of one another?

He wished he could stop thinking about her. Yet

the memories were there, dogging him. Forcing him to remember how responsive she'd been, how perfect.

Damn it, he'd *liked* her. Now that his brain had learned the truth about her, he kept waiting for his body to receive the message. Eva was not for him.

So why did that realization merely depress him?

"You are welcome to wait with the brougham on Canal," he told Sullivan.

Sullivan made a noise. "And leave you alone on these streets? Not bloody likely."

They stopped before a three-story brick row house. Other than the address, the dismal store-front had no sign, no mark to designate what lay beyond. Phillip pushed inside and entered a dark anteroom. After a trip down the stairs and along a dank corridor, he reached his destination. He rapped on the door and waited.

A grimy face appeared. Suspicious eyes assessed the newcomer and a toothless smile emerged. "Why, it's the Prince. What are you doin' here in the daylight hours?"

"Let me in, Joe."

The wood swung wide and Phillip strode inside. The familiar smack of flesh on flesh greeted him, and anticipation hummed in his blood. His muscles were tight and ready, energy coursing through him. He heard Sullivan speak a few Gaelic phrases behind him but paid no attention. Head down, he continued to the small changing area.

It had been Sullivan who introduced Phillip to McGirk's. After attending a boxing match, Phillip had expressed interest in the sport, prompting

Sullivan to suggest a visit here to try it out. The release of aggression and frustration during a bout quickly won Phillip over. The pain and danger caused him to feel alive like nothing else ever had.

The men who visited McGirk's did not box for sport. They boxed because they *had* to hit someone, to burn off the rage and helplessness that could weigh a man down. Each boxer was capable of killing a man with his bare hands, which is why they were only fit to fight each other. If you walked out still drawing breath, you were welcome to return.

He stripped efficiently, pulling on a clean pair of woolen drawers and flat leather shoes, which helped one keep from slipping on the canvas. His chest remained bare. He returned to the main room where he found Joe waiting.

Joe tugged the padded gloves on Phillip's hands then tied the laces. "Anyone here worth my time?" Phillip asked.

"Maybe one or two. Warm up and I'll see who's interested."

Phillip moved toward a large leather bag anchored between the ceiling and the floor. Sullivan trailed behind, reproach hanging heavy in the air. "You sure you want to leave with that pretty face bruised and bloodied in the sunlight, sir?"

"Don't worry about me," Phillip said.

"Does this have somethin' to do with your hotel?"

"You could say that." In fact nothing had gone as planned, not since he'd met Eva. His whole life felt topsy-turvy and he hated it. Her father could not arrive soon enough for Phillip's liking.

Getting through each day—watching her, wanting her—would be agonizing. How was he supposed to keep his distance while overseeing construction of his hotel? She had obviously hoped he'd disappear and leave her in charge. He nearly snorted. As Sullivan had just said, not bloody likely.

Sullivan braced the bag from behind and Phillip started swinging with a series of punches, jabs, and hooks, keeping to the balls of his feet as his arms worked. After several reminders from Sullivan to "loosen up," he finally relaxed and let the movements take over. His mind became entirely focused on the task at hand, the rapid and powerful strikes to the thick canvas. Soon he was breathing hard and a fine sheen of sweat coated his skin.

"Prince! You're up."

Phillip dropped his arms and spun around, eager to spar against a real partner. He froze for a beat when he spotted the man leaning lazily against the ropes framing the ring.

"What's he doin' here?" Sullivan murmured at Phillip's side. "Thought he was doing exhibition matches in the Southern circuit."

The man awaiting Phillip in the ring was none other than James "Brick" O'Reilly, a Tammany favorite and one of the most famous boxers in New York. He'd first gained notoriety as a bare-knuckle brawler in illegal matches over in Five Points. One match had lasted eight hours, finishing only when O'Reilly's blows finally killed his opponent.

Phillip started forward—and then Sullivan caught his arm. "Are you sure, sir? I don't have a good feelin' about this."

"I'll be fine. I could use the challenge." He pulled

free and climbed through the ropes and up into the ring.

Joe stepped forward and glanced between the two men. "Either of you want me to referee?"

Out of habit, Phillip shook his head. "Not necessary." Then he caught O'Reilly's slow grin and wondered over it.

Joe left the ring and O'Reilly pushed off the ropes and sauntered forward. "I've been waitin' for ya," he said through a thick Irish accent.

"Is that so?" Phillip shook out his arms to keep them loose and warm.

"Yeah. I know who ya are, Mr. Mansfield. Misters Croker and Keene asked me t' give ya a special hello."

Ah. Phillip couldn't say he was entirely surprised. Tammany Hall had eyes everywhere—especially on their enemies. Obviously Phillip's refusal to allow them more control over the hotel construction hadn't gone over well and they'd discovered his secret pastime.

He raised his gloves and anchored his feet. "I guess you'd best get to it, then."

THE HANSOM ARRIVED at the construction site just as the pale rose dawn streaked across the Manhattan sky. Eva stepped to the ground, her boot heels sinking into the damp earth courtesy of yesterday's late rain, and paid the driver. She had watched the drizzle from her bedroom window for hours, unable to sleep. With excavation scheduled to begin today, her nerves were frazzled, her body filled with an almost paralyzing anticipation. This project must go smoothly.

There were a host of things to worry about. Mr. Milliken hadn't seemed particularly friendly during their brief chat and she expected no quarter given there. The crew would likely take Milliken's lead, which meant many battles ahead of her.

Then there was Phillip, whose mere presence served as both a distraction and an irritant. How was she supposed to work with a large, handsome man lurking over her shoulder, doubting her at every turn?

Focus on the building and everything else will fall into place.

Her father's words came back to her, the sage advice he'd often repeated during difficult projects. The reminder helped to ease the panic rioting in her stomach this morning. She could do this. She would not let her father—or all the people counting on this project—down. This would be E. M. Hyde's most prestigious, best-known building to date . . . and her secret achievement.

She merely had to survive it. Stand her ground. Assert her knowledge and her intuition.

Most important, she had to stay away from Phillip Mansfield.

Resolved, she slipped through the temporary wooden partition erected to keep the public out of the area during construction. Four giant steam shovels stood silent, waiting, ready to dig toward the granite bedrock underneath the island, and a grin overtook her face. This was the first step in transforming her flat drawings into the most gorgeous hotel America had ever seen.

"Hello, Eva."

She started at the familiar deep voice, her hand flying to her throat as she turned around. *My goodness, where had he come from?* Phillip Mansfield stood behind her, perfectly turned out for such an ungodly hour, hands resting in his trouser pockets, an amused twist to his lips.

Good heavens. A dark bruise marred his cheek, a small cut above his left brow. Brown hair had been slicked off his face as if he'd just emerged from the bath, a suit of slate gray hugging his large frame.

She stared, dumbfounded at the sight of his ravaged profile. "What on earth happened to you?"

"Nothing serious. Just a minor accident. I hadn't expected you here this early."

The smooth switch in topic wasn't lost on her. Was he uncomfortable discussing the injury? Had he been in a fight?

None of your business, Eva.

"I hadn't expected you either. It's hardly a decent hour for society scions to be out and about."

"I am sorry to disappoint you but this scion rises early."

Of course he did. Why was he always so unexpected? Each of her fiancés had slept all day and caroused all night. "I had trouble sleeping and decided to come here."

"Nervous?"

"Hardly." A lie, but she would never admit it to him, not even if someone held a hammer to her head. "More like eager. What is your excuse?"

"The same." He stepped beside her and they both stared out at the vast empty lot. The hotel would span the entire block of Fifth Avenue between

Thirty-Fifth and Thirty-Sixth Streets. "I love to see the bare ground right before we begin. To envision the possibilities."

She had just been thinking the same. "Me as well."

"Shall we walk? Examine the dirt a bit?"

She nodded, grateful for an excuse to start moving. Between Phillip's unexpected presence and her first-day nerves, she was nearly vibrating with tension.

He took her arm and began leading her around the perimeter. "I'm curious. Your father's plans . . . did you contribute any ideas?"

Eva swallowed and considered her words carefully. This was a slippery conversation to have with one's employer. She couldn't admit to a great deal of meddling, else Mansfield would question the source of each and every decision. He wanted the great E. M. Hyde on the cornerstone, not Hyde & Hyde. Or, God forbid, Lady Eva Hyde. "Here and there," she hedged. "He is generously receptive to my suggestions."

"You've studied with him a long time?"

Warm memories flooded her. She had loved watching her father sketch, seeing him pluck an idea from his mind and realize it on paper. The smell of graphite pencils, the feel of his compass and wooden rule. The way he'd asked her opinion when trying to work through a problem. "I trailed him nearly every place he went when I was little. I was forever driving my governess mad with efforts to evade her. When he realized I was serious about learning, he started teaching me himself."

"How old were you then?"

"Eleven when I started following him. Fourteen when he finally decided to teach me." Eight years ago now, which seemed so long in some respects. A lot had changed in that time.

"So you traveled around Europe with him?"

"Quite a bit, yes. Harder after my debut because of my responsibilities in London." Like her father's illness.

"Responsibilities, meaning fiancés?"

There was an edge to his voice that caught her attention. Of course he would bring that up, the Lady Unlucky reputation that threatened his hotel. "Yes, that was one of them."

"More like three of them," he muttered under his breath.

Eva gritted her teeth. Yes, there had been three, but she did not appreciate having her pain and humiliation mocked. Unfortunate that she couldn't utter the proper set down burning her tongue, however. She needed this project, both the money and the notoriety that would result. Arguing with her employer, who already had enough reasons to discharge her, seemed unwise in the extreme.

So she neatly turned it around. "I hadn't assumed you to be the jealous type."

"Three dead fiancés hardly inspire jealousy—they inspire concern."

She patted his arm. "Don't worry—you're safe as long as we never become betrothed." Without waiting on a retort, she strode away, intending to focus on the work instead of this maddening conversation with an even more maddening man.

"You know that's not what I mean," he said behind her.

"Yes, which is why I am choosing to ignore you."

He made a sound, one that closely resembled a laugh. "You are a stubborn woman."

She spun to face him, the heel of her boot grinding into the soft dirt. "Why is it men call a woman stubborn when she disagrees with him? Are we not allowed to know our own minds?"

A challenging light flashed in his dark gaze as he closed the distance between them. She had the strangest urge to back up, to retreat, but held her ground instead, tilting her head back when he stepped in close. His familiar smell—clean, woodsy soap combined with summer sunshine—filled her nostrils and caused her heart to pound beneath her corset.

"If you believe your intelligence and stubbornness are unattractive to me, think again. I cannot shake the memories of the brave and bold woman I encountered on the ship, the lady whom I could hardly keep my hands off. Need I demonstrate—?"

The wooden gate creaked as it slid open and Eva instantly took a step, putting distance between her and Phillip. She didn't need the crew to see her speaking intimately with the hotel owner. Her path was rocky enough without adding that mess to the mix.

Yet part of her wondered what he'd been about to say. He would demonstrate . . . *what*? The range of possibilities caused gooseflesh to erupt along the surface of her skin. A ridiculous reaction, considering they had agreed their relationship was to remain professional. Distant. Respectful.

Under no circumstances would she again find herself in a dark room with his hands working magic under her skirts. And if that thought caused a pang of disappointment in her belly, it was best ignored.

Thoughts of seduction quickly fled as the crew meandered into the site. "This conversation is not over." Phillip's warm breath slid over the shell of her ear as he left to greet Mr. Milliken.

Skin gone aflame, Eva angled away, desperate for a moment to calm down. Damn him. He had the ability to rattle her like no one else. Right now, she needed to appear confident and self-possessed, not giddy and flustered over a *man*.

A handsome, surprisingly charming man. And yet . . .

"Miss Ashford."

It took a second, but a jolt of recognition at the strange name finally went through her. *That's you, silly.* Her head snapped to where Phillip and Mr. Milliken approached. Ignoring Phillip, she extended a hand to the construction chief. "Good morning, Mr. Milliken. I'm certainly looking forward to getting under way today."

Milliken ignored her hand and folded his arms across his chest. "We should be ready with the dynamite in an hour or so. If you don't mind, miss, it's probably best if you clear the area."

Her arm dropped—along with her jaw. "I'm sorry, clear the area? Whatever for?"

"This is dangerous work. We can't have scream-ing and screeching while we're—"

"Screaming and screeching?" Heat broke across the back of her neck as her fingers clenched into fists. A quick glance at Phillip revealed his fur-rowed brow. Had he known Milliken would order her out? "Are you saying you believe the explosions shall cause me to . . . what? *Grow hysterical?*"

"Now, calm down everyone," Phillip started un-til Milliken sent him a determined look.

"Sir, the men," Milliken said. "They might be distracted with her here. Day like today is danger-ous. One wrong move with that dynamite . . ."

Phillip stroked his jaw and watched the laborers stack crates and organize tools. Then he dragged a hand down his face. "Miss Ashford, there is some truth to Milliken's concerns. Dynamite is quite vol-atile and we can't make a mistake, not in the middle of New York City. I am certain you understand."

Understand? No, she most definitely did not understand. They were forcing her to *leave*? And here the English believed the Americans more en-lightened. These two were about as enlightened as a thick slab of granite.

Her gaze shifted between the two men, noting the resolve there. She could argue and complain but what would it gain her? They wouldn't budge and she would further reaffirm their assumptions about her inability to remain calm. Yet she hated giving in, swallowing her pride and her knowledge and walking away. They would never ask the same of a man.

And Phillip. The worst part was that he'd actually taken Milliken's side, instantly validating the construction chief's ridiculous theories about her temperament. She would not forget this.

Straightening her spine, she spoke to Milliken. "I'll return at dusk. If things are not to my liking, I'll be having words"—she sent a hard glare at Phillip—"with both of you. Good day, gentlemen."

Chapter Six

"I am here to see Mr. Mansfield."

Mansfield's butler, an older man with thin lips and a prodigious forehead, opened the door wider. "Of course, my lady. Please come in and I shall see if Mr. Mansfield is home."

"If he is not at home," she said, already removing her gloves. "Tell him I shall wait until he is at home." In other words, she'd not leave until Phillip agreed to see her.

After being summarily dismissed from the construction site, she had walked the forty-plus blocks to Nora's house in hopes of clearing her head. It hadn't worked. More walking through the Cortland gardens also hadn't diminished her anger. Nor had drawing, drinking a glass of sherry, or punching a pillow.

She was still angry.

And her fury was directed in one place. Or rather, at one person.

"That's quite all right, Roberts." A young man

appeared from the interior of the home. "Mr. Mansfield asked that I bring Lady Eva to his office."

Eva tried not to show her surprise. How had
Mansfield known she was here? Had he been at
the window when she arrived? Before she could
ponder it further, the butler disappeared and the
young man came forward with a hand extended.
Then he seemed to turn self-conscious, his skin
reddening. He dropped his arm and awkwardly
bowed instead. "I am Mr. Gabriel, Mr. Mansfield's
secretary. If your ladyship will follow me?"

She nodded and he led her the same way she'd
taken the other day with Phillip, when he'd practically dragged her to his office. Only this time, she
was the one filled with righteous fury.

After a maze of priceless pieces of art and architectural splendor, they arrived at the heavy
wooden door to the office. Mr. Gabriel turned the
latch and escorted her into the thoroughly masculine domain. There were no frills here. Thick
Aubusson carpets covered the floor, with sturdy
and serviceable dark furniture. A huge rosewood
desk, intricately carved, took up one corner, with
a smaller desk—likely Mr. Gabriel's—not far away.
Against the wall, near a plush sofa, was a generous
sideboard that hosted more bottles than a department store perfume counter.

Mr. Gabriel shut the door on his way out, leaving
Phillip and Eva alone. Phillip rose from behind the
desk, placing his pen on the blotter. "Lady Eva. I
cannot say this is unexpected."

Struggling for calm, she smoothed the fabric of

her light cream silk afternoon dress patterned with mauve diamonds along the skirt and half-length sleeves. For some reason, the ensemble reminded her of *Alice's Adventures in Wonderland*, one of her favorite childhood books. She had always related to Alice, a girl stuck in a world where nothing made sense. "You owe me an apology."

"I do?"

"Indeed, you do. Any idea when might I receive it?"

His lips twitched as if fighting a smile. "You have to admit Milliken had a point. These things need to be handled carefully. You must ease into your role on the site else the workers may revolt."

"That is ridiculous and you've merely given Milliken courage for the next time he'd like to send me packing."

"Milliken answers to me. He does not have the ability to send you packing. Not today, not ever."

Phillip remained patient, his battered face relaxed and his voice calm. Somehow that annoyed her further. Of course he was calm. This was a man whose authority had never been openly challenged. He'd never lost or struggled. Never had to prove himself.

"You have awarded the first round to him, Phillip. I prefer to begin as I mean to go on—and in this case I'll be barred from the site any time he deems necessary."

"You are overreacting. If you'd flinched in the slightest today, sneezed at the wrong moment, or even covered your ears during the blasts, you would have done more damage than by simply not being there."

"I would have done none of those things. I'm not a fool and I am aware it's a construction project—*my* construction project. You had no right to send me away like an errant child!"

He blinked a few times, his brows pinching. "First, it is my hotel being constructed, which makes it *my* project. Even so, don't you mean your father's project?"

Blast. Temper had taken hold of her tongue and caused the slip. "Of course I meant my father's project—but I am responsible for it while he is convalescing."

"And I am ultimately responsible for the two of you . . . as well as the men at the site. Meaning, I do not need to answer to you for this or any other decision."

"You are impossible."

He gave her a knowing look. "You are free to return to London at any time, Lady Eva. I'll happily hire another architect to act in Hyde's stead until he arrives."

She studied his expression, tried to see if he was bluffing. Unfortunately, she couldn't be certain. This was her greatest fear, that he'd dismiss her and hire someone local instead. As her father would never arrive, she'd lose the project forever.

That would not do.

No matter what, she had to keep a level head. Her father's illness and financial ineptitude meant that she could push Phillip only so far. Why hadn't her father been more responsible with his money? If he had, then she wouldn't be forced to lie and capitulate to others at every turn.

"Another architect would not understand my father's vision for the hotel."

"Yes, but he—and it *would* be a man, Eva—would not cause the crew to revolt."

"What's more important to you? A docile and obedient crew . . . or having the hotel built to Hyde's designs?"

His eyes narrowed dangerously. "I haven't decided yet."

HE'D LET HER down, that much was clear. Eva had expected Phillip to put Milliken in his place, but he wasn't sure Milliken was entirely wrong. She needed to ease into her role with the crew. Construction workers were extremely superstitious and skittish. If they wanted to keep the laborers happy and on the job then Eva needed to proceed with caution, not barge in like a buffalo.

Yet her disappointment affected him keenly. He had no idea why. He was the captain of this ship, the one whose name would grace the entryway. The one who had financed the entire venture. The one with everything on the line.

If she didn't care for how he handled things . . . that was too damn bad.

And if he'd longed to kiss the mulish set of her mouth before she stomped away . . . well, that was too damn bad as well.

He pushed it all down. Her disappointment. His longing. Milliken's smug expression. The anxiety over the hotel. He wouldn't lie to make this easier on her. He believed in telling the truth, no matter the damage that resulted.

"Eva, this project is bigger than anything you've been involved in before. It's bigger than anything *I've* been involved with—and I must do what is best for the hotel. Not for you."

She studied him intently, searching. "I am curious. Is it your family? Being in New York? You went from a champagne-drinking bon vivant to a business-driven thug in a matter of days." She gestured at his bruised and battered face. "It's as if you are two different people—one personable and fun, the other ruthless and stoic."

This perceptiveness rattled him. Perhaps he'd grown more intense over the years as his responsibilities increased, but he was the head of the Mansfield family. The fortune and the legacy rested on his shoulders alone. In an unforgiving city with judgmental eyes at every turn, there were times when that pressure threatened to overwhelm him, like a pot boiling over on a stove. So he'd learned to adapt, keep under control. The occasional trip to McGirk's helped.

It could explain why he looked forward to trips outside the city to any part of the world where he wasn't expected to behave in a certain manner. Where no one had heard of Phillip Mansfield and didn't give a damn about his family's wealth or influence—or at least was less impressed by it.

Still, he resented her implication.

"I'm quite fun while here," he said, though the words lacked conviction even to his own ears.

She nodded solemnly, pursing her lips to exaggerate for effect. "I've no doubt. Picking fights on the docks, apparently."

That was the outside of enough.

Phillip closed the distance between them, unsure of his intention other than to try to prove her wrong somehow. To show her that, underneath, he was still the man from the ship.

At his approach, she retreated two steps and then planted her feet, as if forcing herself to stand her ground. Exactly what he'd expected her to do.

He came close enough that she had to tilt her head back to see him. The smell of vanilla and roses assaulted him and a low hum wound its way through his blood. Something flared in her hazel eyes, a fleeting thought he wished he could decipher. Was she thinking of how good it had been between them? How heated they'd become that night in his cabin? Or when she'd come on his fingers?

God knew he was having a hard time forgetting it.

The tips of his black leather shoes touched the hem of her dress as he leaned in, his voice low. "You act as if you're not strung tighter than a bowstring as well. You are desperately in need of some reprieve."

She drew in a shaky breath but did not move away. "Not from you—and not in the way you are intimating. We agreed. Professional distance."

He hated that calm composure in her voice when he was so desperate for her. He prided himself on his control, yet she was the confident one tonight. "How do you know what I was intimating?"

The edges of her mouth kicked up and she retreated a step. "I may be unmarried but that hardly means I'm an idiot."

"I've never believed that. In fact, I've always thought you quite clever." From Chinese relaxation techniques and gargoyles, to drawings and her love of design, she had impressed him at every turn, not something he could say often of a woman outside the bedroom.

"There's no need to flatter me. I am your employee. It is best we remain on those terms."

Irritation swept through him, though he couldn't say why. She was correct: he was her employer. Yet that suggested a distance he neither felt nor desired. He couldn't pretend she was a stranger. "Are we not at least friends? I'd like to think we are slightly more familiar with one another, considering." *Considering I've had my hand between your legs and my tongue in your mouth.*

Her gaze narrowed, and he could tell she was skeptical of the idea. As was he. He didn't have many female friends, not ones he wasn't bedding, but he liked the notion of Eva as his friend. They would be working closely together for the next few months, so it made sense. Animosity solved nothing.

"And what would that entail?" she asked.

A fair question. Unfortunately, all the answers that came to mind were salacious. He lifted a shoulder. "I haven't the faintest idea. I've never been friends with a woman, but I'm sure we can muddle through."

"Fine, we're friends."

She said it dismissively, yet he had every intention of holding her to it. "Excellent. The first rule of friendship is you trust your friends. That means you *trust* me to make fair decisions that benefit the hotel. You *trust* that I am not taking Milliken's position over yours."

She let out a huff and crossed her arms. "You manipulated me merely to prove that point."

"No, not exactly—but I want to be clear."

"Clear that I'm to blindly follow your lead and not question you at any point. That's not in my best interest, Phillip. This job means everything, and my entire future is at risk."

"You mean your father's future, don't you?"

She waved her hand. "Yes, but he relies on me when he is not here. Perhaps it's best to consider us the same person, if it helps."

"It doesn't. Downright disturbing, if you must know the truth."

"Be serious—or we're no longer friends."

Her refusal frustrated him, and he found himself lashing out. "Now who is the one acting differently? Where is the bold woman who rubbed my wrists to cure my seasickness?"

"She came to her senses—and what happened on the ship was a mistake." She spun on her heel and marched out the door.

He watched her go, emotion roiling inside him. A mistake? Inconvenient, perhaps, but not a mistake. He didn't regret the evening they spent together, even if it had caused a bit of a headache once he first learned her true identity. But a mistake?

Striding to the sideboard, he poured himself a tumbler of whiskey. No, their night together hadn't been a goddamn mistake . . . and somehow he would find a way to prove it to his new *friend*.

THE RUMBLE AND hiss of multiple steam shovels greeted Eva when she arrived at the construction site. The summer morning was lush with humidity and she'd already begun to perspire under her clothing. Of course her governess would have said ladies do not perspire . . . but Eva knew better. Besides, she'd never been much of a lady.

Once through the wooden barrier, she took a moment to enjoy the chaos. A construction site was like a symphony, with lots of moving parts all working together in harmony. Due to the scope and Mansfield's ambitious timeline for the hotel, two shifts of three hundred men each were working round the clock to dig out the foundation, creating a constant stream of noise and bodies. When they finished, the base of the hotel would contain almost two full acres of solid concrete resting fifty feet below street level.

She searched the crowd for Milliken. In the past few days she'd discovered the contractor preferred to work along with the laborers. He didn't sit idly and watch from a distance. Instead, he rolled up his sleeves and put in long hours aside the crew. Eva respected him for it.

If only he would begin to respect her.

Yesterday, she'd checked the excavation area of the east tower and discovered a miscalculation in Milliken's measurements. Milliken hadn't appreciated learning of the error, telling her she needn't hover over the site like an old hen.

Eva had gritted her teeth to keep from uttering an angry retort. Though it had nearly killed her, she'd instead found Carew and calmly explained the error. He'd listened, verified her findings, and then approached Milliken with the change. Milliken had immediately seen to the correction.

Be patient. You'll win him over eventually.

She spotted Milliken near the west wall where he was talking to a tall brown-haired man wearing a bowler. Her stomach sank as if she'd swallowed a handful of pebbles. Phillip.

He hadn't visited the site in a few days, not since their conversation in his office, and Eva had been glad for some autonomy over the project. Now the boss had returned.

No doubt Milliken was busy lodging another compliant about her, though she'd made every effort to stay out of the way when here. Truthfully, there wasn't much for her to do until the excavation finished. Still, how could she be expected to stay away from the excitement?

Phillip's head snapped up and he locked eyes with Eva. Excusing himself to Milliken, he started toward her. The cut above his brow was now a slash of pink and the bruise on his cheek had nearly faded. The contrast, these different facets of his personality, fascinated her. He was a rogue dressed in a well-fitted morning suit.

"Hello," Phillip said as he reached her. "I'm surprised to find you here."

"I prefer to check in periodically during excavation. Good thing I did, too, as there was a mistake yesterday in the measurements for the east wing."

"Was there? Milliken didn't mention it."

Eva snorted. Of course he hadn't. "Instead of

thanking me, Milliken said not to hover over the site like an old hen."

Phillip's mouth quirked and he thrust his hands in his trouser pockets. "I can imagine how that went over."

"I refrained from kicking him in the shin, though it was a struggle."

"I bet." They stood silently, the chaos of the machines, men, and dirt swirling around them, offering a bizarre sort of privacy. "They've never dealt with a woman in an authority position before, Eva. You must learn patience."

She was the one who must adapt? Wrong. She would keep doing her job and the men would need to get used to *her.* "As long as he does his job—and does it well—then we'll be fine."

She could see the frustration in the tightening of his jaw but his voice remained calm. "Milliken is entirely competent. I wouldn't have hired him otherwise. I hire only the best, as should be obvious considering the lengths I went to secure your father."

"Well, at least you've begun to finally trust in me."

His cocked his head. "Pardon?"

"The last two days . . . you haven't been here. It's none of my concern where, of course—"

"I had to travel to Boston. There was a small kitchen fire at the hotel and I wanted to examine the damage. I returned late yesterday afternoon and came here first. You'd already left."

Goodness, she felt stupid. Here she thought he'd decided to give her a chance and not loom over her shoulder like a vulture waiting to pick at a decaying carcass.

"Miss me, Lady Eva?"

Maybe a bit. Afraid the truth would show, she shifted away from him. "Don't be ridiculous. I foolishly believed you'd finally trusted me enough to leave the project in my hands."

He lost his teasing smile, a frown emerging instead. "It's not a matter of trust. This hotel is my investment, my responsibility, with my name above the door. Every eye in Manhattan is on this city block, waiting to see how it turns out. I won't allow it to fail, fall behind, or go over budget."

Of course, her father's name and reputation were on the line—as well as her future—but she refrained from pointing that out. If this project failed, she would be forced to sell her father's house and move them outside of London in the hopes of escaping their creditors. A familiar anger at her father's financial ineptitude burned in her lungs, along with the wish that he'd sought advice from others on how to invest wisely. If he had, perhaps she'd be spared the need to lie at every turn.

"By the way," Phillip said, "as we are discussing all the ways this project could go wrong, I should tell you Milliken's latest concern. Your father is a licensed architect in New York. You, however, are not. This puts us in a bit of a precarious situation, especially when you're adjusting the plans."

"It's never been a problem before." She'd acted in her father's stead on many jobs across Europe. With a few forged letters containing his signature, her authority and skill had never been questioned.

"In any other city, it wouldn't matter. New York works differently. Corruption here is as plentiful as the champagne. I think it's safe to say that I'll be forced to make another outrageous contribution if Tammany Hall raises a ruckus."

"Another outrageous contribution? When was the first one?"

"I was forced into letting their crew handle the demolition. Tammany Hall likes to keep control over all the moving pieces in this city."

"Sounds like someone else I know," she muttered.

The comment merely made him shake his head. "I suppose that's true, but they're hopeful for anything they can use with which to strong-arm me on this hotel."

Guilt wound through her insides, an insidious snake feeding off her lies. She did not wish to add to Phillip's burdens, and she could only imagine what would happen when it became apparent that her father would never relieve her on this project. But she was in too deep now and she'd not back out. This hotel was too important to her. "I'll try to go unnoticed, then."

"As if that were possible. Even if you weren't incredibly beautiful, your confidence and bearing draw every eye in the vicinity. That's another reason Milliken wishes you gone. He thinks your looks will distract his crew."

Phillip thinks you are incredibly beautiful.

The compliment warmed her, chasing away the guilt from moments ago. Still, she bit her lip and tried to remain professional. "That's ridiculous. No one spares me a glance when I'm here."

"Because Milliken's threatened them—and that's because *I've* threatened *him*. I told him everyone would be replaced if you are harmed or offended in any way."

"Phillip! You cannot do that." Surprise rocked her back on her heels. The gesture both flattered and annoyed her. "They'll all resent me."

"I don't give a damn, Eva. If I cannot prevent you from coming to the construction site, then I need to keep you safe."

Was this merely out of a sense of responsibility? "Everyone will suspect we are intimately involved."

"Again, I don't give a damn—and they're not altogether wrong, considering the ship."

Heat raced along her spine, a fiery longing that settled between her thighs. Would he never let up? "Friends should be too polite to remind other friends of indiscretions."

His mouth curved into a dangerous half smile. "This friend is not quite that polite."

"You're impossible."

"So I've been told. Have a lovely morning, my lady." He tipped his hat and strode toward the gate.

Chapter Seven

He purposely arrived late.

The dinner party guests were assembled in his mother's salon, drinking aperitifs and champagne, when Phillip entered the room. On the sofa, the women tittered over the latest bits of gossip while the men had gathered on the other side of the room, no doubt discussing the exchange.

Phillip's face hadn't yet healed and his mother would be displeased. But one thing he'd learned early in life was to reveal unpleasant things to her publicly, where she'd be unable to make a fuss. Ellen Mansfield was nothing if not proper in front of her peers.

A footman approached with a tray of champagne and Phillip gratefully snatched a glass, downing it in one swallow.

"Phillip!" His mother approached, a wide smile on her face. "There you are."

He turned toward her—and her nostrils flared sharply at the sight of his injury.

"Good evening, Mother. My apologies for being late."

"We'll discuss your face later," she murmured for

his ears only as he bent to kiss her cheek. "Come, let me introduce you to everyone."

As if he were not already well acquainted with every person in the room. "Of course. Lead on." He offered his arm and she took it, bringing him to the ladies on the sofa.

There were five of them, women he'd known his entire life. He greeted them properly, as custom dictated, then decided to procure drinks. Anything to escape the prying eyes trying to make sense of what had happened to his face without outright asking. He had half a mind to tell them merely to enjoy the shock of it.

"May I offer anyone another cocktail?" he asked.

"Rebecca?" Mrs. Hall prompted with a pointed glance at the pretty blonde on her right.

"Excellent idea. I think Miss Hall would care for a refill," his mother announced. "Won't you escort her to the sideboard, Phillip?"

Christ, his mother was as transparent as glass. Wiggling out of it would've been rude, so he nodded. "I'd be happy to. Shall we, Miss Hall?"

Rebecca rose and drew closer, two bright spots of color on her cheeks. The blush complimented the pale pink color of her silk evening gown. "Thank you, Mr. Mansfield." She accompanied him across the room to the sideboard, where they were blessedly alone. "God, Phillip, I'm sorry. This is dashed embarrassing."

He chuckled and took her glass from her hand. "This is what we must endure to humor our mothers. What are you having?"

She threw a glance over her shoulder. "Would scotch be too bold?"

"Not for me." He lifted the decanter and put a dram in her crystal glass. "Go ahead, I'll hide you from the room." He shifted to block her from the rest of the guests and Rebecca tossed the liquor back like a seasoned tippler.

She blew out a breath. "That's better. What the hell happened to your face?"

"Would you believe I ran into a door?"

"Sure, if the door had fists."

"I'm fine. Hardly hurts any longer. Tell me why you're grabbing for the hard stuff." He gestured to the scotch.

"Oh, it's been awful lately. I'm sorry you are the sacrificial lamb tonight."

From one of the best families, Becca Hall was a beautiful young woman with blond hair and green eyes. Moreover, she was intelligent and had a sharp sense of humor. She and Phillip never ran out of conversation and their interactions were always pleasant. They'd known each other so long that he considered her a friend. "I don't mind escorting you, Becca. There are worse ways to spend an evening. So what's upsetting you?"

"Mother's insistence to marry." She tucked a strand of hair behind her ear. "I fear I won't be able to put her off much longer."

"I thought every young woman wanted to marry." He thought of Eva and her three deceased fiancés. She'd insisted her father hadn't been eager to marry her off . . . so had she pushed for the betrothals? His curiosity over the details of those arrangements was bordering on unhealthy.

Becca made a noise in her throat. "No, I do not want to marry."

The way she said it gave Phillip pause. "Because it's me, or anyone?"

"Anyone. You're a handsome, nice enough man, even if a bit intense, but I . . ." She pressed her lips together and cast a furtive glance around them.

"No one can hear us," he assured her. "And I always sensed you were as uninterested in a match between us as I am."

"You sensed correctly. I don't want to marry any man."

"Why?"

"I . . . I can't tell you."

He empathized with her need for secrecy. In their world—a place where anyone who attempted independence was outcast—there were few people in which to confide. God knew it was even worse for women. "You can tell me. I swear, I'll keep your confidence."

She shook her head and refilled her glass—with sherry this time. "It would be quite the scandal if I did."

"Worse than Mrs. Bishop?" Mrs. Bishop had divorced her philandering husband not even two years ago. Society had banished the poor woman, not even acknowledging her any longer.

"Worse."

"Are you in love with a footman? A groom?" Not unheard of, though quite beyond the pale.

"God, no. I almost wish it was so simple."

"A maid, then?" He'd said it as a half jest, but her eyes rounded in panicked surprise before she schooled her features—and he knew. "Do not worry, I won't tell a soul."

"I don't know what you're talking about."

He ignored her. "You know, the Parisians are quite liberal in their thinking on this matter. Have you considered—?"

"No, I cannot leave New York."

"Then I'm sorry, Becca."

She met his gaze, her green depths studying him carefully. "Do you mean that?"

"Without doubt. I would never begrudge you happiness." God knew his body parts had a mind of their own. Eva, naked and sweaty in his bed, was all he could think about these days. "But you have to know your mother will not relent. If you're unwilling to leave for Europe, you'll either need to marry or tell her."

"Out of the question. You know what she'll do if she learns the truth. They'll put me in one of those places."

Phillip had heard of them. Asylums with radical treatments, where unnecessary surgeries were performed under the guise of "medicine." Most women never returned from such places. "So marry a man with a similar secret to keep."

Her brows lowered and she stared at the wall. "I hadn't ever considered that. Where does one find—oh, never mind. Why am I asking you?"

"I'm not entirely sheltered, I'll have you know. While I've never visited them myself, I've heard that places for men of common interests are plenti-

ful in the Bowery." He passed them often on his
trips to McGirk's.

"I . . . I don't know how that helps me at the moment but thank you, Phillip. I cannot tell you what
your understanding means to me."

He poured himself a sherry and toasted her with
the crystal. "I'm just damned grateful you do not
want to marry me."

She patted his arm. "If I wanted a man, you
would be a fine choice."

"Fine?" He sniffed in mock indignation. "You
should be so lucky—"

"There you two are," his mother exclaimed as
she glided up to the sideboard. "Dinner service has
started. Phillip, you'll escort Miss Hall?"

He finished his drink and placed the glass on the
sideboard. "I'd be delighted."

"Oh, excellent." His mother beamed as if Phillip
had just proposed. "I do love the sight of you two
together."

After his mother departed in a swirl of expensive silk, Becca chuckled under her breath. "If they
only knew."

"They'd still try to get their way. It's what all
New York society mothers do."

"I've said it before but I'm a tiny bit afraid of your
mother. I know she means well but I can't imagine what it must have been like growing up in her
household."

He waited as the other guests began rising and
filing out into the corridor. No sense in rushing.
"My sisters had the worst of it. I think I mostly ex-
asperate her."

"With your reputation I can understand why." She put her glass down. "So why don't you want to marry?"

Because I've been burned before. "Not much luck in finding the right woman, I suppose."

"Don't tell me it's because of what happened all those years ago?"

It sounded ridiculous to admit it, that his former fiancée's trickery had put him off marriage for good. But that tended to happen when a woman convinced you she was increasing with your child and you learned another man was responsible. "I just don't see the point. I'm perfectly happy the way things are."

"Hmm. I can quite understand that, I suppose. Your mistress is that actress, Flora Anderson?"

"Was, yes. We are no longer seeing one another, however."

"Any salacious details you'd care to share?"

His jaw fell open. If someone had told him where tonight's conversation would lead, he wouldn't have believed it. "Absolutely not. I never kiss and tell, Becca."

She sighed. "Damn. You're no fun."

"Why does every woman in my life keep telling me that?"

Now it was Becca's turn to look surprised. "Oh, really? So there is a woman in your life. Who is she?"

He shook his head and took her elbow. "Forget I said anything."

They started walking toward the dining room. "I'll forget nothing. Come, you've discovered my deepest, darkest secret. It's only fair I learn one of yours."

"This is New York society, Becca. Not a bit of it is fair."

EVA WIPED THE dirt from her hands. The dying summer sun glowed orange in the sky, and she was more than ready to depart. In fact, if she left now she might be able to join Nora and her aunt for a sherry before dinner.

For the past hour, she and Alfred Carew, the construction superintendent, had reviewed the excavation area for the west portion of the hotel. It was easy to see why Phillip had hired Carew; the engineer was incredibly bright and meticulous in his work. Also, he didn't talk down to her as if she were a child. He explained things patiently when asked, treated her as an equal.

Construction was moving quickly. As expected, water had begun seeping into the giant hole in the earth. Tomorrow, compressed air would be used to create caissons that would allow them to dig deeper, down to the bedrock. "This is moving much more rapidly than I anticipated," she told Carew.

Carew folded his arms and tipped his chin in the crew's direction. "Milliken's an effective contractor. He respects the men and the men respect him. Also, Mr. Mansfield is paying well. Money is a sufficient motivator."

With a timeline as ambitious as theirs, it was a good thing Phillip hadn't decided to be cheap. "What is that going up over there?" She pointed at a wooden structure near the back fence. "The tiny shack?"

"Didn't Mansfield tell you?"

"No."

"Oh, I thought he would've mentioned it," Carew said. "That's for you."

"Me?"

"Yes. He wanted you to have a place to go if it became too hot or too dangerous. A small office, he called it. You can keep your plans there, if you like. It'll be fairly crude, I'm afraid, but should do the job."

Her jaw fell. A small office? Too hot or too dangerous? She didn't know whether to hug him or hit him . . . It was thoughtful, in a condescending way. Did he believe she'd wilt like a precious bloom in the summer sun? Though she had to admit, having a place to sit once in a while would not be unwelcome.

Albeit reluctantly, she was touched. Though her presence had upset him, he was accommodating her, in his own high-handed manner. Ensuring she felt comfortable, even if she didn't wish to be treated any differently than any other architect.

The "office" would stand out among the crew, however, as another reason she shouldn't be allowed here. No wonder the men resented her, when extra effort had been required on her behalf.

She told Carew, "I insist that you use it as well. Please, keep your papers and instruments there. I don't need all that space to myself."

"That's a kind offer, but Mr. Mansfield was very specific. He said—"

"I don't care what Mr. Mansfield said." She gentled her tone. "I would feel awkward if that were only for me. And I wouldn't want the crew thinking I need special treatment."

"Ah. I think I understand. Then thank you, I shall make good use of it."

"Miss?" One of the workers stood there, staring down at his scuffed boots instead of meeting Eva's eyes.

"Yes?"

"There's a lady in a carriage askin' to speak with you."

"Me?"

"Yes, miss. Right there outside the gate." He pointed toward the fence.

She thanked him, said farewell to Carew, and started for the exit. The excavation would roll on, the steam shovels hauling dirt at all hours with the workers rotating in shifts. Everything was moving swiftly—a relief, as Eva would be personally penalized if construction fell behind schedule.

An expensive-looking black carriage waited at the curb, one that had seen quite a lot of use over the years. Though it certainly was not in disrepair, this carriage belonged to a family with old money, not one trying to parade their newly gained wealth around.

What lady had requested Eva's presence? She didn't know anyone other than Nora and her aunt here—and Nora would've just waltzed into the construction site instead of having Eva summoned.

A liveried footman opened the door and assisted a tall brown-haired woman down the steps. She was elegant and refined, with a hard edge that spoke of status and confidence. A woman used to getting her way. Eva stopped on the walk and waited, curious.

When the mysterious matron looked up, a familiar dark brown stare pierced Eva to the spot. She sucked in a sharp breath. Was this . . . Phillip's mother?

The woman wore a stunning violet afternoon dress. A Worth creation, if Eva had to guess. Quite flattering in its simplicity and inventiveness, the dress was a mix of satin and bengaline, with mother-of-pearl buttons along the front of the bodice. Her own dusty beige shirtwaist and matching skirt felt downright dowdy in comparison.

"Miss Ashford?" the woman asked.

"I am Miss Ashford. And you are?"

The woman struck out her gloved hand, which Eva promptly shook. The woman's grip was strong. "I am Mrs. Walter Mansfield. You are working for my son."

So it *was* his mother. Rumor held that most everyone in New York was afraid of her and Eva could well understand why. Still, Eva was not one to be cowed, no matter whom she had to face down. She routinely argued with engineers, contractors, tradesmen, and laborers. She could handle anything. "Indeed, I am. How may I help you?"

Mrs. Mansfield gazed thoughtfully at Eva. "My son speaks highly of your abilities, but I am curious about your qualifications to oversee this project."

Her . . . qualifications? Eva's mouth dropped open. "I beg your pardon?"

"I do have my reasons for asking."

"And I do have my reasons for not answering." Then she added, "Madam."

Mrs. Mansfield's lips twitched ever so slightly. In fact, if Eva had blinked she would've missed it. "Fair enough. You work for E. M. Hyde?"

"Lord Cassell—and yes, I do."

"His lordship, I hear, is not in good health."

Where was this tedious conversation going? Eva dug deep for patience and returned easily, "A minor influenza. No doubt he shall be back on his feet shortly."

"Is he able to work on something new while indisposed, do you suppose?"

Eva thought of her father's slack face, his vacant eyes. The last time she'd seen him, just before she'd sailed for America, he hadn't remembered her name, had believed she was his long-dead wife. The lucid moments came fewer and fewer these days, and every exchange with him felt precious, as if it might be their last. The next time he might not remember her at all—which nearly broke her heart. She was not ready to lose him yet, this man who was still her courageous, brilliant father.

Regardless, she continued the lie. "Yes, of course. I am in frequent communication with his lordship."

"Excellent. I have a small project on which I would like his input. Money is no obstacle. I'm quite willing to pay whatever he requires for the consultation."

Eva considered those words. A consultation . . . where money was no obstacle? She hated to turn that down—on behalf of her father, of course. "I would be happy to meet with you and then seek his counsel on your behalf. When?"

"Would Monday be acceptable?" She produced a calling card and held it out with two gloved fingers. "I shall expect you at two o'clock."

A quick glance at the card revealed Mrs. Mansfield's address. Fifth Avenue and Fifty-Ninth Street, right in the middle of Millionaire's Row. Those were the biggest and most expensive houses in the city. "Very good. I'll bring my notepad and pencil."

The agreement had no effect on Mrs. Mansfield and Eva suspected no one ever said *no* to this woman. It hadn't ever crossed Mrs. Mansfield's mind that Eva would refuse. Exactly like her son.

Mrs. Mansfield folded her hands. "I would appreciate one small favor, however."

"Yes?"

Her expression hardened, the iron will unmistakable. "I wish to keep this meeting between the two of us. There is no reason for my son to know."

Eva pressed her lips together to keep from smiling. Oh, this was too delicious by half. What on earth did his mother wish to keep from him? She quickly nodded, ready to take part in this conspiracy against Phillip. The man deserved revenge after haunting her dreams with his dashed handsome face and ridiculously broad shoulders. "Of course. I shan't mention a thing."

"Excellent. I'll expect you Monday afternoon, then."

"Until Monday. Good afternoon."

Mrs. Mansfield departed in a swirl of purple, leaving Eva standing on the pavement, wondering just what Phillip's mother was up to . . . and why she didn't want her son to find out.

PHILLIP LISTENED WITH only half an ear as Carew and Milliken debated the ramifications of yesterday's terrible thunderstorm. He should be asking pertinent questions about the ground and the timeline but he was distracted. Eva was here, walking around and taking notes, her keen eyes studying and measuring while her dark blue skirts swung back and forth.

This woman fascinated him, with her quicksilver intelligence and stubborn feistiness, all wrapped in a delectable package capable of bringing a man to his knees. She was unlike any female he'd ever met.

He'd tried to forget. Honestly, he'd tried. Told himself a hundred times not to get involved with her again. Remain close, but not *too* close. Stay professional.

God help him, but logic wasn't working. He still craved her. An undeniable hunger for her had buried under his skin to keep him constantly on edge. He could clearly recall the energy between them the night of the storm, how she'd trembled from his touch. The sounds when she'd climaxed . . .

Heat flooded his groin, awareness prickling over his skin. He'd brought himself off to those memories more than once during these past few days. Now he watched as she knelt and pressed the ground with her bare fingers. This was not a woman afraid of getting her hands dirty . . . and why did he find that so damn appealing?

"Mr. Mansfield, are you listening?"

His head swiveled to find Carew and Milliken both frowning at him. What had they been talking about? He raised his hands and took a stab at a response. "Let's not be hasty. We shouldn't rush into anything just yet."

Carew's dark brows lowered until they nearly met. "I asked if you wanted to speak with Mr. Weller. He's standing behind you."

What was the city's superintendent of buildings doing here? Phillip turned and extended his hand to the large man looming behind them. "Weller. To what do we owe the pleasure?"

Richard Weller wore a yellow-and-brown checked suit, a brown vest stretched across his prodigious middle. His gold watch fob sparkled in the morning sun. "Mr. Mansfield. I wonder if we might have a word about your plans."

Suspicion swept along Phillip's spine. "I thought we'd covered that ground. Multiple times, if I'm not mistaken." Weller had gone over Hyde's plans with a fine-tooth comb, asking layers of questions that had required detailed answers from the London architect. Carew had weighed in, verifying that the hotel would be structurally sound, as had other engineers in the city.

"I've had a change of heart. I'm stopping construction until—"

Phillip's body went rigid. "*What?* You cannot do that. We've already started." He swept his hand out toward the giant hole in the ground.

Weller didn't back down in the face of Phillip's fury. "I absolutely may if your building appears to be a danger to the city. I'm afraid that—"

Joanna Shupe

"Is there a problem?"

His chest heaving in outrage, Phillip looked down at Eva, who had just positioned herself between him and Weller. "He's shutting us down," he said through clenched teeth. *Fuck.* Just saying it aloud made him more furious. This goddamn town. Nothing could ever be easy, not even for a Mansfield. He'd soon be a laughingstock if this project failed.

"Shutting us down?" Eva cocked her head, calmly addressing the superintendent. Carew and Milliken also closed in. "What seems to be the issue?"

Weller cleared his throat, glancing over all the anxious faces surrounding him. "The height. Your building will collapse from the weight."

Hyde had come up with a unique and clever plan to support the height of the building. The entire structure would be supported with a grid of Bessemer steel, allowing the interior to carry the weight instead of the outside walls. Phillip had verified the structural viability with no fewer than four engineers, Carew included.

"No, it won't," Eva said. "The weight is sustained by the internal frame. The hotel will weigh one-third of a building constructed in the old manner, where the weight was carried in the outer walls."

"You assume."

She stood up straighter. "No, I *know*. Even if I hadn't run the calculations, they've already used this method in Chicago for taller buildings," Eva pointed out. "Both the Tacoma Building and the Home Insurance Building—"

"Miss Ashford." Weller said the words distastefully, as if he'd smelled a pile of horse droppings left baking in the summer sun. "We are not in Chicago. They may play fast and loose with the rules there, but in New York City we are more careful. We cannot have a fourteen-story building collapsing in midtown."

"Thirteen floors," she corrected. "And two buildings in Liverpool, England, have also used the same method. There is no chance this building will collapse."

He gestured toward Eva but addressed Phillip. "This is pure hubris and considering Mr. Hyde is not even here to defend it—"

"*I* am here." Eva crossed her arms over her chest. "And I'll happily defend it."

"I do not mean to offend you, miss, but why would I take the word of a secretary?"

Phillip leaned in. "She is Hyde's assistant, not his secretary, and is as well-versed with these plans as Hyde himself. She—and Mr. Carew—can answer any questions, allay any fears you might have." God, he hoped that was true. He had three million dollars and his reputation at risk.

"I'll gladly show you my calculations once more," Carew put in. "Hyde's design is solid."

"I happen to know," Phillip said, "that Pulitzer's using the same framing structure—and he's building upward of twenty-three stories." In fact, the engineers for Pulitzer's building had checked over Hyde's plans last year. "Why aren't you downtown, verifying his plans?"

Weller shifted, his gaze bouncing. "We've spoken with Mr. Pulitzer and are satisfied that his building's structurally sound."

Suddenly Phillip knew exactly why Weller was here instead of downtown. Fucking Tammany Hall. Keene and Croker were stirring up trouble to make a point. He took a menacing step forward, crowding into Weller's space. "I don't know how much they paid you," he said softly, "but I'm aware of exactly who is behind this. Think twice before you make an enemy of me, Weller. I also have friends in high places—high *legal* places."

"Mr. Weller." Eva once again stepped in front of Phillip, blocking his path to the superintendent. "Perhaps you, Mr. Carew, and I should retreat somewhere to discuss this. Review the plans once more before we all make rash decisions?"

Weller appeared less sure of himself now. "I don't know . . ."

"Have you ever enjoyed a true English afternoon tea?"

At Eva's question, Milliken's jaw fell open while a heavy frown transformed Carew's usual easy-going expression. Similar surprise jolted through Phillip, though he attempted to hide it. Tea? They were talking about *tea*? Had she lost her mind?

Weller appeared taken aback. "No, I cannot say that I have, miss."

"Then I insist you join me today for proper afternoon tea. Mr. Carew will attend as well and we'll discuss this in greater detail."

Weller glanced at Phillip then back at Eva. "I

suppose we could do that. I must insist that you halt work on the site until we do so, however."

Phillip's fists clenched. "Absolutely not—"

"Fine." Eva placed a hand on Phillip's arm, quelling his argument. "Mr. Milliken, let's give the men the day off, with full pay of course."

A string of curses ran through Phillip's head but he said nothing, merely gritted his teeth and tried not to send an uppercut into Weller's pointed jaw. She'd better have a good reason for all this. Rolling over to Weller's demand went against everything Phillip believed.

"Mr. Mansfield?" Mr. Milliken looked to Phillip for confirmation. He gave a quick nod, and Milliken spun on his heel to shut down excavation for the day.

"I have a meeting at two o'clock, so perhaps you may come at four?" She handed Weller an embossed card, then passed one to Carew as well.

Weller studied the address. "I suppose I can do that."

"Excellent. We shall see you then."

Weller left with a final nod and Phillip rounded on Eva. "Carew, give us a moment."

The engineer raised his hands and started backing away. "I'll see you at four, Miss Ashford. Mansfield."

"I am attending that meeting," he informed her as soon as they were alone.

"No, you are not. Weller doesn't like you and it's clear the feeling is mutual. You also cannot control your temper around him, and I cannot be worried you'll undo all my sweet talk during the meeting."

"Sweet talk?"

She rolled her eyes heavenward. "Phillip, there are times when acting like a bully gets you nowhere. This is one of those times. Did you not see Weller? He expected you to bark and snarl at him, and he was ready for the fight. He has the power here, and we have to find a way to gain a little of our own. That's why I want him off the construction site and in an unfamiliar surrounding."

"You cannot think a pot of Earl Grey and a few crumpets are going to fix this mess, do you?"

"That just proves you've never had really good crumpets. Stay away from this meeting."

"No."

"Do you trust me?"

He set his jaw and tried to think of a careful answer. "Again, it has nothing to do with your abilities. This is my hotel, my money. I cannot twiddle my thumbs this afternoon knowing the fate of such an important decision is out of my hands."

"That is too bad because I'm barring you from the Cortlands' house."

"Eva, I am in charge—not you. If I want to be there, a brigade of armed soldiers could not keep me out."

"You may speak with Weller separately if I am unable to appease him. How about that?"

"No. I need to be at this meeting." He supposed he could bend a *little*. For Eva. "What if I promise to sit quietly and not say a word?"

"Are you capable of such an astounding feat?"

Annoyance rippled through him. "Yes—and since you cannot stop me from coming, it's the best you'll get from me."

"All right, but not one word, Phillip."

"Fine." He sighed and pinched the bridge of his nose. "Where is your two o'clock meeting?"

She lifted her skirts and started to walk away. "That is none of your business. I'll see you at four."

Chapter Eight

The Mansfield matriarch lived in a mansion in the heart of Millionaire's Row. The house was designed in the style of the French Second Empire, with lacy iron edging around a tall mansard roof with elaborate dormers. An impressive stone staircase and balustrade led up to the main entrance. The house was understated when compared to the opulent Vanderbilt and Astor mansions in the neighborhood, but the owner's wealth could never be questioned.

The door opened before Eva used the gilded knocker. "Miss Ashford," the slim butler said, waving her in. "Mrs. Mansfield is expecting you."

"Thank you." The marble entry was impressive, all white Carrara marble, accented with Italian sculptures, lush carpets, and notable paintings. A huge skylight with opalescent stained glass rested four stories above, its colored light bouncing off the crystals of the ornate chandelier below. A majestic staircase swept gracefully to the higher floors, curving to harmonize the space and dominate in a purely theatrical way. Eva would congratulate the designer, if it were possible.

She deposited her parasol with the butler and then followed him to the salon. The house was quiet, with no voices or footsteps save her and the butler. Not even the ticking of a clock could be heard. It was a bit like a tomb—a beautiful, priceless tomb.

The first thing Eva noted in the drawing room was the gold ceiling. She blinked against the brightness. Then she saw Mrs. Mansfield, who wore a pale blue gown that nearly matched the wallpaper. "Miss Ashford. Do come sit down," the older woman said and gestured to the sofa.

As Eva sat, she noticed there were long rolls of paper on the low cherry table. These were traces, the architectural drawings completed on transparent paper. This must be the project on which Mrs. Mansfield needed input. Eva's fingers itched to open the rolls and investigate.

"Thank you for coming, Miss Ashford. I would prefer not to waste time with small talk, if you do not mind."

Eva appreciated the older woman's forthright approach. As she had another meeting in less than two hours, expediency suited her as well. "Indeed not. How may I help you?"

"I wish to consult with your employer regarding a small addition to my Newport cottage."

Eva knew enough about Americans to know "cottage" really meant mansion. And she knew enough about New York ladies to know "small" really meant "obscenely large."

"You've had plans drawn up already, I see."

"Indeed, I have." Phillip's mother reached for the rolls of paper. "I want the east wing torn down and enlarged. The architect has presented me with something absolutely untenable. Your employer has such a remarkable reputation, and I am hopeful that he might be willing to consult on this project."

Eva's curiosity was piqued. "Untenable?"

"Most definitely. I'll show you." She started to unroll one of the traces on the tea table. "The house was built over thirty years ago. We had a small family then and I also hadn't considered how much Newport would change in that time."

Ah, so Mrs. Mansfield wanted bigger and better, a house commensurate with her status in the city. Eva nodded and gestured toward the drawings. "I understand. Let's see what they've proposed."

First she was shown the current floor plan and façade. Stoneacre was an English Georgian in the Palladian style, typical of houses completed early- and midcentury. She let Mrs. Mansfield talk about the new design, how the expanded wing would improve on the livability. Bigger bedrooms, new showers in all the bathing rooms, a new cooling system that would provide relief in the hot summer months . . . There were also several smaller bedrooms, "for the grandchildren," Mrs. Mansfield explained. Eva tried not to think about Phillip filling those small bedrooms with perfect children, undoubtedly created with a prim and proper wife who never dug about in the dirt with her bare hands.

Ridiculous how much that idea bothered her. She

didn't want to marry, not even to a man so hand-some and driven as Phillip. Yes, he understood architecture and had a love of building things, as she did, but they were ill-suited beyond that. He would try to control his wife's every move . . . and Eva would never stand for it.

"So," Mrs. Mansfield finished, "what they've proposed doing is wrapping the current house in sort of a stucco and cocooning it. Then we'll build out with some of the beaux arts details that are so current right now."

Eva frowned at that. "Have they tested the foundation and the center of the house to ensure it's structurally sound?"

"No," Mrs. Mansfield confirmed. "But I'm not happy with any of the exterior design. It looks . . . slapdash to me."

Eva agreed. The idea was a bit like taking an apple pie and wrapping it in sponge cake. Underneath would be a mess. "Was this method proposed to save on building costs?"

"They had a generous budget. All I asked was that they retain as much of the original building as possible but update it."

"In my opinion, what they've proposed is a mistake. The foundation has to be able to support the additional weight. In theory, whatever was built thirty years ago would still be sound but one never knows. I've seen buildings less than ten years old begin to crack."

"So how do we find out?"

"Take the measurements and do the calculations. The structure should be examined carefully." She studied the tracings. "Tell me, if you want a beaux arts style, why not just tear down what's there and rebuild?"

A strange, almost pained look passed over Mrs. Mansfield's face. "My husband had this house built for me as a five-year anniversary present. I am loath to lose it."

Who would have guessed the tough old lady to be so sentimental? Eva had seen it before with other clients. "What if you kept the center portion, this part here?" She pointed to the entrance hall, flanked by the drawing and dining rooms. "Tear down everything on both sides and build out new wings. Perhaps add a loggia in the back to capture the sea air and connect with the bedrooms."

"That sounds wonderful but more than I need. Perhaps your employer would have a solution?"

Eva leaned back against the sofa, reminding herself that Mrs. Mansfield assumed she was nothing more than Hyde's assistant. "I am happy to consult with his lordship, but what you are asking for is a delicate balance. You want to modernize a structure that has emotional value to you, mixing two completely different styles, and therefore nothing will satisfy you. You cannot have it both ways. If you try, the redesign is doomed from the start."

The woman's jaw fell a bit, clearly not expecting Eva to put the situation so plainly. But Eva could tell that Mrs. Mansfield was setting everyone up for failure: the architect, the contractor, herself. No one would be happy with the results—and the house deserved better.

Mrs. Mansfield turned her gaze toward the windows, where the busy Fifth Avenue afternoon traffic passed by. Carriages, carts, broughams, and the occasional man on horseback tottered along this main thoroughfare. Seconds ticked on the clock, loud in the quiet room and even quieter house.

"I suppose you're right," the older woman said after a long moment. "I hadn't quite thought of it that way but it makes sense."

"There's nothing wrong with the house as it is. It's a lovely summer cottage."

"Yes, it is." She glanced at the traces. "So many happy memories there. But I need to look to the future, not the past. My Walter would understand."

"Good for you. I'm certain your architects can revise your plans—"

"No, I'd like you to do it."

"Me?" She nearly laughed but thankfully stifled the reaction in time. "Oh, you mean E. M. Hyde."

"No, Miss Ashford. I nearly always say what I mean. I mean *you*."

Eva didn't know what to say. *Say yes, you fool. You desperately need the money and besides, this could be your first design under your own name.* Instead, what came out was, "Why?"

Mrs. Mansfield settled more firmly into the sofa and folded her hands. "My son speaks quite highly of you and he is not one to suffer fools lightly, especially women. If you were incompetent, he'd already have replaced you. And it's clear from our meeting that you can speak your mind—and God knows I appreciate a strong woman who is able to speak her mind."

Eva couldn't argue. She'd never learned the art

of dissembling or acting polite for politeness's sake. "Thank you, then. I would absolutely love to do this. I'll draft something and have it to you as quickly as possible. Would I be able to visit Stoneacre in the meantime? I'd like to get a feel for the space and what we might be able to salvage."

She could tell the idea pleased Mrs. Mansfield. "Of course. I plan to return to Newport on Wednesday. Come visit anytime."

"I will. Thank you."

"How are you finding working with my son?"

Eva swallowed and tried to think of an appropriate response, all the while willing her pale skin not to turn pink. "He is fair. Well versed in architecture in addition to the construction process. He's much more involved than I imagined."

"You sound as if you aren't certain whether that's good or bad."

"That's because I haven't quite decided," she said honestly and Mrs. Mansfield laughed.

"He's very driven, my son. Didn't use to be that way, you know. He wasn't always so hard. But I'm afraid that's what a broken heart can do to a young man."

"A broken heart?" Eva nearly fell off the sofa. Phillip had been in love?

"Oh, yes. I'm not certain he'd be happy with me sharing the story, however. It was quite well-known at the time. He finds it humiliating, though nothing was his fault. It taught him a valuable lesson, however, that people are often not what they seem."

Guilt thickened Eva's tongue as she struggled to form a response. Phillip had been duped in the past—and by a woman he'd considered marrying? Goodness, she could only imagine the blow to his pride.

And now Eva was lying to him about her father's health and the true architect behind the new Mansfield Hotel. He would be livid if he ever found out the truth.

He must never find out. No matter what happened, she had to ensure he never learned what she'd done. She didn't want to ruin this . . . friendship they had developed. It was important to her.

She realized Mrs. Mansfield was staring at her oddly. "Well, I shall certainly keep that in mind when dealing with him. I should be going, as I have another meeting soon. I'll cable you regarding a visit to Stoneacre. Perhaps Sunday?"

Mrs. Mansfield stood, the long strands of pearls around her neck clacking gently. "That would be lovely. I'll look forward to it."

HE WITNESSED THE entire meeting, but Phillip couldn't have said exactly how she managed it.

Over bland tea and fancy cakes, Eva charmed Weller right out of his concerns over the structural integrity of the hotel. More importantly, she thoroughly won him over to their side. Tammany Hall would not stand a chance in corrupting Weller again.

She and Carew had slowly reviewed the numbers, explained the steel frame system and how it would connect with the supporting beams. Talked through the deflections in place to counterbalance the lateral and vertical forces, such as wind pressure and gravitational pull, and even the sequential load estimates during the build. She had participated fully, displaying an impressive breadth of knowledge.

"Mr. Weller, your wife simply must try the currant jam," the red-haired minx was currently saying. "I'll have the cook send a jar up before you go." She motioned to a footman, who nodded and left the room.

"Thank you." The tips of Weller's ears turned red. "I'm certain she will appreciate your kindness."

"It is my pleasure. A way of sharing things from my beloved homeland. Would you like one as well, Mr. Carew?"

Carew nodded. "Yes, I'd like that. Thank you."

"Were there more questions, sir?" she asked Weller. "You may come back to the site as often as you need, of course, but I trust we've addressed all your concerns."

"More than addressed, I'd say. Hyde is quite clever and clearly has not misplaced his trust in you."

"You are too kind, and the words are undoubtedly a comfort to Mr. Mansfield, who has been quite patient over in the corner."

They all turned to Phillip and he produced a tight smile. Yes, he was profoundly relieved, but far too impressed, too . . . jumbled to join in the conviviality.

Eva rose, calling an end to the interminable visit, and the others came to their feet as well. Phillip was slower to rise, a strange anticipation coiling in his belly. This woman perplexed and enticed him, had from the very start when he'd met her aboard the ship. He'd tried to forget that night, to keep their relationship a working one—not a personal one. He was failing.

Phillip hated to fail.

Of course. The answer appeared with perfect clarity. He would have her *and* his hotel.

He'd convince her to pick up where they'd left off while on the Atlantic. He turned the idea over, allowing it to settle in his veins. The more he considered it, the more sense it made. Why shouldn't they indulge in their attraction while she was still in New York?

She was not experienced, she'd admitted as much that day in his office, but he could ensure she remained a virgin for her future husband. There were plenty of other ways to give and receive pleasure beyond intercourse. He longed to experience them all with her.

Everyone departed. He nodded at the two men on their way out, shaking hands but not speaking, and then he was alone with Eva.

As soon as the door closed, she dropped onto the sofa and blew out a long breath. "That was utterly exhausting."

"No," he said and took the seat next to her. "It was absolutely remarkable. You've worked a miracle, Eva."

Her lips twisted into a self-satisfied, smug smile. "I did, didn't I? It must pain you to admit it after you doubted me so fiercely."

"Not as much as you might expect, actually."

She leaned in to select a tiny strawberry tart. "And why is that?"

"Because I had every confidence in you and Carew."

She snorted and then took a bite of the dessert. Her eyes closed on a moan, leaning back in what he recognized as extreme pleasure, similar to when she'd climaxed in his cabin. A sizzling rush of electricity raced through his blood, along his spine.

Soon, he swore. Very soon.

"I'd like to take you out to celebrate."

She sat straighter. "Take me out? What does that mean?"

He hadn't decided yet, but he knew the usual tricks to entice a woman would fail with Eva. She wouldn't care for flowers or chocolates. Nor did she seem the type for opera or ice cream. This would require creativity. "It means I take you out on the town. That we spend time together in mutually desired company."

"Why would I desire your company? I thought we agreed to remain friends."

Not any longer. He'd moved past friends and was swiftly headed straight for lovers. "I'd like to renegotiate the meaning of that word."

Her gaze narrowed as she studied his face. She put down the rest of her tart and dusted off her hands. "I think you'll need to take up with the etymologists, then, not me."

"There's where you're wrong. You are precisely the person with whom I'd like to negotiate. What sort of friends are we, Eva?"

"Friends that work together and then travel separately to our own homes at the end of the day."

He was close enough on the sofa to easily reach

her, yet he held back. She needed coaxing, but this time without spirits or a life-threatening storm. She had to arrive at the decision on her own, connect the points herself, as only her analytical brain could. That meant going slowly and explaining what he had in mind. Setting parameters and sharing expectations.

"Not good enough. I want to be *close* friends." He dropped his voice to an intimate tone. "The sort of friends who, on occasion, might not go home separately."

She swallowed hard, the delicate lines of her throat working as a flush spread over her lovely pale skin. "That didn't take long. We agreed to be friends only a minute ago."

"Slightly more than a minute, but even so, I believe in adapting when a situation no longer suits my needs."

"Is this where I ask about your needs—which results in the exchange of a litany of innuendos and verbal jabs?"

He grinned, wide and huge without a single ounce of shame. "If you like."

Her hands slapped her knees in exasperation. "I don't know what to make of this. You confound me at every turn. Furthermore, I cannot worry about your needs when I'm struggling to discover my own."

"I feel the same, but I cannot stop staring at you, thinking about you. Remembering that night on the ship."

Her gaze slid away and she shifted on the sofa. Yet she didn't move, and he thought she might be intrigued.

His guess was confirmed when she asked, "And what, exactly, are you proposing?"

"A bevy of delights, my lady." Reaching out, he touched a fingertip to the inside of her delicate wrist, making a circle over the soft skin. He loved a woman's wrist, the fine bones and narrow width that were distinctly feminine, and Eva's was particularly lovely. He gave the briefest caress over the supple, bare surface, and suddenly longed to press his mouth there, to sweep his tongue over that spot. To bathe it, trace the faint bluish veins, and discover if the nerves were as sensitive as he hoped. "Only this time, you'll be entirely sober."

A small tremor went through her and she licked her lips. "It's a terrible idea. I am not . . ."

Interested? Attracted to you? A host of words skated through his mind to complete that sentence when she left it unfinished. "You are not . . . ?"

"Willing to risk everything." She closed her eyes briefly and shook her head. "If you think to manage me by—"

"Stop." He slid his hand up to cup her jaw, tilting her head until he found her eyes. "I'll not mix the two. This would remain completely separate from whatever happens with the hotel before your father arrives." Dipping his head, he brought his nose to her cheek, inhaling the soap and sweet femininity that clung to her skin. "And I have no doubt you'll likely be the one managing me."

Her body swayed and he sensed triumph. He angled his mouth to her earlobe, which he gently bit between his teeth. She gasped, the breathy sound racing through him like fire. "In fact, I'm beginning to fear the lengths to which I'll go for another night with you."

"I cannot." Her chest rose and fell swiftly, yet she shook her head. "My future career—not to mention my reputation—could suffer for this."

"I won't let it, Eva. I swear, I'll protect you with everything I have—by any means fair or foul."

"Not even you are able to control that much, Phillip. If we are discovered . . . No, I cannot take the risk." She rose and crossed to the middle of the room, her arms wrapping around her waist.

"All I'm asking is for you to think on it. We could meet somewhere completely private. No one ever need know."

"No, not even then. I stand to lose in this arrangement."

He came to his feet. Two steps brought him to her side, where he bent to whisper in her ear, letting his lips brush the soft skin of the outer edge. "You're wrong. We both win."

Leaving her to think it over, he left the room without a backward glance.

SHE WAS CONTEMPLATING an affair with her employer.

Well, more like attempting to talk herself *out* of having an affair. It was a terrible idea, for many reasons, yet Eva couldn't get the picture out of her head. Sweaty limbs, deep kisses, his large, rough hands sweeping over her bare skin . . . Her breasts grew heavy imagining what a night together might be like.

And what of her career? She'd never let a man

distract her before, not even her three fiancés. Was she ready to throw away all she'd worked for on a few kisses? Intimacy would complicate her relationship with him, and she would undoubtedly be the one to suffer in the end. He could even go so far as to discharge her or refuse to let her on the construction site. And then she and her father would be destitute.

She should say no.

And yet . . .

Curiosity was killing her, the cause of many lost hours of sleep. *A bevy of delights, my lady.* Heavens, those words sent chills down her spine—even in the blazing summer sun.

As a result, she was distracted and restless. Anxious and uncertain. This should be the most exciting time of her life, in a new city, a new country, overseeing the largest, most prestigious project of her father's career. Instead, she was ruining it by pining over a man.

What was *wrong* with her?

Giving herself a strong mental shake, she continued her stroll about the perimeter of the construction site. The foundation should be completed in another few weeks. Milliken's crew still used the occasional blast of dynamite, with woven steel mats used to muffle the sound, while steam shovels created piles of rubble and dirt to be loaded into carts. It was the fastest excavation she'd ever seen, but efficient, too.

As she navigated through several high piles of debris, she decided to start on her other project, the one for Mrs. Mansfield. At least then she would have more to do. Keep her mind off Phillip and on important matters, like her future. Perhaps she'd travel to Newport tomorrow—

A rumbling sound erupted on her left and her head snapped up. Stone, dirt, and wood began to slide from the giant mountain beside her, the pieces shifting and moving, tumbling toward the spot where she stood. In the blink of an eye, she hiked her skirts, pivoted, and dashed out of the way. Thunder echoed behind her, dirt swirling to sting her eyes as she hurried to put distance between herself and the heap.

When she reached safety, she turned to inspect the destruction. The ground where she'd just been walking was now buried under bits of wood, earth, and stone. She pressed a hand to her chest, trying to calm her racing heart. Heavens, that was close.

"Miss!" One of the laborers arrived, his dirt-streaked face lined with concern. "Miss, are you hurt?"

She lifted a hand. "I am fine. A bit rattled, but fine."

"Oh, thank goodness. You could've seriously been hurt."

Studying the collapsed pile, she could only agree. "Thankfully I have quick feet. Have you seen Mr. Milliken?"

"Um." The worker scratched his jaw and studied the chaos stretched out before him. "Oh, here he comes now." He pointed to the familiar burly figure hurrying in their direction, two other men flanking him.

Eva straightened her spine, wiping any residual

relief or panic off her face. *Show no fear.* "Mr. Milliken, may I have a word?"

"What happened?" the general contractor barked. "Why are you knocking over my debris piles?"

Eva glanced at the other men. "Gentlemen, if you'll excuse us."

They all turned to Milliken, who gave a jerk of his chin and the men departed. She resisted the urge to roll her eyes. When would men stop being so dismissive of women? "You need to better brace these piles. Someone will be hurt."

"My men know better than to poke around these piles. I've never had anyone buried under rubble on any site before and this should be no different, if all things had remained the same."

"If I weren't here, you mean."

"As I've said, a construction site is no place for a woman."

"Yes, you've made that perfectly clear on several occasions. I am, unfortunately for you, not leaving, so you'd best accustom yourself to the idea."

He crossed his arms over his chest, no doubt attempting to intimidate her. "I'll be speaking with Mr. Mansfield about this."

"Please do. In the meantime, I want these piles better supported. Or else I'll be speaking with Mr. Mansfield . . . and I think he'll agree that safety on the site is more critical than gender."

Milliken gave her his back and stomped away. Eva blew out a long breath and decided she needed a cup of tea. No, a glass of sherry . . . or stronger.

She began the long journey toward the exit, ready to put this day behind her. Stares followed her but she ignored them and kept walking. It wasn't the first—or tenth—time she'd been made to feel an oddity. As if women with ambition belonged in cages in the traveling shows, where visitors could obtain peeks for a penny apiece.

A shiny brougham waited at the curb outside the site. For a brief second she considered it might be Nora, but then long legs clad in navy pin-striped trousers emerged . . . and her heart thumped hard in her chest.

Phillip unfolded from the carriage, his brawny shoulders angling to fit through the door. The dying sunlight turned his hair a golden color so befitting this crown prince of New York. He smiled as he strolled toward her. "Just the woman I am looking for."

She squinted at him, using a hand to shield her eyes from the sun. "Here to see today's progress?"

"No, I came to see you."

Her stomach dipped and twirled with giddiness at the words, but she tried to remain distant. She could not allow this man to affect her any more than he already had. "How did you guess I was here?"

His lips quirked. "Where else would you be? From what Milliken tells me, you never leave."

Of course Milliken would say that. "Which is the reason you hired me, you realize."

"The reason I hired your father, yes," he clarified, a not so subtle reminder of who was really in charge. He clasped his hands behind his back. "So if you are always here, then when are you touring our fair city and seeing all those buildings on your list?"

With the project just underway she hadn't even considered it. Her time in New York wasn't to be spent as a tourist but to oversee the hotel construction. "I cannot gad about the city right now. Perhaps after the foundation is—"

"Nonsense. I knew you'd say that." He took her arm and the feel of his fingers gently digging into her flesh caused a shiver to race down her spine. "Come with me. I have a surprise for you."

"Phillip, I really should return home. I'm exhausted."

"No excuses, Eva. This will be worth it, trust me. You'll find this terribly exciting—and besides, you owe me a night on the town."

Without giving her the chance to resist, he helped her up and then had a quick word with his driver. He settled inside, his massive shoulders taking up most of the room in the brougham, her side pressed tightly to his. Heat poured off his body, wrapping around her. There was no escaping him, no way to put distance between them.

She fixed her eyes on the passing buildings and tried to remain calm. Aloof. This was an impossible feat, however, considering the strange restlessness that presented itself only in his presence. All she could think of was burrowing into his side and kissing him again.

God above, the man was turning her into a wanton.

"Are you not even curious where I'm taking you?"

"It appears we are headed south. And there's no use badgering you for a location because you won't ruin the surprise."

He chuckled, a rich, deep sound that wound its way through her stomach, turning her insides to warm jelly. "I hadn't realized you knew me so well. Should I be flattered?"

No flirting. "Hardly. You should be embarrassed over your transparent shallowness."

"Is that it? Well, then tell me." His voice dropped to a seductive rasp. "What I am thinking right now?"

She didn't dare look at him. "I think I have an idea." She dragged in a ragged breath. "And it is definitely not professional."

"You would be right."

"I haven't agreed to anything."

He raised his hands as if to show he was harmless. "I am aware and this outing is not meant to pressure you." She peeked up through her lashes and caught his mouth curving in the most delicious manner. "Not much anyway."

She couldn't help but laugh. This version of Phillip, the charming bon vivant, was hard to resist. "Does this stubbornness serve you well with other women?"

"Never had one resist me, so I couldn't say."

"Then I am happy to be the first."

"Do not worry. I'll wear you down."

If he acted like this, she did not doubt it. This man could sweep her off her feet if she wasn't careful.

But there were too many secrets between them, all that she must keep hidden from him. Guilt weighted her down, a concrete block that only grew heavier as time went on. *It taught him a valuable lesson, that people are often not what they seem.* Eva winced at the memory of his mother's words. She hated lying, believe it or not. Yet circumstances made deception necessary in this case.

He'll never forgive you.

In the end, it didn't matter. She was here to complete the hotel. That was all.

She couldn't worry about anything else.

Chapter Nine

Phillip grinned as the carriage finally stopped at the corner of Twenty-Sixth Street and Madison Avenue. An imposing Moorish-style building dominated the entire city block—a structure Eva's little architecture-loving heart needed to see.

Architecture was a passion for her, much more than just overseeing a project here and there for her father. She knew construction and physics. Knew buildings and angles, materials and earth. She was intelligent, coolheaded, and fairly glowed while at the excavation site.

Considering that, he wanted to show her this particular building, witness the joy of discovery and appreciation in her hazel eyes, one architecture aficionado to another. Beyond that, whatever else happened was entirely up to her.

He hoped, however. Oh, how he hoped.

He angled out of the brougham and stepped to the walk. She emerged, eyes wide, her head tilted up at the yellow pressed brick as he helped her down. He liked the feel of her hand, so small and delicate in his own.

"What is this place? It almost looks like a castle."

"This is the new Madison Square Garden. The amphitheater opened last month and the other parts are still under construction. Would you like to explore it with me?"

"Are we . . . ? That is, will anyone mind?"

"Not a bit. I know Mr. White, the architect, and he's given us permission." They started toward the archways that marked the entrance. A man waited by the interior set of doors. Phillip removed his derby and held out his hand. "You must be the manager."

"I am Mr. Perkins. A pleasure to meet you, Mr. Mansfield. Right this way. I've turned on the lights for you and opened the roof."

"Opened the roof?" Eva exclaimed. "What on earth does that mean?"

Phillip shared a grin with Mr. Perkins then whisked her through the second set of doors. "Allow me to show you."

He'd been inside the building once, earlier in the process, so he had a basic understanding of the layout, though this finished version looked much different. They went under the towering risers of seats and came out into the cavernous amphitheater. Eva gasped at his side, her head swiveling to take it all in. The power had been switched on, so rows of lights illuminated the steel girders above, the effect almost like a circus tent. Private boxes stacked the far end, while lines of seats filled the two levels surrounding the giant center.

"This is astounding. Is that a hole in the roof?"

"The skylight slides to allow in air. It's operated with a mechanical system similar to a bicycle wheel." He pointed to the mechanism. "This main section of the Garden is the biggest in the world. It seats around nine thousand, with room for thousands more on the floor. Additionally, there's a tank underneath the floor that can be filled with water for aquatic events, like water polo and fishing."

He watched her study White's design choices. Her red hair flamed in the yellow electric light, soft strands escaping her bonnet. A natural beauty, Eva was the loveliest woman he'd ever seen, even after she'd spent all day at a dirty, dusty construction site. Milliken feared half the workers were already in love with her, the other half merely in lust. Phillip could understand why, though he'd kill any man who touched her against her wishes.

She faced him, a huge infectious grin splitting her face. He swallowed against the sudden tightness in his throat as she said, "You knew I would love this."

"Yes, I thought you might. You haven't even seen the best part yet."

"Something better than this? I cannot believe it. This is amazing."

He took her hand, laced his fingers with hers, and led her toward the opposite side. Two spots of color emerged on her fair cheekbones but he pretended not to notice as they circled the giant arena. He had no intention of letting her go.

In the back they continued along the mosaic floors, up a marble staircase, until they reached the theater, which was still under construction. "This will be the indoor theater." He pulled open the door for her to peek into the dark interior. The carpet and seats hadn't yet been installed but the proscenium and stage were finished.

Next he let her glimpse the unfinished concert hall, which would eventually seat three thousand. As they rode the tiny metal elevator up to the roof, she nearly bounced on her toes with excitement. "I cannot imagine what else there is to see. I'm already thoroughly astounded."

"Patience, my lady."

She cocked her head, her brows lowered. "How do you know so much about this building? Are you an investor?"

"No, Vanderbilt owns it. I am merely a fan of buildings, as are you."

"But why? Did you want to be an architect?"

He thought about it. "My father built half of Lower Manhattan before he died. I suppose constructing new properties is in my blood."

The elevator stopped and he threw open the metal gate. She passed through first. "Yet you focus mostly on hotels."

"I do. More Americans now travel because of the trains and I want to build a string of hotels across the country."

They went along a covered Grecian-style promenade that overlooked an open space. "What will be down there?" she asked.

"A large restaurant. On this level will be a space for smaller performances. Here we are." They turned the corner to reveal the roof garden and its charming Chinese pagoda. Eva stopped dead in her tracks, her head tilted up at the incredibly tall tower. Her mouth fell slightly ajar. "It's . . ."

"Do you recognize it?" He knew damn well she did, so he let her say it.

"The Giralda Tower in Seville, Spain," she breathed. "I cannot believe it. It's stunning."

"You've seen the original, then?"

She nodded, still fixed on the tower looming over them. "Yes, many years ago my father took me. There's nothing more magnificent on earth than the Cathedral of Seville. What is that at the top there, that copper figure?"

"Diana, the Roman goddess of the hunt. Quite nude, too. The conservatives are making a hue and a cry over it."

"Oh, they mustn't take it down. How do we—?" Her head swiveled as she tried to find a better angle to see the statue.

"Come along." He held out his hand, curious if she would take it. Without blinking, she slipped her hand into his large grip. He smothered a smile and guided her to where he'd been told the stairs could be located. The tower would be inaccessible to the public once the Garden officially opened so he was glad they were able to enter it now.

After another elevator ride, they climbed a spiral staircase up the center, a slight breeze blowing in from huge open windows cut into the brick on all sides. The sun had set, leaving twinkling lights to illuminate the city around them. They went up and up, higher and higher, to just below the tall spire. Both of them were breathing heavily by the time they reached the observation point, a narrow stone platform not deep enough for two.

Eva strode out onto the platform and gripped the balustrade. "Phillip . . . my goodness. It's the entire city."

He remained inside the tower itself, content to merely watch her. The backdrop of the island, miles of flickering light and dark sky, stood behind her, mesmerizing him.

Or perhaps it was merely this unusual, compelling woman.

"Come see." She beckoned with her hand. "This must be the tallest point in Manhattan."

"Second tallest, actually. And I'm fine where I am." *Watching you.*

She turned, one brow arched. "Why, Phillip Mansfield. Are you afraid of heights?"

"Not afraid of heights, per se. Just afraid of falling."

"What if I promise to hold your hand?" She strolled toward him, clearly enjoying this bit of superiority over him. "I won't let you fall." Strong fingers threaded his own, her face now close enough that he could bend and kiss her without much effort.

So that's exactly what he did.

THE KISS SURPRISED her. It shouldn't have, of course, considering the isolated romantic setting, but one minute they were discussing his aversion to heights and the next he captured her mouth. She didn't fight it. There was no use denying she wanted him to kiss her again. Had been looking forward to it for days, in fact.

So she relaxed, surrendered, as he yanked her closer, their lips molding and shifting over one another, a wicked dance that needed no words, no air. His mouth was soft, so unexpectedly lush for a man his size. He was all finesse and technique, not brute strength, coaxing as opposed to overpowering her. She'd never been kissed this thoroughly— unless she counted the night in his cabin.

Her arms wound around his neck, fingers sliding into thick, silky hair. His tongue traced the seam of her lips and she parted them eagerly, allowing him to lick inside, to find her tongue and stroke it with his own. The effect was like a jolt of brandy, warming her everywhere while weighting down her limbs. She held on, lost in him, lost in this moment where nothing else existed but the two of them.

Determined hands slid over her ribs and hips, everywhere he could reach, and she could feel her resolve melting, all the feeble reasons for resistance evaporating as the kiss dragged on. Her fingers dug into the heft of his wide shoulders, enjoying the shift of muscle and bone through his clothing as he moved.

His breathing labored, he drew back and stared into her eyes. Large hands cupped her face, fingers gentle on her jaw, as if he were desperate to keep her in place—not that he needed to worry. She had no intention of running away. "Yes," she whispered to the unspoken question in his gaze.

His nostrils flared ever so slightly. "Why?" His brows lowered in confusion. "Not that I'm complaining, but why now?"

She understood perfectly. A few days ago she'd insisted on professional distance. Yet how could she explain it? They were high above the city, just the two of them, in a cocoon of warm July air. "Does it matter?"

"It does to me. I'd like to know why you've changed your mind."

Because she felt reckless and daring again, just as she had that night on the ship. And because she wanted him, wanted to experience the same wicked things he'd done to her before. The area between her thighs grew slick just thinking on it.

Her reputation in England was ruined anyhow; no decent man would marry Lady Unlucky. What was to prevent her from having fun while in America, especially when he'd promised no one would find out?

She went with a coy answer instead. "Isn't that what women do?"

One side of his mouth kicked up. "Most women, perhaps. However, you're not most women. There's no one else who can begin to compare."

Before she could wrap her head around that heady compliment, he kissed her again. She felt herself being pulled under, mindless to what was happening, all instinct and urges as the kiss wore on. Soon she grew restless, the craving for him a fever in her blood. She pressed closer and he grasped her hips, bringing them flush with his own, and his erection pushed against her pubic bone. She hadn't touched him at all during their night on the ship—at least that she remembered. Now she longed to undress him and map every detail before she lost the chance.

Because, honestly, a woman with three dead fiancés in her past knew exactly how everything could change in an instant. What if she never had this opportunity ever again?

Decision made, she slipped her hands inside his coat and started to push the fabric off his shoulders. Large fingers wrapped around her wrists, stopping her. "Not here," he panted.

"Yes. Right here."

He made a disbelieving noise in his throat. "No. There's no room to ravish you properly here. I need to thoroughly consume you, to wreck us both. I want to destroy you for all other men in both England and America. Hell, any country on the planet." His thumbs caressed her wrists, his espresso brown stare nearly black in the moonlight. "Let me take you to my home. We'll be alone there."

Her knees wobbled, bones gone liquid at the provocative words. Oh, the temptation . . . She could almost see them together in his bedroom, on a bed probably as big as an island, their bare limbs entwined. Skin hot and sweaty as the pleasure built higher and higher. *Sweet heaven . . .*

Reality quickly returned, however. She could not be seen skulking in and out of his home. Servants talked and there was always the risk of someone catching her. Her career—her father's career—lay in her very hands. "No, absolutely not."

He frowned and maneuvered them so her back was to the stone. Then he dropped a string of kisses along her jaw, over the skin exposed above her collar. His teeth sank into the tender flesh of her neck, gently biting. Tingles shot through her limbs, white-hot stars that pulsed in her veins and settled between her legs. "I loved seeing that mark on your creamy skin," he murmured into her throat, referring to the love bite he'd left on the ship.

"It certainly was a surprise."

"For me as well. I've never lost control with anyone like that. Were you angry?"

Not as much as she probably should've been. It had served as a reminder of one of the best nights of her life. "No." She leaned up and nipped his jaw. "But don't do it again."

He chuckled. "Fine. Shall we find a hotel?"

With all those prying eyes? How did one even manage such a rendezvous? "No."

"Eva . . ." He rested his forehead on her temple. "Be reasonable. I'm about to incinerate."

As was she. Here, it had to be here. Where no one would discover them. Where they could be alone in a city full of over a million people. To convince him, she did something no proper lady would ever consider: she snuck a hand between them and placed it directly on his erection. He jerked, surprised, and then exhaled, rocking his hips into her grip. *"Oh, Christ."*

She hadn't ever touched a man so intimately and the intoxicating power of controlling his pleasure appealed to her instantly. Phillip's eyes remained closed, jaw clenched, as she continued to smooth her palm along his thick length. He shivered when she added more pressure. He gasped when she used her nails. When she reached for the fastening on his trousers, he stilled her wrist. "Come with me."

He led her down the circular stairs to a landing

where a carved wooden door was nearly hidden off to the right. Phillip tried the knob and the latch turned, revealing a secret room. "What is this?" she asked as he ushered her into the semi-dark space.

"The architect's apartments." Moonlight filtered through the uncovered windows to reveal bare floors, Roman columns, and unpainted walls. Dust billowed beneath their feet, most likely a combination of plaster and sawdust. The familiar smell of raw wood and sweat hung heavily in the air, with only a few pieces of furniture to break up the emptiness. "He said most of the rooms are not finished, but I am hoping—Oh, thank God."

He came to a halt in a large room, where a wooden bed frame supported a mattress covered in plush white bedclothes. The walls were painted a deep scarlet and a great Japanese fan hung from the ceiling, thick carpets covering the wood floor. Goodness, it was like a Covent Garden bordello. This was not a residence for a wife, that was for certain.

While tawdry, the surroundings did not dissuade her in the least. "Will he mind that we are here?"

"Not a bit, considering his purpose in building this space as his own." He faced her, his body crowding her smaller frame in the most delicious way as he held her gaze. "I meant what I said, Eva. I want you to be sure. I won't give you any cause for regrets."

She appreciated his concern, though it was for naught. There would be no regrets. Doubtful a man existed who'd overlook her reputation or her career choice. She might as well be searching for a unicorn. "I want this. I want *you*."

"May I undress you?"

The earnest question gave her a moment's pause. She had the sensation of standing at the edge of a cliff, one step that would forever change her life, but she knew he would not hurt her. She hadn't been in the frame of mind to refuse him that night on the ship, yet he hadn't forced her, hadn't taken advantage of her in any way. Whatever happened between them tonight was up to her. He would respect her wishes and not push her further than she desired.

The realization emboldened her. How had he known exactly what she needed to hear to proceed? Putting that thought out of her mind for now, she reached for him. "I'd rather undress you."

HER WORDS WENT through Phillip like a jolt of direct current and he swallowed hard. "Perhaps it'll expedite matters if we each tend to ourselves."

"I sort of fancied playing your valet." Her mouth curved in the most seductive, alluring way and he found himself kissing her. She met him eagerly, her lips attacking his with a hunger to match his own. Hands shoved the coat off his shoulders, the fine cloth dropping to the carpet. He unfastened his cuff links and slipped them in his trouser pockets while she loosened his necktie.

He liked her boldness. It had been one of the first things he'd noticed about her aboard the ship. For a proper lady, she could quite easily bring him to his knees. Then his necktie was on the ground and she attended to the buttons on his vest, slipping them free of the holes. Her knuckles brushed the thin cloth covering his stomach and his cock jerked.

Breaking off from her mouth, he trailed kisses over her jaw and throat while he removed the strip of cloth around her waist. His clumsy fingers, rough and callused from boxing, were shaking with need as he began to work on the ties of her skirt, anticipation strumming in his veins. He considered savoring the experience, unwrapping her slowly and carefully, but he was too damn desperate.

From there, he peeled apart her high-necked shirtwaist, undoing the tiny pearl buttons between her breasts, down her stomach. His vest disappeared at some point. Her cotton corset cover came next, leaving her in a silk and cotton beige corset. He drew back to stare at her. With one finger, he traced the delicate lace edge at the top of the garment, her ample bosom heaving with labored breaths, arms now at her sides. "You are incredibly lovely," he whispered.

She ran her hands over his shoulders, her eyes tracking the progress. "You are quite handsome yourself."

He slipped his hand under the light material of her chemise and stroked the top of her breast. Smooth and supple. Irresistibly soft. "I cannot rush this. I feel as if I've been waiting years for you."

As if ready to move things along, she untied her petticoat and then her bustle. When she stepped free, he quickly spun her around and unlaced her corset. Thankfully she had the cumbersome thing half unfastened by the time she turned back around. When it fell to the floor he bent and lifted her in his arms, carrying her to the bed and placing her on the crisp bed linen.

She didn't let go. Small fists clenched in the material of his shirt and she pulled him down atop her, where the heft of her breasts met his chest and his cock ground into her thigh. They both inhaled sharply. "You minx," he growled against her cheek, rolling his hips as his body screamed for friction. "This is not going slow."

Her hands moved to his throat, where she focused on his collar and then his shirt. "You have on far too much clothing." She pushed the suspenders off his shoulders, gathered his shirt in her fists, and shoved it higher. He whipped the white cotton off and let it fall. Her fingertips traced his chest through the tight undergarment he wore. "You look nothing like the other American gentleman of leisure."

Instead of offering an explanation, which would reveal far too much, he began nibbling and sucking on her skin, moving steadily downward, over her collarbone, sternum, and the slope of her breast . . . Her back bowed, eyes falling closed in sweet surrender, fiery red hair tumbling free of her coiffure, and he suddenly wanted to bite her, to mark her again. God, what was it about this woman that brought out the primal beast in him?

Her chemise was off in a blink, leaving her magnificent breasts exposed, pale mounds that were full and round, topped with the prettiest pink nipples. Bending, he teased her with his tongue, fingers kneading the supple heft, until she writhed beneath him, her hands clamped around his head.

Then he wrapped his lips around one of those peaks and drew it deep into his mouth, relishing the moan that rumbled out of her chest.

It wasn't enough. He wanted to bury his face between her thighs, taste her sweetness on his tongue, but didn't wish to scare her. He broke off and loomed over her, pushing a lock of hair from her forehead. "Do you trust me?"

"Yes," she answered quickly, not even requiring a moment to consider it, and something in his chest turned over.

"I plan to remove your drawers and pleasure you, but I don't want to frighten you."

Lines creased her forehead. "I had assumed that would be included."

He nearly laughed, her answer so forthright and *Eva*. He leaned down to gently nip the lobe of her ear. "A bevy of delights, my lady. As promised."

"Then you'd best get busy," she rasped, turning her head to meet his mouth with her own. They kissed for a long moment, during which he tried to keep his wits about him. He was painfully hard and nearly delirious with need, but he'd promised to take care of her. Watching her come had been the highlight of that damned sea voyage and he couldn't wait to taste her pleasure on his tongue this time.

He rose up on his knees and went to work. Removed her boots, then untied her drawers and slid them down her hips, taking the stockings as well. This left her exquisitely bare, a feast for his eyes with her pale, unblemished skin, long legs, and red thatch of hair on her mound. *Sweet heaven.* He ran his palms over her calves and along her thighs, pushed them apart to make room for himself.

Now on his stomach, he used his thumbs to part the outer lips of her sex, revealing every delicious part of her. She was wet and swollen . . . and he hadn't even touched her yet. His lids drifted shut as he inhaled, the sharp scent of her desire more arousing than any perfume ever created.

"What are you doing?" She shifted, trying to see him and close her legs at the same time. He didn't move, just kept his shoulders squarely between her thighs.

"Patience, my dear." Using the flat part of his tongue, he gave a long lick through her folds to the treasure beneath. She squeaked, a noise he definitely hadn't expected but didn't deter him in the least. Another long swipe and she dropped onto the mattress. "Oh, God," he heard her whisper before he continued using his mouth, his tongue, his lips . . .

After a few seconds she no longer formed words but uttered sweet, incoherent sounds of pleasure that had his cock throbbing. When he began sucking on the little bud at the top of her sex, her thighs started to quiver so he worked a finger inside her, then two, and pressed the sensitive spot on her inner wall. The result was instantaneous. She shouted and her muscles clamped down on his fingers, her body rocking and shaking as she came, and he used his tongue to prolong her pleasure as long as humanly possible.

Forever. I could do this forever.

When she pushed on his head, too sensitive for

him to continue, he fell onto his back and closed his eyes. Christ, he wanted to shove deep inside her so very badly. He'd never craved a woman like this, with a blinding, all-consuming need to have her. But he couldn't. She was an innocent and he could not first take her like a brute.

Without thinking, he opened his trousers and took his cock out of his undergarment. He began stroking himself, fast. The familiar feel of his hand, the right pressure, her tangy sweetness still on his tongue . . . It wouldn't take long—and as soon as he came he could function once more.

Movement registered beside him before gentle lips pressed to his throat. Her hand swept down his belly and covered the hand flying over his shaft. "Let me help you."

He was burning alive, desperate. "Eva," he groaned and bucked his hips. Fuck, he was so close but he didn't want to scare her. "Are you certain?"

"Yes." She began pulling on his erection, moving with him, trying to learn. "Show me what you like."

All his common sense, his gentlemanly instincts, disappeared like smoke. "Harder," he panted. "As hard as you can—and faster. *Yes. Like that.*" Pressure built between his legs, his balls tightened, and he switched places so her grip was against his skin with his hand on the outside. He kept the pace, her soft hands on his erection, and his muscles clenched.

That was when she released his cock . . . and climbed on top of him.

Chapter Ten

He was the most beautiful man, rumpled and wild with pleasure. Eva couldn't resist him or this need to ease the ache deep inside her. She knew the basics of intimacy between a man and a woman, and she was desperate to experience it with him.

Throwing a leg over his hips to straddle him, she lined her core up with his erect shaft. His eyes, half-lidded and dark with lust, focused on her face. "Are you certain?"

Instead of speaking, she nodded. Her palms found his chest, nails digging in as she rocked her hips experimentally. The slipperiness between her legs helped her glide over his hardness, and they both gasped.

"God, I want you. So badly, Eva."

He reached between them and positioned himself at her entrance. With his other hand, he found her hip and nudged her slightly. The blunt crown pressed inside, then more, a thick heat that scraped over her sensitive tissues, stretching her slowly.

When the fullness became too much, she paused and he waited, agonizingly patient as her body adjusted. He gave her time and she took it, knowing the reward was soon coming. After all, why would anyone engage in intimacies more than once if it were such a terrible experience?

She sank down, bit by bit, her breath labored and choppy. Sweat broke out on her forehead. Everything clenched in anticipation as she enveloped him, the deep invasion hitting sweet spots she hadn't known existed. He massaged her breasts and rolled her nipples, his strong, capable hands arousing her with every caress. When their hips joined she let her lids fall and threw back her head, taking a moment to *feel*.

It was so much more than she'd ever imagined. He was inside her, a part of her, connected in a way she'd never been with another before.

"You are gorgeous," he murmured, leaning up to take one of her nipples in his mouth. He sucked and stroked the tip of her breast, until she was compelled to roll her hips, her body urging her to move.

"Yes, more," he breathed against her skin. "Just like that."

"What does it feel like for you?"

He dropped onto the mattress and gripped her thighs. "Tight. Hot. Like absolute heaven. Move, Eva." He showed her how to rock and slide to bring them both the most pleasure. She ground down, the pressure building as she rubbed over his pubic bone.

"I want to see you." Her fingers began unfastening the remaining tiny buttons of his undergarment, the ones he hadn't bothered to undo earlier. He reached to help and soon he'd slipped both arms free and pushed the cloth to his waist. Her breath caught. God above, he was . . . solid. Corded muscles gleamed with perspiration and shifted with every movement. Hollows and ridges outlined bone and tendon. Silky dark hair covered his chest, leading down toward his groin. She'd never seen anything more beautiful in her life.

Not that she planned to tell him. Undoubtedly, he was aware of his effect on the opposite sex, Mr. I've-never-had-a-woman-resist-me.

Instead, aroused beyond belief, she quickened her pace. Phillip grunted his approval, then slipped a thumb between her legs to rub the swollen nub waiting there. A rush of pleasure started in her toes, white-hot sensation overcoming her, limbs trembling as the orgasm dragged her under.

Dimly, she felt him driving upward—hard, powerful thrusts that jolted her entire body. He shouted, jerking and shaking as he came, his shaft thickening and pulsing inside her. She loved his desperation, this loss of control in such an otherwise rigid man.

Then they were panting, limp and exhausted. Eventually, she collapsed atop his heaving chest, and his softening penis slipped out of her core. Shadows cloaked the dark room—a place Eva would never forget. She felt sticky and sweaty . . . but utterly transformed. Knocked down and then rebuilt, stronger and wiser, as if she'd been let in on one of life's biggest secrets.

Bringing her to his side, he held her in the crook

of his arm and she stroked the soft mat of hair covering his wide chest. A peaceful moment, the quiet said more than words. Though she was tired, she couldn't ever remember being happier.

"I should not have finished inside you. I apologize."

Oh. Yes, that.

Tranquility shattered with very real consequences, she rose up on her elbow to see his face. "It never occurred to me."

He winced, his expression twisting with true regret. That hurt more than anything else he could have said right then. Not that her virginity was any sort of gift or prize, but she had allowed him *inside* her. Him, no one else. And already he regretted it.

No doubt her inexperience offended him, quite unlike the ladies he normally bedded who knew how to prevent conception. Women who need not be shown how to please a man. In this lazy postcoital glow, she'd expected praise and affection . . . not contrition.

Lady Unlucky. How could she have forgotten?

Ignoring the swift pain in her chest, she pushed off the mattress and sat, her legs swinging over the side as she tried to collect herself. *Casual and professional, Eva. There's no need for an emotional scene. It's an affair, not a relationship.*

"You needn't worry," she said in an attempt at bravery. "I'm quite certain no complications shall result." Where was her chemise? She peered into the darkened room, moonlight her only guide.

"No one can be certain," his deep voice said behind her. "Not at this point."

Rising, she bent to grasp her stockings. "Well, I am."

"Eva, I am attempting to express concern over your well-being, about something that affects us both. The least you could do is look at me."

No. What she needed to do was leave. To put distance between them and regain her equilibrium.

She yanked on her stockings and garters, then her drawers. As she tied the strings, Phillip stood in front of her, hands on his hips. "Eva, stop."

Ignoring him, she spun to retrieve her crumpled chemise on the floor. Strong fingers wrapped around her shoulders and forced her to stand. "What is wrong with you?" he asked, not letting go. "You are rushing out of here as if the building is on fire."

Wasn't that what he expected? This was no love affair, like in the romantic novels, with tender affection and words of everlasting devotion. No, tonight had been about his promised bevy of delights, which had been quite thoroughly demonstrated. "I assumed you would prefer to leave now that we are finished . . ." She waved her hand in the direction of the bed.

"Finished?" His mouth flattened into an unhappy line. "You are completely shutting me out. I am trying not to feel—"

"Trying not to feel what?" she asked when he cut himself off.

Releasing her, he dragged a hand through his hair. "I've never . . . Well, I didn't expect you to want to escape me so soon."

She thought of the way he'd winced earlier. His regret. *Shore up your walls, Eva. Build them high. Protect yourself.* "You are being silly. This was lovely but I must now return home. I'm expected for dinner."

He made a sound of disbelief and stared out the window. Tall and broad, he'd pulled his trousers up but hadn't fastened them. They hung off his hip bones in the most sinful manner. Even annoyed, he was delicious.

"And," she continued, "I'd say we both got what we wanted. No one was hurt." *Except my pride, of course.* "Isn't that how these things work?"

"Yes, I suppose so. I just . . . I normally have some sort of understanding with a woman. There are practical matters to be discussed ahead of time."

"Such as?"

He bent down and plucked her chemise off the floor. "Here, put this on. I cannot think straight when you're half-dressed."

She lifted her arms and he drew the material over her head and down her hips. "Better?" she asked when he finished.

He nodded and sat on the edge of the bed. "Are you . . . ? Would you like to do this again?"

"With you?"

Dark eyes narrowed, his jaw hardening. "Yes, *with me.*"

She liked that spark of anger. A hint of emotion that eased her bruised heart. Perhaps he hadn't regretted every part of tonight.

She considered his question. Did she want to engage in sexual congress once more? Even with her body sated from the most recent bout, she already craved his touch. What was the point in resisting him, especially now that the deed had been done?

She answered honestly, "I think I would, yes. Would you?"

"Most definitely yes. As often as possible."

Well, that was flattering. Still, she could not allow this man to overrun her life. She had a job to do—jobs, if one took into account his mother's cottage—and she did not have time to bow to his whims. At least not outside the construction site.

Most important, she could not develop feelings for him.

"Perhaps we should come up with a schedule. To make things easier."

His brows lifted, as if the suggestion surprised him. "I was about to propose the same thing."

"Convenient we think so alike, then."

"Yes, quite."

He stroked his jaw, regarding her, and her heart beat faster. She busied herself by slipping into her shoes. "So once a week? Every other week?"

"What am I, fifty years old?" He chuckled. "No, Eva. I'm thinking three times a week. Perhaps more."

More? More than three times a week? No wonder men were always so busy, rushing about the city as if on important errands. Who'd have guessed a majority of those "errands" were lascivious in nature?

Still, she didn't presume to think she was the only woman currently in his orbit. The idea of him with another twisted her stomach, but she had to ask. "Are there not . . . others?"

His mouth opened, then closed. Reopened to ask, "Do you *want* there to be? I had assumed we would be exclusive."

Exclusive was good. Exclusive worked for her. She shook her head. "No, I don't. Nevertheless, I believe twice is sufficient for now."

"Twice? Come now. I know you enjoyed yourself with me. Think of how much better it will become once we sort our likes and dislikes."

Goodness, if this got any better it may very well kill her. "Twice, Phillip. I am quite busy these days, but we may revisit the schedule if we both feel it's insufficient."

He cursed and rubbed his eyes with the heels of his hands. "Stop acting like . . ."

"Acting like what?"

"Like such a *man*. I feel as if our roles are reversed."

Her first instinct was to apologize . . . and she suppressed it. She did not owe him an apology for being logical and careful, especially when she had the most to lose. "Then you must understand how I feel."

"Yes, I rather think I do," he muttered. "And it is certainly putting these matters into a very different light for me."

She wasn't sure what he meant, so she brought them back to the issue at hand. As today was Thursday, that made sense to include it as one of their days. "So we've agreed on twice a week. How is Monday and Thursday?"

"Fine. Where?"

"I . . ." She trailed off. Where, indeed? A hotel was too risky. Their houses were out of the question.

"Forget it," he said with a slash of his hand. "I'll take care of it. Now, I assume you do not use any kind of sponge or syringe?"

She shook her head wildly. What were those things? Did all women know of them?

"No worries. I will procure some condoms." Her face must have shown her confusion because he said, "Rubber sheaths that encase a man's erection during intercourse. It will protect you from conceiving."

Heavens, this was complicated. "Thank you. I assume that means you have no unwanted children running about New York?"

"You would be correct. I am always careful, which is why tonight was such an aberration."

An aberration. If only he meant that in the positive sense. *Build those walls higher.* She folded her hands. "Is that all you cared to discuss?"

"One more thing and then we'll depart." He stood and closed the distance between them. Cupping her face between his hands, he kissed her softly, swiftly. "Thank you for tonight. Whatever went wrong between us, I'll fix it. This matters to me. *You* matter to me."

Oh, dear. Her heart melted, the organ turning a soggy mess inside her chest. No, she must not allow this. He was her *employer.* She could not risk losing her greatest work to date and her father's legacy.

Swallowing the emotion clogging her throat, she patted his cheek. "You are sweet. Now let's hurry. I shouldn't like to be late for dinner."

PHILLIP SLAMMED THE front door behind him, the wood rattling on the hinges from the force. He tossed his hat and cane on the table and started for the stairs. A tangle of emotions rioted through him, confusion at the forefront. Eva's abrupt change in demeanor baffled him. One minute, they were basking in an intimate glow, her limbs warm and pliant against his. The next minute she'd turned into an ice queen.

You are being silly. This was lovely but I must now return home.

What on earth had he done wrong?

Roberts arrived, a word of greeting dying on his lips when he saw his master's face.

"I'll be in the ballroom," Phillip told his butler. At least he could let off some steam there. More than a year ago the giant empty space had been converted to hold boxing equipment. He had gloves, several heavy bags, and a speed bag there to help him work up a sweat when the occasion called for it. If he wanted to spar against a real partner, however, he traveled down to McGirk's.

Tonight he just needed to use his fists and expel some of the frustration burning in his chest.

"Please wait, sir. Mr. Milliken is here, awaiting you in your office."

Phillip heaved a sigh and stopped halfway up the steps. Shit. "What does he want?"

"He has been waiting for the better part of an hour."

Turning, he stomped down the stairs, returned to the main floor, and found his way to the office. Milliken rose from a chair, his derby in his hands. Phillip continued to the sideboard and poured two glasses of whiskey. "Milliken, this better be good."

"I need to speak with you, sir. About this unconventional set of circumstances you've created at the site."

Phillip carried the glasses over and handed one to Milliken. He dropped into the chair behind his desk and took a long swallow. The whiskey burned all the way down, taking a slight edge off his anger. "Well, what is it? What happened today?"

"We cannot have a woman strolling about on the site any longer."

This was not the first—or tenth—time Milliken had raised the issue. "We've had this discussion. You know where I stand. I must wait this out until her father arrives."

Milliken lifted his glass and threw back some liquor. "Yes, but I fear the situation has turned dangerous. Today, she was walking through the piles of debris near the east wall and one collapsed."

Phillip shot straight in his chair, the wooden legs rocking with his weight. "Collapsed? Jesus, she could've been killed." The idea of it made him sick to his stomach. Why hadn't she mentioned the accident tonight? *Because you had your face between her legs. And then your cock.*

"Precisely right, sir. She was quick on her feet, apparently, and escaped with nothing more than some dust on her skirts. But this kind of thing could happen at any moment. We're not used to having a woman on the site. It's bad—"

"I know, it's bad luck." He drank more whiskey, wondering what Milliken and the laborers would say if they knew Eva's moniker. "There's no such thing as luck, however."

Milliken shook his head, and Phillip didn't bother trying to change the Irishman's mind. The notion of luck was bone-deep with some people. "Bad luck or not, she's a distraction to the men."

"Has anyone . . . ?"

"No, not that I've seen or heard. That doesn't mean it couldn't happen, sir."

Phillip finished the liquid in his glass and set the crystal on his desk. "I don't like it, either. I never expected to face these problems, as I'd always assumed Hyde would helm the ship. However, in Hyde's absence, she's the architect's liaison. I cannot bar her from the site."

"Even if someone gets killed because of her? You know how easily accidents happen when men aren't paying attention to what they are doing."

"No one will be hurt. But let's better brace those piles to prevent anything like this happening again."

"Already done," Milliken said with a nod. "I have the night shift working on that. Be finished by morning."

"Good. And circulate word with the men once more about staying far, far away from Miss Ashford. I don't want them talking or looking at her. Any man who touches her—or, God forbid, hurts her—will be answering directly to me."

His general contractor frowned but jerked his head. "I wish you would reconsider. I know you and Miss Ashford are fond of one another—"

"Stop right there," Phillip snapped. "She is Hyde's employee and therefore my employee as well. There is nothing untoward happening between Miss Ashford and me." He knew the statement to be false, but he couldn't allow anyone to suspect an affair between the two of them. "There's no preferential treatment happening."

"I meant no offense, sir. But the safety of the men is my first concern, not the hurt feelings of a pampered Englishwoman."

Phillip nearly laughed. Hurt feelings? Pampered? Eva was the toughest woman he'd ever met—and that included a Bowery boxer named Mad Maeve, who he'd once seen knock four teeth out of a man's mouth. "This is not about feelings, Milliken. The woman is here to do a job, a job we need, I remind you, until her employer arrives. And you've said yourself, she is competent."

"I just hope her employer arrives soon. I'm hearing rumblings from the men about a strike."

Prickles swept over the back of Phillip's neck. This had been his greatest fear in letting Eva stay on as Hyde's representative. He leaned in closer. "Who in hell is talking about a strike?"

Milliken shifted, not meeting Phillip's eye. "Some of the men. They are talking about walking off the job until she's replaced."

Christ, that would delay them for months. He had no intention of replacing Hyde or any other member of his team, so a strike would mean negotiating with the union or firing all the laborers—including Milliken. Phillip needed to shut this down, stall as long as he could until Hyde arrived. "There had better not be a goddamn strike—and if that's a threat, I do not take kindly to them."

"Very well." Milliken's expression remained sullen. He'd clearly hoped for a different outcome from today's meeting, but Phillip couldn't help that. This was his project and he wasn't about to bend to ridiculous demands, no matter what happened.

"I know this is an unusual situation," he told his general contractor. "But Hyde's name on the hotel is integral to its success. Bear that in mind when you're dealing with your men. Some moving pieces can be replaced, but Hyde isn't one of them."

"I understand."

Milliken didn't appear happy but Phillip wasn't here to coddle the man. "Now, if that's all . . . ?"

With a nod, Milliken rose and swiftly departed. Phillip stood and rolled his shoulders, the stress of the evening wearing heavily on him. Between Eva's bizarre reaction earlier and Milliken's thinly veiled threats, he needed to relieve some tension. Oh, and he couldn't forget that he'd come inside Eva. He sighed, appalled at his own stupidity. He was always so careful, took every precaution with his partners. After what happened with Caroline, he never wanted to be uncertain as to a child's parentage ever again.

Strange, though, that the thought of Eva heavy and round with his child did not cause him to break out in a cold sweat as with previous affairs. If she conceived he would be honorable and do the right thing. He could almost see the two of them together. Marriage to a woman such as her would never be dull, that was for certain.

Not that she would agree. No, the woman had run away from him faster than a fox with a pack of hounds on its heels. His fists clenched just remembering it.

He set out for the ballroom, determined to punch something.

THE SATURDAY EVENING dinner crowd at Sherry's contained table after table of the most well-dressed people in New York, with diamonds and ostrich feathers each way one turned. Everyone ate tiny delicacies and drank champagne, the atmosphere loud and raucous, like a posh circus. This was her first outing to the legendary restaurant and Eva couldn't stop staring as she followed Nora to their dining table, Julius Hatcher directly behind them.

Once they were seated, she leaned over to her elegantly turned-out friend. "Are they all celebrating something?"

Julius snorted. "Yes, being wealthy and lazy." Julius, Eva had learned, worked hard for his fortune, not having been born to a well-off family. The man rarely left his office, except to spend time with Nora, the two still posing as betrothed until their wedding this autumn.

Nora smirked at him. "You had your share of celebrations, my love. Let's not forget how we met."

He shook his head and tilted his gaze toward the ceiling. "A birthday party, once a year. She'll never let me live it down."

Nora glanced at Eva. "Don't listen to him. One does not acquire a reputation such as my husband's from one bacchanal a year. Regardless, this is a typical evening in New York. It's quite gay all the time."

No wonder Nora was so fond of her newfound city. Her friend craved excitement and fun. Eva was much the opposite, more serious, focused on architecture and overseeing her father's projects. She'd never cared for the balls and soirées. The best part of her three betrothals had been the ability to skip all those tedious social events.

Was this chaos what Phillip enjoyed about New York as well? She hadn't seen him since she climbed into a hack after their . . . encounter at Madison Square Garden the other night. His absence at the construction site turned out to be a blessing. She couldn't think of him without her skin going up in flames.

Twice a week. Was the entire thing a mistake? She had agreed to intimacies but doubt had crept in since then. *Stop acting like such a man,* he'd told her. Well, why not? Men approached these things with distance and reason, not emotion and expectation. Should she not do the same to protect herself while enjoying their physical attraction?

Marriage was not in her future, but she did not need to give up companionship. Desire. Gratification. Phillip offered all those things and was committed to not siring any bastards on her. Why not take advantage of the opportunity? No man had ever affected her as he did . . .

If only he'd been a bit . . . gentler after the deed had concluded. That wasn't asking too much, was it?

You want to work in a man's world, Eva, then you must learn to act like a man. She could almost hear her father's voice giving this advice, he'd said it so often.

So, no. She required no coddling, in either the affair or at the construction site.

But she would force him to promise the affair would not impact her role on the project. If one of them grew dissatisfied with the arrangement, she had to know those issues would remain separate from the work.

After all, the work came first.

The menus were delivered and Eva grasped hers eagerly, ready to take her mind off her employer. Julius asked for a bottle of champagne and Nora ordered nearly everything on the menu, saying Eva "positively must" try a bite of each dish.

After the champagne had been uncorked and served, Nora held up her glass in a toast. "To good friends and extended visits."

"Here, here," Julius said and clinked his glass to both of theirs.

Eva touched her glass with Nora's. "An extended visit that is merely temporary."

"Oh, of course," her friend said, though the sparkle in her eyes suggested she didn't quite believe it. "By the way, how was your visit with Mrs. Mansfield?"

Eva's throat closed on a mouthful of champagne and she began choking. Nora patted her back delicately, no doubt enjoying catching Eva off guard. When she could breathe, Eva studied her friend's sly expression. "How on earth did you know about that?"

"Our driver, of course."

"She has all of Cortlands' servants eating out of the palm of her hand," Julius said. "They tell her everything."

"True, so there's no use in lying. Now what did Mrs. Mansfield wish to discuss with you?" Nora reached over and put a hand over her husband's eyes so he couldn't see. *Phillip?* she mouthed.

"No. She has need of an architect."

Nora dropped her hand. "For?"

"She's interested in adding on to her Newport home. The plans have been drawn up by a local firm but she's unhappy with what's been proposed."

Julius shook his head. "The house is already huge, and rumor has it Mansfield's forbidden the alterations altogether."

It was Nora's turn to be amazed. "Where did you hear that?"

"You are not the only well-informed one," he said through a satisfied grin.

"The most knowledgeable hermit in New York City." Nora patted his arm affectionately. "Now, Eva, how did you respond? Did you agree to get your father to help her?"

"Not exactly. She wants to hire me."

"You?" Nora clutched Eva's forearm. "You mean as *yourself*?"

"Yes." She grinned, unable to hide her glee. "I was as surprised as you are."

"It's quite the coup, but what if your current employer has a problem with this? I would hate for you to jeopardize anything to do with the hotel project."

The thought had occurred to Eva, but she honestly did not see how Phillip could complain. The two projects had nothing to do with one another—not that she had any intention of telling him. Let his mother share that news. "I'm not doing anything to jeopardize the hotel. Merely drawing up an idea for her to consider."

"So what did you think of her?"

Eva considered this a moment, sifting through her impressions of Phillip's mother. Mrs. Mansfield had acted entirely properly, with rigid politeness, but there was a steely determination underneath that Eva could relate to. "I liked her. She's forthright and has a no-nonsense approach that I appreciate. And she's intelligent. She had no difficulty in explaining the issues to me or following the discussion of possible problems."

"Interesting," Nora murmured before sipping her champagne.

"Do not get ideas, Nora."

When Nora merely smiled cryptically, Julius stepped in. "I believe Nora is smirking because not many people in New York say positive things about Mrs. Mansfield. She's rather terrifying, in a Lady Macbeth sort of way."

"Lady Macbeth? That's ridiculous. She's hardly sinister. I sense she's a lonely older woman who needs to keep busy."

Food began arriving at that point, black-coated waiters arranging small plates for them to share. Champagne was refilled, napkins settled on laps. Eva surveyed the array of sausage, cheese, olives, caviar, and mackerel in white wine . . . Goodness, it all appeared delicious.

As they ate, no fewer than three gentlemen approached their table at various times to speak with

Julius about the exchange, clearly fishing for tips on stocks. Eva leaned over to her friend during the third visit. "How does he stand it?"

"He hates it, truth be told. He tolerates them for my sake, but I think it's one of the reasons he hardly leaves the house anymore."

How . . . sad. She remembered going out with her father and people stopping him to ask for unsolicited advice. Free consulting, her father used to call it. As she started to relate that to Nora, she noticed movement on the stairs near the front door. A tall man with light brown hair was leading a woman up the stairs toward the private dining salons. *Phillip.*

She froze and watched his long legs easily handle the steps as he smiled down at the woman in an open and warm manner. He seemed . . . enraptured. Completely engrossed in her. Eva knew the look well, as he'd given her the same smile two nights ago.

"That is Miss Rebecca Hall."

Eva did not take her eyes from the pair. "I suppose he's taking her to dinner."

"Yes, it appears so. Those are her parents directly behind them. I hear their families are keen on a match between the two."

Eva's stomach dropped somewhere on the dining room floor, then she chastised herself for the reaction. He meant nothing to her, merely a pleasant distraction from the loneliness of staying in a new city. Phillip would get two nights of her time each week and beyond that, they would lead their own lives. She had no hold over the man.

Besides, she couldn't afford to care about someone who lived an ocean away. Her father and her life were back in England. She had every intention of returning as soon as possible. *The other night didn't mean anything. You both have responsibilities and expectations that do not include the other.*

"What happened? What did I miss?" Julius had concluded his conversation and turned back to the table.

Nora tipped her chin toward the stairs. "Mansfield's just arrived with Miss Hall and her parents."

"Oh, yes?" He craned his neck to see the front entrance but the couple had already disappeared. "I know her father. Family made their money in shipping some years back. She seems like a nice enough girl. Oof!" The table rattled at Julius's grunt. "Why'd you kick me?" he asked his wife.

"Because not everyone wants to hear you sing the praises of other women." Nora flicked her gaze toward Eva.

"Oh, I don't mind," Eva quickly said. "I'm certain she is a lovely person. It doesn't bother me at all. Honestly."

"Thou doth protest too much, methinks," Nora noted.

"No, I haven't. I've protested the exact proper amount considering the situation."

"Wait," Julius said. "Are you saying you've developed some level of affection for Mansfield?"

"Don't be ridiculous," Eva said.

"Yes, that's right," Nora said at the same time.

Eva narrowed her eyes on Nora, the woman who was supposed to be her friend. "Stop it. You're the one who hopes I develop affection for him. You want me to stay in New York."

"Of course, because I'm the most selfish woman on the planet." Nora rolled her eyes. "That is not the reason. I have eyes and I also know you better than anyone else. You have developed affection for him, Lady Eva. Past tense."

"You're wrong."

"Is that so?" Nora quirked a brow then leaned in and lowered her voice. "Then why did you arrive home so disheveled on Thursday evening?"

Eva gasped, her skin blazing. She reached for her champagne, desperate to cool off her suddenly dry throat.

"Nora, darling," Julius said gently. "You're embarrassing her, and this is not really the place for such a private conversation."

"You're right. I'm being crass and I apologize, Eva. I'll drop it." She plucked an olive off one of the gold-rimmed plates. "For now."

Eva nearly groaned. "You're worse than a matronly chaperone."

"Only because you think I'm not paying attention to what's going on . . . but I am."

"For what it's worth," Julius said as he speared a pickle. "Mansfield's a good choice. I've always liked him. He isn't afraid of hard work, unlike most of these gents. He could just live off his trust and bet on the ponies, but he's more interested in trying to build up cities. Dashed respectable, if you ask me."

"See?" Nora gestured toward her husband. "And Julius doesn't like anyone."

"That's not true." Julius snatched his wife's out-stretched hand and brought it to his lips. "I like you."

Nora's face flushed and Eva was pleased to see her friend so loved and adored. Would she ever have that with a man? The lump in her throat expanded into a boulder inside her chest. All she wanted to do was leave, to forget about perfect Phillip and his perfect dinner companion. Undoubtedly they would marry, live in his perfect Italian home, and have perfect babies.

Perfect, perfect, perfect. The exact opposite of a woman like her, who never quite fit in anywhere.

She dropped her napkin on the table and started to rise. "I think I'll go home."

Nora's head swiveled, expression full of concern. "Wait, Eva. Don't leave. Is this because of . . . ?" Her eyes flicked to the ceiling.

"No, no. Just feeling unwell all of a sudden. You two enjoy your—"

Nora clasped Eva's hand to stop her. "Have I ever told you how well acquainted I am with Sherry's second floor?"

"What, to spy on them?" The very idea caused her to feel pathetic. She wouldn't do it. "There's no reason to go up there. I have no claim on him and, more importantly, I'm soon departing for London. I cannot leave my father for good. He still needs me."

"Eva—"

She pulled her hand free of her friend's grasp. "Thank you for dinner, Julius. I shall see you at home, Nora. Good night."

Chapter Eleven

"I'm quite relieved you are here," Becca whispered near Phillip's ear. Waiters hovered around the dining table, making adjustments, while the four guests settled into their chairs. To rescue his friend from matchmaking efforts, he had agreed to accompany Becca and her parents to dinner tonight. At least the private dining suite on Sherry's second floor would shield them from the prying eyes in the main dining room downstairs.

"Of course," he murmured. "Besides, you've promised to return the favor at the opera on Friday."

He and Becca had come to an understanding of sorts the other night during his mother's dinner. Neither of them had any interest in marriage yet their families were insistent. Therefore, they decided to play along for a short while, accompanying each other to required social events to keep their parents from matchmaking. If they stuck together—and remained well within the bounds of propriety—then this would buy them time. Rumors might circulate but would come to naught. They had no intention whatsoever of marrying.

Phillip thought it a genius plan.

"Yes, I have," Becca said as the champagne was poured. "And I hate the opera."

"I promise to smuggle as much scotch as you can handle," he murmured and she laughed.

"It is so lovely to see you two getting along," Mrs. Hall said, beaming across the table at Phillip and her daughter. "Mr. Hall and I are quite pleased."

"Yes, indeed." Mr. Hall picked up his glass. "Let's toast to a promising future."

The rest of them lifted their glasses. "To the future," Phillip said with a small smirk in Becca's direction.

A food order was placed and the group relaxed with drinks, chatting easily about events and people they shared in common. Phillip listened with half an ear. He'd never cared for polite society or following who was in or out of favor this particular week. That was his mother's world, not his. His focus remained on ensuring the Mansfield name was remembered for far more than hosting the annual Debutante Ball.

"How is your hotel project coming along?" Becca's father asked him.

"Very well, actually. We're continuing with the excavation for another few weeks. Then they'll pour the foundation."

"Do you really think you can fill all those expensive rooms?" Mrs. Hall sipped from her crystal glass. "Are there enough people who can afford it?"

"Yes, I think so. Large events will help subsidize

the costs, as will the revenue from the restaurants. But it's my hope to create a new standard of luxury travel in America."

"I think it's very clever," Becca said. "I cannot wait—"

"Excuse me." A waiter approached the table with a small slip of paper offered to Phillip. "Mr. Mansfield, a message."

"Me?" Who on earth knew he was even here? He took the paper and quickly read the note. Baffled, he glanced up at his party. "If you will excuse me for a moment, Mr. Hatcher is dining downstairs and wishes to have a word."

"Hatcher, you say?" Mr. Hall leaned closer. "See if you can ask him about where he predicts oil prices going, will you?"

"I'll do my best. Forgive me," he told the women. "Please, begin eating without me." He stood and strode out of the room. When he was halfway down the corridor a sound stopped him in his tracks.

"*Mansfield*," a female voice hissed.

A woman's face peeked out from one of the side rooms. Curious, he went over. "Yes?"

She motioned him inside the room. "Hurry, in here."

"Do we . . . I'm sorry, have we met?" When he crossed the threshold, she shut the door behind him. He found himself in one of the larger event rooms. A man he recognized was leaning against the wall. Not surprising, as women weren't allowed to wander about alone on the second floor. "Hello, Hatcher."

"Mansfield, hello. Have you met my fiancée?"

He indicated the woman who'd called Phillip in here. "This is Lady Honora Parker."

He'd heard of her, of course. Daughter of a powerful earl, she and Hatcher became betrothed after the two had nearly been burned alive in a theater fire. He gave a quick bow. "My lady, a pleasure. I am Phillip Mansfield."

The brown-haired beauty struck out her hand. "Also a pleasure, Mr. Mansfield. And please, just Nora."

"Call me Phillip, then. This is a rather odd place for a meeting." He glanced between them. "Is there something I may help you with?"

"I apologize for the subterfuge," Nora said. "That's my doing. I wanted to have a private conversation with you, one best not conducted in the main dining room."

"Oh?"

"Yes." She studied him carefully, her eyes searching for something in his expression, almost as if she were trying to see under his skin. Her flat gaze held no teasing light or welcoming warmth. Had he offended her somehow? "You might have guessed from my speech that I am English."

"It had crossed my mind," Phillip drawled.

"Not a shocking revelation, I realize. The reason I mention the fact is because our society is not like yours. Girls there are not afforded as many freedoms as your American girls. It's . . . harder for women to blossom in our country."

Where in the hell was she going with this? Too polite to interrupt, he merely nodded and waited for her to continue.

"I am a bit outspoken"—her fiancé snorted, which earned him a stern glare—"and a bit of a bluestocking, so making friends was never easy for me. I had only a few friends my own age that meant anything to me."

A sinking feeling began to expand in Phillip's chest, the weight of dawning realization.

"Lady Eva is one of those friends."

She let that statement hang there and he had no idea what to say. "I see," he settled on.

"Good. She is like a sister to me and she's not had an easy time of it. I'm quite protective of her, which is why I thought it past time you and I met."

"Because you're worried about her?"

"Yes, specifically when it comes to *you.*"

He shook his head. "I don't understand. I've agreed to let her serve in her father's absence. I've even threatened the crew to stay away from her."

"Yet you haven't applied the same rules to yourself."

"Nora," Hatcher said, but his fiancée held up a hand.

"Let me finish. I do not know what game you are playing with her, but I'll not allow her to be hurt."

Phillip slipped his hands in his trouser pockets and shrugged. "With all due respect, I am not playing any game. I have no wish to hurt her."

"While that may be true, your actions speak volumes." She gestured toward the private dining room he shared with Becca and her parents. "If you have intentions elsewhere do not amuse yourself with Eva at the same time."

"Dear God," Hatcher muttered under his breath. "That's it. Come along, Nora. You've said enough."

Nora held Phillip's stare and he saw a depth of knowledge there. Clearly she'd learned about what had happened aboard the ship and at Madison Square Garden. This must be the friend with whom Eva was living while in New York.

He could feel his skin heating in embarrassment, the shame of his ungentlemanly behavior settling between his shoulder blades. He had bedded Eva, taken liberties reserved for a husband. Consensual liberties, but liberties all the same. And yet he wasn't sure he could stop, even realizing how wrong it had been.

He wanted her still.

And he couldn't very well explain why he was escorting Becca, the private reason the two of them were nothing more than friends.

Hatcher clasped his wife's arm and began tugging her out of the room. "Apologies, Mansfield. Let's forget this ever happened."

Nora narrowed her gaze at Phillip as if to say, *I won't be forgetting.* He tried to give her a reassuring nod but his heart wasn't in it.

He had no intention of staying away from Eva, not unless she ordered him to do so herself.

ON MONDAY, EVA raised her parasol higher to block the afternoon sun. The removal of dirt seemed never ending, cart after cart carrying away piles of brown earth from the site. Milliken and his crew ignored her, but she hardly cared. She'd spent most of her childhood alone, no siblings or mother to interact with, only servants. And her father when he'd been at home.

She'd purposely come later today, as Phillip tended to visit in the morning. She hadn't been entirely eager to see him, not just yet. The vision of him smiling at the pretty blonde girl the other night hadn't exactly vanished yet, even though she told herself she had no reason to be upset. He was her employer and her lover, not her betrothed. There was no future for the two of them beyond their two-night-a-week arrangement.

And today was Monday.

Did she still want to see him?

Yes. She closed her eyes, almost embarrassed by the admission. Despite seeing him with another woman, she did wish to continue their arrangement. She had enjoyed the other night, at least the part before the awkward conversation afterward. Perhaps it was the same for every pair of casual lovers, but the entire experience had been wondrous. Electric. The memories had kept her up late at night, her body tingling at the notion of doing it all again.

Enough. She had a job to do here. Such was the reason for her visit to New York, the project she and her father needed to survive. And she was leaving for Newport tomorrow. Thoughts of Phillip could wait.

Unable to stand still, she headed toward the farthest end of the construction site. She liked to see the excavation from all angles once every few days, just to ensure the measurements were correct. There had already been one distance mistake, a simple miscalculation Milliken should have caught, and Eva wasn't keen on sitting idly by while another happened. She was well versed in how to use the survey equipment, and had Carew's permission to appropriate it as needed.

The wooden shed for her "office" had been finished last week, per Phillip's instructions. She'd insisted Carew and Milliken use the tiny windowless space as well, however, so there were now copies of the building plans, Milliken's records, and the survey equipment contained within.

She pulled the iron latch and entered, sunlight streaming through the slats to prevent her from tripping in the tight quarters. The scope and tripod were leaning against the far side.

With the door closed, the cacophony from the steam shovels receded slightly, though it was still quite noisy inside. She gathered the cumbersome pieces of the scope, trying to lift them all in her arms, when she heard a metal scraping sound at the door. She turned and waited for Milliken or one of his assistants to enter.

The door remained shut.

"Is someone there? Hello?" Unlikely they heard her over the din, so she put down the scope and went to investigate. She pushed on the handle— and it didn't budge. What in heaven's name . . . ?

She shoved harder this time but the door would not open. It was jammed from the outside somehow. Had it locked when she entered? The scraping sound`. . . Had someone locked her *in*?

Using the heel of her hand, she beat on the thick slats. "Help! The door is locked. Is anyone able to hear me?" She kept up the noise for another few minutes, hoping someone might walk by and discover her. Unfortunately, the steam shovels moaned and hissed all around the tiny shack, so until they quit running it would be impossible for anyone to hear her.

Worry sank deep into her bones. This was very bad indeed. The interior was hot. Sweat was already pooling under her collar and between her shoulders. Worse, what if the steam shovels never stopped? What if no one came to the shack, if she had to stay here in the dark? A shiver went through her, a bolt of true fear.

She had to get out, no matter what it took.

There must be something inside to aid her escape. A weapon, a tool . . . anything to break down the door or pick the lock. *Think*, she told herself, squinting into the gloom. *You know how things are built, which means you know how to take them apart.*

Unfortunately there were only papers on Milliken's desk. She opened the drawers to find more papers, nothing hard or sharp. Not even a letter opener. *Dash it.*

The air in the shack was oppressive, a steamy cocktail that drenched her in humidity. Sweat rolled down her temples and over her face, every breath like a damp blanket. She had to escape or risk passing out from the heat. The wooden tripod caught her eye, specifically the spindly legs. If she could break one off she might be able to use it as a lever to pry some of the wooden slats apart and squeeze through to freedom. She wasn't sure it would work but she had to try something.

Grabbing the tripod, she unscrewed the heavy scope and set it on the desk. The piece was expensive and well constructed, its wooden legs affixed to the base with sturdy brass. Pulling it apart would not be easy. She'd need to kick the wood in hopes of snapping it below the metal.

She wiped her forehead with her petticoat, sopping up as much of the sweat as she could. Then she put the tripod on the ground, lifted one leg, and stepped on the thin wood. She winced. Her foot had slipped and she ended up stomping on the brass instead. Ignoring the sharp ache radiating up her leg, she tried once more. Another kick, higher this time, and she splintered the wood, freeing one of the tripod legs.

Carrying it with her to the wall, she placed the thickest end between two slats, where they had been nailed into the frame. She pushed up with all her might, trying to dislodge the iron nails. The wood groaned but held. *You didn't think it would be easy, now did you?*

For twenty minutes she struggled and strained, finally rewarded when one end of the nailed slats popped free. She kicked at it, pushing it as far from the building as she could. Then she went to work on the slat directly below, shoving and rocking the wooden stick, until that piece also came loose. With more kicks, she was able to create a fairly large opening.

There was no time to revel in the victory. Her clothing soaked from sweat, she began working to free another piece of the exterior. With one more she'd likely be able to slip outside.

Fatigue settled in, a combination of exertion and the heat, and her arms ached. It seemed like eight hours had gone by, though it was probably closer to one. *You're so close, Eva. Don't give up.*

Through sheer force of will she dislodged the third slat and kicked it out of the way. It splintered and she quickly wriggled out of the hole she'd created, never more grateful to see dirt. As she pushed through, her foot caught on a slat and she lost her balance. Crashing to the ground, she rested there with her eyes closed, exhausted, breathing as if she'd just swam the length of the island.

"Eva!"

Her lids cracked open at the sound of the familiar male voice. Running toward her was Phillip, horror etched on his handsome face, followed by Milliken and Carew.

She'd be damned if these three would see her beaten. Digging deep for strength, she came to her feet and straightened her skirts, brushing the dust as best she could. Then she pushed sweaty tendrils of hair off her face and attempted a smile.

Phillip nearly skidded to a stop in front of her, his hands gripping her arms. "What on earth happened to you?"

She pointed at the wooden shack. "Someone locked me in."

He jerked with surprise. *"Locked you in?"*

Carew immediately strode around to the door, while Milliken moved behind Phillip, his arms crossed over his chest. "It's bolted shut," the engineer yelled from the side.

"Good God." Phillip's shrewd gaze searched her

face. "You could have died in there, considering the heat today."

"I'm fine. I dislodged a few of the slats and slipped out. Nothing to be concerned about." She shot an apologetic glance at Carew. "I had to break your tripod and use one of its legs as a jimmy. I'm sorry."

"Don't go apologizing," Carew immediately said. "If the tripod helped you escape then that's what matters. It can be replaced."

Phillip's chest heaved, an angry flush covering his neck. He spun on Milliken. "You will find the man responsible for this. I want him ferreted out and sent to me. *Today.*"

"Sir, you know there's not a man here who'll admit to such a thing, knowing the consequences." Milliken jerked his chin in Eva's direction. "And you know how they feel about her."

Her. As if she weren't standing right there. Still, Milliken was right. If they made a big deal over this, resentment would merely escalate. That was the last thing any of them needed. "Mr. Milliken is right. It's unlikely we'll learn the identity of the culprit and a witch hunt serves no purpose other than to brew discontent."

Milliken blinked as if he hadn't expected her to agree with him, but Phillip's scowl deepened. "I don't give a damn. This type of behavior will not be tolerated on my job site. If I let this slide he'll only try again."

She had to stop this. An investigation would not bode well for her relationship with the crew. "Phillip, please. I'm dirty and sweaty but none the worse for wear. Let's all forget this happened."

Phillip's nostrils flared slightly and she could see the indecision in his eyes. He faced Milliken once more. "Shut everything down for the day. Everyone goes home and no one gets paid . . . unless the man responsible comes forward." He wrapped his fingers around Eva's elbow. "Come with me, Miss Ashford."

"THAT WAS A mistake."

Phillip ignored Eva's rebuke as his brougham slowed along Twenty-Fourth Street. They were the first words she'd spoken since leaving the construction site. She was clearly furious he hadn't let the incident go, angry that he'd dragged her away in front of the men . . . but he would not apologize. He didn't give a damn how the men felt about losing a day's wages. Whoever was responsible for locking that door had better hope Phillip never found him alone in a dark alley.

The wheels stopped in front of number Twenty-Two, an unassuming four-story brick building, and Phillip flipped open the brougham's door. He descended, and then helped Eva down to the ground. "You needn't stay," he told his driver and shepherded her toward the front door. He withdrew a key from his jacket pocket.

"What is this?" Her neck craned as she took in the façade. "Where are we?"

He unlocked the front door and held it open. "Inside you go."

"Phillip, I'd really like to go home. I'm dirty and—"

"Patience, my lady. Just trust me." She entered, albeit unhappily, and he latched the door behind them. Taking her arm, he ushered her up the steps. "You wanted privacy. Privacy you shall have."

"You rented an apartment for us?"

"No." They turned at the first landing and he smiled down at her. "I bought the building."

"You . . . bought this entire building? Just to have a place for us to meet?"

"Don't sound so surprised. It's a good investment. Area's a bit rough now, but there's talk of cleaning it up. The property should only climb in value in the next few years."

"It certainly appears well constructed," she said, her gaze sweeping the walls and stairwell. "Who were the tenants?"

"You'll see." He anticipated witnessing her reaction. The purchase had happened quickly so there hadn't been time to remodel except to replace the bed frame and mattress. He had his priorities, after all.

When Eva faltered on the final landing, Phillip reached down and lifted her in his arms. She clung to his neck. "Put me down. I can walk."

"I know, but I'd rather carry you."

She stopped complaining and put her head on his shoulder. He bounded up the remaining steps, set her on her feet, and opened the apartment door.

He flicked the switch to turn on the electric as Eva stepped across the threshold. She gave a long whistle. "My, my. No mystery as to the identity of the former occupants. I do hope the girls weren't too put out at their displacement."

A former brothel, the main room was papered a deep red color and had matching velvet furniture. Colored lights hung from the ceiling, a kaleidoscope of hues that bounced off the mirrors strategically placed at various points. Phillip dropped onto one of the sofas, where the men would have congregated to meet the various women of the house. "They were not, considering I compensated them quite handsomely. Do you like it?"

She took it all in, her head swiveling this way and that. "It's appalling. And yet oddly perfect."

"You haven't seen the best part." He rose, took her hand, and led her deeper into the apartments.

"Let me guess. The bed."

He chuckled. "Second best, then." Once through the dining room they entered the largest of the bathing suites. A huge tub sat in the center of the blue-and-white mosaic tiled floor, mirrors surrounding them from all sides. It was decadent and tawdry, a delicious find he meant to put to good use. Right this minute, in fact.

She gasped. "This is . . . Men would actually pay to *bathe* in here with a woman?"

He shrugged. "Of course."

He strode to the taps and turned them until water began spilling into the bottom of the enameled cast-iron tub. Then he poured a splash of the new bath oil he'd brought earlier into the water.

"Wait, you don't expect me to . . . In *there*?"

"Why not? I've had the place thoroughly cleaned, including the tub. Wouldn't you care to wash after being locked in that shed for God knows how long?"

She bit her lip, staring at the water longingly. What was her hesitation?

Crossing the room, he tucked an errant strand of

red hair behind her ear. "Are you worried about the cleanliness of the tub, because I swear—"

"No, I believe you if you say it's been properly cleaned. However, it's a bit decadent of me to lounge in a bath while you twiddle your thumbs, wouldn't you say?"

"Not if I am decadent with you."

"You mean . . ." Her brows jumped. "Oh."

Ah, his little innocent. How he loved corrupting her. He shrugged his coat off his shoulders and tossed it to the ground. Then loosened his necktie. "I promise I'll make it worth your while."

She watched his hands with rapt attention, a flush blooming along the neckline of her shirtwaist. "But I have no clean clothes to wear."

"Who said anything about requiring clothing?"

Her lips curved and she reached to unfasten the strip of cloth around her waist. "This may be a terrible idea but I desire a bath too desperately to argue with you."

They both removed their clothing, piece by piece, eyes lingering on the other, until she needed help with her corset. Now bare-chested, Phillip unlaced her, and she let the heavy garment fall to the floor. From there, things progressed quickly until they were both completely naked.

Not wanting to embarrass her with his half-hard erection, he shut off the taps, stepped into the bath, and sank into the warm water. This had an added benefit in that it allowed him the perfect view of her entrance into the tub after she disrobed.

Eva was glorious, all creamy skin and fiery hair. Full breasts with dusky nipples. Long legs and a slightly rounded stomach. Exquisitely female, like an Italian Renaissance painting come to life. His heart pounded, his tongue thick and dry with anticipation.

"Wouldn't a decent gentleman avert his eyes?" she asked as she stretched out on the opposite side, her legs brushing his under the surface of the water.

"I suppose he would. I noticed you took your time, however. I think you enjoyed teasing me."

Her toes trailed along his calf. "You might be right."

"Shall I wash your hair?"

"Fancy yourself a lady's maid, do you?"

"Just fancy getting my hands on you as rapidly as possible."

"You'll have to wait until I am clean." Water lapped the mounds of her breasts, drawing his eye. Christ, how he wanted this woman. His cock was already heavy and needy, even in the buoyant water.

"I met a friend of yours the other night at Sherry's," he said, sliding his leg alongside hers.

Eva's eyes widened. "Oh, no. Was it Lady Nora?"

So her friend hadn't mentioned the conversation. Interesting. "Indeed, it was she. Charming woman, Lady Nora. Fiancé's a good man, though he's not really out on the town much these days."

"What did she say?" Eva leaned in, her teasing mood now gone. "If she said anything about me, you shouldn't pay a lick of attention to it."

Now that was a curious comment. He wondered what about him Eva had shared with her friend. "And why shouldn't I pay attention if it pertains to you?"

"Did she say anything about me?"

"Are you answering my question with another question?"

"Yes. And I'll keep doing so until you tell me what she said."

He wrapped a hand around her foot and began massaging her instep with his thumbs. She groaned and closed her eyes, reclining until her shoulders met the tub once more. "I was attending a dinner with a friend and her parents. Your Nora is worried I am playing a game with you, that I'm leading you on while I romance another woman."

Eva peered up at him through her lashes, her gaze intense. "And are you?"

Ah. This came as no surprise to her. Had Eva been there that night as well? "Absolutely not. Miss Hall is merely a friend, though her parents might wish otherwise. There is no romance between us."

"I heard there are rumors. About the two of you."

"As I said, there are some who would approve of that match. Neither of us wishes for it, however."

"Good."

Her relief pleased him, a dark satisfaction of knowing she had been jealous, and he had to be completely honest with her. "However, we will be seeing more of one another in the upcoming weeks."

She blinked and sat up a bit straighter, her foot falling out of his grasp. "I don't understand. I thought you said . . ."

"I did. Miss Hall and I have a mutually beneficial arrangement."

"Another mutually beneficial arrangement?" She started to rise from the tub. "Good heavens. In just how many of these are you involved?"

He yanked on her ankle, drawing her back into the water and across the tub. When she was within reach he lifted her atop him, so her legs straddled his waist. His cock was trapped under her heat, the pressure nearly driving him mad, yet through some miracle he retained his focus. He cradled her face in his palms. "Not that type of arrangement, Eva. You are the only woman with whom I am entertaining in such a manner. Just you."

"Ah."

"Do you believe me?"

Her piercing gaze traveled his face, lingering on his eyes, searching for the truth. "Yes, I think I do."

"Good. Now, kiss me."

Chapter Twelve

       In the end, he did much more than kiss her.

Large soapy hands swept over every inch of her with remarkable thoroughness, almost as if he were fastidious about cleanliness. Yet he wasn't one of those men always in gloves and afraid of getting his hands dirty. No, he merely enjoyed the teasing—though her squirming and writhing on his lap elicited many gasps and groans from him in return. At least she hadn't suffered alone.

He took his time in washing her, stroking and caressing, talking quietly between kisses about the things he liked most about her. Places like the inside of her elbow . . . the skin of her wrist . . . a ticklish spot under her ribs . . . the slope of her collarbone . . . By the time he soaped and rinsed her hair, she ached with wanting, her pulse a steady beat between her legs.

Just when she couldn't take it any longer, he reached to stroke the slick, swollen heart of her, his fingers deft and steady. Two thick digits slipped inside her, his palm pressing on the bud at the top of her sex. "Rock your hips on my hand," he told her. "Use my fingers to come."

She hardly knew what he meant but her body took over, chasing the bliss, each roll of her pelvis sending little shocks along to her toes. His mouth found her nipple, sucking and biting, the scrape of his teeth causing a quiver in her womb. She began a frenzy of nonsensical words, daft pleas and promises that spoke of urgency, as water sloshed out of the tub. Using his free hand, he pressed her hips down to create more friction and she detonated, her body convulsing as she cried out into his neck.

When she stopped shaking, he lifted her from the water and stepped out of the tub. Droplets rained onto the tile as he continued toward the door, carrying her into another room where a huge four-poster bed awaited. He placed her onto the soft bedclothes, his body following to cover her.

She sighed, the weight of him unexpectedly delicious, his crisp and silky body hair rubbing over her limbs, while wide shoulders blocked out the dying afternoon light. She wrapped her arms about his neck and dragged his mouth down, desperate to feel his lips on hers. Though his erection lay hard and insistent against her thigh, he kissed her thoroughly, sweetly, his hand cradling her jaw to keep her where he wanted, his tongue slick and hot against her own. He was an excellent kisser, the technique maddeningly mercurial, shifting between rough and gentle, demanding yet giving. She tried to keep up, to match him, but it proved impossible, her need obliterating all rational thought.

His fingers found the wet heat between her legs once more and he circled her entrance until she canted her hips, seeking. He smiled against her mouth. "Anxious for more, are you?"

He was too smug, too certain of his prowess . . . too male. So she pushed on his shoulder until he rolled onto his back. When she crawled on top of him he brushed the wet hair out of her face, saying, "I take it this means we are done with teasing."

"Not even close. I haven't yet begun."

So she did as she pleased, trailing her fingertips along his jaw, his shoulders, over his ribs, feeling every peak and valley that made up his exemplary frame. She hadn't had the opportunity the other night and she meant to commit the shape of him to memory.

Lord above, the man was too perfect by half. When touching became not enough she dragged her lips over those spots, tasted the clean, rough skin. She quickly learned what caused him to groan, (a nip of her teeth on his throat), and what caused him to gasp (a brush of her tongue over his nipple). The lower she traveled the more restless he grew, his breath choppier.

He froze when she kissed the flat of his stomach, and she wondered if he would stop her from continuing on. She'd studied enough drawings and paintings to be curious about using her mouth on him. Would he enjoy it?

A few more kisses brought her mouth to the tip of his erection, lying stiffly against his belly. She swiped her tongue over the crown, hardly anything at all, yet his body jerked, nearly dislodging her.

"Christ, Eva," he rasped. "I hadn't expected that."

"Shall I continue?"

"Oh, God. I may very well expire if you do."

Not an answer, not really, so she kept going. Perhaps this would shake his control and give her a bit of the upper hand. She licked the taut flesh, running the flat of her tongue down the silken skin of his shaft. His hands curled into the coverlet, the knuckles white with strain. She nearly smiled. *A heady power, indeed.*

Sliding his erection in her mouth, she took in as much as was comfortable. Phillip hissed, his muscles clenching. She dragged her lips toward the tip, intent on doing it again.

Instead, strong arms lifted her up. His face etched in stone, he rolled her underneath him and settled between her legs. Reaching between them, he lined up at her entrance and then pushed inside, slowly and steadily, the fit much easier this time around. She marveled at the difference, how her body bloomed and accepted him, widening and stretching, until he was fully seated.

He paused, dropping his forehead to hers, supported on his elbows, both of their chests heaving. The fullness, the way she could *feel* him deep within her . . . it eased something, an emptiness she hadn't realized existed. As if he unlocked a secret part of her, a part she'd never known about. It both thrilled and terrified her.

They each began moving, working together, hips churning, and the pleasure took over. He palmed her breast and she clutched his buttock. He sank his teeth into her shoulder, she scratched his back.

When she wrapped her legs about his waist, he started thrusting faster, harder, sweat building on his forehead as the bed frame creaked beneath them. "Oh, God. I cannot stop. It's too good."

So, so good—but not quite enough. "More, Phillip. Please."

He groaned and claimed her mouth, his kiss wild and demanding as he continued to drive into her body with none of his earlier finesse—and she loved it. "Yes," she breathed, her muscles drawing tight. She was so close, right there on the edge. "God, yes."

"Goddamn it, now, Eva." He pushed up onto his hands, his hips churning, the slap of wet flesh filling the room, and she incinerated in a wash of heat and light, her inner muscles clamping around him, the crest taking her under like a wave.

"Christ, I can feel your walls . . . milking me. Wait, no, no, no . . ."

His hips stuttered as body seized, his own pleasure overtaking him. He thickened and pulsed inside her, a hoarse moan escaping his mouth, lids screwed tight.

The room fell silent except for their panting breath. There was no noise at all, no ticking clock or footsteps. No street noise or servants. He shifted and withdrew, slipping easily out of her channel, before he dropped onto his back, the heels of his hands pressing onto his closed eyes. "Jesus. I don't think I've ever come that hard. Or that fast."

Eva had no response, especially since he did not sound happy about the fact. And she wasn't about to apologize.

"I even had a condom on hand." He heaved an unhappy sigh. "Yet I spilled inside you once again. What in hell are you doing to me?"

She hated the accusation in his tone. Hated the way her stomach clenched at the harshly uttered words. The bubble of happiness cocooning her popped and hurt filled her chest like wet cement. She tensed but remained still. "None of that is my fault."

"I know." He turned his head to see her. "That's not what I meant, Eva."

"But that's what it sounded like. In my experience, men often blame women for their troubles. A woman with three dead fiancés? She must be cursed. Cannot concentrate on your work because a woman's in the vicinity? Yes, let's force the woman to leave instead of telling the man to keep his eyes off her breasts."

He rose up on an elbow. "I don't believe any of that. For God's sake, I've been your biggest supporter—"

"Until we're alone and then your loss of control is somehow my fault."

"No. This is my fault. All of it. And whatever consequences arise you may rest assured that I'll—"

She levered off the bed, not wanting any part of this conversation. It was reminiscent of the other night and she had no desire to repeat it. Yes, they had both been reckless and foolish, allowing the heat of the moment to cloud their judgment. And she was every bit as responsible as he. So when would he start treating her as an equal?

"I don't wish to discuss fault and blame and consequences before my skin's even cooled."

"Fair enough, but the consequences are quite real. You cannot ignore them."

Once on the floor, she noticed the inside of her thighs were sticky and wet. *Consequences, indeed.* The bath. Even if the water had turned cold, she had to wash all this . . . secretion off before she returned home.

"Where are you going?" he demanded as she marched toward the bathing chamber. "We need to discuss this."

"No, we most definitely do not." She grasped the connecting door and stopped to glance over her shoulder. "Or, better yet, have the conversation without me. You seem to do better that way."

She slammed the wood, closing herself on the other side.

BY FRIDAY PHILLIP'S mood was downright black.

After barely speaking during Monday night's ride home, Eva had disappeared on Tuesday, leaving word she'd traveled out of town. Phillip had it on good authority that Lady Nora remained in the city, so he wasn't sure where Eva had gone . . . and with whom. The uncertainty pricked at him all week, growing worse as the days progressed without a message from her. Their Thursday assignation had come and gone, with him waiting at the Twenty-Fourth Street house for hours, only to spend the evening alone.

Yes, he'd bungled their post-coital conversation. Again. But that did not mean she could ignore him.

They had to work this out, especially as she was working for him.

Christ, what a damn mess.

He reached for one of the champagne glasses resting on the silver tray and winced. His shoulders ached from hours spent at McGirk's this week. He'd fought so much that Joe had finally ordered him home, saying Phillip couldn't return until he promised not to take out his frustration on the other boxers. Sixteen opponents had gone down in the ring the past few days, causing Joe to grouse that Phillip had ruined all their best fighters.

"You don't appear happy," Becca murmured as she sidled up to him, selecting a glass for herself. "Sorry you came?"

They were at the Metropolitan Opera House, as he'd promised, surrounded by her family. Though summer, many members of society were in attendance, all sitting in the "diamond horseshoe" tier. The performance had started but Phillip, eager for a drink and some respite, had retreated to the salon in the back of the box.

He faced Becca, who positively glowed tonight. "No, and it's nothing a few stiff drinks won't cure. You've obviously had a good day. I don't think I have ever seen you this radiant."

"Your flattery won't work on me, Mansfield. You've got the wrong parts."

He laughed, the first since Monday. "Hardly flattery and fair enough. Tell me, why are you so chipper?"

"I've merely had an excellent week." She coyly dropped her gaze and sipped her champagne.

Must have something to do with the maid. He was happy for her, even while miserable himself. "Bully for you, then. At least one of us has."

"What happened to put you in such a sour mood?"

He had no idea how to explain it, so he lifted a sore shoulder. "Women are dashed complicated."

"That's because we are more intelligent than men give us credit for. You assume we're something we're not." Mirth danced in her eyes. "So tell me, what has she done now?"

"Disappeared on me. She's gone out of town, which is a bit odd since she hardly knows anyone in the city."

"Is this a mistress? Or . . ."

A lover. A friend. An employee. Instead of filling in the word, he said, "Definitely an 'or.'"

"The lady who claims you're no fun?"

His lips twisted in amusement at the reminder of that conversation. "Yes, her."

"And the two of you had an argument?"

"More like a disagreement."

"You're dissembling. If she's hied it out of New York City, it was an argument." She finished the rest of her champagne and placed the empty glass on the table. "Which means you need to properly apologize."

"Just how do you know I'm at fault?"

Her face transformed into a look that said Phillip might be the slowest man in Manhattan. "Because if you had felt wronged, you'd have been the one to run away."

She patted his arm and returned to the box, but

Phillip wasn't ready to follow quite yet. Perhaps he'd visit the smoking room first. A quality cigar sounded nice about now.

He stepped into the corridor that ran behind the boxes and found it blessedly empty. Before he'd taken two steps, however, he discovered James Keene strolling toward him. Keene spotted him and his brows rose in recognition, a smug, satisfied smile emerging.

Phillip's skin began to burn with anger, as if someone had lit a match to it. He headed toward the other man. "I'd like a word, Keene."

"Mr. Mansfield, good evening. I hear you've been having a bit of trouble on the hotel site." He leaned a shoulder against the wall. "That is certainly a shame."

Phillip thought of Eva, sweaty and disheveled, as she'd emerged from that shack the other day. Had she not been able to escape on her own, God only knew when she would've been found. A few hours enclosed in severe heat could kill a man, let alone a slight Englishwoman.

Fists clenched, he stepped in close, not afraid of using his size to intimidate the other man. He was pleased when a flash of fear widened Keene's gaze. "If I learn that you or any of your cronies have been causing said trouble, I will bury the lot of you in a pit so deep and so dark you'll never be found. Do you understand what I'm saying?"

"Now, why would we bother sabotaging your project when you're doing such a damn fine job of that on your own?"

"Because you're spineless, sniveling cowards who think they can harass and blackmail to get what they want."

Keene held up his hands, palms out. "There's where you are wrong. We only want what's best for the city and its inhabitants."

"While getting rich in the process."

"You say that as if you're not partial to earning a dollar yourself. When your father was alive, he worked *with* us—not against us. You'd do well to work in the same manner. Certainly would accomplish a lot more that way."

"The days of Tweed and rampant corruption are over, in case you haven't noticed. We're in a new era, one where the people expect their government to work *for* them, not steal from them."

"Now you're just trying to hurt my feelings, calling me a thief."

"I'd call you worse if we weren't in public."

Keene chuckled. "You do have a temper. Must be what makes you an outstanding boxer. They say you can beat nearly anyone in the ring."

"Which you'd do well to remember. I'm not someone you'd care to anger."

Keene stepped back and brushed his sleeves with his gloved hands. "I could say the same, Mansfield. After all, what would society think if they knew the true purpose behind that building you bought on Twenty-Fourth Street, the one you and Miss Ashford—?"

Phillip's arm shot out and he pushed Keene against the wall with a thud. The other man swallowed as Phillip snarled, "You do not want to finish that sentence. And if I find out you're having me followed, I'll destroy everything you know and love."

They stared at one another for a long minute, Keene's hard expression not easing for one moment. Finally, the other man brought his arm up and dislodged Phillip's hold, putting space between them. "So bloodthirsty for a proper gentleman. You are quite surprising, Mr. Mansfield. Quite surprising, indeed."

"Take care not to forget it."

"Oh, I shan't. You have an enjoyable rest of your evening."

He said nothing as Keene strolled away, the other man clearly pleased with himself. He'd set out to rattle Phillip and had succeeded.

Phillip dragged a hand through his hair, marching back to the Halls' box. He needed another drink to wash the acrid taste of that exchange from his mouth. Clearly he'd underestimated his enemies. They were determined to cause destruction and mischief at every turn.

Once he'd fortified himself with a glass of Hall's whiskey, he dropped onto the velvet settee. Undoubtedly Tammany Hall had been responsible for Weller's attempt to shut the project down. Quite likely they were behind locking Eva in the shack as well. Were they also having him followed?

The idea enraged him, these men knowing his intimate secrets. While owning space for the purpose of meeting or keeping a mistress was nothing new for him, the identity of the woman was not something he wished to become public. Eva would be furious, for one thing. Her reputation, both personally and on this project, would suffer, with their working relationship irrevocably changed.

Perhaps after her father arrived and assumed the reins they could renegotiate the terms of their arrangement. Until then, he must protect her in every way possible.

Because he had no intention of giving her up.

OH, DEAR. EVA measured the length of the crack once more, writing the number down carefully in the journal. Mrs. Mansfield would not be pleased at these findings.

Stoneacre was falling apart.

Eva had gone over every inch of the property. Twice. In the past four days she'd crawled in the attic and inspected the foundation. She'd evaluated the exterior walls, stood on the roof. Short of removing plaster and floorboards, she'd done a thorough job in her assessment.

One thing had become clear. The entire place needed to be rebuilt.

Eva hated to be the one to tell Mrs. Mansfield. The older woman loved this "cottage" for sentimental reasons. Yet sentiment wouldn't guard against the unforgiving ocean salt or the rough winds. The original builders hadn't used quality materials to withstand all Mother Nature could dole out.

Yet she had to tell Phillip's mother the truth. As her father had often said, wrapping bad news in a bonbon never helped: it was still bad news at the core. Better to just get it over with.

She checked the watch attached to her skirts.

Mrs. Mansfield would just be sitting down for afternoon tea. She politely invited Eva each afternoon, but Eva usually declined, as she preferred to make the most of daylight hours instead.

In addition to being a practical use of her time, remaining busy prevented her from thinking about Phillip.

Yes, he'd apologized more than once for ruining their night, and she had quickly forgiven him. What else could she have done? They had to continue working together and she couldn't lose this position. She only hoped that in time he'd come to see her as an equal, stop blaming her for every little thing. That he'd recognize her abilities and afford her a bit of proper respect.

He thinks he's hired your father. E. M. Hyde would have Phillip's respect, not you.

Give it time, she told herself. In a month or two, he'd be so enamored of her work and intelligence that she'd finally be able to deliver the news about her father's illness. After she explained he'd undoubtedly be grateful and astounded, so much so that he'd forget any anger over her subterfuge.

Grateful and astounded? Now you've really gone round the bend.

She would need to tell him eventually. The guilt continued to eat at her, an ache in her stomach every time she saw Phillip. Yes, he was quick to temper but he could be made to see reason. He would come to understand why she'd lied, the importance of maintaining her father's legacy.

Just . . . not yet. A few more weeks. Then she'd tell him.

She set off for the conservatory in the east wing, Mrs. Mansfield's favorite room in Stoneacre. Even in structural shambles, the building was a beautiful one. She could well imagine Phillip here as a small boy, tearing through the halls and running on the back lawn. The silence now must only remind Mrs. Mansfield of what the place was lacking. Love and laughter. Activity and bustle.

Where were Phillip's sisters? Did they not wish to enjoy the ocean and the sun?

And why did Eva care? Hadn't she enough problems, with the recent trouble on the construction site, her father's illness, and her employer's pigheadedness?

Had Phillip waited for her at the apartments Thursday night? Likely he hadn't bothered, taking the opportunity to go about with Miss Hall instead, the woman he *could* be seen with in public.

Pain bloomed in her chest and she resolutely pushed it down. The subterfuge had been at her insistence, after all, so no use getting upset over things she could not control. She merely wished . . . Well, she wished a great many things were different.

She wished she did not miss him quite so much.

I suppose constructing new properties is in my blood. Hers, too. Had she ever met a man who so thoroughly understood her passion for architecture?

If only that understanding echoed across all facets of their relationship.

She hadn't decided if continuing as his lover was smart or foolhardy. That he'd purchased an entire building for their affair astonished her, though the expense was likely nothing to a man of his great wealth. The apartments felt very scandalous, very illicit . . . and she loved it.

She blew out a breath, determined not to let this affect her. Theirs was not a long-term arrangement. Her career was flourishing and she had a real chance to make a mark for herself—as an architect, not as a wife or society hostess. Whatever happened between her and Phillip, she planned to be renowned the world over for her designs. And she'd be based in London, near her father . . . not New York.

She nodded to the footman standing at the conservatory door. Inside, she found Phillip's mother pouring herself tea. Her head shot up at the sound of Eva's footsteps.

"Miss Ashford, hello. I hadn't thought you'd be joining me."

"I decided to stop by after all. I hope you don't mind."

"Not a bit. Please." She held out a hand toward the sofa directly opposite her chair. "Have a seat and I'll pour another cup."

"Thank you." Eva settled on the soft cushions, setting her journal down beside her. The long row of glass windows stood open to allow in the most glorious ocean breeze. Though the temperature was high outside this room felt downright cool. Eva made a mental note to include something similar in the new plans.

Mrs. Mansfield came to the point. "I notice you've been revisiting areas already once covered. Is there some question as to the findings?"

Eva appreciated the woman's astuteness. "I wanted to be certain. I do not like to make recommendations unless I'm absolutely positive of the facts."

"I certainly appreciate thoroughness." The older woman sipped her tea. "And what is your recommendation in this case?"

"You must tear it all down and build from scratch."

Mrs. Mansfield choked, coughing around a mouthful of tea as she set her saucer on the table. Concerned, Eva started to rise, but Phillip's mother waved her away. "I am fine," she rasped and then cleared her throat. "Just caught me by surprise."

"I apologize. I've often been told I am too blunt. I should have tried to soften that news."

"Nonsense. News is news and I'm old enough to survive the worst of it." She wiped the edges of her eyes with a linen handkerchief. "Now, tell me why you believe this to be the case."

Eva went on to describe the cracks she'd discovered, both in the foundation and the walls, and why these were a problem. Then she went over the wear and tear a building can endure in this type of climate and environment, how more modern materials and techniques better guarded against the elements. Mrs. Mansfield listened intently, not saying a word.

When she finished, Eva sat back and drained her now-tepid tea. Phillip's mother stared out the window pensively and the silence stretched. After a few minutes, Eva worried that she'd offended the woman. Would Mrs. Mansfield rescind her offer to have Eva design the new house?

If she did Eva would have no regrets.

Better to sell a pile of gold than a pile of dung, her father once said. *Otherwise, you can never get rid of the stink.*

She would not ever tell a client anything other than the truth.

"Fine."

After uttering that one word, Mrs. Mansfield rose and started for the door. Eva's jaw fell open slightly. Were they done? Had she been discharged? "Wait, what does that mean?"

The older woman dragged in a deep breath before turning. Eva was horrified to see that Mrs. Mansfield's eyes were shining with unshed tears.

"Forgive me. I am being quite rude but I need a moment alone." Her voice quavered but her shoulders stood strong. "Please begin drawings for an entire new house. I feel we understand each other well enough and I am confident you'll give me what I need. I shall see you at dinner."

The door closed behind her and Eva could not help but let out a little squeal as she bounced on her toes. Design an entire house! Under her own name!

Good heavens, it was too perfect. She'd been longing for this moment for ten years.

She must get started straightaway. Tomorrow she'd return to New York and sketch ideas. She could almost picture the finished product, taking into account Mrs. Mansfield's request for a more beaux arts style. Windows with arches. Pilasters on the façade. Corinthian columns adorned with volutes. Ornate cornices and balustrades. Oh, and a loggia in the rear.

A twinge of regret colored her happiness, the

memory of Mrs. Mansfield's face before she walked out. She'd obviously been saddened at the thought of losing the house her husband built for her, even as she'd ordered it demolished.

Eva knew what she had to do. A small bit of Stoneacre's history must somehow be preserved in the new design. A tricky prospect, as there wasn't much worth saving and all the structural pieces needed replacing.

Thankfully she was up to the challenge.

Chapter Thirteen

Phillip kicked a piece of rock with the toe of his boot. He'd wandered around the construction site most of the day, roasting like a Christmas goose in the hot summer sun. He had no reason to linger, other than the silly desire to see one particular woman. With no word from her, he had no idea when—or if—she planned to return.

He refused to believe she'd left for good. This project was too important to her. No, she was upset with him and merely taking time to cool down. Eventually she would come back and he could apologize for upsetting her.

Then all would resume as normal.

The interminable wait was killing him, however.

Thankfully construction continued at a steady pace. No rumblings of a strike, no sign of any threats. It was calm and steady, except for the occasional blast of dynamite and the hiss of the equipment.

Milliken had given both the day and night crews lectures regarding the safety of everyone on the site, including any woman present. Never mind that there was only one woman who would ever—

A flash of yellow caught Phillip's eye. *Eva.* She was just coming through the main gate with her ever-present ledger in hand. Relief flooded him and he hurried toward her, dodging workers and dirt as he went, the heavy chug of the steam shovels drowning out his labored breath.

She wore a yellow skirt with a white cotton shirtwaist, a large hat shielding her face from the sun. She was like a bright spot of perfect sunshine amidst all this dirt and grime, one he'd sorely missed.

"Miss Ashford," he called as he drew near.

Her head snapped up, expression giving nothing away as she spotted him. "Hello, Mr. Mansfield."

Less than a rousing greeting, but he supposed he deserved that. "May I have a moment of your time?"

Lips compressed, she did not appear pleased at the request. Her gaze darted at the surroundings before she nodded. "Of course. I assume this is about the ongoing work here?"

Not even close. He gestured to the tiny shack. "In there?"

She led the way, chin high, ignoring the men as she sailed by. They all pointedly ignored her in return.

With the lock on the shack now dismantled, anything valuable belonging to Carew and Milliken had been removed. So when they entered, the space was mostly empty. The air was still and heavy from the humidity.

Her head swiveled to take it in. "Seems much larger."

"I had them leave a chair and desk for you, but I wouldn't keep anything of worth in here. We removed the lock."

"That explains why there's nothing about." She removed her bonnet and set it on the desk. "What is it you wish to discuss?"

"I wanted to apologize."

Tiny lines creased her forehead. "For what, exactly?"

"For the other night. I never should have said any of that."

"You apologized—repeatedly—on the way home and I've already forgiven you."

"Then why . . ." He took off his derby and ran his hand through his hair. "Then why did you disappear?"

"Is that what this is about?" He dipped his chin and she let out a sigh loaded with exasperation. "I had to visit a friend. I was not running away or avoiding you."

"A friend?" God, was it a man? His stomach plummeted to the bedrock some thirty feet below. "Who was it?"

"Just a friend, Phillip," she repeated, not meeting his eyes.

Emotion churned inside his gut, none of it welcome. She was keeping something from him, he could feel it. He'd never experienced jealousy before and he hated every second of this bleak doubt. But he had absolutely no right to be possessive of Eva—especially when he was the one publicly escorting another woman about town these days.

"Oh, my goodness. You're jealous." She came closer, peering at his face carefully.

Clearing his throat, he decided to be honest. "I've never been in this position before, Eva. I've never cared about my partners and whether they were with others outside of our time together. I don't feel nearly as relaxed about where things stand with us, however. This is all quite unsettling."

"You have your Miss Hall. I wouldn't think you'd concern yourself about my social schedule beyond Monday and Thursday evenings."

"Well, I do. Very much so. And I've explained the true nature of the relationship with Miss Hall. We are friends. Nothing more."

"And I believe you."

"Do you?"

"Of course. I'll not play games with you. If I were worried about your motives I would speak up. Though I think it best to remember what this is between us."

Wariness crept into his gut, a discomfort that had him frowning. "And what is this, exactly?"

"A casual affair, nothing more. We both have our reasons for not pursuing anything serious."

He supposed that was true, but he hadn't expected such bluntness from her. Most women agreed to his terms but tried to circumvent them by pushing for more of his time. Or they professed their feelings in the hopes he'd reciprocate. Followed him and faked a chance meeting to pressure him in a public setting.

Yet Eva ran from him every chance she got. No matter how much she gave, he always wanted more. He was quite greedy when it came to Lady Eva Hyde.

If only she were as greedy in return.

"This may not be serious," he said, "but I do worry about you. I would never want you coming to harm, whether on my construction site or crossing the street. And with no word from you for five days, I thought I'd go out of my mind from the panic."

Her face softened and she put a hand on his chest. "I was visiting a friend in Newport. An older woman. No man anywhere in sight, I swear it, and no risk to my person at all."

He was embarrassed by the huge wave of relief that swept over him. Lifting her hand, he brought it to his mouth and kissed her knuckles. "You think I'm being ridiculous."

"No, I would worry if the roles were reversed in this case, and I apologize for my thoughtlessness. I was quite busy but that's no excuse for ignoring you or my duties here."

"If you mean your duties at the site, then do not concern yourself. If you mean your duties at Twenty-Fourth Street . . ."

One side of her mouth lifted and she peeked at him through her lashes, her body leaning into his. "Did you wait for me on Thursday?"

"Only for six hours or so."

"Oh, Phillip. I never guessed you'd wait that long."

He heard the unspoken truth in the last sentence. "But you hoped I'd wait. As penance."

"Perhaps an hour. Two, at the most. Six is absolutely absurd."

Cupping her jaw with his palm, he angled down. "No, absurd would be not waiting long enough and missing the chance to spend the evening buried inside you."

He heard the swift intake of her breath before she moved in closer, her front nearly flush with his. "Perhaps I could make up for all that lost time."

"You could," he started, gripping her hips and grinning down at her. "However, it's only Saturday."

"Would you rather wait until Monday?"

"Definitely not."

"Then come along, my dear man. You've waited long enough."

EVA ROSE FROM the sofa as the trio of ladies marched through the door. Nora had invited two of her new American friends over for tea, insisting Eva take time from the construction site to meet them.

Though she had a multitude of more important tasks on her mind, Eva had agreed. How could she refuse Nora when the two of them had spent such little time together in the past few weeks?

Between the hotel project, Mrs. Mansfield's summer cottage, and Phillip, Eva had hardly been available for visiting. So one afternoon of society gossip would not kill her.

Probably.

"Eva, it is my pleasure to introduce Miss Kathleen Appleton and Miss Anne Elliot. Kate and Anne, this is my dear friend, Lady Eva Hyde."

The two young ladies stopped and performed an awkward curtsey. "No, none of that," Eva said, coming forward. She thrust out her arm and shook hands with both girls. "It is lovely to meet you both. Nora has told me so much about you."

Not a lie, as these two were Nora's closest friends here in New York. Nora had said the girls were "blunt and mischievous . . . in other words, perfect."

"And we've heard all about you, Lady Eva," the one named Kate said. "You are astounding. A female who aspires to be an architect! I am amazed."

Anne gestured toward her cousin. "Especially since she can't trace her own hand, let alone draw up plans for an entire building. But I'm impressed as well, Lady Eva. You give us hope that women will one day be equal with men."

Eva nearly snorted. She felt anything but equal most days, as the men never let her forget her gender and all she lacked. Namely, a penis.

"Perhaps one day. Mostly it's a struggle." She gestured to the seating area. "Shall we sit?"

Soon, everyone was seated and Nora poured tea. They talked of the weather and Eva's first impressions of New York as they settled with cups and saucers. Kate and Anne were obviously very close, often finishing each other's sentences, and Eva quickly felt right at home with them, just as Nora had promised.

"Please tell us all about the hotel project," Kate said. "I ride by there frequently and I'm dying to know what's happening behind the wooden fence."

"Is it true they used dynamite to build out the bottom?" Anne asked, her eyes wide.

"To excavate the foundation, yes. We use dynamite because it is the fastest method available. Once the excavation is complete we'll start building."

"I think it's all terribly exciting. Have you gone

to see it, Nora?" Kate reached for a piece of poppy seed cake. "It must be fascinating."

"The men are skittish with a woman around," Eva told them. "I haven't invited visitors because I hesitate to give them more reasons to despise me."

"Despise you? How could such a thing be possible?" Anne asked.

Eva told them of nearly getting swept under the debris pile and then being locked in the wooden shack. "So it's probably best not to rattle the men any further at this point. Perhaps in a few weeks' time."

Nora set down her saucer with a slap. "Eva, I had no idea. Why did you not tell me? You could be seriously hurt—or worse. What has Mansfield done about this? It is his responsibility to keep you safe."

Eva hurried to reassure her friend. The last thing she needed was for Nora to accost Phillip on Eva's behalf. Again. "He's doing everything in his power to ensure I remain so. He was furious I'd been locked in the shack. He sent all the men home without pay, shutting construction down for the day."

"That hardly seems enough," Nora snapped. "Was the man responsible ever caught?"

"No, not yet."

Brow lined with unhappiness, Nora drummed her fingers, nails tapping on the side of her porcelain teacup. "I don't like this. And I don't like *him*."

"Oh, really?" Kate rushed out. "What is Phillip Mansfield really like, then? He's quite handsome and—"

"Intense," her cousin said.

"Yes, but also handsome," Kate said.

Anne made a noise. "You said that already."

"I know," Kate agreed, "but it bears repeating. By the way, I hear he boxes." She waggled her brows as if the idea were salacious.

Boxes? Eva pictured his bare shoulders and arms, well-defined muscle no wealthy scion should rightfully possess. Yes, boxing made sense. And that would explain the cuts on his cheek and brow a few weeks back. "Where did you hear that?"

"Servants. They say he's turned his ballroom into a sort of . . . boxing equipment area."

"You don't appear surprised," Nora noticed, peering carefully at Eva's face. "Have you seen said ballroom?"

No, but I have seen him naked, she wanted to say. Saturday evening, in fact, when he pleasured her to within an inch of her life. They had stayed for hours at the Twenty-Fourth Street apartments, talking and touching between rounds of lovemaking. At the end, he'd been sweaty and wrung out, spread on the dark bedsheets like a marble statue come to life. They had lain there, in silence, the warm summer breeze blowing across their skin, and she'd been . . . content. It had been quite nice.

And in a few hours, they'd do it all over again.

A sizzle of anticipation went down her spine and settled in her toes. She forced her attention to the conversation at hand. "I have not been in the ballroom, though I have been inside his house."

Nora's gaze sharpened with disapproval and curiosity, but Kate and Anne whooped. "Please tell me it was his bedroom," Kate said. "I am picturing dark cherry and deep greens."

Anne smacked her cousin's shoulder. "Don't be

ridiculous. If she'd been in his bedroom it wouldn't be to note the color scheme."

Eva put the bedroom idea to rest. "I've only been on the main floor, the entryway and his office specifically."

"That's a shame," Kate muttered. "I was hoping the rumors about him and Miss Hall were false."

"The rumors of a match, you mean?" Eva had no intention of breaking Phillip's trust by speaking the truth, revealing that he and Miss Hall were merely friends, but she was curious what the gossips were saying.

"Yes. They say he's going to offer for her."

Not likely.

"How lovely for them," Nora said dryly, the tone flat and insincere. "Do any of you know the story behind his first engagement?"

Eva jerked slightly. How had Nora learned of this? She hadn't been in New York long enough to hear old scandals . . . unless she'd been purposely digging. She shot her friend a questioning glance, but Nora merely raised one haughty brow. It was her smug *I'm-up-to-something* look.

"Oh! Goodness, yes. I daresay that's one they still whisper about." Anne noticed the blank stares from Nora and Eva, and leaned in eagerly. "Of course you haven't heard it, so allow me. He was not yet twenty, I think. Met a girl near his college, a Boston blue blood. Miss Caroline Kerry. They say she was a scheming social climber but incredibly beautiful. She'd already turned down two proposals, so Mansfield knew he'd have to pursue her hard to win her hand."

"And pursue her he did," Kate added with a nod. "Followed her everywhere both in Boston and New York. Sent her gifts. Chased away the other suitors. He never tried to hide his feelings or his intentions. Told everyone, 'That is the girl I am going to marry.'"

"How . . ." Romantic. And unbelievable. That hardly sounded like the man Eva knew.

"Isn't it?" Anne agreed with a dreamy sigh. "Her parents naturally pushed for the match—"

"Not hard to see why with Mansfield's wealth and pedigree," Nora said.

"Yes, but his mother was quite cool to the girl. No one thought Mrs. Mansfield would ever approve."

"He wouldn't have cared," Eva said softly, her stomach twisted in knots. "He would've married her anyway."

"Exactly," Kate said. "So he proposes. Takes her on a picnic in Central Park, just the two of them—"

"I've heard it was on his yacht in Newport," Anne corrected.

Nora waved her hand. "Doesn't matter. Get on with it."

"She accepts and they're betrothed. Within days the match is touted as the wedding of the year. Boston society meets New York society. Mrs. Mansfield throws a lavish betrothal ball to celebrate."

Kate and Anne paused and exchanged a glance, as if deciding who would share the rest of it. "And?" Eva said sharply.

Gaze sparkling, Kate continued. "Just as the wedding preparations are almost complete, her dress has to be refitted."

"Well, that's nothing unusual." Nora lifted one shoulder. "My dress has already been altered three times and we're several months away from my wedding."

"No," Anne said with a meaningful lift of her brows. "It had to be *refitted*." She pointed to her abdomen.

Nora gasped. "Do you mean to say she was . . . increasing?"

Eva's mind whirled as she tried to put all these pieces together. His fiancée had been with child? Where was said child now? He'd led her to believe—

"She was indeed. And would you care to guess as to the identity of the father?"

"Well, I assume it wasn't Mansfield," Nora said. "Otherwise the wedding would've proceeded."

"Correct. The girl only accepted Mansfield's proposal because she'd conceived a child with some butcher's son. Fancied herself in love with the young man."

Oh, no. Eva closed her eyes, sympathy swelling in her chest like a bubble. Poor Phillip. He would've hated the embarrassment above all else, the public blow to his pride. This was clearly what his mother had been referring to when she'd mentioned Phillip's broken heart.

No wonder he shied away from marriage.

And why did that knowledge sadden her? She had no intentions of marrying, not after three failed attempts. While she knew she wasn't truly cursed, perhaps fate had been telling her something with those failures. That perhaps she was meant for greater things than household accounts and hosting dinner parties. That she should focus on her career and passion in architecture instead.

A knock on the door interrupted them. The Cortland butler emerged with a silver tray carrying what appeared to be a cable. "I beg your pardon, but this telegram just arrived for your ladyship."

He came to Eva's side and held out the salver. "Me?" He nodded and she scooped up the message. The only cables she ever received were from her father's secretary. Tearing it open, she paled as she read the words inside.

When she finished she could barely breathe. Could barely think. Cold fear had wrapped around her heart.

Nora clasped her hand. "Eva, what is it? You're scaring me half to death."

"My father," she rasped. "He's taken a hard fall and is bedridden. He—he may not live."

"Oh, no. Eva, I'm so sorry." Nora's grip tightened on Eva's hand. "What can I do?"

"I . . . I must pack. I need to return home." She had to see him, needed to sit at his bedside. She started to rise, but Nora grabbed her arm to stop her.

"I think you should wait a day or so. Leaving immediately feels rash."

Eva frowned, surprised at her friend's comment. "Rash? What if he dies? I'll never forgive myself for not being there."

"The trip will take you three weeks, longer if you find yourself in bad weather. If he recovers in a day or two, there's no turning back once you're on the ship."

She pressed a hand to her chest, hoping to alleviate the ache there. "But if he dies . . ."

"You still won't make it in time." Nora's eyes were gentle. "Darling, I know this is upsetting but think what your father would want you to do. What did he always tell you?"

Eva swallowed. "The work comes first."

"That's correct. The work comes first. So wait a few days. Cable your staff as often as you like to keep abreast of his condition. The truth is, he won't ever know if you are there with him or not—even if he is awake."

Tears pooled in Eva's eyes, a hot, stinging flood of emotion. Unfortunately, Nora was right. Her father's memory had deserted him. Even if Nora were there, he wouldn't recognize her. "But I will know," she said, wiping the moisture from her cheeks.

"He's too stubborn to die from a fall. He's hardheaded, just like his daughter." Nora rubbed Eva's back in long, calming strokes. "Give it two days. If he's the same, then book your passage home."

"All right. I'll wait. I hope this isn't a mistake."

"You'll see. This will all work out."

Eva wished she shared her friend's confidence. If they were wrong, she'd never recover. Perhaps her father had been wrong all these years about his priorities because, right now, it did not seem like the work should come first.

THE CURTAINS TO the private dining suite parted and in entered Mr. Ogden Doyle, the renowned Boston architect and designer. Phillip rose from the table and closed the distance between them, his hand outstretched. "Mr. Doyle, thank you for coming."

Doyle, a lanky man in his early thirties, shook Phillip's hand. "Mr. Mansfield. I appreciate the invitation."

They settled in chairs and a waiter appeared to take drink orders, vermouth cocktail for Doyle and a whiskey for Phillip. "And please bring a bottle of champagne for our third guest."

Doyle removed his gloves and tucked them in his coat. "Third guest?"

"My architect's representative."

"Ah. I had heard E. M. Hyde is your primary architect."

Phillip couldn't keep the smug smile from appearing. "Yes, I was fortunate enough to land him."

"Especially before he became ill."

"Indeed. He is expected to recover soon, however, and will join us here in New York."

Lines of confusion dotted Doyle's brow. "Oh. But I had heard his condition was—"

Eva burst into the room at that moment, a vision in an emerald green silk evening gown. Just the sight of her curves had Phillip's blood heating. He hadn't been able to stop thinking about her today, not after she canceled their Monday evening rendezvous. She'd begged off, saying she was unwell.

She looked exquisite tonight, however. Perhaps he'd have luck in convincing her to join him at the apartments after dinner. He quickly pushed the reaction aside. There would be time enough for that later.

Both men came to their feet. She hurried to the table, her gait purposeful yet feminine, a large case in her right hand.

"I apologize for my tardiness. There was a streetcar accident on Forty-Second Street." She thrust her hand at Doyle. "I am Miss Ashford, his lordship's secretary."

Doyle froze for a brief second then quickly bowed over her hand. "How lovely to meet you, Miss Ashford."

When Doyle released her, she gifted Phillip with a soft, heart-stopping smile. Something inside him turned over. "And good evening to you, Mr. Mansfield."

He also bowed over her hand, kissing her gloved knuckles for good measure. "Miss Ashford. Thank you for joining us tonight."

"Of course, though I am a little befuddled as to the purpose."

"All in good time. Let's enjoy our drinks and order dinner first."

The waiter returned as they were discussing Boston, the people they shared in common. Doyle came from a good family there, his uncle a long-practicing architect in the Northeast. Phillip resolutely avoided any discussion of the Kerrys or their daughter—his former fiancée—Caroline. That business had long since ceased to be important to him.

A dinner order was placed and the staff gave them privacy. Phillip leaned back in his seat, ready to get to tonight's purpose. "I was impressed by what you did inside the Back Bay Club, Doyle. I had the occasion to visit earlier this year."

"Thank you. It was something a bit new for me."

Eva interjected to ask, "What exactly did you do?"

Phillip liked that she was not shy about inserting herself into a conversation or asking questions. He let Doyle answer.

"They hired someone else to design the exterior, but allowed me to handle the interior. I had complete control over every detail, from the draperies, to the furniture, carpets, and paintings."

Eva's brows went up, and Phillip knew what she was thinking. With most projects, the interior was left to upholsterers, who believed the more furnishings used—which all had to be upholstered, naturally—the better. There was no eye for taste or continuity, just gewgaws every which way one turned.

"You have a talent for it," Phillip added. "Which is why I wanted to meet with you. I'd like for you to design the interior of the new Mansfield Hotel."

Doyle's eyes rounded, his face going slack. "Your new Fifth Avenue hotel? I would be a fool to say no."

"Even still, you should think it over. As you may have heard, I can be a difficult employer. I'm exacting and don't care to be deceived or placated. This project is important to me for various reasons and I plan to be very involved."

"Mr. Mansfield," Eva said, gaining his attention. "Before Mr. Doyle provides an answer, I have a question. What of the rooms I've already earmarked with a certain design theme? Some cannot be altered."

"For example?"

"Well, the ladies' drawing room on the main floor. We agreed to recreate Marie Antoinette's apartment."

"How clever," Doyle said, stroking his chin. "All round, with mirrored walls?"

"Exactly." She leaned in, excitement fairly glowing on her face. "The ceiling will be inset and covered by a large fresco. I've already made inquiries into replicating the furniture."

"Sounds as if you have a majority of the work planned out." Doyle looked between Phillip and Eva, clearly wondering where he would fall in line.

"Not even close. You would, of course, consult with both Miss Ashford and E. M. Hyde about the space and any plans they had. But there's much to be discussed outside those common areas, such as decisions on the rooms, from the most expensive suite right down to the cheapest single."

Three waiters entered, their arms laden with china plates and bowls. The food was arranged in front of them, drinks refreshed, and then the waiters disappeared once again. Phillip nodded for Eva to begin, and she started on a plate of clams. He'd selected cream of artichoke soup, and Doyle had gone for the bisque of shrimp.

"I am intrigued," Doyle said. "But I've only decorated a few homes and the Back Bay Club. Why me? You could hire almost anyone for this project."

"You sell yourself short. You come highly recommended, and I've also seen the home in Newport you decorated. I believe you have an eye for this kind of thing. My hotel must have the right atmosphere, one unparalleled in this country. I want luxury but also want accessibility. Jaws should drop, but it shouldn't cost so much that only a handful of people can afford it."

"That is quite a lofty goal."

"I realize as much, which is why I only hire the very best people. The ones who can accomplish the impossible."

"Well, I'm no E. M. Hyde," he said, dragging his soup spoon through the bisque. "Or even Miss Ashford, it seems."

Eva flushed under the compliment. "You are too kind. And I suspect humble, as I know Mr. Mansfield's standards."

"When would I need to start?"

Phillip leaned back in his chair. Doyle would say yes, he could feel it. "As soon as you're able. The foundation will be poured the week after next and then we'll start framing the floors. Hyde will arrive in a few weeks or so, once he recovers. Having your input from the beginning will be critical."

A familiar face appeared in the doorway. Phillip pushed back from the table and rose. "Miss Hall. Good evening."

Becca's eyes darted around the room, taking in the scene before her. "Good evening. I apologize for the interruption, but I wondered if I might have a moment to speak with you, Mr. Mansfield."

He nodded and then turned to his dining companions. Eva had gone stiff, her gaze pointedly on her clams. She wasn't upset over Becca's arrival, was she? Eva knew there was no reason for jealousy. "If you'll both excuse me, I'll only be a moment."

Doyle waved his hand in Eva's direction. "No rush. This will give Miss Ashford and me time to get acquainted."

Phillip didn't care for the sound of that, but how

could he complain? To the outside world, Eva was
merely Hyde's secretary and Phillip's employee.
Without further comment, he followed Becca into
the corridor. Electric lights framed with glass
sconces hung on the walls, throwing a soft yellow
glow onto the patterned wallpaper. No one else
was about, thankfully.

Becca was wringing her gloved hands. "I'm
sorry. I had to warn you, and when I heard you
were dining upstairs I came as quickly as I could."

"I don't mind. I'm with business associates." He
rolled his shoulders, suddenly uncomfortable with
referring to Eva in those terms. Acting as if she
were unimportant to him, as if he wasn't burning
to bury himself inside her once again.

"It's my father," Becca said, reclaiming his attention.

"Your father?"

"He's growing anxious." She motioned between
the two of them. "About us. He plans to seek you
out to determine your intentions."

He winced. This had been the consequence he'd
feared most. With him and Becca spending so
much time together, her parents had every right to
make assumptions about an imminent betrothal.
"What did you tell him?"

"I told him there is nothing serious between
us, that I do not wish to marry you. I'm afraid he's
heard it before, unfortunately. This time he doesn't
believe me, especially with all the rumors flying
around the city."

"Perhaps he'll believe me."

"And if he doesn't?"

"He cannot force us to marry, Becca. He has no leverage over me and I'm hardly a green lad. The worst is he tries to retaliate in some manner, but I doubt it. My family is too venerable to strong-arm."

She mulled this over a moment. "He's desperate to marry me off. I think . . . I think they suspect something between me and *her*."

"I'll deal with him if he approaches me. In the meantime, we should just continue to go about our business as usual—with a bit more circumspection."

"As long as you're prepared." She ran a hand over her stomach, smoothing her gown. "I must find a way out of that house. Move someplace where no one knows my name."

"I can assist you with that. Merely say the word."

The lines in her forehead eased and she rose on her toes to press a kiss to his cheek. "You're a good friend, Phillip. Thank you."

"No thanks are necessary. Just keep it in mind if your situation becomes untenable. Now, hurry back to your table before they notice you're missing."

Chapter Fourteen

The instant Phillip left, Mr. Doyle put his knife and fork on the edge of his plate, his boyish expression turning shrewd. "So, tell me. Why are you lying, Lady Eva?"

Eva's jaw dropped, the comment catching her by surprise. "How did you . . . ?"

He leaned in. "Because I am a student of architecture. I have studied his lordship for years. He's . . . something of a hero to me. And that is why I suspect E. M. Hyde did not design the Mansfield Hotel."

Eva swayed in her seat, all the blood draining so quickly that she felt dizzy. Her heart pounded behind her ribs, a powerful drumbeat of doom. Mouth gone dry, she swallowed. "He did."

"It's obvious from your reaction he did not." He chuckled. "You must be worried I'll tell Mansfield. I won't, you know. I have too much admiration for E. M. Hyde—and for you. There has been talk for some time in the community about your talent."

"Why would you keep such a secret—if it were true, I mean?"

"Mansfield is no fool. He's obviously carefully reviewed what you've done. If you made him believe it was your father's work, you must be as talented as the rumors. Does he know you are Hyde's daughter?"

Her chest swelled, the compliment filling some of the cracks in her confidence, the ones formed from years of doubt and frustration. "Yes, Mansfield knows. We thought it best to conceal my true identity from the workers because of the moniker I've acquired in London."

"Ah, yes. Lady Unlucky. The superstitious fools. May I see the plans?" He gestured to the satchel by her feet.

Reaching, she found the satchel and withdrew the traces of the hotel, while Mr. Doyle moved their plates to a nearby table, giving them room to spread out the drawings.

He bent to examine the front exterior, following the angles and markings with his finger while mumbling under his breath. "Loggias, gables, tiled roof. All of these top-floor rooms will have balconies?"

"Yes."

Turning to the floor plan, he asked, "What do you plan here, in this interior garden courtyard?"

"White terra-cotta and frescoes. Three fountains in a line."

"Beautiful. And this room here, this large one on the main floor? It merely says State Room."

"Mansfield plans to turn that into a restaurant. We're thinking mahogany and green marble."

He continued through each level, concentrating on the details and flourishes she had included. The touches that would make this design *hers*. When he finished, he straightened and gestured toward the drawings. "This is absolutely stunning. The city—and the country—has never seen anything like it."

"Thank you. He wanted it to be the best in the world. An unlimited budget helped as well."

"The towers, these with the mansard roofs, they're very Second Empire. Nicely done."

Eva grinned, pleased he'd caught that. "Yes, I thought so."

"And the domes over the corner turrets . . . I am quite impressed. It is easy to see why Mansfield loved your design."

She admitted nothing, but she assumed her face was the color of a tomato, her chest nearly bursting with pride. Doyle hadn't belittled her or mocked her at all. She liked that about him. He seemed kind and thoughtful, not one to overtake a project with his own ideas. "Does this mean you want to work with me?"

"Of course. As I said, I'd be a fool to refuse. Tell me, how is your father's health?"

Grief knotted her throat. Since receiving the news of her father's fall, she'd hardly been able to eat or sleep. Two more cables had arrived from her father's secretary to say her father was resting comfortably, having awoken a few hours after the fall. He'd hit his head and was confused, but alive.

As Nora had predicted, he hadn't died and remained unaware of his surroundings. He wouldn't have known if Eva returned or not, a fact that broke her heart.

Her *father*. Her protector, her mentor. Her family.

And he no longer knew her.

Eva kept hoping his condition would improve, that the doctors were wrong. Sadly, this seemed unlikely as time passed. Still, she needed to be with him in these final years, for however long he had. She had decided to see the foundation poured and then return to England for a visit.

Of course, she hadn't told Phillip of her plans. Perhaps she would invent another reason for her trip home. Financially, she had to remain employed.

"I apologize," Doyle said when she remained silent. "It's none of my concern."

Eva sent a nervous glance to the doorway where Phillip had disappeared moments earlier. "No, I am just not used to answering honestly. His health is quite poor, actually."

"I am truly sorry to hear that. I met him once, six or so years ago when he spoke at the Royal Institute. A genius, your father."

She had been in the audience, the only woman in a room full of men. Her father had refused to speak until they admitted her. Perhaps this was where Doyle recognized her. "Yes, he is that."

"When will you tell Mansfield? He believes your father will arrive in a few weeks' time. From what I understood that will be nigh impossible, and Mansfield does not seem the type to appreciate a lie."

"I haven't decided yet—"

The curtains parted and Phillip, tall and deliciously brawny, entered. "You haven't decided, what?"

Eva froze, her brain stuck on a lie. Mr. Doyle came to her rescue, his answer smooth like dry plaster. "On whether to attend the grand opening celebration. I assume you are having one?"

"Of course." Phillip joined them at the table, slipping his hands into his trouser pockets, dark eyes sweeping over the traces. "But that's two years away. Miss Ashford has time to decide before then, though I do hope she'll join us. Along with her father, of course."

Eva struggled not to react. *Mansfield does not seem the type to appreciate a lie.* Her stomach clenched, the guilt twisting her insides. She did not know how much longer she could go on lying to him. Phillip cared deeply about this project, and having E. M. Hyde's name attached to it mattered to him. A lot. Eva did not want to face his disappointment when he learned she'd been behind the entire design.

Coward. You'll need to tell him eventually.

Yes, but that didn't mean it must happen today. Or tomorrow. Or next week.

"You know busy architects," she said. "Always flitting from one job to the next. I have no idea what his lordship will be working on by then."

The waiters arrived with entrées and the traces were rolled and packed away. Eva promised to send copies to Mr. Doyle, who confirmed his interest in the project.

Phillip looked entirely pleased with himself, so handsome and dashed appealing as he cut into his roasted lamb. She watched his hands—rough and large, and incredibly strong—and shivered. They were capable of delivering such delicious pleasure, the memories enough to make her dizzy.

A boxer. Yes, she could see those fists pounding

another man. Raw strength and power behind his punches. Heat licked through her veins, and she suddenly longed for a fan to cool off.

Glancing up, she caught his eye. A dark brow quirked in amusement. He'd obviously caught her staring. Well, they were having an *affair*. They were supposed to desire one another, correct?

Yet it was becoming so much more than physical. She liked talking to him, making him laugh. Discussing buildings and designs, the progress at the site. He was intelligent and kind, protective and intense. She hadn't met anyone like him, not in England or New York.

And that scared her.

She had to remember her purpose here, the nature of their relationship. He was her employer, nothing more. She would soon return to England, to her father. When in London, she would cable Phillip with news of her father's inability to travel and offer to handle the rest of the build herself. He must never learn of her duplicity.

You merely want to continue the affair.

Yes, she did. For the most selfish reasons, too. Though the affair was temporary, she planned to enjoy every minute of it.

She raised a brow at him in return, challenging him, and the side of his mouth hitched. *Later,* he mouthed, and gave her a bold wink that turned her bones to jelly.

Her gaze darted to Mr. Doyle, who was thankfully engrossed in his soft-shell crabs. She breathed a sigh of relief. At least he hadn't seen her act like an utter fool over their employer.

Above all else, no one must learn of the affair. Not only would she be humiliated, the world would assume she'd used her charms to get favors from Mansfield. That she'd allowed him in her bed as a way to influence her role on the project. The idea was ludicrous, but there would be some who believed it—even if it were untrue.

She had to try harder to hide her feelings for him. From everyone . . . especially herself.

DOYLE LEFT SHORTLY after dessert, but not before declaring his eagerness to work on the hotel. Phillip had shaken his hand and promised to follow up tomorrow. Now, it was time to celebrate.

Plus, a particularly luscious redhead had been staring at him all evening, her long gazes full of hunger and longing. He understood, his mood much the same. It seemed years since he'd last touched her and he might go mad if he didn't satisfy this insane craving straightaway.

He excused himself to have a quick word with the staff before locking the suite door and returning to the table. Anticipating they would be left alone for the night, he inched his chair closer to hers until their thighs were nearly touching. "Did you enjoy meeting Mr. Doyle?" He draped an arm over her chair back, fingertips skimming the nape of her neck.

Her breathing hitched and two spots of pink appeared on her cheekbones. He loved her unblemished pale skin. Every thought and emotion was clearly visible, like the perfect telegraph into her mind.

"I did. But then, you knew I would. For the record, he knows who I am."

Phillip hadn't expected that. "He knows you're Hyde's daughter?"

"Yes. Apparently he's an ardent fan of my father. Will that pose a problem for you?"

"For me? No, as long as he does not tell the crew."

She nodded, her gaze sliding away as her mouth tightened. Puzzled, he caught a finger under her chin and forced her to meet his eyes. "Is that frown about hiding your identity from the laborers?"

"No. We agreed to keep it a secret." The shadows in her eyes gave her away. She was growing unhappy with the lie.

He let her go, his mind racing as a knot formed in his belly. They hadn't even poured the foundation yet, and her reputation could very well jeopardize the entire project.

However, this was *Eva*. Her unhappiness affected him, even as he'd told himself to keep a distance from her. Despite those noble intentions he . . . cared for her, more than he'd ever dreamed possible. She had slipped under his skin that night on the ship and he'd been unable to recover ever since.

Perhaps he didn't want to recover.

Wait, what was he saying? He and Eva, together? *Publicly?*

The idea no longer filled him with dread. Instead he imagined pulling her skirts up inside his box at the opera . . . Showing her the inside of the New York World Building when it was finished downtown . . . Seeing her red hair spread over his pillows every night . . .

Christ, he ached for that.

Standing, he shoved the coffee cups and dessert plates to the other side of the table. Then he helped her stand. "I am going to kiss you," he warned. "For a long time."

"Here?" Her gaze darted to the door.

"It's locked and the staff won't interrupt us. You're mine, Lady Eva."

He sealed his mouth to hers, her body instantly relaxing into his frame, a delicate hand curling into his vest to hold on. She tasted of sugar and champagne and everything he'd ever desired.

His tongue found hers as he pulled her closer, his arms tightening around her. He loved how she reacted to him, the way she shivered and pressed her breasts to his chest. The marked difference in their sizes never seemed to bother her. In fact, she seemed to like his bulk. It was yet another reason why he adored this woman.

She moaned into his mouth, a faint yielding that stoked his blood like a furnace. Cupping her buttocks, he lifted her until she rested on the linen-covered table, the china and crystal rattling gently. She drew back, her glance darting to the door. "What are you doing?"

"What we're both craving." He bent his head and nibbled the side of her throat.

"Phillip, there are hundreds of people below us—people who would be scandalized to learn what we are doing right now."

He dropped kisses lower and lower, over her collarbone, the smell of her creamy skin drugging him, until he reached the plump mound of her breast. "It would not be the first time pleasure was sought in these private dining suites, I'm sure."

She clutched him, her breath coming fast and harsh. "But I cannot stroll down the stairs all sweaty and disheveled, looking as though we've just gone three rounds in bed."

He knew this. He would not give her cause for embarrassment . . . yet he needed to taste her everywhere. Right now.

Flicking her skirts to her knees, he slid her thighs apart and stepped between them, the fabric of her drawers scraping the wool of his trousers. He was hard, his body demanding and ready, but his pleasure would have to wait.

"Phillip, stop. You are not listening to me. We are in a restaurant. A very public restaurant, with most of New York society one floor below us."

He reached down to cup between her legs. She was warm and soft and lust rolled through him, a burn that settled in his groin. "Just let me feel you."

Her thighs fell open in tacit approval and he slid a finger inside her. She gasped and let her head drop to expose her neck. He began peppering kisses along her jaw, scraping his teeth over the sensitive skin. "You're so wet. So tight. I never get tired of touching you."

He pumped his hand and added a digit, stretching her. "All those people downstairs and no one would suspect I have my fingers inside you. Pleasuring you. What would they say if they knew?" He dragged his thumb over her clitoris, gratified when she moaned. "That's it, sweetheart. Let them hear you. Let them hear how much you love what I'm doing to you."

More wetness coated his fingers, her grip tightening on his shoulders. *She likes this.* Was it the danger of discovery? "How quickly can you come, I wonder?" He rubbed faster, pausing to curl his finger and find the spot deep inside that drove her wild.

She tensed, her hips tilting slightly. "Phillip . . ." It was said like a prayer, a benediction, and he knew she was close.

A third finger and she began panting, the tops of her breasts heaving. He bent his head to kiss and lick the soft mounds. "Do you wish I was inside you right now? Thrusting into you over and over? Would you like everyone downstairs to know that you're being pleasured by my c—"

Before he could finish the crass word, her body clenched around him, walls pulsing. He quickly sealed his mouth to hers, swallowing her cries. God, she was so perfect. No one made him harder, not even in his youth. He couldn't wait to get her to Twenty-Fourth Street tonight.

A long moment later, she slumped back on the table, her eyes glazed and skin flushed. He grinned in triumph. He loved seeing that well-pleasured look on her face. Leaning in, he kissed her. "You're beautiful."

"You're the devil," she breathed. "How does a society scion learn to speak that way?"

"It's you." He withdrew his fingers and slipped them into his mouth, groaning at the musky, delicious flavor of her. "You've turned me into a barbarian."

She smiled shyly and then smoothed her skirt. "Well, barbarian, we should continue this at the apartments. I'll leave first. Then you may follow in twenty minutes or so."

A prickle skated along the back of his neck. Subterfuge no longer sat well with him. Why hide how he felt about her? This was unlike anything he'd experienced before and he didn't care who knew it.

Had there ever been a woman more perfect for him? They made a good team, even outside the bedroom. He'd sworn never to marry after the disaster with Caroline, but that had been a bitter promise borne of humiliation and heartbreak. He could see that now.

Besides, if Eva were increasing, the babe would definitely be his. She was nothing like Caroline and the two situations were entirely different. There were no secrets or hidden agendas here. Eva cared nothing about his money or his position. In fact, she'd resisted him at every turn.

Moreover, he was not a green nineteen-year-old overcome by lust. He wanted more than just to bed her. He longed for early morning coffee and rides in the park. Trips to Newport and London, discussions on their favorite buildings. Arguments and laughter.

He wanted her, in every way. Damn the consequences.

Trusting his gut instinct, he blurted, "No. I'm leaving with you."

"You cannot." She stared up at him, eyes wide, her hand clamped over his forearm. "Everyone will see us."

"I don't care who sees us together, Eva. I don't care who knows. Let's tell all of New York, in fact."

Her brows drew together and she twisted away from him, sliding off the table until her feet hit the floor. "What on earth are you talking about?"

He lifted a shoulder. Undoubtedly he was not articulating this well, but he had to try. "If keeping your identity on the construction site a secret bothers you, let's tell everyone. I am able to protect you."

"Tell everyone? You are not making any sense. You cannot protect me without ruining my reputation."

Hardly. A public relationship would only help her. The only question was how serious a face they put on it. The one thing he knew was he wanted to do this right. She was English aristocracy, the daughter of one of Britain's most famous men. There were rules, protocols, for this sort of thing and he'd abide by them. She deserved no less. "I don't want to ruin it. I'd like to court you. Properly."

"Court me?" Eva's face lost most of its color as she backed up. "Have you gone mad?"

"Not at all. My name will protect you, both in society and on the construction site. No one will dare harm or slander you if we are linked together."

Instead of relief, horror washed over her features. "I do not require your protection. I am perfectly capable of protecting myself."

Her unexpected reaction began to sink in and an unfamiliar awkwardness quickly turned into annoyance. "Well, the episode in the shack says otherwise. Besides, we're already having an affair. Why not do this right, more formally?"

"For many reasons," she snapped. "For example,

I do not have time for courting. I like our arrangement precisely as it is."

"And it would remain as such, but with a few more public outings."

"Taking time away from other tasks, not to mention I would lose all credibility at the construction site. They would see me merely as an extension of you."

Exactly. And his word was law there. "Why on earth would that be a problem?"

She let out an exasperated noise and threw up her arms. "Because it would. I'm the architect, Phillip, not some errand girl there to relay her man's wishes."

"You mean your father is the architect. Technically you're his errand girl."

Anger sparked in her gaze, though he couldn't say why. "Exactly. How could I forget? So you want me to go from being his representative to acting as yours."

"Would that be so terrible? The men would all respect you, despite your fear of losing credibility. Don't you see? This gives you *more* credibility."

"No, it does not. This ensures no one sees me as Eva Hyde. I essentially disappear, lost in your shadow. First, my father's shadow . . . and now yours." She put her hands on her hips. "How is that better for me?"

What was she talking about? "Eva, I won't try to prevent you from working on the project or stop you from visiting the site. You may continue your duties until your father arrives from London."

"Oh, how generous of you." Her tone dripped

sarcasm. "All under your careful watch, of course. You still wouldn't trust me with any appreciable responsibility."

His muscles clenched as they did before he stepped into the ring. "I've told you, the project is too important to leave in—" He shut his mouth but it was too late. The words were out there, and they both knew it.

"In my hands?" She gave a mirthless laugh. "Precisely."

"Eva, I'd be saying the same to your father if he were here."

"I honestly doubt that," she shot back. "You still don't believe in me. But that's all right because I believe in myself—and I will prove my worth to you before I return to London."

She strode toward the door, the silk layers of her train whispering over the carpet. "Just so we are clear, I am not interested in marriage. Ever. Everything is skewed to benefit the man in that institution and I have too much to lose."

EVA'S MOOD WAS as dark as tar the next day as she and Nora trotted toward the massive open park in the center of Manhattan. "The only reason I'm agreeing to this absurd early morning excursion is to see Olmsted and Vaux's design." Central Park was widely considered the finest park in the world, an egalitarian masterpiece that made common green space accessible to all citizens regardless of social standing or wealth. It was worth getting on the back of a horse to see it. Maybe.

Nora smirked, the feathers in her jaunty riding

hat bobbing as they rode. "Then I consider myself lucky to accompany you. No doubt you'll tell me all the details that make the park unique."

Eva didn't care if Nora wanted to hear her commentary or not. She would spout the details, if only to have someone share in her joy at the discovery. *If only Phillip were here, he'd appreciate the details.*

She ground her back teeth together. *Stop it. Stop thinking about him.* The rebuke almost caused her to laugh. Stop thinking about him? She might as well order the earth to stop spinning.

In case I haven't been clear, I want to court you.

Had he gone mad? The two of them currently had a lovely arrangement. Why ruin that with talk of anything serious?

He hadn't proposed marriage, but that generally followed a courtship, and marriage meant she'd never have a career of her own. She'd forever be Mrs. Phillip Mansfield, wife of the wealthy and powerful hotel developer. Any project she undertook would need approval from him. Approval! As if she were chattel, incapable of making her own decisions.

No, thank you.

Besides, she'd tried courting three times with disastrous results. Why attempt a fourth go-round?

They entered the park at Miner's Gate, off East Seventy-Ninth Street, then headed north along the drive. Shaded footpaths twisted and turned through the rocks and fields, green stretched out as far as the eye could see. A few other riders were enjoying the near-empty main drive, as well as some cyclists, but otherwise the space was quiet.

Birds could be heard all around them, their morning song loud and strangely soothing.

"You're awfully quiet," Nora said, maneuvering her horse alongside Eva's. "Were you out late?"

"No. I arrived home before you, in fact." Nora had been with her husband all evening, not returning until well after midnight. Eva had still been awake and had heard the carriage pull up.

Her friend sighed. "I swear, leaving him only grows more and more difficult." They nodded at a passing rider, a man dressed smartly atop a glorious black stallion. "Speaking of difficult, how are you coming along with Mrs. Mansfield's design?"

"I've made some rough sketches. I have a good idea what she wants, so it shouldn't take long to complete the traces."

"And how are things coming along with Mr. Mansfield?"

There was no use in hiding it. Nora would drag it out of her at some point anyway. "He asked to court me. Properly."

Nora maneuvered her horse around a divot. "And what did you tell him?"

She gave a dry laugh. "That I had no interest in anything serious—with him or anyone else."

"Eva!"

"It's true. I'll never have any sort of career of my own if I marry him. I'll go from being E. M. Hyde's daughter straight to Phillip Mansfield's wife."

"It's different here. Women are allowed slightly more freedom—"

"It's not that much different. I would still be overshadowed and dismissed outright. My money becomes his, not that I have any currently but I will one day. He'd have all the rights and I would have none. Besides, people would always wonder if I had been hired because of my husband, not my talent."

"Nonsense. Once they saw your brilliant work no one would dare question your abilities."

"You are kind. Misguided, but kind."

"And you are impossibly stubborn. What if you find yourself with child?"

Eva's jaw fell open, her breath catching in her lungs. "How did you . . . ?"

"Please. It was written all over your face the other day when we had tea with Kate and Anne. Where is he taking you, a hotel?"

"No, he bought a town house."

"Clever bastard," Nora muttered under her breath. "So what, you're content with being his mistress?"

"I'm not a mistress. It's an affair, not a financial transaction."

"Semantics. Again, what happens if you conceive?"

"Shh." Eva glanced around them, ensuring no one could overhear. "Must you bring that up?"

"Yes, I must. I hope he is taking precautions with you."

Eva said nothing, merely straightened her shoulders and tightened her grip on the reins.

Nora growled, scaring their horses into side-stepping. "Good God, I really want to strangle that man. How dare he be so careless with you! And why on earth would you put up with such behavior?"

"It was only twice. He's been careful ever since."

"Oh, only twice. Well, that absolves him of any wrongdoing."

"Your sarcasm is noted, Lady Nora. And I do not need you approaching him again, taking him to task. Promise me you'll stay away from him."

"I cannot do that." Nora lifted her chin. "I only have your best interest at heart. I fear he's taking advantage of you. He's your employer. Can you not see the gross imbalance of power between you? He holds your future in his very hands—both personally and professionally."

Phillip did not wish her harm, Eva was certain of it. But sometimes people could be hurt regardless of good intentions. "I started my courses this morning, so there's no reason to fret about a baby."

"What about the rest of it? Your reputation, your safety on the construction site? Your heart?"

"As I've said, he has offered to court me. And my heart is not at risk."

"Bollocks," Nora said and started her horse forward once again. "You may force yourself to believe that drivel but you cannot convince me. Not after the other day."

What on earth had she done to give her feelings away during that tea? "Fine. I care for him. It hardly matters as nothing will come of this relationship. He'll never forgive me for lying to him. Once he learns the truth about my father, he'll never speak to me again."

"If he loves you, he will understand your reasons for lying."

How Eva wished that were true. "No, he won't. He abhors liars. He was angry enough that I was here in my father's stead. I can't imagine what he'll say when he finds out I've posed as my father all along."

"You're so talented. If he cannot see that, then he is not the man for you."

"I do hate lying to him. Some days I want to just blurt out the truth so this awful guilt will go away."

"Perhaps you should. Perhaps Mr. Mansfield would surprise you."

"With how quickly he discharged me? No, thank you. I think I'll continue the lie for a little longer."

"And how long do you intend to continue lying?"

She rubbed her chest with her gloved hand. "I thought I would write to him from London with news that my father is too ill to travel. Then I shall offer to see the project through until completion."

Nora's expression turned dubious. "And you actually believe that will work?"

It had to work. There was no other choice. She kicked her heels into the mare's sides. "Let's circle the reservoir. I want to explore the park, not depress myself even further." She raced off, leaving Nora to catch up.

Chapter Fifteen

Phillip entered the Gotham Club at midday, the neo-Renaissance entryway tasteful and discreet, a mere hint of the luxury awaiting inside. Soft lighting hung from crystal chandeliers overhead, the staff quiet and efficient as they assisted with overcoats, canes, and hats.

An attendant opened the door and Phillip went inside. At one end, the grand staircase—twin sets of marble stairs angling toward a common landing before diverging in opposite directions—dominated the main floor. Stained-glass windows overlooked the space, the colors reflecting off an intricately carved wooden ceiling. He'd always loved the imperiousness of the space.

Grasping the ornate iron railing, he climbed the stairs to the third-floor dining room. Gilded accents adorned red velvet-covered walls along the way. The frescoes and plaster carvings lent a baroque feeling, with molding and inlay each way one turned.

He wished Eva were here to see it. She would love the tiny details no one else noticed, the craftsmanship that appeared so effortless in the finished product. Both of them knew, however, the work that went into a space such as this. It was the same sort of talent he'd soon see inside his New York hotel.

That line of thought reminded him of the other night. He hated the way she'd left, the conversation that went round and round with no resolution. He hated no resolution.

Just so we are clear, I am not interested in marriage. Ever.

He hadn't even proposed and she'd already rebuffed him. Why? Clearly, she did not oppose marriage in general. After all, the woman had three betrothals in her past. So what had those three men possessed that he did not? More charm? Better looks? More money? He hadn't ever envied a dead man before now.

It was time to contact her father. Ill or not, the man needed to get on a steamship. The sooner E. M. Hyde arrived, the sooner he and Eva could arrive at some understanding about their future. Perhaps her father could talk some sense into her where Phillip had failed.

In the dining room he was greeted by an attendant and led to a square table on the far side. Mr. Hall rose and thrust out a hand. "Mansfield. Thank you for coming."

"Hello, Hall." They shook and Phillip lowered himself into a chair. "Nice to see you."

They placed orders for drinks and the waiter suggested the chef's fish special for lunch, to which they both agreed. When they were alone, Phillip let Hall steer the conversation, since he knew the direction they were headed and was in no hurry to get there.

"How is your mother?" Hall asked.

"Full of vim and vigor. She's in Newport now, tending to her garden and indoor plants." And lamenting the lack of grandchildren, no doubt. Phillip's sisters were not visiting this summer, one remaining in Chicago and the other traveling in Spain with her family. Perhaps he should pay a visit to his mother, who'd been suspiciously silent since his refusal to allow construction on the cottage.

"Mrs. Hall is anxious to return as well. What is it with women and the ocean air?"

"The same could be asked of men and their yachts."

Hall chuckled. "Too true. By the way, I have a new yacht this year. Sixty-five feet. She's a beauty. You should come down, take Becca for a sail."

"I'd like that," he said, not committing to anything.

"With my wife anxious to leave the city, I'll have no choice but to bring Rebecca with us to Newport. I do hope the two of you will continue your association in such a case."

"Of course. However, it might be tricky to schedule time away from New York, with the hotel construction under way." *And Eva in my bed.*

Hall placed his crystal glass on the white linen cloth and then folded his hands. "I have no easy way of asking this, so I'll be blunt. We are anxious to see Becca settled with you. The two of you make a fine match, and I couldn't ask for a better husband for my daughter. What can we do to move this forward?"

Phillip sat, momentarily stunned. He'd known this was coming, but not quite so baldly. Clearing his throat, he took a long swallow of wine and debated his answer. He decided forthrightness was called for in this situation. "I appreciate your regard. However, I must be honest. While I am fond of Miss Hall, I do not see a permanent match in our future."

The edges of the older man's mouth turned down, his mustache drooping. "Why not? Has she given you any indication that your suit would not be—?"

"No, no. Nothing like that. It's just that I'm not anxious to marry. Your daughter is aware of my feelings on the subject. Perhaps in a few years I'd be willing to reconsider."

"My daughter does not have a few years to wait." Eyes flashing, he leaned in. "You have monopolized her time and made it known you are courting her. Do you think another man will have her now?"

For Becca's sake, he certainly hoped not. "Her reputation is intact. We've been entirely circumspect in our behavior." He couldn't say the same for his behavior with Eva, which had been reckless from the start.

"Circumspection hardly matters and you know it. Other men will wonder why you never married her."

"Your daughter is strong. She will find someone who cares for her, who makes her happy."

The older man rocked back in his chair, jaw open slightly. "I cannot believe this. You are actually refusing."

"If you thought to browbeat me into marrying her, I am sorry to disappoint you. My mother's been attempting it for years and I've been able to resist her." And few were as fearsome as Ellen Mansfield.

"Perhaps I should speak with your mother. Appeal to her sense of societal responsibility."

Threatening him with his mother? *Really?* He lifted a shoulder. "You are welcome to try, but I fear her threats never work on me. Miss Hall and I have an understanding, one that works for both of us at the moment."

"What does that mean, an understanding?"

"Neither of us are keen on making this association permanent."

"Yes, but if we allowed young people to marry whom they wished, our society would fall apart. You, better than anyone, know how this works."

Indeed, Phillip knew. He'd grown up surrounded by the rules, by the tradition. Had selected the "right" type of girl to marry once upon a time . . . to disastrous results. This go around, he'd settled on an independent British aristocrat, one with ambition and intelligence. One who wanted neither marriage nor courting. A challenge, for certain, but Phillip was persistent when he set his sights on a goal.

And arguing for a loveless marriage because "that's the way it's always been done" was not enough, not in these days of progress and invention.

Perhaps society needs to catch up with modern ideals, he thought, surprising even himself.

The cocoon of New York society had always served him well. He'd profited hundreds of thousands of dollars off his contacts and connections, the investors in his hotel projects. The home in Newport, the mansion on Fifth Avenue, his yacht, all the Mansfield properties in the city . . . Much of his wealth and luxury had been derived from this so-called Knickerbocker society.

But were any of them happy?

Eva made him happy. When he was with her, he wasn't focused on the future or his legacy. Not even the family's standing concerned him. He could lose himself in her, and live in the moment for the first time in his entire life.

He took a sip of his drink. "I think young people should be allowed to decide their own matches."

Hall shook his head as if he'd just been given bad news. "Your mother would cringe to hear you speaking in such a manner. I expected better from you."

Irritation swept across the nape of Phillip's neck like talons. "It's nothing I haven't already expressed to my mother many times when she has tried to force me into a match."

The food arrived then, the waiters oblivious to the tension between the diners. Phillip rose and tossed his napkin on the table. "I believe I've lost my appetite. Thank you for lunch, Hall."

"This isn't finished, Mansfield. You've wronged my daughter and my family. There will be consequences."

Staring Hall directly in the eyes, he said softly, "You may certainly try, but I wouldn't advise it." With that, he headed for the exit.

He needed to find Rebecca. Fast.

JOE JERKED A thumb over his shoulder at the woman behind him. "Prince, you've got a guest."

Phillip glanced up from the heavy bag and dropped his arms. He'd kept his shirt on in anticipation of this meeting at McGirk's, not wanting to embarrass her with his near nakedness. He was happy to see she was on time.

"Rebecca, hello. Glad to see you arrived safely."

It was the middle of the afternoon and he'd asked her to come to the Bowery boxing hall. There was little chance of being recognized here.

"Hello." Becca's wide eyes surveyed the surroundings. "When your note said to meet you here, I hadn't really expected this to be a boxing hall." She cut him a look. "Or to find you boxing."

He lifted a shoulder. "I like the physicality of it."

"Why, Phillip Mansfield . . . I do believe you have a wild side."

The side of his mouth hitched. That sounded like something Eva might say. Would Eva like to see him box someday?

"May I try it?" Becca asked, eyeing the canvas bag.

"Boxing?" She nodded, and he said, "Perhaps in a moment. I need to first tell you about my lunch meeting."

Taking her elbow, he drew her into the shadows for privacy. He then related the conversation with her father, during which Becca's lips compressed tighter and tighter. When he finished, she appeared visibly shaken. "This is awful. Exactly what we feared," she whispered.

"Indeed. However, I can handle myself. I'm worried about *you*."

She inhaled deeply. "As am I. What am I going to do?"

"Has he hurt you? I don't like the idea of you staying in that house."

"He has not hurt me. But he's been . . . angry. More irrational than before."

He came to a swift decision. "I want to send you away. To Europe. Canada. Wherever you'd like to go, as long as it's far away from your father."

Hope flared in her irises but was quickly extinguished. "I cannot let you do that. It's too much, Phillip."

"I promise you, I can well afford it and I'd much rather give you money to escape than worry about you every day. What does she say?"

No need to explain to whom he referred. Becca chewed her bottom lip. "She wants to go. She's worried they will follow through in having me committed."

The way her father had acted today, Phillip would not dismiss the idea. "I share that concern."

She let out a shaky breath. "I have to admit, I never expected you to be so understanding about all of this. About my . . . choices."

He frowned. Was he seen as so staid, then? So inflexible and traditional? He well understood the pressures of society, of familial expectations. But Becca deserved happiness. Just because she'd taken an unconventional path did not mean she should be denied the right to love and commitment. The right to be treated equally—

Unconventional path . . . Equally. The words rang in his mind like a church bell. Isn't that exactly what he'd done to Eva, who had embarked on an unusual path herself?

He hadn't fully accepted it, this idea that she wanted to be an architect. By offering her his protection, his name, he'd thought to influence and guide her. He hadn't understood how important it was for her to remain her own person, to retain her individuality. To remain independent.

Yet he'd accepted Becca, trusted her to know her own mind.

The realization did not sit easy with him. With two sisters and a strong mother, he'd assumed he possessed a great deal of respect for women. Hell, he regularly donated to the Women's Suffrage Coalition of New York City. Except he hadn't shown that side to Eva; instead he'd discouraged her at every turn. And all she'd wanted was to be treated as an equal. Seen for her talent and not her gender.

He dragged a hand through his hair. Later. He could deal with this later. Right now, Becca was his first priority.

"Becca, whomever you love is none of my business. I only wish for you to be safe and happy. Neither of those things is possible here."

She rubbed her eyes with her fingers. "Fine. Europe then. I'll see about a boat next week—"

"Tonight. You must go tonight."

"I cannot possibly . . . There's too much to organize. What of my things?"

"Do you have any sentimental items that cannot be put in a carpetbag?"

Her brow furrowed. "No, none that I recall."

"Good. Go home and pack a light bag. No trunks, only one change of clothing. I'll have everything else you need sent ahead to the ship. As soon as I book two passages, you and she will come to the docks in a hackney. Do not give your family a way to track you."

"I cannot say good-bye or tell them I'm leaving?"

"I wouldn't recommend it. They may prevent you from meeting the ship. If you're committed to escaping New York, then cable them from Southampton when you arrive."

She nodded. "You're right, of course. This is all just so sudden."

"It's perfectly reasonable to feel overwhelmed, but I have every confidence in you, Becca. You'll be fine. I must be certain, however. This has to be what you want."

"To live openly and freely . . . with her? Of course that's what I want. I don't need to consider it."

"Excellent. Then return home and wait for my cable. My footman will be instructed not to hand it to anyone but you."

She touched his arm, emotion brimming in her eyes. "I will, and I cannot thank you enough. For everything. You have already done so much for me and I haven't a clue how I shall repay this kindness."

"No repayment necessary," he told her. "If you are happy and well, that is all the repayment I need."

Becca pushed up onto her toes and kissed his cheek. "You're a good man, Phillip Mansfield. I am so grateful our parents tried to push us together."

He laughed. "Me as well. Now, go. We'll be in touch."

Becca hurried from the boxing hall, leaving Phillip behind. He quickly strode to the dressing area. There were normally several steamships departing for England each day. He had to ensure Becca and her friend ended up aboard one. The sooner she left New York, the better.

That problem was easily solved. Eva, however, was another matter altogether. What they each wanted differed drastically and he wasn't certain how to bridge that gap.

Though he did owe her an apology for the closed-minded way he'd treated her.

Was this the reason she refused to let him court her? Would an admission of his behavior change her mind?

There was only one way to find out.

EVA DASHED DOWN the front steps, ready to hail a hackney, when the sight of a familiar elegant black carriage stopped her cold.

Phillip.

Before she could decide whether to turn around or ignore him, the door opened and his bulky frame emerged. A dark brown suit highlighted his tanned skin and rugged features, a delicious package no able-bodied female would be able to resist. Least of all her.

For the sake of your career, you must try.

Long strides brought him close, his coffee-colored eyes sweeping her pale green morning dress, heating every inch of her underneath her clothing. No one had ever affected her as he did, with the ability to liquefy her insides with one glance.

She swallowed, her tongue thick. Nothing would please her more than to throw herself in his arms and kiss him right here on the street. She had missed him the past two days. The short separation had only illustrated how important he'd become in her life.

He holds your future in his very hands—both personally and professionally.

Nora was right. The question was, could Eva trust him with both? Perhaps . . . but perhaps not. Could she bet her career and future happiness on such a gamble?

"Good morning." His tone was low and silky, his full mouth hitched in a purely masculine, purely arrogant, expression. He knew what he was doing to her, she realized, even as her nipples tightened inside her corset.

She lifted her chin. "Out for a drive?"

"No. I was waiting on you. Would you care for a ride to the construction site?"

"With you?"

His teeth, even and white, sparkled in the morning sun. "Yes, with me."

A quick peek revealed no hacks in the vicinity,

and wilting in the heat to prove a point hardly appealed. "All right. Thank you."

Within moments, he had her settled in the cool carriage interior and they set off for downtown. "Still upset with me?" he asked, stretching out his legs to brush against hers. Tingles erupted where they touched and she didn't immediately pull away. *You're a glutton for punishment,* she told herself.

"No," she answered, "as long as our conversation from the other evening is concluded."

"Does it bother you so much, the idea of me courting you?"

There was a hint of insecurity in his voice, one she hadn't heard before. "Not just you. Courting in general."

"Yet you've almost married three times."

"True, but that was before I knew what I'd be missing." And before her father's illness. He'd been the one to push for a marriage, not Eva. Now that his health had declined, losing her independence hardly seemed worth it.

"Ah, now we are getting somewhere. Tell me, please. What would you be missing out on if you married? Other men?"

"No!" The vehemence of her response took them both by surprise. She wished she could take it back, but there was no hope for it.

"Well, I'm certainly glad to hear that," he said a little too smugly. "I would hate to think I wasn't enough for you."

She thought of his large body poised over hers, hips rocking as his shaft tunneled deep, filling her. A flutter materialized in her lower abdomen.

No, he was more than enough for her. In fact, she doubted she'd ever tire of his lovemaking.

Another reason this affair was so dangerous.

She slid her legs away from him, breaking their contact. Even still, her skin burned, a phantom touch she already missed. Heavens, she was in trouble with this man.

"Who said the husband would be you?"

His lips pressed together and she couldn't tell if he was annoyed or trying not to laugh. In a flash, he shifted to her side of the bench, crowding her with his large frame. His knuckles swept gently over her jaw. "A man can hope. Besides, I know you care for me. You never would have agreed to sleep with me otherwise."

She opened her mouth to refute it, but could not force out the words to deny what they both knew as fact.

He continued, "And I'm not asking to marry you tomorrow. I'd merely like the opportunity to court you in public. Let everyone see that you're mine."

A dark thrill raced through her. Part of her liked that idea, of belonging to him. But she'd much rather belong to herself. Phillip Mansfield, the city's beloved prince, would overshadow her.

Then she thought of walking away from him. The idea twisted hard in her chest, made it nearly impossible to breathe. She couldn't end this, not now. What did that mean? Did she *love* him?

"And before you complain," he said, "this also allows everyone to see that I am yours. We're equals in this, Eva."

She hadn't considered that, and it did take the

sting out of the proposition. "Equals until marriage, in which case I cease to exist."

His palm cupped her jaw. "No, my dear woman. Marriage, in which case we join together to become something far greater than just ourselves." He bent his head, his mouth hovering directly above hers. His breath feathered over her lips, seductive and insidious. "I'll wait as long as necessary until you accustom yourself to the idea. Months. Years. However long you need."

"You are relentless," she whispered, her defenses crumbling like rotted wood.

"And be glad for it, considering your stubbornness."

Did he mean it? Could she honestly have him *and* a career of her own? The proposition sounded almost too good to be true. She would need to return to England, but hopefully not too soon. Her father was stable and well cared for so, barring another injury, she had at least another month here. "You'll not pressure me to marry you?"

He shook his head. "No pressure—but that doesn't mean I've changed my mind. I'll never give up on you, Eva."

The words wrapped around her heart, a fragile hope that took root in her soul. She believed him, heard the truth in his voice, this man who'd never lied to her. The weight of her own lies dimmed her happiness slightly—and she decided then to finally tell him the truth. She could not begin this new stage in their relationship with the weight of her lies between them. As soon as they finished checking over the construction site, she would take him to Twenty-Fourth Street and reveal everything about her father and how the hotel plans were truly hers.

She shifted, tilting her head to kiss him, their mouths meeting and opening as she melted against him. Soft lips worked over hers, his tongue invading to stroke her own, the familiar taste of him sending a buzz beneath her skin, scorching. Burning. She would never grow tired of this, the way he made her feel.

He groaned, a deep rumbling sound, and she tried to get closer. She was restless, her hands testing the meat of his shoulders, the flat planes of his chest, the ridges of his ribs . . . anywhere she could reach. She wanted to clamber onto his lap and lift her skirts . . .

The carriage stopped, breaking through her haze. Had they arrived already? Perhaps he'd be willing to ask his driver to take another turn—

A sound outside caught her attention. Was that chanting? The words sounded angry. Spoken by a large group of men.

Leaning forward she looked through the carriage window. That's when she saw the signs and the mob gathered just outside the construction site.

"Oh, my God." She clutched his arm. "Phillip, the workers are on strike!"

Chapter Sixteen

A goddamn disaster. The entire thing was a goddamn disaster.

Phillip paced, so furious he wanted to kill someone. In fact, if not for Eva's cool head, he very well might have.

Workers lined the long block in front of the construction site, chanting over "unfair" working conditions.

A fucking lie.

The conditions were far better than anywhere else. His workers were treated fairly, paid a living wage and not pennies, as some of these construction projects often did. He gave them time off. They were a diverse group, from all walks of life, hired based on ability and not any preconceived notion about ethnicity. Working conditions were safe and injuries generously compensated.

How, exactly, was that unfair?

He watched as Carew darted across Fifth Avenue, to where Phillip had been waiting for the past twenty minutes, banished. Eva had taken one look at his face upon arrival and dragged him to the opposite side of the street to cool down before making the situation worse.

Probably wise, but definitely not his style. This hotel was his baby, his masterpiece. The future of the Mansfield name. Allowing others to resolve any crisis underfoot rankled. Still, he was willing to trust her on this. Temporarily.

"Mr. Mansfield, any comment on the strike?"

He glanced down and found a reporter waiting, a journal and pencil in his hand. *New York Citizen*, if memory served. "No comment."

Eva suddenly stepped in front of the reporter and steered him away from Phillip. "Hello, Mr. Murphy, is it? We have no comment at this time, but Mr. Mansfield will cable you with a printable quote before the afternoon edition goes to press."

Murphy tipped his hat. "Thank you, ma'am. Just doin' my job."

"Bloodsuckers," Phillip muttered as the reporter skulked away. "And how did you know his name?"

"He asked a question at the press conference when we broke ground." She said this as if the answer were obvious. "Now, are you ready to hear what Alfred has learned, or are you going to continue snarling at everyone?"

He ignored the jab and faced Carew. "Well?"

Carew cleared his throat, wiped his forehead with a linen handkerchief. "I thought it might have something to do with me but, when pressed, it comes down to one issue. They're opposed to having a woman on the site."

Phillip swore creatively, raising brows from both

Eva and his engineer. Eva put a hand on his arm, addressing Carew. "How is that an unfair working condition?"

"Same thing Milliken's always claimed. That it's dangerous and distracting."

"Christ," Phillip muttered and dragged a hand through his hair. "That is ridiculous."

"The union is citing the three recent injuries as examples."

"But I wasn't even there!" Eva exclaimed. In the past two weeks, three men had suffered various injuries. Eva hadn't been present during any of them.

"This is ridiculous," Phillip repeated. "I cannot believe the union is allowing this. I should fire every man out here picketing and hire scabs to finish the job."

"I, uh . . ." Carew wiped his brow once more. "I ascertained that someone powerful is behind the union's decision. Someone with a grudge against you."

Fuck. Keene and the boys at Tammany Hall. Phillip would bet his life on it.

A carriage rolled to a stop at the curb. Gabriel, his assistant, exited first, followed by a well-dressed man. Mr. Frank Tripp was Phillip's longtime attorney, one of the best in the city. Placing his derby on his head, Tripp cast a glance at the chaos across the street before joining Phillip and the others. "Now I see the urgency of your cable," he said, shaking Phillip's hand. "You've got quite a mess on your hands."

"Frank Tripp, this is Miss Ashford, the architect's representative, and Mr. Carew, my superintendent. Mr. Tripp is my attorney," he told Eva and Carew.

Handshakes were traded and then Carew filled Tripp in on what they'd learned about the reasons behind the strike. "Ah. So you're the trouble-maker?" Tripp said to Eva, a teasing smile on his face.

"She's done nothing wrong," Phillip snapped, even more irritated for some reason. "The whole thing is Tammany's ploy to get me to buckle to their demands." Milliken's betrayal in participating in the strike was another matter altogether. Phillip would be having harsh words with his general contractor at his first opportunity.

"And what were these demands?" Tripp asked.

"To hire their crews for the job instead of bringing others in from the outside."

"They're clearly hoping you'll use their scabs to break the lines and get work back under way."

"That's my assumption, but I have absolutely no intention of doing so."

"But that doesn't explain why Milliken is striking. Wouldn't he want to keep his own workers on the job?" Eva asked.

"Unless he's being paid handsomely to strike by this powerful backer," Carew said.

Tripp held up a hand. "Let's deal with the immediate problems first. We need to get some Pinkertons down here to keep the peace and guard the site. You don't want another B&O strike on your hands."

The B&O Railway strike in '77 had been long

and bloody. Thousands of workers had laid waste to materials, buildings, and equipment, and then resisted the federal troops brought in to secure the peace. The idea of it happening here caused a shiver to run down Phillip's spine. Looking to his secretary, he said, "Gabriel, inform the Pinkerton office of what's happening. Hire as many as they deem necessary."

The young man nodded, writing the directive down in a small pad.

"Good," Tripp said. "Now, I think we should sit down and try to negotiate as soon as possible."

Eva spoke up. "I agree—and I'd like to be the one at the table."

"Absolutely not," Phillip instantly replied. "Why would we put the very issue they object to at the table?"

"Wait a minute, Mansfield." Tripp held up a hand. "I'd like to hear the lady's reasoning. Why would you be the best person to iron this out, Miss Ashford?"

"People fear what they don't know. If we show them I am competent and reasonable, they'll back down."

"You hope," Phillip said. "That is a huge gamble on a very expensive project."

She angled toward him, her expression serious. "I have a lot to lose, every bit as much as you do, if this falls through."

"I highly doubt that."

Hurt flashed over her features before she masked it. "If you don't send me, they'll assume it's because you agree with them, that you believe I'm not capable of doing my job. The only way to show them they're wrong is to let me be there."

Tripp chuckled. "Oh, I like this woman. You are as devious as they come, Miss Ashford." High praise coming from Tripp, who could wriggle his way out of any legal argument known to man.

Phillip ignored his attorney and addressed Eva. "I still don't care for the idea. How do you know they'll even agree to a meeting if you're involved?"

"They'll have no choice," Eva said, her chin lifting with confidence. "When they see who we hire as scabs, they'll be anxious to get back to work."

He was almost afraid to ask. "And who are we hiring?"

"I don't want to say just yet. I need to do some research, see if the idea is even plausible."

A knot formed in Phillip's stomach. This situation was careening out of his control, and he didn't care for it. Not one bit. "Do not do anything without my approval."

"Of course," she said sweetly. Too sweetly. "I wouldn't dream of it, Mr. Mansfield."

Tripp tried to hold back a laugh and failed. Phillip scowled at him and his attorney instantly sobered. "Right. Seems we all have a bit to do. I'll get started on an injunction to demand the workers cease striking or risk being fired. I've got a few judges who owe me favors so I should have it signed by tonight. Keep me posted on any developments. We should try to resolve this in the next day or so, to keep the bad press to a minimum."

"We'll handle the press from my end," Phillip said, nodding at Gabriel. "And believe me, I want this resolved as quickly as possible. Every day the work is stopped pushes us that much further from meeting our deadline."

"I understand. Good day, all. I'll be in touch."

"Thank you, Frank," Phillip said, extending his hand.

"Of course, though this is the reason you pay me a ridiculous amount of money." After shaking hands with everyone, Tripp disappeared into the waiting carriage and drove off.

"Gabriel and I will return to my office. May I drop either of you along the way?"

"Think I'll stick around and keep an eye on things here," Carew said.

That was smart. "Just send word if you need help. Miss Ashford?"

"No, thank you. But before you go, may I speak with you a moment, privately?"

Though he itched to do something, Phillip sent Gabriel ahead in his carriage. At least then the Pinkertons could be dispatched before the situation grew out of hand. Carew excused himself and wandered down the block, out of earshot.

Exhaling, Phillip scrubbed his face with his hands. This project had been cursed from the start. He hadn't known building in his own backyard would turn into such a headache. Boston and Chicago had been nothing like this.

"Phillip, I'm terribly sorry." Eva touched his forearm. "I never dreamed anything like this would happen."

That made two of them. "I know. No one is blaming you."

"How could they not? I'm the reason the workers are unhappy."

"No, you're merely an excuse. This is about Tammany Hall trying to strong-arm me into doing what they want."

A ghost of a smile passed over her face. "They don't know how stubborn you are, apparently."

"Apparently not. Any chance you'll tell me what you're planning?"

"No. It's just an idea, and I need to see if it'll work first."

"I don't like you keeping secrets from me."

Her eyes widened, almost panicked, but she quickly masked it. "I promise to tell you everything when the time is right."

"Everything? Meaning, there are other secrets?"

"Let's straighten this mess out first, then we can work on us."

Something in his chest loosened, the dread easing just a little. Remarkable, this power she held over him. Leaning in, he said softly, "I like the sound of that, working on us. I'm holding you to that promise."

A blush worked its way over her throat, the pulse in her neck hammering. "And I'm holding you to your promise as well, that we'll be equals in whatever happens."

"I wouldn't have it any other way, my dear."

IT TOOK HER two days but Eva finally managed to organize a very specific group of workers. An all-female construction crew.

With Nora's help, she had rallied every woman

in New York City, Brooklyn, and New Jersey with the ability to hold a hammer to come to the Mansfield Hotel construction site. They had started with the women's associations and word had quickly spread. Any woman was welcome, whether she had experience or not. The point was to send a message to the men outside, the men who refused to work because the architect was a woman.

So let them see how eager women were to take their jobs.

That morning, the Pinkerton agents, as well as the city's police, held the striking crew members aside to let the women pass, Eva at the front of the line. Curses and rocks rained down on them, but each woman remained firm, her chin high. They had known what to expect, the hate and vitriol the men would spew, and they were ready for it.

You whores!

Go back home, cunt!

Stupid fucking cows!

Eva tried not to flinch at the words, even as a particularly large stone bounced off her shoulder. She refused to let them see her rattled. Nor did she want to give Phillip any reason to doubt her plan.

He was here somewhere, having insisted on accompanying the women through the picket lines. She suspected this was mostly an effort on his part not to let her out of his sight. He hadn't wanted her to participate today, preferring instead to keep her far away from the chaos, but she had remained firm. This was her fight as much as his.

Perhaps more so.

Once through the gates of the construction site,

she led the group to one side. All told, there were about seventy-five women. Some stared at the big machinery nervously, while others eyed it with an eager gleam. The men continued to chant and yell on the other side of the fence, so Eva raised her voice. "Thank you all for coming. Most of what we're doing today is digging and hauling dirt. Take breaks as necessary and drink adequate amounts of water. Anyone have experience with a steam shovel?"

One woman's hand went up. "I do, miss," she called out. "Drove one nearly like it on my father's farm."

Eva pointed to her. "You're up there, then. Anyone else?" No one raised their hand, so she let it go for now. Perhaps they could teach someone else at some point.

"I'll take another one," Carew said, now at Eva's elbow. She hadn't seen him yet this morning and hadn't known if the engineer would approve of this plan.

She smiled gratefully at him. "Thank you, Alfred."

He ducked his head, almost embarrassed, and started for the far side of the excavation, where another steam shovel awaited. Eva quickly put the women to work. None complained, all eager to earn a decent day's wage. Spirits were high, even in the hot sun.

Phillip hardly stopped moving. Throughout the day, he talked with groups of women, demonstrated the safest way to accomplish a task—even helped haul dirt on the ladders at one point. The women seemed to like him, their grins wider, posture a bit straighter when he was near. One woman fanned herself when he turned away.

Eva well understood the feeling. The man was too handsome by half.

This also allows everyone to see that I am yours.

Hers. She quite liked the sound of that. A lot, in fact.

It was a lost cause. She had officially fallen for Phillip Mansfield.

The idea settled in, her chest filling with happiness and possibility, with none of her usual panic. By the way he kept stealing glances at her today, giving her secret, knowing smiles, she suspected he might feel the same.

Could her luck finally be turning after all?

As the sun lowered in the sky, shadows lengthened around the surrounding buildings, stripes of burnt orange over the ground. Eva was explaining to a small number of workers how the foundation would soon be poured, the metal framing that would shore up the skyscraper, when four men walked through the main gate. Mr. Milliken and three men she recognized as union representatives.

Excusing herself from the ladies, Eva approached them. "Good afternoon, gentlemen. Have you come to check on today's progress? As you can see, the new workers are quite competent."

Milliken said nothing, merely stared down his crooked nose at her. One of the men stuck his hand out. "Miss Ashford, I am Mr. John Debs, head of the union for the workers outside. Perhaps you and Mr. Mansfield would be willing to meet with us."

Giddiness fluttered in her chest, though she tried not to show any reaction. This was better than she'd even hoped for. The union was already caving, ready to come to the bargaining table to hammer out the issues. The idea of women stealing their jobs must have been the slap in the face she'd intended. "When?"

"Two hours? We'll meet you at the Fifth Avenue Hotel."

"I shall ensure Mr. Mansfield and I arrive on time."

Debs nodded and then led the group back out of the construction site. She could still hear the noise from the men on the other side of the gate. Would they all return home now, or wait to yell at the women on their way out?

She assumed the latter.

"Was that Debs?" Phillip arrived at her side slightly out of breath. "What did he say?"

"They want to meet with us in two hours' time at the Fifth Avenue Hotel. I think they are ready to negotiate."

Phillip's brow wrinkled. "What makes you think that? Did he say anything about a negotiation?"

"No, but he said they wanted to meet with you and me."

He stroked his jaw thoughtfully and stared off into the distance.

She said, "I thought you'd be happier about it. It means this is over."

"Means nothing of the sort. If they were ready to discuss terms, then why not include attorneys? They know Tripp will handle the contracts."

"Maybe they assume you and I are capable. That lawyers aren't necessary."

He gave a noncommittal sound. "I still wish to invite Tripp. What time are we sending the women home?"

"Best to do it now, while it's light outside. Many have a long journey ahead of them."

Reaching out, he swept blunt fingertips over her jaw. "I don't know how you accomplished this in such a short amount of time, but you have my thanks."

Warmth settled in her veins in a rush of tender affection. She adored this man. "We're all eager to get Milliken's crew working again. But perhaps you'll pay the women extra? I had promised them at least two days' wages."

"I'll make good on that promise. I'm a man of my word." His dark gaze sparkled, the clear reference to their courting bargain not lost on her. "I'll find Carew and the Pinkertons. We'll set up a table, pay the women, and then load them into the wagons."

"Excellent." She beamed up at him. "I'll round them up."

THE FIFTH AVENUE Hotel loomed across from Madison Square Park, its plain Italianate brick façade stretching across the entire block. The outside was large and handsome, but by no means beautiful or whimsical. *Boring* was the word that came to Phillip's mind.

He knew his new hotel would easily outshine this one, with his offering unprecedented luxury and grandeur—both inside *and* out. He had E. M. Hyde to thank for that.

While Eva had worked magic on an all-female crew, Phillip had been seeing to Becca, securing her passage on a transatlantic steamship. He'd instructed Lord & Taylor to deliver a month's worth of dresses and personal items for both women to the ship, and he'd provided money to get them started in Europe as well as a place to stay. The Mansfields owned a house in the French countryside and he'd given Becca leave to use it until the two women found their own home.

No word from her father yet, but Phillip expected a visit imminently.

One problem at a time, he told himself.

The carriage stopped. He alighted then assisted Eva down. Her gloved hand curled around his fingers, the contact burning straight through him. He was looking forward to the conclusion of this meeting, after which he planned to steal her away—

"Exactly on time," he heard Frank Tripp say from behind him.

Tucking Eva close, he regarded his attorney. "Thank you for coming. I hope to put all this to rest tonight."

"I bet. How did your stunt go over today?" He glanced from Eva to Phillip. "Any riots break out?"

"No riots," Eva answered with a lift of her shoulder. "Merely rocks and insults. Nothing we couldn't handle. The men seemed quite unhappy, however, so I am hopeful the union will be ready to negotiate."

"Suppose we'll find out in a minute." Tripp's arm swept out. "After you."

Under the portico, they strolled through the front door. At a small desk, he found an attendant and introduced himself. "Yes, Mr. Mansfield. I've been instructed to bring you this way."

The three fell into line behind the attendant, and Phillip assumed they would be led into the dining room. Instead, they were shown through one of the common areas to a broad, private corridor with two sofas positioned adjacent to one another at the corner. Three men sat waiting, one of who was Milliken.

"Ho, the Amen Corner," Tripp muttered.

"What does that mean?" Eva asked softly.

Phillip leaned down. "It's said every big deal in the city is concluded in this spot. One must come to the city's political powers and get an 'amen' on your project—or it won't go through."

"So that's good for us, right?"

Phillip couldn't say. Meeting here, instead of over drinks or dinner, did not lend itself to an air of relaxation or lingering. The union reps expected the meeting to be short . . . but why?

He tightened his hold on Eva's hand where it rested on his arm. Whatever happened, he would not back down. As the architect's representative, she had the right to inspect the work done on the site.

Even still, he'd cabled E. M. Hyde again yesterday. The sooner the architect arrived, the better.

The other gentlemen stood, hands extended. Everyone was quickly introduced, the two union reps all smiles, while Milliken wore his usual sullen expression. Phillip, Eva, and Tripp sat on one sofa with Debs, Gray, and Milliken on the other. The configuration was intimate, the sofa edges nearly touching in the corner.

"Thank you for coming down to meet with us tonight," Debs said. "Quite a spectacular stunt you pulled off today."

Phillip lifted a shoulder. "We found a group of workers eager to earn a day's pay rather than stand about complaining. And the women will return as many days as we need them, if the men refuse to work."

Debs held up his palms. "Now, no one is refusing anything. Our men simply want a safe, respectable space in which to labor. Hardly seems a lot to ask for."

"It is when my architect's representative is no longer allowed on the property."

"Yes, let's speak of your architect and his representative. Mr. Gray?"

Phillip braced himself. Had they learned Eva's true identity? If so, did they hope he would fire her? More fool them, as he'd been aware of her connection to E. M. Hyde almost since they'd disembarked.

The other union official opened a satchel and began withdrawing papers. "Are you aware of Miss Ashford's background?"

Eva bristled beside him. "I hardly see how this is—"

"Tell me, what is her background?" Phillip remained calm. If this was the worst of it, then they'd have a resolution in minutes.

"Well, for starters," Gray said, holding out a piece of paper, "her name is not Ashford at all. She's actually the daughter of E. M. Hyde, Lord Cassell. A real English lady."

Phillip didn't even bother reading the paper. "If you were hoping to surprise me, I'm afraid to disappoint you. I've known Lady Eva's identity from the beginning."

The men gave no outward reaction. "We suspected you might," Gray said. "There are so many rumors going around, it is hard to keep them all straight."

Rumors? About what, exactly? Phillip wasn't certain, but he suspected this was a thinly veiled reference to the affair. His fingers curled into fists. If someone dared allude to anything improper . . .

"More important is the information we discovered on her father," Debs said.

He frowned. This he hadn't expected. "What about E. M. Hyde?"

Gray removed more papers from the satchel. "We have signed affidavits here from the physicians that have been caring for his lordship in London." He presented a set. "E. M. Hyde is incapacitated. Alive, but incapacitated. Completely unable to work and has been for some time. Some say for at least sixteen months."

Chapter Seventeen

The news hit Phillip like a punch to the jaw. "Sorry, incapacitated?"

"You had no right to look into my father's affairs," Eva snapped to the union representatives. "And I doubt the validity of those affidavits."

"They are quite legal, my lady," Debs drawled. "Perhaps Mr. Tripp would care to verify them?"

Gray handed Tripp the packet of papers while Phillip tried to get a handle on the conversation. Eva's father . . . unable to work? And for the past sixteen months?

No, that made no sense whatsoever.

They had to be mistaken. If Hyde were incapacitated, then whom had he been dealing with this entire time? "You are wrong," he told the other men. "I have correspondence. Furthermore, I have his signature on the contract as well as on the plans approved by the city."

"Clear forgeries, most likely by the woman who has presented her work as his own for almost two years now."

"Presented her work as his?" He chuckled and shook his head. "She would not do such a dishonorable thing."

When no one else joined in, his amusement quickly faded. Eva remained mute, her lips pressed tightly, and a sense of foreboding crawled along his spine. Why wasn't she disputing these outlandish allegations?

"These look completely legal to me," Tripp said, handing Phillip the affidavits. "Perhaps they are telling the truth."

"This cannot be the truth. If it is . . ." He shifted to better see her, his throat tight with dread and confusion. "If this is true then you drew up the plans for the hotel and passed them off as your father's."

Eva shot to her feet, a murderous gaze fixed on the union representatives. "You did not come here with any intention to negotiate. You merely wished to stir the hornet's nest."

Debs raised his hands, placating. "We merely thought everyone ought to have the same information when we sit down to resolve this strike. You cannot blame us for that."

"This meeting is over," Phillip snarled, his voice laced with menace. The world had just gone topsyturvy on him and he required a minute to think this through. Debs and Gray would need to gloat elsewhere. "We're done for today."

Everyone stood, except him. Tripp led the union representatives out of the corridor, Milliken silently trailing behind. Eva took a step away from the sofa, as if she planned to leave.

"Do not even think about it. You owe me answers,"

he said, his attention squarely on the carpet. His stomach roiled with a heavy weight he'd never thought to experience ever again. *Goddamn it.* Why hadn't he insisted on meeting with E. M. Hyde in person? If he'd pushed harder then he would have discovered the truth.

How easily he'd believed her lies. Dazzled by her beauty and fire, he hadn't even questioned them. She must have laughed quite heartily at him, at how stupidly he'd behaved.

Jaw tight, he tilted his head and fixed her with a stare. "Well?"

"I was going to tell you." She folded her hands in front of her, fingers knotted until the knuckles turned white. Apprehension?

Apprehension she'd been caught, no doubt.

"When, exactly, were you going to tell me? After I put his name on the cornerstone?"

"I know you won't believe this, but I had planned to tell you tonight."

He crossed his legs and brushed imaginary lint from his trousers, struggling to gain control over his emotions. "You're right. I don't believe you. You've had ample opportunity for weeks to tell me and yet you chose to keep it a secret. Indeed, why ruin a good thing by letting me in on your swindle?"

"This was *not* a swindle. I did not lie to you out of malice. My intentions were good—and you loved the designs I presented you with."

"Designs drawn by your own hand." He needed to hear her say it.

She straightened her shoulders, standing taller. "Yes. I sketched the entire thing."

"And put his name on it. Tell me, how long has it been since he's been able to work?"

"Twenty-two months since he's drawn or sketched anything useful."

Right before Phillip had reached out to offer the hotel project.

Christ. What a fucking mess. His skin felt as if it were on fire, the anger a living, breathing storm barely contained inside him. This was far worse than what Caroline had done to him. Eva had not only humiliated him, she'd taken this project—the hotel to bear his name and serve as his legacy—and ruined it. He'd never be able to step inside it without remembering this awful feeling.

Betrayal.

That was all he could see, taste, and smell right now.

"But he grew increasingly forgetful a few years before that," she added. "I do apologize for deceiving you, Phillip. It was wrong of me to do so. But I knew you'd never give me a chance if you knew the truth."

"You're right. This was to be the only E. M. Hyde–designed hotel in America. You've stolen that appeal. No one will come to New York to stay in a hotel designed by Lady Eva Hyde."

"They'll stay in the hotel because it's the finest there is—regardless of the architect."

"You are wrong. Furthermore, not only have you robbed me of your father's cachet, you've made me a laughingstock in my own city. Everyone will learn of how you duped me, the lies that you've told."

"Not if you don't tell them."

Don't tell them? His mouth fell open slightly. "If

you think the union representatives will keep this secret, they absolutely will not. They've probably spread word to all the newspapers by now."

"That's not what I mean. You could say you willingly hired me. That you were aware of my father's condition and, knowing he could not design your hotel, asked me to do so instead."

"Even if I were so inclined to join in your parade of lies, it would be hard for anyone to believe that story when E. M. Hyde's signature is all over the official paperwork."

"Not when my initials are also E. M. Hyde. Eva Margaret Hyde."

How convenient for her. He pinched the bridge of his nose between his thumb and forefinger. While that solution might help him salvage a bit of his pride, it did not solve what upset him most: her lying to him.

Hell, he'd wanted to court her. To *marry* her. And he hadn't known a damn thing about her.

Just like Caroline.

Agitation drove him to his feet. His chest heaved, air bellowing in and out of his lungs, muscles clenched with the urge to hit something. "I need to know why. When you decided to take on the project in his stead and lie to me, tell me why you did it."

"We needed the money."

He stopped short. "That cannot be. Your father is one of the best-known architects in Europe. Additionally, I know what he's been compensated for other jobs. I researched his income before making an offer. He's exceedingly wealthy."

She drew in a shaky breath. "No, he's not. Over the years, he spent nearly as much as he made. All our remaining savings have gone to doctors and treatments. We are in dire straits. I have been accepting small jobs under his name just to keep us afloat."

If that were true, Hyde was an idiot. He'd been paid handsomely in the past twenty years. More than handsomely, in fact.

And, while Phillip found the story sad, it did not excuse what she'd done. Not by a long shot.

"And here I was, your goose laying golden eggs."

"I never thought that. I desperately wanted this job and worked incredibly hard on my designs. To imagine something so luxurious and timeless was a challenge and I did not want to disappoint you . . . or those familiar with my father's style."

She had succeeded. The design definitely honored her father's legacy, not that Phillip would admit it now. "Let's not forget you had one other reason to lie. Passing your work off as your father's conveniently allowed you to skirt your reputation."

She swallowed, but acknowledged the hit with a dip of her chin. "That's true. It's doubtful anyone would hire an architect dubbed Lady Unlucky."

Including Phillip. Damn it, he should've sent her packing the instant he learned of her identity. His gut had told him a woman in such a position of power was a mistake, yet he'd let their history and his desire dissuade him from firing her. *Idiot.*

God knew the workers would never come back once they heard her moniker. They'd believe the worksite was cursed.

He could hardly blame them. He was beginning to believe it himself.

Eva took that opportunity to move closer. The hem of her dress brushed the top of his boot as she laid a hand on his arm—causing him to freeze. "Phillip, I know this is a shock and I deeply apologize for lying to you. I never meant to hurt you or the hotel."

"I don't believe you." Her eyes widened in surprise and she opened her mouth to argue. He moved away and her hand slipped from his arm. "Oh, I believe you didn't want to disrupt construction or affect the job you so desperately needed. But you didn't give a damn about me. If you did, you wouldn't have lied to me. No wonder you pretended to abhor marriage. I guess I should be grateful you didn't trick me into marrying you as well."

"I did not pretend to abhor marriage. Everything I said was the truth. I have no intention of ever marrying and giving up my career."

"So sleeping with me was just a way of keeping the boss happy in case he discovered your secret? Christ, was anything between us real?"

She sent a nervous glance down the corridor, presumably to ensure they were alone. He didn't give a damn; he wanted answers. "That is not why I slept with you. Everything between us was—is—real. Utterly inconvenient and absolutely real. I've . . . fallen for you."

The declaration irritated him. He didn't trust anything she said. She was angling to keep her position, no doubt. To not lose out on the chance to see her design realized. She'd say anything to placate him, wouldn't she?

And while she might not weep and cajole as Caroline had, Eva saw him as the means to an end . . . just like his former fiancée.

Failure washed over him, like a thousand tiny stings, burning his insides. "Admit it. You knew who I was aboard the ship. That's why you followed me to the dining room, to start getting into my good graces in case I learned about your father."

She shifted back, hurt flashing over her face. "You know that is not true. I had no idea who you were on the ship."

"I wish I believed that. But I cannot tell what's true anymore when it comes to you." Tenderness no longer accompanied the memories of that night in his cabin. She had destroyed those as well.

"Phillip—"

"Stop, Eva. Just stop talking. I do not care to hear any more lies—"

"I am not lying," she protested. "Not any longer. You must believe me."

He could not take this. The desire to escape, to get far away, rushed through him. He needed time to sort through all of this and begin to fix the damage she'd caused. The work came first.

Steeling himself, he snapped, "You are not to return to the construction site until further notice. I shall discuss my legal options with Tripp and how I might best proceed. You will hear from him as to my decision."

"Phillip, you cannot possibly—"

"Wrong. I can do whatever I damn well please when it comes to saving this project. You'd do well to remember that."

He spun on his heel and departed Amen Corner, feeling anything but blessed.

SO MUCH FOR trust. So much for equals.

Eva struggled to retain her composure as she waited in Mrs. Mansfield's reception room. Reminders of Phillip surrounded her, even here in Newport. Photographs, paintings, bric-a-brac . . . the great Mansfield legacy loomed large over Stoneacre's every square inch.

Eva hadn't wallowed since yesterday's disastrous meeting. Instead, she'd spent each waking minute on Mrs. Mansfield's design, desperate for any task to take her mind off Phillip and the hotel.

She should have told him the truth, of course. Hoping he wouldn't discover her secret had been a risk from the moment she'd arrived in New York. And she didn't blame him for being angry. Now she lived in constant fear of being discharged, awaiting the papers from Frank Tripp that would terminate their agreement.

Stupid, but she'd never expected him to turn his back on her.

I will discuss my legal options with Tripp . . . You will hear from him as to my decision.

So he didn't plan to ever speak to her again?

A lump rose in her throat and she forced it down. Feeling sorry for herself solved nothing. Phillip would either forgive her or he wouldn't. He would either take her to court or he wouldn't. He would allow her back on the site or he wouldn't. She couldn't control any of that.

The one thing she knew for certain? Their affair

was over. For good. She had expressed her feelings, told him she'd come to care for him . . . and it hadn't mattered to him. The timing hadn't been perfect, but she meant those words, words she'd never spoken to another man in her life. And he hadn't believed her.

Now they were done. The ache in her heart felt a mile wide. Their last conversation played over and over in her head, compiling the hurt and the guilt. If only she'd done things differently . . .

Mistakes last forever, her father had often said. *That's why you must get it right the first time.*

She'd always assumed he meant measurements, not relationships. Yet another mistake to add to the list.

"Miss Ashford, this is quite a surprise." Mrs. Mansfield swept into the room. "I am anxious to see what you have come up with."

Eva blew out a long breath, clutched her satchel tighter. "And I am anxious to show you."

A maid entered and set up tea while Mrs. Mansfield bade Eva to sit on the sofa. "Now," she said as she poured, "why don't you show me what you've done."

Clearing her throat, Eva accepted a cup and saucer from the older woman. No reason to beat around the bush. She might as well get right to it. "Before we get to the designs, there is something I need to share. My name is not truly Miss Ashford."

Mrs. Mansfield paused, her eyes rounding. "No?"

"I am Lady Eva Hyde, the daughter of E. M. Hyde, Lord Cassell."

"Well." Phillip's mother sat back and sipped her tea. "I hadn't expected that. I thought you were going to tell me you were unwilling to continue on the project."

"No, definitely not," Eva rushed out. "That is, unless you cannot forgive my duplicity and would prefer to work with another architect."

"Goodness, no, though I am curious why you used a different name. Was it because of that Lady Unlucky nonsense?"

"So you've heard."

"Of your deceased fiancés? Yes. Circumstances beyond your control from what I understand. Does my son know?"

"Yes, he knows. When I arrived, he was reticent about allowing me to stay on in my father's stead, so I suggested the secondary name to conceal my identity from the crew."

"Clever of you, though I am surprised Phillip bought into any of that superstition. He's usually levelheaded, unless his temper is provoked."

Eva needed no reminders of Phillip's temper. There had been enough demonstrations of that at the Fifth Avenue Hotel.

Now she had to confess the rest, lest Mrs. Mansfield find out from her son.

"You should know he has removed me from the Mansfield Hotel project. The laborers have gone on strike, claiming my presence led to unsafe working conditions—"

Forehead creased, Mrs. Mansfield set her cup and saucer down with a snap. "And Phillip sided with them? That hardly seems fair. I will speak with him immediately. He cannot possibly allow that to stand."

"With all due respect, he learned something else that upset him. You see, my father has been ill for some time. His mind is failing him. I have been accepting and carrying out jobs in his stead for the last two years."

"Oh, dear. That includes . . ."

"Yes, that includes Phillip's hotel. He was most unhappy to learn that the E. M. Hyde who designed the hotel was me, not my father."

The older woman's gaze brimmed with sympathy. Eva found that puzzling. Shouldn't Mrs. Mansfield side with her own son, instead of Eva? Based on the other woman's unforgiving reputation, Eva half expected to be shown the door at this point.

"My son hates to be deceived, especially by a woman. Harkens back to years ago, so try to not take it personally. He will come around, Lady Eva."

Unlikely. He'd stared at her with utter disgust—and with good reason. She had deceived him more than once. How could they both move forward after that? "Please, just Eva will do."

"Then you must call me Ellen." The older woman smiled kindly. "Now, was there anything else I need to know before we get started?"

"Then you're still planning on moving forward with me?"

Ellen rocked back slightly, as if surprised. "Of course, my dear. You've been forthright with me and I daresay I appreciate working with a woman. And if your work was able to fool my son into thinking you were E. M. Hyde, then you are quite talented indeed. I shall be proud to tell the world the new house was designed by Lady Eva Hyde."

A hot, stinging sensation started behind her eyes and Eva blinked rapidly. Relief flooded her, making her both weepy and incredibly grateful. She hadn't realized how on edge she'd been, expecting to be sacked from this project, too. "Thank you," she managed.

"Oh, no thanks are necessary. Women do not have an easy time of it in our world, especially for those who possess a modicum of ambition. Any tiny amount of help I can lend is heartening. Incidentally, what do you plan to do about the hotel?"

Eva lifted a shoulder. "Wait to hear from Phillip, I suppose. Or his attorney, Mr. Tripp."

The other woman dropped her pearls and reached for her teacup. "That almost sounds like giving up. While we do not know one another well, I have the impression that you don't surrender easily. So, why now? Why not fight for what you want?"

Because her heart was bruised right along with her pride. She hadn't developed feelings for an employer before and the situation was all tangled up in her mind. Anger, regret, hurt . . . the combination was overwhelming. "I'm not certain our relationship can be salvaged."

The word slipped out before Eva thought better of it. Phillip's mother showed no hint of surprise, however, her face a mask of cool reserve. "Anything may be salvaged if it is valuable enough. If this is something you want, then take matters into your own hands and make it happen."

Did she mean with Phillip or the hotel job? "Resolve the strike myself, you mean?"

"If that is what it takes to set things right. Tell me, why are they striking?"

"The union claims my presence causes an unsafe working environment. They want a man to take my place."

"For heaven's sake, men are so confusing. They respect their mothers and daughters, sisters and grandmothers. But any other woman is unqualified and unworthy. It makes no sense. Are we not all someone's mother or daughter?"

A valid point. Eva hadn't ever looked at it that way. Doubtful the men had either. If only there was a way to confront them with this hypocrisy, to show how not all women were a danger . . .

An idea came to her, one so insane that she almost discounted it. Then she considered it a bit longer, intrigued. After all, the union reps must have women in their lives, strong women who would not appreciate the claims behind the strike. Women who might side with Eva. Hope blossomed in her chest for the first time in days, though it had nothing to do with Phillip. Yes, she could take matters into her own hands. Why hadn't she thought of this angle?

"Even if I do resolve the strike," she said carefully, "I am not certain your son will rehire me. And I'm not certain I deserve his forgiveness. I lied."

Mrs. Mansfield frowned and set her teacup down. "Eva, everyone deserves forgiveness if they are truly sorry. My son has always preferred to look ahead, never behind. You mustn't let him. Force him to focus on the present."

Eva had no idea how to accomplish that. Perhaps if she could bust up the strike and get the project under way, he might reconsider her role on the project. It wasn't much, but it was more than she'd had an hour ago.

Feeling lighter, she grabbed the satchel at her feet. "Shall we take a look at the designs?"

Ellen nodded. "Indeed, I'd like that. But please, do not give up on my son, Eva. The hotel needs you. *He* needs you."

Eva's tongue thickened with emotion, her brain not entirely certain how to respond. So she merely nodded and picked up her drawings.

PHILLIP STRUCK THE heavy bag with a series of blows, alternating his fists, his arm muscles burning with the effort. Sweat rolled down his torso and face, his chest heaving.

Unable to focus on work, he'd come to the ballroom in the middle of the day and wrapped his hands in boxing gloves. The physical release of boxing had saved his sanity the past three days. Work on the hotel site had been shut down completely, the laborers still on strike. He hadn't hired the women again, a seemingly impossible task without *her* assistance.

And he absolutely would not think about *her.*

He hadn't decided what to do about the dilemma she'd caused. Should he fire Milliken and the entire crew? They'd turned against him, now in league with the Tammany-backed union. How long would it take to find a new crew to replace them all?

Thus far, the news of her father's illness had not

been made public. The union was likely sitting on the information, ready to use it as leverage over Phillip should they not get what they wanted. Perhaps he should release that tidbit himself, to wrest back a bit of control in this calamity.

Jesus, what a mess. He never should have let her stay on.

And the worst part? He *missed* her. Like a lovesick schoolboy.

It was disgusting.

"Ho! Ease up on that poor bag."

Phillip dropped his arms and found Frank Tripp sauntering across the ballroom. "Please tell me you've brought some good news."

Tripp frowned and the knot in Phillip's stomach tightened. "There's not much good news to be had, I'm afraid," Tripp said.

Phillip bent at the waist and put his hands on his knees, taking a minute to catch his breath. "Let's have it, then. What have you leaned?"

"First, the contract. That's a bit of a gray area. She was careful not to use her father's signet ring, seal, or make any reference whatsoever to Lord Cassell in the correspondence or contract. Everything is as 'E. M. Hyde,' which legally could refer to herself."

Clever of her. "So in your opinion?"

Tripp lifted a shoulder. "The city has no basis to revoke the permits. As far as I can tell, everything is binding and legal. This also means you'll have a hard time winning a breach of contract case in court."

Phillip exhaled harshly. Part of him was relieved. He hadn't wanted to pursue legal action against her for a variety of reasons. "You're saying I am able to do nothing?"

"You could withhold the payments. Let her try to take you to court, if she so chooses. Doubtful the Hydes could afford a protracted trial. She wasn't lying when she said they were in dire straits. The estate barely has two farthings to rub together."

That was astounding. Her father should be horsewhipped for squandering so much money and leaving Eva in financial peril. "What of the union? Have you spoken with them?"

"I have. They are willing to return to work, with full compensation for days missed, as long as Lady Eva is not allowed on the construction site. Ever."

While Phillip had barred her temporarily from returning, allowing the union to make this permanent rankled. The decision should be his, not anyone else's.

"I don't like giving in," he told Tripp. "They'll be emboldened by the victory. Who knows what may cause them to strike next? It could be any damn thing."

"I agree."

"You do?" He had expected his attorney to push for a quick resolution. Plus, every day without construction on the site meant the entire schedule had to be adjusted. The project wouldn't move into the black until the hotel opened to paying guests.

"Yes, I do. This sets a dangerous precedent." Tripp thrust his hands in his trouser pockets. "Also, I am not certain it will do your romantic life any good."

A choked noise erupted from Phillip's throat. "My romantic life?"

"Yes. It's obvious there is something between you and Lady Eva. Doubtful she'd ever forgive you for not taking a stand on her behalf."

"First of all, there's nothing between us." The lie scraped over his throat. "Second, I've been taking a stand on her behalf for weeks now. Dashed lot of good that's done me."

Tripp shook his head. "You may lie to your mistress, your priest, and your mother . . . but never lie to your attorney. If you think it isn't obvious when you are both in the same room, let me be the one to disabuse you of that. Besides, you forget who reviewed the deed for Twenty-Fourth Street."

"Which could've just been sitting empty for all you know."

"But it wasn't." Tripp winked.

Annoyed and frustrated, Phillip punched the heavy bag again, desperate for something to do. "Have you spoken with her?"

"No, I had no reason to do so. Plus, I assumed you would speak with her."

He should have. Ignoring her had been cowardly, a result of his stinging pride. But he was still too angry, too hurt by her deception. He'd thought to give it a few more days, until he was calm. "I haven't decided what to do. I don't know what to say."

Tripp sighed and Phillip heard him walk away. He kept at the bag, moving his fists, waiting for clarity to strike him like a thunderbolt. That, or exhaust himself into a stupor.

His attorney leaned against the wall. "Are you unhappy with the designs for the hotel?"

Phillip answered honestly. "No."

"So why does anything change now that you've learned she is the architect? I realize she lied, but you know why. Not only is she the wrong gender, she has that nickname to contend with. It cannot be easy having everyone disregard you when you clearly possess the talent."

"I don't want to feel sorry for her," he snapped. "She deceived me." *More than once, in fact.*

"Yes, I realize that. But are you ready to have another architect take over in her stead? Are you ready to never see her again?"

Both notions sat heavily in his chest, making it even harder to breathe. He stopped boxing and stood there, panting. "You say that as if the choice is simple."

"Because it is. Either you are willing to forgive her or you aren't. And in case you're making the comparison, this isn't anything like what happened with Caroline."

"Really? And how exactly are you so certain?"

"Your former fiancée planned on taking everything from you to cover her misdeeds. Your name, your home, your money. Lady Eva may have deceived you but she was giving you exactly what you wanted. Your hotel, your legacy. You would have been better off in the end."

Interesting way of looking at the problem. He hadn't considered that before. "Only an attorney could spin the facts so handily."

Tripp lifted his hands, a small smile twisting his lips. "It's what I do best. But you should think about it because the longer you let this go on, the harder it will be to win her back."

He nearly snorted. "Who said anything about winning her back?"

"You didn't have to. The sorry state in which I found you did. By the way, I did learn who was behind this strike, if you care to know."

Phillip's head snapped up. "What do you mean? I assumed Keene and Tammany were behind it."

"To an extent," Tripp said. "Keene's been talking to the union and making promises. But there's someone giving large payoffs to ensure the hotel project does not move forward."

Goddamn it. "Who?"

"Mr. Mortimer Hall."

Becca's father. *Jesus.* Phillip's shoulders sank. He never would have guessed. He smacked the bag with a devastating right hook.

"Yes," Tripp said grimly. "I thought you might enjoy that news, which is why I gave it to you last. We'll be in touch, Mansfield. I have a meeting to attend."

Tripp strolled out of the ballroom, his arm raised in a half-hearted wave.

Furious, Phillip stood leaning on the punching bag. He would find a way to deal with Mortimer Hall. No one tried to sabotage his project and got away with it.

Chapter Eighteen

Three men entered the Cortlands' receiving room. Eva stood as the butler announced them. "Misters Debs, Gray, and Milliken, my lady."

She waited until they crossed the room, and then struck out her hand. "Thank you, gentlemen, for coming. I am most grateful. I realize this was a last-minute request." The meeting had come together quickly once she had returned from Newport. "You recall Mr. Tripp, I'm sure." She gestured toward Phillip's solicitor, who stood beside her.

"Of course," Debs said as he shook hands with Mr. Tripp. "Where is Mansfield?"

Eva motioned to the footman, who came forward to offer glasses of sherry from a silver tray. All three men accepted the spirits. "He was unable to join us, so Mr. Tripp is here as his representative."

Not quite the truth. She hadn't invited Phillip. This meeting was a gamble and better to have fewer witnesses if it failed. Most important to her was getting the project up and running again. Every other concern was secondary.

Still, she hated to add one more secret between them, even if he likely never planned to speak to her again.

"I suppose that'll be all right," Mr. Gray said as everyone settled into chairs. "It's not as if we're ready to arrive at a resolution."

Oh, she wouldn't be too certain about that, if today went as planned.

"First," she said. "I wanted to discuss in greater detail the issues you have with me. Let's address them one by one, shall we?"

The two union reps shifted in their chairs, clearly uncomfortable with being put on the spot. "Well, now, Lady Eva," Debs finally said. "We wouldn't care to hurt your tender feelings."

"My feelings are far from tender, Mr. Debs. Please, let us hear these concerns."

"You must be aware that you are a woman," Mr. Gray said, as if that was all the explanation required.

"I am quite aware of that. I am curious as to what that has to do with my abilities to perform the job."

"Please, my lady. This is a waste of everyone's—"

"Excuse me, Mr. Debs, but this is hardly a waste of time. I'd like to go through your grievances regarding me and address them. It's only fair."

"Mr. Tripp," Gray appealed. "Certainly you can see this is a most unconventional conversation."

The solicitor lifted one dark brow. "I see nothing of the sort. In a labor dispute, the two sides must come together to discuss their grievances. Unless, of course, Mr. Milliken would like to pack up and return to Chicago. I should tell you that we have three construction crews waiting, one from Boston and two from Philadelphia. All are ready to travel to New York City at a moment's notice." He brushed the sleeve of his jacket. "And an interesting fact? None belong to your union, Mr. Debs."

Debs's mouth flattened into an unhappy line. "That won't stop us from picketing."

"We'll see," Tripp said with a small, mysterious smile. Eva had informed him of her plan beforehand, and he'd pronounced her "brilliant."

She hoped he didn't come to regret that praise.

I never should have allowed a woman to take charge of this project. After everything, Phillip still saw her as a mistake. How she longed to prove him wrong today.

Gesturing at the union reps, she said, "So back to the issue at hand. Let us hear your complaints, gentlemen."

Debs and Gray exchanged a smug look, as if to say, *Well, she asked for it.*

It was Gray who spoke first. "You must admit you are hardly qualified. Your experience is lacking, my lady, and that raises concerns about the soundness of your structure."

She'd expected this. "Would you accept an independent review of the plans from an architectural firm?"

Debs cleared his throat. "I suppose we might, if it were independent and the firm itself was a reputable one."

"Excellent. Because I have authorized statements from not one, but three, architectural firms. Mr. Tripp?"

The solicitor withdrew three documents full of legal jargon and began slapping them on the low table. "These are sworn statements from Mr. McKim of McKim, Mead and White; Mr. Charles Coolidge of Boston's Shepley, Rutan and Coolidge; and Mr. Richard Morris Hunt, who I believe needs no introduction whatsoever."

Eva tried not to gloat. She'd gone to see Hunt, an old friend of her father's, in Newport herself, a visit she'd never forget. Hunt had called her work "inspired."

The two union reps wore shocked expressions before they carefully masked them. Then Mr. Gray waved his hand at the papers. "This may speak to the design but it does not solve the issue of her presence at the site."

"Ah, yes. My presence at the site." Eva resisted the urge to rub her hands together in anticipation. "Let's discuss why that is a problem."

Everyone looked to Milliken, who had yet to speak. The edge of his lip curled as he said, "The men are distracted by you. They should be watching what they're doing instead of following you around with their eyes."

"And how many injuries have I caused in these first few weeks of construction?"

"I couldn't say," Milliken said with a frown.

"But you can," Tripp said. "Each accident must be recorded and reported to the owner, as stipulated in your contract with Mr. Mansfield. So how many injuries have been sustained because of Lady Eva?"

"We've had thirteen injuries." Milliken lifted his chin.

Tripp pulled a stack of papers out of his satchel. "I counted fourteen in total, but who's to quibble?" He flipped the pages. "And all of these are normal injuries that occur at any construction site in the height of summer. Nine overexposures to heat, two abdominal pains, two ringing in the ears, and one migraine. Do any of those sound like they were related to Lady Eva's presence?"

"Not directly, but indirectly . . ." The general contractor let his voice drift off, as if that were all the explanation required.

"Indirectly, how?" Tripp asked. "Because not one of these occurred when Lady Eva was actually on the premises."

"It doesn't matter," he snapped, pointing a finger at Eva. "They call her Lady Unlucky, and that's what our site has become."

"Really?" Tripp located a few more papers in his bag. "Because not only is the project ahead of schedule, it is under budget. Well, before the strike, of course. How is that unlucky?"

"Women should not work!" Milliken snarled.

Now they were getting to the meat of it. Eva asked the union reps, "And do you agree, sirs? That women should not find gainful employment?"

"I'm afraid I do," Debs said. "At least not around men. You should work in a factory with other women. Where it's safe." Mr. Gray nodded at this, adding his approval.

Eva rose. "You already know I disagree and the numbers Mr. Tripp has produced prove otherwise. However, sometimes proof is not enough. A personal touch is required."

She strode to the door that led into the dining room. Sliding it open, she beckoned her guests. "Ladies, if you'll join us now."

Three women walked into the receiving room—and all three men shot to their feet.

"Good God," Gray breathed.

"What is the meaning of this?" Debs choked out. "What is my *mother* doing here?"

"I have a very good reason for bringing these women here today. Allow me to perform the introductions." She gestured to the woman on her far left. "This is Mr. Debs's mother, who works in the family grocery in Brooklyn. Next is Mr. Gray's mother, who owns a saloon with her husband in the Lower East Side. Lastly, this is Mr. Milliken's sister, who came in from Ohio. She is employed at a bank. Ladies, thank you for coming here this afternoon."

"What are you hoping to prove?" Gray asked.

Eva ignored him. "Ladies, do all of you work in an environment where men are also present?"

They all nodded.

"And have any of the men suffered injuries in your presence, because you are too distracting?"

Two rounds of "no" were heard, while Mrs. Gray said, "Hell, no. My lady."

Somehow Eva kept from smiling at that. "And do any of you believe that a woman's mere presence in the workplace causes it to be unsafe?"

Each issued an emphatic *no*, and then Mrs. Debs added, "Son, I should hope you don't believe that. If you do, then you must think I shouldn't work, either."

"I don't believe that about *you*, Mother," Mr. Debs said. "But a construction site—"

"Construction site, nothing." His mother snorted. "All men want is to tell women what they can and cannot do. Smart, pretty thing like Lady Eva . . ." She shook her head. "You should all be lining up to let her work there."

"Thank you, Mrs. Debs," Eva said.

"George," Mrs. Gray said, "I worked my fingers to the bone in that saloon to send you to a fancy college. What if someone had prevented me from providing for you? What then?"

Mr. Gray had the grace to turn red. He didn't even attempt to argue with her.

Milliken's sister stepped forward. "John, I know we aren't as close as we used to be, but I'm certain Mother would be disappointed were she still alive. Our parents believed everyone deserved a fair chance, no matter their background."

Milliken crossed his arms over his chest and stared at the wall, his jaw tight. Eva had suspected he would be the hardest to reach.

If she couldn't change his mind, so be it.

"So, gentlemen." She clapped her hands together. "Have we addressed all of your concerns? Are we able to end the strike and get the men back to work?"

Debs and Gray glanced at each other, then at their respective mothers. "Allow us a few moments to discuss this privately," Debs said. "I'm certain we can come to some sort of an agreement."

"Excellent. I'll just keep your family members here so they may hear the outcome as well."

All three men winced. Feeling victory close at hand, Eva crossed to the bell pull to ring for the butler.

THE GOTHAM CLUB bustled with early evening activity, gentlemen coming and going before the whirl of parties and soirees began. Phillip hadn't entered the social club, however. Instead he lurked in the shadows, waiting. He felt like the thug Eva had once accused him of being.

How had she seen through him so clearly?

He missed that about her, her keen perceptiveness. It was one of the qualities that made her a great architect, the ability to see things others could not. But that wasn't all he missed. He had come to look for her everywhere in the city, each splash of red hair drawing his eye.

Mostly he missed her at night. He could not go past Twenty-Fourth Street without recalling some of their evenings spent there, her warm and willing body wrapped around his own. Kisses that drugged him, made him delirious with want and need. Her scent, her taste . . . Damn it, he ached for her.

What could he do about it? Had he ruined everything between them for good?

A carriage pulled up and Phillip tensed. Sure enough, Mortimer Hall descended the steps to the walk. Phillip slipped out from the alley to trail him. Before they reached the club stairs, Phillip grasped the other man's elbow. "A word, if you please."

Hall's entire body jerked. His gaze rounded when he spotted Phillip over his shoulder. "What do you want, Mansfield?"

"To talk."

"I don't have anything to say to you." Hall tried to extract his arm from Phillip's grip.

Phillip held fast and began towing the other man toward the alley. "Oh, but I have plenty to say to you."

"Unhand me. Good Lord, Mansfield. Have you lost your mind?"

Though Hall tried to resist, Phillip was bigger and much stronger. He forced Becca's father into the dim alley and shoved him against the rough brick. "I haven't lost my mind but apparently you have."

Hall straightened and adjusted his necktie. "This is beyond the pale. What do you think to do, pummel me?"

"What I want to do is impart my unhappiness with the havoc you've caused. I'm told you financed the union's strike efforts."

"I did. I warned you there would be repercussions for playing with my daughter's affections, Mansfield."

"There were no affections, you idiot. None whatsoever on either side—and you well know it." Phillip gave the other man a pointed look. They were both aware of where Becca's true feelings resided . . . decidedly not with Phillip.

"Nonsense. She would have married you. I just needed a bit more time to convince her."

"You mean threaten her, don't you?"

Hall's expression hardened, his jaw clenched. "She is my daughter and therefore under my guidance. She'll do what I say or—"

The silence stretched, the only sound a rat rustling in some trash nearby. Phillip leaned in, snarling, "You'll what? Have your own daughter committed to a sanatorium? Subjected to ice water baths and a straitjacket?"

"We'll never know. It's too late now. The girl's disappeared."

At least he didn't suspect Phillip had aided Becca's escape. "Can you blame her, with the way you treated her?"

"It's none of your business, Mansfield."

"But it is my business, Hall. You made it my problem when you took your frustration out on my hotel project. Do you know how I handle problems like you?"

Hall lifted his chin but wisely kept silent.

"I bury them. Did you know I have friends at the Manhattan Central Bank? Interesting fact: with enough money, one can buy mortgages from the bank. Might you guess whose mortgage I purchased today?"

Hall paled, then turned red with fury. "How dare you! You had no right to do that."

Phillip shrugged. "I dared. And you had better not piss me off ever again or I'll be calling in the full amount due."

Hall began sputtering, his mouth working, spittle flying as he tried to form words. "You . . . How . . . I cannot . . ."

Phillip cupped a hand to his ear. "Sorry, I couldn't quite hear you."

Pushing off from the wall, Hall shoved a finger into Phillip's chest. "This is all because of that woman, that tart you've been seeing, the one working on your construction site. Strutting around and lifting up her skirts—"

Phillip's fist cracked across Hall's jaw, dropping the other man like a stone. He shook out his now throbbing hand and regarded the prone man on the ground. "If you ever speak ill of Lady Eva again, I'll do worse than hit you once. I'll break every bone in your goddamned face. And if you don't think I can, just ask the boys down at McGirk's in the Bowery."

Hall said nothing, merely blinked up at the sky as he undoubtedly tried to get his bearings. Phillip wasted no time in departing. He'd said his piece. If Hall had an ounce of sense, he'd stay out of Phillip's way for the rest of their lives.

Better yet, he'd move.

Errand completed, he found his carriage. A quick ride uptown brought him to his doorstep. His hand required ice, the knuckles already swollen and red. He crossed the threshold, ready to request the ice and a stiff drink, when a visitor stopped him short.

"Mother?"

Ellen Mansfield stood in the doorway to his salon. Never one to dress down, she wore a deep green dress with extensive beadwork that shimmered in the soft electric light. "Hello, Phillip."

"I thought you were in Newport."

"I was, but I had to see you." She faced him, her expression somber. "Are you injured?"

He shoved his hand into his pocket as he came forward to kiss her cheek. "Nothing to worry over. Shall we sit?"

He led her into the salon where she settled on

the sofa. Handing her a sherry, he poured his own whiskey and then joined her.

She took a sip. "She is giving up nearly everything to save your precious hotel."

"Sorry, what? Who?"

"Lady Eva. She is busy saving your hotel at great personal cost to herself."

There was much he didn't understand about that sentence but he started with the name. "You called her Lady Eva."

"She told me her true identity, Phillip. To where do you think she went when she fled the city?"

None of this made sense. He shook his head as if clearing the cobwebs from his brain. "Are you saying she traveled to Newport? I wasn't aware the two of you were acquainted."

"Yes, we are acquainted. I hired her ladyship—"

"You *hired* her? For what?"

"To redesign Stoneacre."

His shoulders bunched, muscles tensing. "I told you to leave Stoneacre alone, Mother. You had no right to hire an architect without consulting me."

"Do not presume to order me about," she said, her blue eyes snapping fire. "I am not one of your servants or employees. I may do anything I please with that house, Phillip, and we've enough money to build twenty Stoneacres if I so choose. Lady Eva has an amazing gift and I am more than pleased with the design she's presented."

Eva had already presented designs? Yet another secret she had kept from him. He rubbed his forehead tiredly. Christ, how many more were there?

"Incidentally, I am the one who asked her not to

say anything to you. So if you are thinking of laying the blame for that at her feet as well, you may forget it."

Had his thoughts been so obvious? "What did you mean, she is giving up nearly everything to save the hotel?"

"Do you not know of the bargain she's struck?" He shook his head and she continued, "I hear she has agreed to limit her visits to the site to one hour a day during the dinner shift change if the union agrees not to raise a ruckus over who actually authored the plans. The men will resume work tomorrow."

The hair on the back of Phillip's neck stood up. "One hour? At the same time each day? I never would agree to that."

"I've no doubt that's true. But she has agreed to it—for *you*. You, Phillip. No one else. The girl is in love with you."

I've . . . fallen for you. He hadn't believed her declaration, assumed her selfish motives had prompted it. Now he wasn't sure what to believe. "I'm assuming she consented because she didn't want to lose the project."

"Wrong, my dear boy. She shall use her own name on my Newport house, which means she won't have to hide under the E. M. Hyde identity any longer. Also, she stands to pocket quite a bit of money as well. In short, she doesn't need your hotel project, not for those reasons."

He didn't quite know what to say to that. Eva deserved success and notoriety. Of course she did. But a strange sense of disappointment rose inside him, almost as if she'd cut him out of her life.

No, you cut her out of yours.

He winced. He hadn't meant to, not permanently. Yes, he'd said things, angry things, he now regretted. Disappointment and hurt had clouded his mind, making it impossible to process anything else and he'd lashed out. He truly had intended to apologize . . . once the sting had ebbed.

Now he'd learned of other bits of information she'd withheld. Why was he always on the outside with Eva? *Because she sensed you didn't trust her, that you wouldn't forgive her.* He hadn't given her any reason to believe in him. In them.

Yes, he'd asked to court her but hadn't confessed how he felt about her. Hadn't told her he'd never cared about a woman this deeply, this . . . completely. She'd stolen into his life aboard the ship, and since then she'd slid under his skin and wrapped around his heart.

And she'd been brave enough to tell him, a declaration he'd thrown back in her face. How could she ever forgive him?

His mother watched him carefully, so he cleared his throat. "How do you know all this, about the negotiations and the agreement? Why are you better informed than me?"

"I've just come from the Cortlands' home. I needed to see her before she left for Newport. So do you plan to fight this resolution and fight for Lady Eva?"

"I plan to, but she's made her feelings on the subject very clear. I'm not certain she'll forgive me."

His mother's sigh echoed in the large room. "Nonsense. Anyone could see that she's the perfect woman for you. Understands all the construction nonsense, stubborn, intelligent . . . Classy and beautiful. You'd be fortunate to have her. That is, if you can grovel sufficiently enough."

Could he win her back? Groveling hadn't ever been necessary before. "I would think you'd disapprove, considering her scandalous string of dead fiancés."

"Fools. She told me all of them discouraged her interest in architecture. A talent such as hers should bloom, not wither on the vine."

That was surprising but still he forged ahead. "She's informed me on several occasions that she has no interest in marrying. She believes she'll lose her independence. Go from being in her father's shadow into mine."

"Then you must make certain to step aside and let her stand in the sun. A strong man does not need to strap his wife to his side. A strong man gives her a long tether, allows her some breathing room."

"Is that what Father did with you?"

"Of course. We never lived in one another's pockets. In a marriage, you must maintain your own interests but develop common ground upon which to stand. Your father knew how to accomplish this, to not complain when I hosted events and parties. He hated society but I loved it. We compromised."

Compromise. He could get used to that word, if it meant keeping Eva around. Could he convince her to forgive him?

His mother patted his arm. "You're a Mansfield. Compromise won't come easy, but the right woman will make it worthwhile. Now, catch the next train to Newport and get her back."

EVA WALKED ALONG the perimeter of Stoneacre with Mr. Jacobs, the engineer Carew had recommended, the morning ocean breeze a relief after yesterday's sweltering heat. They were discussing soil erosion and the wind, how it had affected the old stone exterior. "I suggested marble for the new house," she told Mr. Jacobs. "Costly, but it's able to withstand the elements better than other types of stone or brick."

"Agreed," the engineer said. "Though Fall River in Massachusetts has some marvelous, unique granite. I'll get a sample to show you next week. You might decide to use it somewhere, if not here."

She liked the idea of using a nearby quarry. Jacobs was smart and never shy about offering opinions—respectfully. He wasn't condescending or smug, which she appreciated. "Excellent. Shall we go back inside? I'd like to get your thoughts on the—"

"Good afternoon."

That voice. Eva's head snapped up to find Phillip approaching, his long legs easily eating up the distance of the green lawn. The brisk wind ruffled his dark hair and molded his clothes to his large frame. The sight of him after so many lonely days caused her battered heart to leap in her chest.

And here I was, your goose laying golden eggs.

She exhaled slowly. That he'd believed her so calculating, so callous, had cut deep. As if she were some fortune seeker, hoping to fleece a man out of his wealth. All she'd wanted was a chance to prove herself, but Phillip hadn't been willing to overlook their past or her gender, even after she'd apologized for her deceit. Not even after she'd revealed her feelings for him. Instead of reciprocating, he'd walked away . . . and that spoke volumes as to his regard for her.

Build up your walls, Eva. Protect yourself.

"Mr. Mansfield," she said coolly as he joined them. "Your mother is not here."

"I came to see you, actually."

That caught her by surprise. Schooling her features, she quickly made the introductions between the two men.

Phillip shook the engineer's hand. "Jacobs, you said? You did the work on the Haverton House here, correct?"

"Yes, sir." Jacobs beamed, clearly pleased that Phillip had heard of his work. "As well as Chateau Bellevue."

"Impressive. It seems my mother's new home is in very good hands."

She studied his expression. He . . . knew about the redesign of Stoneacre and wasn't angry over it? Ellen must have informed Phillip of the project at some point in the past few days. What was that wily old woman up to?

"Mr. Jacobs," Phillip said. "Might I have a moment alone with Lady Eva?"

"Oh." Jacobs looked at her. "Your ladyship?"

Did she want to speak to Phillip alone? They still had the hotel project in common—for now. Perhaps he was here to fire her.

Best to get it over with, then.

"If you'll wait in the library, Mr. Jacobs, I'll be but a moment."

The engineer nodded and tipped his cap before hurrying around the side of the house to the main entrance.

Eva faced the ocean, closing her eyes against the bright sun and enjoying the faint sea spray on her skin as she waited for him to speak.

"I heard about the deal you struck with the union," he said. "I wish you had involved me. I never would have agreed to such restrictions."

She'd resolved the strike and he was complaining? "I wasn't sure it would work, to be honest. And the restrictions hardly matter if you're here to discharge me."

"I don't want to fire you. I came here to apologize."

She cast a glance at him, his familiar handsomeness causing her throat to close. "Oh?"

He thrust his hands in his pockets, his shoulders hunched and stiff. "For what I said the other night. How I reacted about the news regarding your father. I'm sorry, Eva."

There was little reason to hold a grudge, not when they might still be working together. "I accept your apology. Was that all you wished to discuss?"

"I . . ." He blinked a few times. "I was angry and lashed out. I didn't mean any of it. I hope you know that. You're welcome to come back to the excavation site—and to me."

She was *welcome* to come back to him? Was he *serious*?

The top of her head throbbed with an oncoming ache. "I have a few things to do here first, but I should be able to return to work on the site next week."

What had been left out would be plain even to an idiot—and Phillip was no idiot.

"But you'll not return to me? To us?"

"It's best we not resume that part of our relationship."

His gaze narrowed, sparks of gold flaring in the dark depths. "So we're back to this? Professional distance?"

She drew in a deep breath, squared her shoulders. "The affair was lovely but we both knew it would end. There's too much distrust between us now and I have no interest in going backward. Only forward."

"You said you had fallen for me. Was that also a lie?"

No, but she almost wished it had been. "I'll get over it."

His mouth compressed into an unhappy, flat line. "What if I don't want you to get over it? What if I confessed that I had fallen for you as well?"

Happiness burst inside her chest, an explosion of hope and excitement—but then she sobered. This was too late, all too late. "It would not change a thing. I must do what I feel is right for me, and continuing an affair with you is not in my best interest."

"I want to marry you, Eva, not continue an affair."

She blinked at him, dumbfounded. Hadn't they

settled this issue already? And that was before the fragile trust between them had been broken. "Heavens, where did marriage come from again?"

"It never left. I never stopped wanting to marry you."

"Well, I haven't changed my mind about not wanting to marry you."

"I don't understand. There are no more secrets between us. I've forgiven you and I've also apologized for my behavior." He studied her face, scrutinizing every detail as if searching for clues. "What am I missing?"

"No, it's rather what I am missing." Like, a proper proposal. A firm declaration of his true feelings. A guarantee she could retain her career after marriage. Seeing her father once again. No, she stood to lose everything while he would only gain. "I know you'd rather not have the Lady Unlucky name haunting your new hotel, but I'm afraid there's no help for it now."

His brows slammed down. "You think this is about the hotel? I am not concerned about the future of the hotel. I had hoped to convince you to trust me, believe that I'll do right by you as a husband."

Trust him? After he'd tossed her aside so easily? "I know this is about the hotel, about giving me credibility and your protection. But I need a partner, not a keeper. I cannot marry, give away my rights and my work, on such blind faith—not to a man who has shown me very little reason to trust him."

He winced. "I realize that's true. I've handled much of this badly. And no one said you must give anything away."

"So you no longer believe it was a mistake to let me stay? To let a woman oversee the building of your hotel?"

The question seemed to catch him unaware, as if he hadn't remembered making the comment. "You've done a fine job, Eva. The project is under budget and ahead of schedule. How could I complain?"

A nice way of evading the question. "Why not send me back to London? You have E. M. Hyde's plans. You don't need me any longer. Hire another architect to see it finished."

"I'm trying to tell you why, you daft woman. I want to *marry* you. Have you by my side. Forever."

All of this just felt wrong. Every instinct, every bit of intuition was telling her *no*. The foundation of a marriage had to be strong, and there was nothing but weakness—hurt and distrust—between them now. "I cannot. None of that is good enough. I deserve better." A knot settled in her chest, making it hard to breathe, and she turned to walk to the house.

"Wait." He grasped her wrist. "Tell me what you need. Tell me how I can be good enough. Please, don't walk away from me, Eva."

She couldn't do this. She couldn't change him into someone else, force him to put her needs equal with his. Couldn't have made him bare his heart. "I'm sorry," she said, pulling free of his grip. "But you should return to the city."

Without glancing back, she ran into the crumbling house.

Chapter Nineteen

Eva was shoving her papers into a large leather case when Nora burst into the room. "Am I understanding this correctly? You're going to Newport for the rest of the summer—without *me*?"

Eva had returned to the city late last night after Phillip's disastrous visit to Stoneacre. All she wanted now was to pack her things and escape to the seaside for a few weeks. Go to a place where she wouldn't need to see Phillip or the hotel, where work would keep her busy.

"Hello, Nora. You are welcome to come, of course, though I'll be working. We start demolition on Stoneacre in two weeks."

Nora dropped onto the bed. "Oh, boo. You won't go with me to any of the parties. Neither will Julius, so I might as well stay here, then." She watched Eva pack for a long beat. "I'll miss you. I wish he hadn't driven you out of the city."

"Don't be ridiculous," Eva said quickly. "He didn't drive me away. Another project is taking me to Newport. And I'll be going to London in a month or so to check on my father. None of that has anything to do with Phillip."

"I wish I believed that, but I know you too well. The man has broken your heart and you're running away. Again."

She hated that Nora knew her so well. "He came to see me yesterday."

Nora's eyes went wide. "He did? What did he want?"

She lifted a shoulder. "To apologize. And to ask me to marry him."

"Marry him? Goodness! What did you say?"

"It wasn't a proper proposal, really, more like an idea. And I said no, of course."

"Oh." Deep grooves emerged in Nora's forehead as she contemplated this. "I don't understand."

"He said I was welcome to come back to the excavation site . . . and to him."

Nora's jaw dropped. "That's a bit short on the romance. Did he say how he feels about you?"

Eva's chest tightened like a fist. "No, he didn't. Though he did ask what I would say if he confessed he'd fallen for me."

"Talk about beating around the bush. Was he afraid his feelings wouldn't be returned?"

"No. I had already confessed that I'd fallen for him. He is well aware of how I feel."

"Oh, Eva." Nora's gaze swam with sympathy. "Undoubtedly Mansfield thought you would swoon at his feet after the marriage proposal. Most women would have, you know."

"He is welcome to them, then. I won't marry a man who doesn't trust and believe in me. And who isn't willing to put me first."

"Shall I kick him in the shin? Better yet, we could have Julius ruin his finances." She wiggled her fingers ominously.

"Not necessary, but thank you for the kind offers." Eva smiled at her closest friend. "If I change my mind, you'll be the first to know."

Nora smoothed her skirts, not meeting Eva's eye. "Do not take this the wrong way, but are you certain you shouldn't talk to him again? Perhaps after the two of you have had some time to think."

"I hardly see the point. What's done is done."

A knock on the door sounded and Nora went to open it. A footman held out a salver. "A cable for your ladyship."

"Which one?" Nora asked.

"Lady Eva," the young man said, his ears turning red.

Eva thanked him and picked up the paper. Unfolding it, she read the message.

You are needed at the hotel site. Come quickly.

Signed, Frank Tripp, Esq.

She tapped the paper against her hand, thinking. "What is it? What does it say?" Nora asked.

"It's a request to come to the construction site."

"So what are you waiting for?"

"It's strange, is all. This is from Phillip's attorney, Frank Tripp."

"Oh, I know Frank. He's one of my husband's close friends. Devilishly clever, that one."

Eva glanced at the clock on the mantle. If this didn't take long, she could still make the afternoon train to Newport. "I guess I had better hurry." She plucked a bonnet from the pile in the dressing room, found a pair of matching gloves.

When she returned to the bedroom, Nora was waiting there, her own bonnet and gloves in hand. "I'm coming with you."

"Why?"

"Intuition." Her friend was nearly bouncing on her toes. "Something tells me this is going to be worth seeing."

A CROWD HAD spilled onto Fifth Avenue, almost completely blocking the busy thoroughfare. "What is happening?" Eva peered out the window of the brougham. "We'd best get out here and walk."

Nora agreed and ordered the driver to pull over. When the wheels finally stopped, the two women descended to the street.

"What on earth . . . ?" Eva took Nora's arm and began threading through the throngs of people.

"Is this normal?" Nora clasped her parasol higher as if ready to defend them at any moment.

"No. This appears to be Mr. Milliken's crew." Not that she recognized the multitude of diverse faces, but their hats and working clothes were similar to the men who had toiled on the excavation these past few weeks.

As they edged toward the main entrance, the shouting increased and the crowd grew thicker. Eva didn't hear any of the machinery that usually dominated the site. Why weren't these men at work? The deal with the union had been struck two days ago.

The laborers lingering on the walk moved aside as she passed, letting her through. That was . . . odd. No hostility, just open curiosity. "Why are they all staring at you?" Nora whispered at her side.

"I have no idea."

She spotted Frank Tripp near the front, his arms raised as he tried to calm a group of angry workers. "Frank!" she called.

His head swiveled and he nearly sagged at the sight of her. "Thank God," he said, starting for her. "Lady Eva, I am incredibly happy to see you. Hello, Nora."

"Frank, what is happening?" Nora asked. "Did the workers strike once more?"

He gave a dry, humorless laugh. "No. It's the owner on strike this time."

"The owner?" Eva blinked. "But that means . . ."

"Yes," Frank confirmed. "He's gone and lost his damn mind, if you'll pardon the vulgarity."

Eva waved it away. She'd certainly heard worse. "Where is he?"

"At the gate. Which he's locked. He refuses to turn over the key, and no one quite knows what to do."

"Why on earth would he do that?" Nora asked.

"Because of her." Frank pointed at Eva. "Says he won't let the workers back in until they agree to allow Lady Eva back in as well."

"What?" Eva rocked back on her heels. "That is foolhardy."

Frank lifted his hands in surrender. "I won't disagree with you. However, he's a man possessed. I've never seen him like this."

"Go," Nora said, shooing Eva with her hands. "Find a way to fix this."

Eva twisted and turned through the men mulling about, most of the laborers grumbling about the strange owner and wondering why he wouldn't allow them to just work. Eva had to agree. This went against everything she knew about Phillip's personality.

Was he really doing this for *her*?

At the gate, Mr. Milliken was there, engaged in a staring contest with Phillip. Neither man blinked, their intense gazes locked in a battle of wills. Good Lord. The last thing they needed was a brawl erupting right here.

She stepped between them, her back to the general contractor. "Phillip, what are you doing?"

He didn't glance away from Milliken. "Taking a stand."

"But this is madness. Open the gate and allow the men inside."

"Yes," Milliken agreed. "Open the gate and allow my men inside."

"No, not until they agree to give my architect complete access to the site, whenever she likes."

"She already agreed to the terms, Mansfield," Milliken snapped. "The deal's done."

"Then we need to renegotiate because I'm not satisfied."

"We cannot do that!" Milliken said, slapping his bowler hat against his thigh.

Eva turned toward the general contractor. "Mr. Milliken, if you'll give me a moment to speak with Mr. Mansfield in private?"

Shaking his head and mumbling, Milliken stalked off into the crowd. Eva approached Phillip, who appeared on the razor's edge of sanity this morning. Dark circles lined his eyes and his hair was disheveled. He hadn't shaved either, the dark stubble causing him to look roguish and deliciously dangerous.

Stop. Absolutely no thinking along those lines, Eva.

"Phillip, what are you doing?"

"I'm trying to help you. Are you truly satisfied with the deal you struck?"

No, she wasn't . . . but she'd been desperate to end it. To keep Phillip's hotel on schedule. To finish and return to her father in England. "I had to get them back to work. The strike was my fault, so I deserved whatever stipulations they put on the resolution."

"Wrong—and I *never* would have agreed to that. You are the architect. You deserve to be here, no matter the hour. This is your project."

She could hear the conviction in his words, could see the truth blazing in the dark depths of his eyes. And while the sentiment touched her, the deal had been done, papers signed. They could not go back on the agreement now, not unless they wanted to risk the entire project.

Closing half the distance between them, she said, "I appreciate your support. It means a great deal to me. But if this is some ploy to get me to change my mind about us, you are wasting your time."

"It's not." A muscle jumped in his strong jaw. "I know I've lost you, that I muffed the whole thing up. I deserve that for the way I've treated you. You're right—I didn't trust you because you're a woman, and when you lied to me that last time I felt like my fears were vindicated. It was wrong of me. So I have to fix this for you, this one thing that's still in my control." He hitched a thumb over his shoulder toward the silent construction area.

"Mansfield!"

Eva looked over to see Debs and Gray swiftly approaching, their faces mottled with anger. Milliken trailed not far behind.

"What is the meaning of this?" Debs shouted. "Milliken tells us that you won't let the men inside to work."

"Have you lost your mind?" Gray asked.

"More like I've found it," Phillip said, crossing his large arms over his massive chest. "You two struck a bargain I never would've agreed to. I'm here to fix it."

Debs pointed at Eva. "She agreed to it, and your lawyer signed for you."

"I'll take you to court," Phillip said. "That agreement will never hold up."

Gray threw him arms up. "This is absurd. What exactly is it you're after, Mansfield?"

Phillip took a step forward, toward the laborers gathered in the street, and then put his hands in the air. "Everyone, may I have your attention? Please. A moment."

Silence rippled through the crowd as the men all waited to hear what the hotel owner had to say.

"Many of you objected to this woman's presence at the worksite." He indicated Eva. "Her name is Lady Eva Hyde, and she is the daughter of Lord Cassell, E. M. Hyde. Not only that, but *she* is the true architect of the Mansfield Hotel."

Murmuring noises floated in the air, the men glancing at one another in surprise.

"The hotel design is completely hers, and no one else's. So you see, she has more right than any of us to be here, overseeing the plans. She is brilliant and talented, every bit as gifted as her father—perhaps more so because she must put up with men everywhere who doubt her abilities. Like me. I doubted her but she's proven herself time and again. Therefore, I will not allow her visits here at the site to be limited in any way. She has free rein to oversee the project as she sees fit . . . or I will not open the gates ever again."

"Ever again?" Debs said. "You'll shut the whole thing down?"

"That's right." Phillip gave them a cold smile. "If she is not accepted as a member of the team, with all the rights and responsibilities afforded the men, then I'll take her plans to the West Coast and build my hotel in San Francisco instead."

She gasped, the meaning settling in. The loss of time and money would be staggering if he did so. Also, the city would need to find another developer for the huge piece of land, losing out on the revenue the hotel would generate for New York. This would not endear him to the locals. Was he truly willing to risk all that for her?

The walls she'd built up to protect herself began to

crumble, folding in on themselves like paper. She'd never had anyone do something so . . . selfless for her. This meant more than flowers or chocolates— even jewelry. Perhaps he did value her more than the hotel.

Before she could say anything, Debs said to Phillip, "This is ridiculous. You'd never shutter this project, not when it's so far along."

"You're wrong. I won't tolerate any disrespect of her ladyship and I'll gladly go broke trying to prove it. So, what's it going to be, gentlemen?" Phillip shouted this out to the crowd en masse.

Feeling overwhelmed, she moved closer. He dropped his head to gaze deep into her eyes, and the fierce determination reflected there wound through her blood, warming her. "Phillip, you don't have to do this."

"I do," he said quietly. "I've let you down in every other respect. You're worth a hundred ruined hotels to me."

Her chest swelled, emotion clogging in her throat. "That is the nicest thing you could ever say."

"Perhaps we should let the men take a vote!" Frank Tripp yelled, and the men cheered, ready for some kind of a resolution.

"Fine!" Debs threw up his hands in disgust. "Vote, then."

Tripp cupped his hands around his mouth. "All those *not* in favor of giving Lady Eva full access to the site, raise your hand."

About thirty men out of the hundreds present raised a hand—including Mr. Milliken.

Phillip frowned at these men. "Everyone with

your hand raised, you're fired. Everyone else, we appreciate your support of our architect. Welcome back."

Turning, he unlocked the gate and dragged it to one side. A cheer went up before the laborers began streaming into the site.

By the time Eva reached Phillip, Milliken was already there, the contractor's face nearly apoplectic with rage. ". . . cannot fire me! These are my men. They won't stay and work if you fire me."

Phillip looked calm and collected, every inch the powerful New York scion. "I think I've just proven they will, Milliken. And I have indeed fired you. If any of your men want to leave, they have my blessing to go. I'll hire another general contractor and more laborers, as many as I need. But you are no longer allowed on my construction site."

Eva tried not to gloat as Milliken stormed off. Astounded at the morning's events, she covered her mouth to stem the giddiness from bubbling forth. He'd really done all this . . . for her.

She couldn't reach his side fast enough.

He watched her carefully, tracking her approach. His brows lowered in confusion when she didn't immediately speak. "Eva?"

When she was close enough, she rose up on her toes and whispered in his ear, "Your presence is requested at an urgent meeting. Number Twenty-Two Twenty-Fourth Street." Then she drifted away, desperate to find a hack.

NOW OUT OF breath, Phillip arrived at the top floor of the town house. Was she here? He hadn't allowed himself to hope on the ride downtown, too worried he'd misunderstood her intentions.

The door to the top set of apartments stood ajar. He pushed through and entered the former bordello. "Eva?"

A small shape moved one instant before a woman launched herself at him. *Eva.* His arms banded around her, holding her tight in case she changed her mind. He breathed her in, the familiar smell of earth and her flowery scent like heaven after all these days. God, he'd missed her.

Her face buried into his throat, she mumbled, "I cannot believe you did that. You're utterly mad!"

"I meant what I said. I did not shut down the site as a ploy to get you back." Though that would certainly be a nice side effect, one he would not turn down. "I did it because you deserve to be treated equally."

He heard her drag in a shaky breath. "And I am grateful. That was the nicest thing anyone has ever done for me. Thank you."

Pride filled him as he hugged her. "You are quite welcome."

She withdrew, unwinding her arms from his neck, and he forced himself to let her go. Disappointment filled him as he shoved his hands in his trouser pockets, waiting.

"Did you see? Almost all of them went back to work. Hardly any of the men cared that I'm a woman."

"I figured the majority didn't care, that there were only a few bad apples in the group. Frankly, I should have fired Milliken as soon as he voiced his first complaint about you. I'm sorry, Eva."

"You are forgiven. For all of it."

"I am?"

"Yes. I am sorry I deceived you about the plans. I was certain you'd never hire me otherwise. Also, the longer I hid my father's illness the better chance I had of securing more projects in his name."

"I had no idea your finances were so dire. Why did you not tell me?"

She bit her lip and looked away. "I didn't want anyone to know. My father was a brilliant architect but incompetent when it came to money. And now with his care . . ." She shrugged. "I'll find a way to keep us afloat."

He didn't doubt it. Eva could do anything if she set her mind to it. He'd never met a woman more determined or resourceful.

Marry me and I'll help you.

The words were on the tip of his tongue. Yet he withheld them. He'd asked her before and her refusal had been clear. Just because they were here did not mean she had changed her mind about marriage.

Though he would wear her down eventually. Losing her once more was *not* an option.

"I know you will," he said, "and anything you need, merely ask. I'll give you anything."

Her lids swept down and she peeked up through dark lashes. "Anything?"

"Yes, anything."

"Will you give me another chance?"

His heart thumped, blood racing at the idea. "To resume our affair?"

"If you like." She drew closer, laying her palm on his vest. "Or perhaps more."

"Such as?" The need to touch her burned through him, his muscles clenching at the effort to remain still. He had to discover what she meant first. "Courting?"

"Is that what you want?"

"I want to marry you, but I'll take whatever you're offering." His cock was rapidly swelling, her nearness affecting him like no other woman ever had. He longed to press his body to hers, to feel her softness against him.

Her fingers trailed over his jaw and up his cheek, threading into his hair. "Why do you want to marry me?"

Is that what she'd needed? A proper proposal in which he bared his feelings?

Without missing a beat, he dropped down onto one knee and took her hand. "Because I never dreamed I'd find a woman like you, one with intelligence and fortitude. One who loves architecture as much as I do. One who knows how to ease my *mal de mer* with a simple touch. You've captivated me from the moment we met and I don't ever want to be apart, not for one single day. I love you and I need you by my side. That is why I must marry you. Please, marry me, Eva. I promise I'll learn to compromise and never block you from the sun."

She said nothing, just stared down at him with wide eyes. He grew nervous as the seconds stretched. Wasn't she supposed to say something?

Embarrassment washed over him. She remained mute and he felt like a fool. He started to push up.

"No, wait," she said, stopping him. "I hadn't

expected all that. I'm . . . well, I'm flabbergasted. I merely wanted to hear if you loved me or not."

First he hadn't said enough . . . and now he'd said too much?

"I love you," he said again. "I'll say it as many times you'd like, if you'll marry me."

She covered her mouth with her hand, eyes brimming with emotion. "I will want to build my career as an architect."

He tried to contain his grin as he rose. "As well you should—and I'll not stop you."

"And my father? I'd like to bring him here."

"Of course. He'll have the best care available."

She took in a deep breath. "I have three dead fiancés. Are you certain you are willing to risk being number four?"

He couldn't help but chuckle at that feeble argument. Cupping her face in his hands, he said, "I don't believe for a second that you're cursed. Furthermore, I plan to stay alive for many years, long enough to grow old with you and our children."

Her gaze watery and bright, she nodded. "Then yes, I'll marry you."

"Thank God." Bending his head, he kissed her for a long moment, relief and promise in every shared breath.

When they finally drew apart, she tilted her head thoughtfully. "I've been Lady Unlucky for so long. What will everyone call me now?"

"They'll call you Eva Mansfield, the most talented architect in the world."

"I like that. But don't you mean the most talented female architect in the world?"

"No, I don't. My wife will outshine every other architect, no matter the sex."

Grabbing his necktie, she began walking backward, dragging him toward the bedroom. "I like that answer. But right now, your future wife would like to demonstrate her talents in other important areas . . ."

*Two years and
four months later*

It had taken them four months longer than expected to hold the grand opening of the Mansfield Hotel in New York City.

The reason had nothing to do with schedules or strikes, but instead a chubby little angel named Edward Mansfield, who'd been born just as construction finished. The hotel owner, and baby's father, had insisted on pushing back the opening celebration, refusing to host it until the architect had recovered from the birth and was able to attend.

It hardly needed to be said, but Eva loved her husband to distraction.

"I cannot wait to see all Mr. Doyle has done in the last few months," she said as the carriage brought them downtown, her body nearly vibrating with excitement.

"I think you'll be quite pleased." Her husband

held her hand, his large fingers laced with hers. "He's honored your extraordinary design."

"I wish my father could see this."

Edward Michael Hyde, Lord Cassell, had passed away six months ago. Eva had been heartbroken that her father would never see her finished work. She missed him dearly, though his memory had only deteriorated further after coming to New York. It had been Phillip's suggestion to name their son Edward, and Eva had readily agreed.

"I know, sweetheart." Phillip squeezed her hand. "But he knows. Wherever he is, he knows."

Tears threatened and she beat them back. No crying allowed tonight. She tried to lighten the mood. "Edward would have enjoyed this. I still think we should've brought him."

Phillip shook his head as he leaned in to kiss her cheek. "I want you all to myself tonight. It has been too long, Eva."

A shiver worked its way down her spine at his husky words. "Considering there will be four hundred guests tonight, I hardly think you'll have me to yourself."

He merely hummed and turned his gaze toward the window.

The carriage slowed and she spotted the hotel's cornerstone, a sight that still choked her up. Phillip had insisted her name, not her father's, was inscribed on the stone, right beneath his own name. *Our legacy*, he'd told her at the time, which had caused her to cry happy tears.

They arrived at the edge of the red carpet streaming under the portico. Well-dressed New Yorkers were lined up at the entrance, eager to see the inside of the world's finest hotel.

The exterior had been finished months ago, the design everything Eva had envisioned. And the result had rendered her speechless. It was truly one of a kind, with amenities the world hadn't yet seen in a hotel, such as bathrooms and electricity for each room. Despite this, the newspapers had expressed doubt that the rooms would actually rent. They called it "Mansfield's Folly," and had openly mocked the owner.

Fools. No one should've ever doubted Phillip Mansfield. As of yesterday, the hotel was sold out, every room booked, through the end of next year. In fact, the King of Prussia was expected this week.

Friends and society members, dignitaries and politicians, bombarded them on the red carpet. It seemed everyone of import was attending the opening gala. Mr. Weller had given Eva a hearty handshake and his congratulations from the city's buildings department. Even Debs and Gray from the labor union were here, accepting praise from guests as if they hadn't been trying to shut the whole thing down.

Mr. Doyle waited for Eva and Phillip just inside the front door. They all shook hands and then Doyle proceeded to give them a tour of the interior. Phillip had seen it all already, of course, so it was really just for Eva's benefit.

And she was suitably impressed. Doyle had a bold flair, one that suited the structure well. The common rooms were eye-catching yet comfortable.

Her favorite was the Turkish smoking room, done in a Moorish style with mosaics, ancient suits of armor, and heavy reds.

"This is outstanding work," she told Mr. Doyle. "I almost want to live here."

Doyle beamed at her praise. "Thank you. It has been a labor of love. I am very fond of the place as well."

Out of the corner of her eye, Eva saw a woman striding toward them. "Becca!"

Doyle excused himself to see to his grand opening duties just as a grinning Rebecca Hall joined them. Her skin fairly glowed under the soft electric lights, her hair twisted high on her head. "Mr. and Mrs. Mansfield, hello."

"None of that formality, not from you." Phillip embraced the woman. "Paris clearly suits you. I've never seen you look happier."

"I am," she confirmed. "Leaving New York was the best decision I ever made."

Now Eva's turn, she kissed Becca's cheek. "Well, we are so pleased you returned for the grand opening."

"I wouldn't have missed it for anything, even without your assurance that my father won't be attending."

"He was definitely not on the guest list," Phillip drawled. "He's been quiet since he learned I hold his financial ruin in the palm of my hand."

"I wish I'd seen his face." Becca sighed wistfully. "Oh, congratulations on your son. I heard the news this morning."

"Thank you," Eva said. "Please come and visit him tomorrow, if you'd like."

The head of the hotel, Oscar Boldt, approached. Phillip had lured the legendary maître d'hôtel away from Delmonico's to run the Mansfield Hotel. Eva had quickly seen why, as the Swiss man was a force of nature himself. Even before construction had finished, Boldt had weighed in on improvements to strengthen the appeal of the hotel, such as including a more varied menu in the restaurant and allowing women to enter unescorted. *How can a hotel designed by a woman not allow women to enjoy it as well?* he'd said.

"Oscar," Eva said after introducing him to Becca. "Everything is lovely. You and the staff have outdone yourselves."

The maître d'hôtel preened under her praise. "That is my job, madam. Mr. Mansfield expects nothing less than perfection."

Phillip grinned, clapping Oscar on the back. "I do, and you've made me very proud tonight. The crowd is sure to be impressed."

"I do hope so. The performance should start in twenty minutes," he told them, then addressed Phillip directly. "Everything is as you requested, sir."

"Excellent. Thank you, Oscar."

The maître d'hôtel hurried away, on to more important tasks, and Becca excused herself to see old acquaintances. Eva accepted a glass of champagne from a passing waiter. "Well, husband. Shall we find our seats for the performance?" The New York Symphony Society was set to play for the crowd, followed by a lavish meal in the dining room. Eva had seen the elaborate menu and she could hardly wait.

Phillip took her elbow. "I have a better idea." He began leading her toward the private elevator in back, one that only royalty and heads of state would use once the hotel opened. This elevator, powered by the generator in the sub-basement, led to the very best suites within the hotel.

"Where are we going?" She glanced over her shoulder as they left the chaos behind. "Shouldn't we continue to shake hands? Don't you want to revel in your success?"

He nodded to the elevator operator as they stepped inside the steel cage. The operator closed the opening and then set the lever, whisking them upward.

Phillip glanced down at her. "It's your success every bit as much as mine. Would you like to stay down there, accepting your congratulations?"

"No, I don't need to stay. I design for the joy of it, not the public adulation. But I thought you'd love that, considering how hard you struggled to get it done." Between the baby and the hotel, they'd both run themselves ragged in the past two years. She had also overseen Stoneacre's redesign, which was shaping into one of Newport's most stunning properties.

"Oscar and Doyle will see it all handled," he said enigmatically as the elevator came to rest on the second floor.

The steel opened and Phillip led her toward the state apartments, ten lavish suites designed for the most important guests at the hotel. Each was decorated in the style of a famous European palace or landmark. She, Phillip, and Doyle had chosen

372

these ten locations together during a long dinner at Sherry's, one of her very favorite memories of the entire process.

Phillip unlocked the Francois I Suite, decorated in the style of the Château de Fontainebleau in France. "Why are we going in here?"

He merely held the door open and waved her inside. "I am surprising you. That's what we are doing."

Surprising her? She stepped inside the suite's drawing room, an Italian Renaissance delight, and stopped short. A small dining table with two chairs had been set up in the middle of the space. Covered dishes rested on the surface, along with candles and a small arrangement of flowers.

The click of the lock regained her attention. She turned to find Phillip leaning against the wall, hands in his trouser pockets, eyes locked on her face.

"I don't understand. We're having dinner here?"

He began closing the distance between them, a predatory gleam in his gaze that she hadn't seen in many months. Not since before she'd grown heavy with Edward. A thrill raced through her, along her thighs, settling between her legs.

"We'll eat dinner later. For now, I thought we'd examine the bed. Ensure it's up to the standards of the hotel."

"Oh, so this is about the hotel," she teased.

He caught her around the waist and pulled her tight to his frame. "Not in the least. This is about having my wife to myself. Pleasuring her until she can't possibly take any more."

She clung to his shoulders as he dragged his nose along her temple, inhaling her. "But there are hundreds of people downstairs. What would they say if they knew you were shirking your duties as owner to bed your wife?"

"They'd say I'm the luckiest man in New York City." Bending, he caught his arm under her knees and lifted her up, carrying her to the bedroom. "And they'd be right."

Author's Note

Every now and again, a historical tidbit will spark my creativity. Such was the case for Eva and Phillip's story. My dear friend Diana Quincy mentioned in passing one day that the architect of Hearst Castle, built by William Randolph Hearst at the tail end of the Gilded Age, was a woman. Skeptic that I am, I had to look this up immediately. Yes, in fact the architect was Julia Morgan, the first woman architect licensed in California. My mind was blown and the basis for Eva's character was born.

Architecture is not something I am familiar with, so many hours were spent researching techniques and engineering of the day. The most detailed information I could find was on the building of the Empire State Building, built in 1930. I have taken artistic license to apply some of the figures and details of that project to the Mansfield Hotel (which wouldn't have been nearly as high as the ESB).

All the errors are my own.

Acknowledgments

My sincere thanks to Michele Mannon, Diana Quincy, and JB Schroeder for their help with the shipboard romance and with shaping Phillip's character.

Thank you to Tessa Woodward for loving Phillip and Eva as much as I do and helping to strengthen their story. Also thanks to Laura Bradford for all her expert guidance and support.

My deepest gratitude to the team at Avon Books, especially Elle Keck, Pamela Jaffe, and Angela Craft, for all you do for my books.

As always, thank you to the Gilded Lilies for sharing my enthusiasm for this time period (as well as Justin Trudeau photos). And I'm so grateful to all the readers, bloggers, reviewers, and authors who help to spread the word about romance. You are all rock stars.

Lastly, love and thanks to my family, especially my husband, who is my best friend and biggest supporter. Couldn't do it without you, babe.

In the gilded world of The Four Hundred, love is never simple. Don't miss the next breathtaking romance from Joanna Shupe,

A Notorious Vow

Coming Fall 2018